THE GHOST THEATRE

The Ruins

THE GHOST THEATRE

A THRILLING ADVENTURE BY

MAT OSMAN

STARRING A CAST OF CHARACTERS INCLUDING...

Flapper Shay
Lord Nonesuch
Alvery Trussell
Jean Blank
Flanders Alouette
John Chappell

John Motteram
Nathan Field
Philip Pykman
Thomas Grymes
Saloman Pavey

BLOOMSBURY PUBLISHING

LONDON · OXFORD · NEW YORK · NEW DELHI · SYDNEY

BLOOMSBURY PUBLISHING
Bloomsbury Publishing Plc
50 Bedford Square, London, WC1B 3DP, UK
29 Earlsfort Terrace, Dublin 2, Ireland

BLOOMSBURY, BLOOMSBURY PUBLISHING and the Diana logo
are trademarks of Bloomsbury Publishing Plc

First published in Great Britain 2023

A catalogue record for this book is available from the British Library

ISBN: HB: 978-1-5266-5440-3; TPB: 978-1-5266-5441-0;
EBOOK: 978-1-5266-5439-7; EPDF: 978-1-5266-5438-0;
GOLDSBORO EXCLUSIVE EDITION: 978-1-5266-6692-5

2 4 6 8 10 9 7 5 3 1

Typeset by Integra Software Services Pvt. Ltd.
Printed and bound in Great Britain by CPI Group (UK) Ltd, Croydon CR0 4YY

MIX
Paper | Supporting
responsible forestry
FSC® C171272

To find out more about our authors and books visit www.bloomsbury.com
and sign up for our newsletters

For Anissa

Act 1

London, 1601

IF THE MEN HAD brought dogs rather than their fancy trained
wolves then Shay would be dead by now. Dogs could have been let
off the leash and they'd have made short work of her up here on the
roofs. Wolves though were worth a sovereign and that was too rich a
prize to be risked on a flapper like her. Gilmour had begun chasing
her back in Eastcheap, where it was easy enough to leap from rooftop to rooftop. The roads there were barely wide enough for a cart to
pass through and the houses leant towards one another like plants
seeking the sun. There Shay had stepped between the roofs as easily
as stepping across a stream. But the men drove her westwards. At first
she'd relished this; west London roofs were tile rather than daub and
she worried less about crashing through into the rooms below. But as
they forced her towards grander streets wide enough for carriages, the
jumps were becoming hard work. Her legs throbbed with the effort.
She threw herself across St Peter's Hill and barely made it. Her leading foot caught the edge of the thatch and it was only momentum
that carried her body on to flatten against the slope of the roof. Grit
bit her hands and knees. She scrambled around the building's edge,
leaning into its slope, and cursed the loss of rhythm. Below her, three
storeys down, the rest of Gilmour's men careered along the street. She
flung herself across a short gap between domed roofs and scampered
across a rare glass skylight. A glimpse of faces turning up to watch
her feet and then she slid down a bank of mossy tiles onto the house's
flat border. A ten-foot gap gaped in front of her. She scanned the roof
for a ladder to bridge the space: nothing. Gilmour was close now. His
whistles came more frequently and when she turned she could see the
wolves straining against their leashes, snouts tasting the air in front
of them.

She turned back along the gutter, looking for another path. The houses down by the Thames were bunched closer together again so she edged along the peak of the roof and then threw herself across a thin alley. Her landing place was a row of older houses with boards on top, and the wood bowed under her weight; if it collapsed then she'd break a leg, or worse. The jumps were manageable here but now she was running at an angle to Gilmour and he was closing in. For the first time she could hear the panting of the wolves and the sound of his feet clattering over the boards. At this rate he could afford to wait until the dead end of the river.

Legs complaining, Shay leapt from the board-houses onto a sturdier roof. She came down with a crash, sending a flock of pigeons skywards in a soft explosion of feathers. They spread like a fountain and she repeated the catechism under her breath: *The gods are birds and the birds are gods.* She let its cadence guide her feet. *The gods* – step – *are birds* – step – *and the birds* – step – *are gods* – leap.

Gilmour to the right, the river to the left and the end of the city ahead. She spun around: a church spire, a flash of grass, the turrets of a gate. She turned east towards a plain of thatched roofs and ran harder. Gilmour was near enough that she heard his commands to the wolves: 'Come by, come by. There's my girl.' He let out a long whistle and it was instantly echoed from the streets below.

Each step tore strips of breath from her body. The thatch was ragged, and twice she caught her foot under a loose section. Straw-ends burned her hands. She looked for landmarks. St Paul's Church rose from the carpet of the city and behind it, obscured by smoke, sat the old bell tower. No good to her now, either of them. She looked right and saw a still figure sitting on a flat roof with a hand shielding its eyes. For a second the figure watched, then it raised a hand, stood, and began to run parallel to her.

The birds are – leap – *GODS*. Nearly eight feet that one, arms thrown out to catch the central ridge of thatch and pull her up and over. She slid down the other side and narrowly avoided going over the edge. Gravel fell to the street below. The figure now ran on a course that would inter-cept her. Friend or foe? No way of knowing. Then a boy's voice sounded across the rooftops. 'Go right for three houses, then head for the spire.' She hauled herself upright and stepped over the thinnest of alleyways. Thirty feet below, a river of noise pulsed. She took off, not daring to look back, and made for a longhouse with a peaked top that would surely be too steep for the dogs. That gained some precious moments. She scuttled across the slope, keeping one eye on her footing and one on the boy. He was twenty feet away but closing in. Just a lad, with hair to his shoulders, dressed in scarlet and black. Once he was level with her he kept a street's width between them. 'Three jumps ahead there's a roof with a smoking chimney. Stop there, and then do as I do.' Shay tried to nod but the pain in her lungs wiped her strength away.

Three leaps – *gods, birds, gods* – and they converged on a square of roof barely large enough to hold the pair of them. A rickety chimney puffed fragrant white smoke: a sweet smell, almost sickly. The boy lay on his front and reached over the side. Shay heard a click and a creak of wood.

'Watch me.' There was no urgency to his voice. Shay lay down and looked over the edge. They were higher up than she expected and the street below was too far for any noise. A drop of sweat fell from her brow and spun lazily downwards.

'Look.' The boy squatted, held onto the edge of the roof, and then rolled over while still grasping the rim. His body somersaulted and then disappeared. Shay held her breath, waiting for the crash.

'Now you.' His voice was close. She edged out further. A window stood open underneath the lip of the roof. He'd flipped over and inside the tower in one movement. His face peered up. 'Quick, don't think about it.'

Frantic whistles behind her and the wolves howling with anticipation.

She grabbed the edge and threw herself forward. The world spun as the weight strained against her aching shoulders and she began to fall back into the window, but then her left leg slammed into the frame and her hand slipped. For a second she dangled there by one arm, legs flailing for some kind of purchase, before he grabbed her around the waist and pulled. Her back and arm scraped hard against the window frame and she fell backwards into the building.

Shay wanted to lie there for a moment, but the boy set off down a spiral staircase so tiny that the steps were no larger than roof tiles. He jammed his hands against the walls and half slid, half fell down the spiral. She followed as fast as she dared, breathless and dizzy with her vision blurring. The stairs seemed to go on forever but just as the nausea was making her stumble, his footsteps stopped ahead of her. She collapsed to her knees in a larger room with two doorways and an open serving hatch in the wall. An enormous woman was wedged into a chair by the door, stroking something in her lap. The boy knelt at her side and talked quickly into her ear. Then the two of them looked over at her and Shay was about to thank them when she heard the sound of splintering wood from above. The boy said something more to the giant woman, kissed her gently on the ear, and then pulled the serving hatch open. It was a small lift, no bigger than a chest of drawers. 'Inside,' he said.

Shay placed her hands on the frame. 'I can't. It's too small.'

The fat woman laughed at that. 'Little scrap of rag like you? It's your choice. You could take your chances with whoever's up there instead.' The splintering stopped, and the ensuing silence was more frightening than the noise had been. Shay lifted a knee into the hatch and then pulled one shoulder and her head inside. She smelt cooked meat and that same sickly smoke from the chimney. The box creaked under her weight and again hands grasped her waist. The boy lifted up the rest of her body and shoved, jamming her head against the wall. She looked out, sideways, at his hands and the murk of the room, and, she now realised, the long silver machete that lay in the woman's lap.

'Don't move, and don't touch anything when you get down there.'

The box lurched and scraped against the wall as it descended. She was wedged in tight; when the box stammered to a stop she had to push with her legs to get out and she fell awkwardly onto the floor. A moment to catch her breath. She was in another room, more shadowy than upstairs and oily with smoke. The serving lift disappeared back up with a jerk and the room echoed to a low hubbub of voices that hadn't stopped upon her arrival. She pulled herself up and found a man standing over her, older, and dressed in clothes that had been expensive once. He leant down and took her by the chin, turning her face towards the candles. Their eyes met for a moment and then he let go and smiled. 'Well, I definitely didn't order *that*.' Laughter came from over his shoulder as he walked back into the room. The serving lift juddered back into place once more and the boy slid gracefully out, landing on his feet. He tutted and brushed himself down and then took Shay's hand and guided her into the shadows.

The room was divided up into small cabins, each lit by a single candle. Men smoked and slept, one to a booth, and the air was muddied with thick haze. The boy found them an empty booth. He pulled over some cushions and regarded her with interest. Shay was unused to such close scrutiny. She worked hard on being unmemorable: her clothes, her manner, her voice. She'd learnt to bounce off the surface of people, to slide between the rough edges of life, but he didn't look away.

She knew what he'd be thinking: 'What *is* this?' She'd lost her cap somewhere, so her two wings of hair stuck up in tufts around her tattoo lines, and there were cuts on her neck and shoulders. Her breasts were taped down, and she wore sailor's culottes and buckle shoes. She'd heard all the questions – 'Are you a boy or a girl?' 'What happened to your hair?' 'Why are you dressed for the poorhouse?' – so she set her face as hard as she could manage, her heart still racing, and tried to stop her legs trembling.

The boy kept examining her, and then shook his head as if to dislodge something.

'So rude of me.' He reached out a hand, like an adult.

'Shay.' She kept her voice as flat as possible, deepened it a little. The act was almost unconscious now.

He clasped his other hand over hers. 'Well, hello, Shay. I'm Lucifer, the very Devil come to earth.'

2

I T WAS AN HOUR before they dared venture back above ground.
Out, blinking, to an autumn sky so thinly blue that it might shatter if you threw a stone. It was market day and clear skies on market
days meant crowds; the city would be full of Gate People, up for the
day, gawping and hesitating and examining every head on the Newgate
spikes. Shay preferred the dull days when only Londoners were about
and the crowds flowed like birds.

The pair walked under the awnings of Westcheap Market, keeping
to the edges in case any of Gilmour's men were still around. The boy
walked with an odd, shuffling step, trying to slow his pace to match
Shay's struggle through the throng. He was tall enough that he could
have rested the point of his chin on the stubble of her scalp, and those
extra inches were like second sight when Cheapside was this busy. He
sidestepped and knight's-moved, ducked under eaves, scaled barrels and
pulled Shay diagonally across four lanes of traffic.

At Shay's eye-level London was a kaleidoscopic barrage: the sharp
shoulders of prentices and a flash of stacked cherries on a cart, horses'
breath at her neck. Of course, she felt hands on her too. They mostly
guided her out of the path of the more hurried walkers, but once she
felt the briefest grab of buttock, so quick as to be unattributable, and
once the gentle, but unmistakeable, touch of a practised hand scanning
her waistband for a purse. She unsheathed her knife with a snick and
the hand withdrew. St Nicholas Shambles was so crowded that the jam
of people lifted her off the ground and her feet didn't touch earth for
nearly ten feet. Fine by her; a constant acrid stream of animal piss ran
down the centre of the street, racing for the Thames. As she tilted her
head back for some fresher air, Shay caught segments of sky between
the shoulders and stalls. It looked blank and welcoming amid the dung

and the muddied sleeves and the rotten fruit and sweat and shouts. They scuttled through a tavern on Old Change so slender that she brushed both sides with her outstretched fingertips, then ducked out the back into an alleyway.

That first quarter-hour Shay only caught the boy in snatches: the prow of his chin pushing through the crowd, the dance-step of his fussy black velvet shoes. But as he blocked her path with an outstretched arm to allow an emptying of chamber pots above them, she could see him properly. He was tall, or at least tall to Shay, and slender too. Slope-shouldered and thin-waisted, topped with a nest of curls that ran from treacle at their roots to the blond of roof-straw at the tips. A face and body where everything came to a point. His nose was an arrow towards his attention. Thin brows and elbows like scissors. They weren't the fine features of an aristocrat but he was still pale and unblemished: a city boy. His outfit confused her. He wore an unstarched ruff, deliberately, so it appeared, which hung down as if he were on the way to his laundress. A leather tunic, well made but worn at the elbows and seams, decorated with a hundred tiny diamond-shaped slashes so that the shirt below could be pulled through. Shay had seen the look before on the plumed and perfumed Italians who stalked St Paul's Walk of a Sunday, but she'd never seen it done with such stylised extremity; his back looked like a flotilla of sailing boats on a black sea. His hose and knife-sheath were a matching dull scarlet and his blade had a silvered hilt. The hose looked overly feminine on him, especially atop those button-lined velvet shoes. Who could he be? A down-on-his-luck gentleman's son, forced into hand-me-downs? A gang leader longer on funds than taste? She couldn't exactly place him, a fact which frustrated and excited her in equal measure. A final spout of water poured from overhead and as he lowered his arm Shay said, 'I like your jacket.'

He looked down as if seeing it for the first time, and Shay liked him a little less – those tufts of shirt alone meant he'd spent at least a quarter-hour on his look. He plucked a triangle of snowy linen to a peak and said, 'You know the Earl of Anglesey? He died in it.' He poked a finger through a slit in the side and waggled it at Shay. 'Lanced right through like a pig on a spit. There's another hole in the back.'

'Oh. I'm sorry,' said Shay. 'Was he a relative?'

The boy snorted with pleasure. 'Hah, Lord no. The earl left three outfits to the theatre.' His voice deepened. 'To be worn solely on the occasion of playing royalty.' He snorted again. 'In his dreams. This would do for a minor nobleman at best. We're not supposed to wear them off stage but I do feel that I should be an advertisement for the place.'

The theatre then. She should have guessed. Young, well dressed and loafing on a work day; he was a Blackfriars Boy. Even back in the marshes, where London was little more than a rumour, Shay had heard of them through schoolfriends who followed the boy actors with a dreamy obsessiveness. The idea of lads little older than themselves being household names before they could shave, performing before the highest of society, was a glorious, freeing aberration. No matter that the flapper girls were too young and too poor to see them perform. The boldest saved up for the London ferry and hung around the stage door to badger playgoers with questions. They learnt the whole troupe by name, knew their likes and dislikes, devoured their histories. It was only once Shay started working in London that she heard other, whispered stories about the troupe: plays so satiric that they had to be performed by invitation only, and secret liaisons with noblemen and noblewomen.

He slowed the pace. 'Why were they chasing you, back then?'

Shay was surprised that hadn't been his first question. 'You know the bird shop on St Laurence Lane? The man with the wolves is its owner, Gilmour. And I'd just set all his birds free.' She waited a beat. 'Again.'

She saw it unfold one more time. Her fishhook lowering like a well-bucket through the gap she'd made in the shop's ceiling, lowering three times, each a little nearer to the handle of the birdcage. The *tink* of hook against metal, lost among the caws of thirty birds. The shop boys were focused on a woman customer whose sable alone said that she could buy the entire shop with the contents of her purse. Shay's target was the hatch on the top of the biggest cage. One more time the hook crooked around its handle and this time it caught. She spooled the line in and watched the hatch. It rose vertically and then fell, striking the top of the cage with a noise like dropped cutlery. The shop boys looked around. The woman looked around. But the birds didn't move until Shay tugged so hard that the wire dug into her fingers. The hook bent under the cage's weight, and as it rocked, the birds panicked. There was a flash of scarlet wing, almost too fast for human eyes, and the warbles of the songbirds turned to shrieks of alarm. The cage see-sawed back and hit the table with a shudder. The first escapee was a lovebird, downy and sunset-coloured. Up, out of the hatch and through the shopfront like it was sucked on a tide. There was a moment of balance as the cage settled and the shop boys swivelled. Then, with a card-shuffle sound, the rest of the birds streamed from the cage. Shay was back out onto the roof in an instant. The birds, unnerved by their sudden, gaping liberty, rose in a waterspout of noise and colour, and then, on some unknown signal, spread out, throwing scraps of bright, living silk out into the sky.

The boy kicked at the floor and grinned as if he'd been the one who'd done it. He craned his neck to look at the sky. 'How many times have you done that?'

'Four. The first two were easy.' Back then she'd just walked in, undone the cage at the front, and walked out.

'You'll need a disguise then. Let me get you something from the theatre.'

Something must have shown on her face because he laughed. 'We're not as black as we're painted, I promise. The owner's not there today so you're not going to get press-ganged.'

She tried a laugh. 'I thought if the Devil offered you a gift, then you were supposed to turn it down.' He raised an eyebrow and she said, 'I still don't know your name, Lucifer.'

'Ah, of course. I'm Nonesuch.' He shook her hand again and then he was off without waiting to see if she was following, sidestepping down a body-wide alleyway between houses, into a shop selling candle ends and out through a back door into a courtyard full of horses still steaming from their morning's work. Somehow they were back on Cheapside.

Shay loved Cheapside, loved it more than any other place in London. The world was laid out here like a living map. Silks from India were stacked in riotous pyramids, rough edges hinting at the jungle within. Dutch merchants wore heavy, buckled hats over heavy, troubled faces, and squatted behind a forest of tulips. Seville oranges were labelled, hopefully, *Morisqo*, so that buyers' patriotism wouldn't be questioned. Reynolds' spice shop warmed one whole side of the street with a burnt, throat-catching aroma and she took Nonesuch's arm and slowed him, nose to the air, with her eyes closed. Cinnamon, cayenne, cloves and pepper. 'You taste it? India. Panama, Madeira. On your tongue for free.' He barked a quick laugh but still he stood with his mouth ajar.

Wiltshire ham, Anglia wool, Cornish tin. In ten minutes' walking they heard five languages, twenty accents. Even the swallows overhead had travelled thousands of miles to get here. In Shay's view of the world, London was the bullseye at the centre of an archery target and Cheapside was a miraculous, once-in-a-lifetime, dead centre shot.

They walked the back streets for a while and Nonesuch wound stories around their route. It was convulsive storytelling, each tale more outrageous than the last. He flung his arms wide, or hunched over like a goblin when performing some evil character. Outside a puppet show he copied the marionettes, making Shay laugh with a jerky dance. But he was a listener too. He listened with his whole body, often stopping, blocking traffic to scan her face urgently or put his hands on her shoulders. That brought a heat to her face. She prized her anonymity above everything and usually such attention would have felt invasive, but the boy had an openness that was infectious. He told her, unprompted as far as Shay could tell, about a countess's daughter who paid him a shilling an hour to teach her street talk. How he'd ridden the rapids between the arches of London Bridge on a log, throwing up before and after. Shay's stories were smaller but he watched her face intently as she spent every interesting part of her: her father and his snow-white swan-boat; her rooftop messengering and falcon taming; the fortune-telling and card-reading.

'It wasn't your first time up there on the roofs then?' he asked.

'God no. I pretty much live up there. I can cross London faster than any messenger in the city. But I love the rooftops anyway. My father worked up high. In dovecotes and places like that, so I got a taste for it.' Snatches of memory floated down. Her father's glove, so large that she could fit two fingers in each hole, gripped by the falcon's knotty claws. Him facing the wind with his mouth half open, tasting it, a smile creeping across his face every time. Her favourite moment was the unhooding of the falcon and the way that the bird's eyes were instantly, unblinkingly alive; the unsheathing of a knife. The moment the falcon took off, your hand, relieved of its weight, followed. It leapt after the bird as if the updraught of wings might pull you along behind it. Shay would stand on tiptoe, trying to keep the connection between her and the falcon for as long as possible.

Nonesuch nodded. 'I sit out on the theatre roof most days. A pipe and a book. And all the secret conversations of the street rising up to you.' He mimed picking an apple.

They walked south towards the smell of river and the streets grew more crowded again. Gate People everywhere: up from that sprawling second London that squatted around its walls, makeshift villages that huddled in as if the cold stone might give off warmth.

The quarter bell rang. 'Shit,' said Nonesuch, 'I still have chores.'

He dragged her across a furious stream of farmers' carts, down into a shaded side street where he rapped at a high door. After the shortest of pauses it was thrown open and a man in an apron so drenched in blood that Shay could smell it – sweet and rotten – grinned down at them. 'If it isn't Beelzebub himself. Wait.'

He closed the door carefully and shouts came from within, then a deeper, ominous chopping sound. The man reappeared with a bucket and a sack that was stained and damp at its base. Nonesuch took it and held it carefully away from his body. 'It's definitely lamb? The cow's was too thick.'

The man laughed. 'Slit its throat myself.' He handed the bucket to Shay. A stick protruded from a few inches of viscous blood.

Nonesuch said, 'Keep stirring as we walk, if it hardens there'll be hell to pay.' Shay must have looked stricken because he added, 'For me, not you.'

She swirled the stick in time with their footsteps. The bucket was heavier than it looked and flies already bombarded its surface. 'What's in the sack?'

'I *hope* it's sheep intestines.' He switched hands and flexed the one that had been holding the bag. 'For a fight scene tonight. The silk merchant wears them inside his tunic, I spring—' He lurched forward and thrust out an imaginary sword. 'I slice, and out they come. Except last week they only had cow's intestines. Too big. The damn thing burst before I even had my sword arm up. It looked like he was giving birth.'

'And the blood?'

'For later on. You fill a pig's bladder and stitch across the top. Tuck it under here,' he gestured to his armpit, 'and when you're hit, you squeeze.' He wore a rueful grin.

'We're still late,' he said. 'I swear there are more of these hayseeds every day. How do you feel about a little emergency, at least until Blackfriars?' When Shay looked quizzical, he reached into the bucket and smeared a thick glut of the blood across his neck. Shay smelt iron and shit.

He squeezed out into the street and yelled, 'Oh God. Bastard cut-throats,' and collapsed backwards into Shay's arms. With his face upside down he looked younger still, until he winked up at her. The crowds parted at the noise, and a shiver of excitement ran ahead of them. Nonesuch spluttered and gurgled in her arms, looking like a dead weight but somehow his legs were helping propel them. The fiction percolated through her. 'Out of the way, damn you,' she shouted, and her voice sounded odd, hard. 'Let us through.'

People jammed themselves against walls and under awnings. Faces expectant with looks that said *oh thank God it's not me, it's some other poor sod* and Shay was swept along by their relief. 'Left here,' Nonesuch whispered between death throes, and when they were in the quiet of an alley he straightened up and wiped his face clean. He pulled Shay close; she couldn't imagine what for. Their faces were inches from each other.

'Do I look all right? My public awaits.' His voice was back to its drawl. She wiped a thumbprint of dried blood from his temple and nodded. A sweep of eyes across her face. 'And you, do I introduce you as boy or girl?' The question was asked more casually than anyone had managed it before.

'Boy, here in London. It's for work. It's illegal for girls to run messages, see.' She saw no reason to go into it further.

He laughed at that. 'Fine. You don't have to tell me about the roles we play.'

3

T HE COBBLES OUTSIDE THE theatre had been washed clean, leaving a semicircle of sheen protruding out into the murk of the street. Bystanders huddled in small groups, pointedly ignoring one another. Serving girls mainly, and a couple of whores out early, even a trio of gentlewomen standing primly to one side with their neat little feet on pristine squares of handkerchief. Nonesuch pulled his hat down over his eyes but that, if anything, drew more attention to him. A ripple of calls went up: 'Nonesuch, Nonesuch, what are you playing tonight? Any spares? Any backstage?' They talked over Shay's head as if she wasn't there.

He held up a hand and said, 'Not now, apologies. I'm late for rehearsal,' and as he and Shay ducked into the dark of the theatre there was an audible rush of disappointment from outside. 'Sorry about that, it's a peril of the profession. It's crazy that they arrive here so early.'

He didn't look particularly disappointed, and Shay asked, 'Why doesn't the theatre have a back entrance, then?'

For the first time since they met, she saw embarrassment in him. He said, 'Well, I suppose there is one, actually.' The double doors cut off the street's racket so completely that inside felt like a church and Shay let herself believe that his entrance might have been purely to impress her.

A smell of sandalwood and incense spiced the air. Blackened candelabras hung from the ceiling, yards above her, but they were so sparse with candles that the room was as shadowy as a confessional. Nonesuch guided her deeper into the auditorium and the shape of the place coalesced: two tiers of boxes lining a room cambered in such a way that every seat had a view. A crack of light from the rear illuminated a high stage where a knot of boys recited lines, speaking over one another. A desultory sword fight was taking place in the aisle and the weapons rang like bells. Real swords, Shay noted.

Nonesuch pulled her into the grimy light with a finger on his lips and the swordfighters stopped. He beckoned one over. 'Where's Evans?' he asked.

'He's out counting his money. He'll be a while.'

The boy who replied was mousy and small-featured. His armour was made of thick paper and up close Shay could see rips forming in the tighter pieces. He placed the tip of his sword onto his shoe and rotated it, watching Shay.

Nonesuch said, 'Call me if he arrives,' and led Shay up onto the stage.

The boy called after him. 'Oh, Mr Lucifer?' Nonesuch turned with a grin and the boy said, 'No devilry tonight, I'm afraid. Special request from some pal of Evans'. You're giving us your Cleopatra, darling.'

Nonesuch stopped dead. 'Cleopatra? Really? We're on in two hours and I haven't played it since the spring. A little warning would have helped.'

'Don't blame the messenger. The others are learning their lines as we speak.'

Nonesuch grabbed another boy and unloaded the sack and bucket onto him. He opened a shoulder-high door at the back of the stage and ushered Shay through. It was a tiny tiring room, taller than it was wide and stained the dark brown of ale-dregs. It was darker still than the auditorium and two boys sat face to face in the corner, trying out lines on each other. Nonesuch lit candles in the wall holders either side of a silvered mirror and talked under his breath. 'Cleopatra. I bet the costume smells like a midden. And that make-up. You'll stay, won't you?'

The last was aimed at Shay and she found herself nodding yes without knowing why. She sat by a second mirror and watched him get ready. Nonesuch scooped two fingers of a thick paste the colour of plums from a tub and began to smear it across his face. There were more colours too: a bright red for his mouth and eyes, daubed so sloppily that his features broke their banks, and a convalescent yellow for his cheekbones and brows. He recited as he worked, so quietly that Shay had to watch his lips to catch the words.

'Oh, may these eyelids never close again, till with my sword I have that conjuror slain.' His face tightened in the candlelight. Even before the make-up his features looked ornamental: arches of eyebrow and philtrum, sharp-angled nose and cheekbones. He had skin the deep white of new mushrooms, gentleman's skin. Shay knew that some Blackfriars Boys were sons of the gentry, press-ganged, bribed or plain kidnapped. In certain well-to-do streets the sight of the theatre owner's black-plumed horses elicited the same terror that bailiffs did where she grew up. Nonesuch spoke well, dressed better and his hands looked like they'd never seen hard work, but Shay couldn't quite see him as a gentleman's son. There was a preparedness for danger about him that she had never seen in anyone of comfortable means.

The smallness of the room and the mirrors meant it was hard for Shay to look elsewhere as Nonesuch undressed. He seemed unworried by her presence anyway. She got an impression of tautness. White skin and muscles like tree roots. Flat-stomached and trim. He dressed in black and gold. Black hose, a black gown and gold bands at his temples, wrists and ankles. In the mirror his body disappeared into the gloom while his face shone. There was a new suppleness to him. The boys in the corner dropped to their knees and prayed with hands on each other's shoulders. Nonesuch plucked off one lad's cap with the tip of his sword and lowered it onto Shay's head without a word. Flowers were delivered silently and ignored. A Moor polished a trumpet in the mirror, turning it this way and that to catch the light, and Nonesuch gave him a silent bow. He was, Shay realised with a prickling of pleasure, the only adult she'd seen backstage. When the stage door opened again it let in a bubble of noise and the sword-fighting boy from before. He said, 'Nonesuch, it's almost time. I think we'll sell out again. Westland and Rodrigo are about to come backstage to say hello.'

Nonesuch took a long look at himself in the mirror and sighed. 'Fucking vultures. Why can't they wait until afterwards like all the other bloodsuckers?'

'Don't complain, they brought wealthy friends. Anyway, *sharp eyes, blunt knives.*'

Nonesuch repeated the phrase and said, 'Wait. Trussell, this is my friend Shay. Where can he watch from?'

Shay hadn't asked to stay for the performance. Trussell looked her over with the questioning gaze they all gave each other a hundred times a day. The look that asked, 'Where are you from? And where are you allowed to go?' He was slight and bony with piscine eyes and unruly hair. 'Every good seat is taken, I'm afraid, even on the stage. You might have to listen from here.' He was about to leave when he said, 'I don't suppose you can read?'

Pride battled with her desire for anonymity. 'I can read.'

His interest pricked. 'You can read properly? You could read this?' He passed over a sheath of loosely bound pages and Shay flicked through. Hand-inked lines and stage directions with marks all over in pencil. She chose a page at random. 'The stars align on paths eccentric, our fates are tugged like drunken horse-carts.'

Trussell laughed. 'Well, that sounds like the kind of bollocks I hear every night. Ladies and gentlemen, it appears we have a prompter, like at an actual theatre.'

A bell rang out and Trussell hurried her down the steps and through the curtains before she had time to say no. Even walking across the stage made her feel desperately conspicuous. The room in front of them sparkled and the air of wealth was unmistakable. It was in the glint of rings and the flash of lace. People looked lit from within. A lady sat flanked by two male servants, one of whom cracked walnuts for her. A whore in whiteface glinted everywhere: pearls in her hair, pearls at her ears. Shay tried to block out the sight of feathers in hats but they were everywhere. It was all too much, like being drunk. She concentrated on her feet as she walked and her shadows raced across the stage. There must have been a thousand candles around the theatre, each reflected in the gleam of gold and leather and diamond and mirror. Candles were strung on wires across the ceilings in convoluted patterns too, and she recognised a couple of the shapes: the Plough, Orion's Belt.

A long, raised slit bisected the front of the stage and a face gazed out from inside. Trussell told her, 'Down you go,' and Shay slid her legs through the slit until hands twisted her around. It was tight in there: a low bench, racks of props and effects, and a pale, long-faced girl. She was dressed in a black bodysuit with a high neck, giving her the appearance of a cameo in a locket. 'What are you? Not a prompter?'

Shay tried to get comfortable. 'Yes. Well, apparently. I'm Shay. I've been roped into this. I've never done it before.'

'Of course you haven't. Typical. Never mind, you're better than nothing.' Her frown suggested that might not be the case. 'I've been doing both for weeks. I'm Alouette: lights and props. I apologise that I don't have time to show you the ropes, but it is pretty simple. Follow along what they say with the script. If they forget a part, they're supposed to whisper "line" but mostly they will just moon at you like a heifer. If they skip a page or two don't worry, but let them know afterwards.' She gestured with her lantern. 'Keep your eye on Trussell, the boy who brought you here. He's playing Julius and I have a bet with Lord Nonesuch that he won't get through a single act this year without making a mistake. Easy money.'

'And what about Nonesuch?'

Her sniff was one of pleasure. 'Him? He is absolutely guaranteed to go off-script, I think it's a point of principle with him. But that doesn't mean he needs prompting. Drying up is not that boy's problem.'

Alouette settled herself. 'A prompter and curtain-up only a quarter-hour late. It must be my lucky day.' She locked her eyes on Shay's and said, 'Sharp eyes, blunt knives.' Shay repeated it back, self-consciously.

Conversations were snuffed out with the candles and there was a weight to the darkness then, like the room had filled with oil. A wedge of scenery was wheeled onto stage before eyes got used to the dark. There was a last, delicious moment of calm before Alouette lit the lamp in front of them.

There it was. The prow of a ship, cresting and burrowing into waves. Aquamarine silk undulated across the floor. It was at once profoundly unrealistic and utterly beguiling. Alouette worked a bellows laid side-ways with its spout angled towards the bow and she sent up a glimmering spray of water. Shay caught the smell of deep sea with no land in sight. The ship curtseyed to meet the waves and when it rose again Nonesuch was on deck with his hands on his hips. He was Cleopatra. Bird-eyed and horse-maned. Black silk that captured ripples of sea-light and gold at his ankles and wrists. Gold that was too plain for jewellery, but too rich for shackles. He turned a degree so that the light split his face in two. His first line, according to Shay's script, was, 'The waves know my fate, and Caesar's too,' but he continued to stare out in silence. There was a reverie to it: the creak of wood and the smell of salt, the candle-light and hushed breaths. Shay tugged at Alouette's hem, 'Should I?' but Alouette shook her head.

'Our hearts are ships.'

He didn't say it the way she was used to hearing players talk. Rather, he threw the line to the front row of the audience, quietly enough that they had to lean in a little closer.

'Our hearts are ships,' he said again, 'and when life's weather is fair, we tell ourselves that we are our hearts' captains. It is us who steer the course. We set sail for new lands. We explore.'

He flung his arms wide and turned so that he was almost entirely in darkness. There was the tiniest glint of light from his eyes. Alouette dimmed the lantern until he was little more than a voice and a gleam of gold.

'But that is an illusion. When true storms come, they pluck the ships of our heart up and toss them this way and that. We are no captains. Instead, we hang on for dear life, clinging to the mast as the winds rage around us.'

He blew out his cheeks against the squall of the spray. His hair was damp and flustered.

'Our hearts are ships,' he said, louder now as Alouette worked the bellows. 'And tonight the tempest is here. The storm is upon us and my heart is lost on a killing sea.'

Shay looked in vain at her script; not a word of the speech appeared there. Nonesuch stood taller, extended a hand, and blew. Tiny paper boats, as small as thistledown, streamed from his palm, and all over the theatre hands reached up into the light, and then, in one moment, Alouette killed the lanterns and a curtain fell.

'Well, I suppose that was scene one,' she said.

The play unfolded with a dreamlike imprecision, Nonesuch the centre of every scene. Cleopatra came to Rome to plead for her country, truffling for power. One minute he rolled, untouched, from a carpet to land propped on an elbow, the next he flattered Rome like a courtier. Caesar's part was taken by a brute of a boy, six foot tall and wide as a door, whose toga rode up while his laurel crown bulged at his temples. No matter; he was pure foil. Nonesuch worked in and out of his shadows with a voice half for himself and half for the audience. He flitted between the sexes, sometimes in the space of a sentence. His body lied and cajoled, flattered and fretted, and Shay found herself tangled up in him. When his words tumbled like rainwater, her heart rate rose with his. When he dropped to his knees, it was Shay's gut that clenched.

She missed her first prompt. In the middle of a long speech, Trussell simply stopped. Shay had been watching four gentlemen who sat in chairs set on the edge of the stage, close enough to the action to reach out and touch the actors. Indeed, in the middle of a knife fight one had pulled out his rapier and offered to help Trussell out, a suggestion which won a smattering of weary laughter from the main seats. Two of the gentlemen were engaged in a game of dice and Shay was distracted until Alouette elbowed her in the ribs.

By the time she'd found her place another actor had taken over the speech. She checked the script and found that the cast had missed out a chunk. She cursed herself. Alouette's expression was unreadable in the dark but Shay was sure that she'd moved away from her. She had other chances though. In a long soliloquy a soldier stopped for a moment and bit his lip. She whispered his line to him and he went on without pause for the rest of the speech. The next scene was riddled with corrections in her text and three times actors lost their way. Each time she nudged them back.

Near the end of the act Nonesuch went out among the audience. He trailed fingers over bare shoulders as he walked. He whispered something into a gentleman's ear that won a blush and he sat in laps. He looked so fragile among the heft and luxury of the noblemen that, when the interval came, Shay found she'd been holding her breath; she was damp with sweat.

The black-clad boys of the chorus slipped onto the stage as the musicians started up over their heads. Fiddle, lute and hand drum stepped around one another until a loose volley of trumpet notes sounded out, tiptoeing across the bridge of sound. It was the Moor from backstage, standing among his sitting comrades, sending forth curling breakers of frothy, bubbling notes.

Shay asked, 'Is Nonesuch really high-born? I can't place him at all.'

Alouette turned the lantern onto her. It was blindingly bright. She scowled and then relaxed. 'That is what they say. He's certainly as lazy as a gentleman. And he does have a taste for the finer things. But I've never heard him talk about his past.' She considered the question again. 'There are whispers that he was taken from a very wealthy family.'

There was a Nonesuch Palace in Ewell. A Nonesuch Hall. It was a name made of stone and glass. 'Surely a family of means would have the power to get him back. The owner, this Evans, he can't be untouchable.'

Alouette worked as she talked. 'Evans has the Queen's ear. More importantly, he has the Queen's Warrant. Who knows what happened? Maybe his people fell out of favour, maybe this was a warning. Still, I've never seen Nonesuch with kinfolk so it could all be nonsense. Don't ask him.'

Shay nodded and then felt the heat as Alouette turned the lantern back towards her. 'Seriously, don't ask. They have so little, these boys.' The Moor's trumpet stepped down through a scale to land, breathless, on the hush, and Alouette dimmed her lantern. 'This, here, is his family now.'

The second act began with a long speech from Nonesuch. There was a weight to his words that she'd not noticed earlier. His voice was a blade returning to a sheath, a pigeon coming home to roost. And his power was doubled, trebled even, by Alouette's lighting. Her lanterns were mirrored and directional, throwing beams of light that always caught Nonesuch's face. She could dim and brighten, flattening his features or throwing him into the shadows. She played with the light the way Nonesuch played with words and the two of them warped the very air to their bidding. At one point, with Cleopatra alone on a storm-tossed hillside, Alouette slid a sheet of cracked tin in front of the lantern, dropped a greyish lump of something behind it and, as the scene reached its crescendo, lit it. There was a blinding flash and a throat-tearing pall of smoke in the box, but on stage the effect was unmistakable: lightning, splitting the backdrop from ceiling to boards and fixing Cleopatra's agony in an eye-blink of white light. Alouette's face was taut until there was a chorus of gasps and then a round of applause so loud that Nonesuch had to halt his speech. Shay was so caught up in the action that it was only when she turned over a page and saw the next was blank that she realised the play was over.

Even if she'd been up on stage, Shay didn't think she could be more drained. She sat, winded, as Alouette tidied and the chatter of the crowd drained away behind them. She loaded up a clever wooden box with drawers that folded out like a fan containing wicks as thick as fingers and others as delicate as thread. A drawer lined in lead was packed with twists of paper that smelled of gunpowder. The tin stencils slid into a series of slots and she read out the names as she replaced them. 'Dawn, Storm, Dusk, Battle, Hell.' Once the last stencil had gone back into the box Alouette turned to Shay. 'So? How was it?'

'I loved it.' It was true. She was thick with the weight of the drama, drunk on it. 'I'm so sorry that I missed that first cue.'

Alouette nodded. 'You have to let them hang at least once otherwise they wouldn't bother learning the lines at all.'

She had an accent that Shay didn't recognise. Rounded but hard, like river stones. 'Where are you from?'

She said something in a language that Shay didn't understand, and then, 'Flanders, near Ghent.'

Shay didn't know much about Flanders except Anne of Cleves and marsh warblers, neither of which seemed likely topics of conversation. She tried another tack. 'What brought you to London?'

'What brings anyone here? Work. Certainly not the food.'

Shay sensed that Alouette was torn between talking, and appearing over-eager, and remaining silent. She found that she wanted this girl to like her, she wanted to be invited back. 'The lantern and the … tricks, are they your own work?'

'All mine; my family are clockmakers, it's in my blood. And they should be only the start. If Evans had any foresight, I would turn this theatre into a palace of wonders.' The auditorium was nearly empty – there were scraps of conversation and the swish of a brush somewhere behind them.

Shay asked, 'What wonders?'

Alouette didn't miss a beat. 'A bonfire that doesn't char, a sea that stretches for leagues. Forests of crystal. Atlantis rising from the waves.'

Each phrase set images coursing across Shay's mind and she let them play as Alouette finished up. She worked in silence but when she was done she said, 'Would you like to go down to the dorm and say good-bye? The boys should at least thank you.'

The room had the smell of musk and sweat and penny scent. Shay sat on the edge of a bed and marvelled at how the boys could throw off a performance like that. Lads who minutes earlier had been plump-lipped Egyptian handmaidens now tussled over toys and play-ing cards. Boys did boy things in boy ways: rough with each other, careless. Everything too small for them like plants outgrowing their pots. Most lay on grubby cots with rectangles of dust underneath, while one boy read theatrically out loud. He stumbled over a couple of words and a boy threw balled-up hose at him. Junk collected in the corners of the room: a drum with a broken skin, clothes in piles, wooden swords. And at the far end a ladder led up to a curtained-off bunk. Alouette called up, 'St Nonesuch. Are you coming down off your cross?' A hand slipped out from between the curtains and raised two fingers. Alouette was unoffended. 'I'll come up there with my rag and vinegar, then.'

Nonesuch poked his head out, bringing with it a cloud of smoke. He raised a hand. *Wait.*

He levered himself out onto the ladder. He was wearing the costume from the performance and his hair was still powder-dark. He'd wiped off most of the paint but there were crusts of purple and red in his face's corners: behind his ear, in his eyebrows, where his nostrils met his cheek. 'How was I?'

Alouette laughed. 'I've seen better. You have to step forward more for the sea scene. Otherwise the rain looks too thick.'

Nonesuch waved away the criticism and fixed Shay with a quizzical smile.

'It was … magical.' She was still blindsided.

'Thank you. You were pretty good yourself. Might we persuade you to visit us again? Tomorrow, even? I think I can get Evans to stretch to tuppence a performance.'

Tuppence. That was more than she got for an afternoon's messages. She pretended to think about it, even though she would have happily come back for free.

Nonesuch kicked at a table. 'Anyway, here's the lad who should be thanking you, seeing as you saved his bony arse.'

Trussell was drawing quickly. His right hand drummed on the table while the left worked steadily on a sketch taking shape. A naked woman, lying on a couch with her right arm thrown backwards and her head turned away. Her hair was down and pearls accentuated her nudity. Shay thought it might be the whore who she'd seen in the audience. There were drawings tacked up over nearly every bunk and they all looked like his work. There were girls and ladies in swanlike, sinuous poses. Giant bears fought with dogs and wolves, a bull tossed a gentleman on its horns. The smaller boys had more innocent work: sleeping dogs and rural cottages, mothers and fathers, and one boy had a heart-rending mixture of flashy nudes and huge-eyed kittens. Trussell finished with a flourish, looked up, and realised they'd been talking to him. His blush was instant and comprehensive. 'Oh. I'm sorry. Yes, thank you, Shay.'

She took the drawing from him. *I'm just one of the boys*, she told herself. 'It's beautiful,' she said. 'Is it the woman in the box earlier?'

'Yes. I didn't get a proper look.' He was embarrassed, she thought. 'You can keep it.'

She had to offer. 'What do I owe you?'

'Nothing. You saved me out there with your prompting, thank you.' Alouette laughed but a gleam came over him. 'Oh, actually there is something you could do. You're a flapper, right?' He blushed again. 'Sorry, an *Aviscultan*.'

Shay's heart dropped. She didn't know what had given her away. The borrowed cap was still pulled over her horns of hair so he must have caught a glimpse of the sparrows tattooed on her inner wrists. Uselessly she tugged down her sleeves. Now would come the questions. Did she really worship birds? Could she speak with magpies? Could she *fly*?

She wiped the worry from her expression and said, 'Yes, I am.'

Trussell's nose twitched. There was something rabbity about him. 'And you have the fortune cards?'

Everyone knew that flappers meant fortune-telling and everyone thought that fortune-telling meant the cards. Shay could read them well enough, if need be, but they were childish things compared with the real mysteries. But she *was* a guest.

'Of course,' she said, checking her pockets for her cards. 'Think of a question that consumes you.' Even the ritual words tasted musty.

'No, sorry, I don't want a reading.' He looked around the room: the clamour, the dust. 'I'm not sure I want to know my future at the moment. But I would love to see the drawings on the cards.'

She handed them over and Trussell fanned them out and picked through them, making involuntary, guttural noises at ones that he liked.

'This is ...' he isolated a card that showed an empty carriage, pulled by slavering dogs, speeding through the night. 'It's so beautiful. Who painted them?'

Shay'd never thought of the cards having a creator; they had always been part of her life. 'I'm not sure, sorry. They've been around my home for years. I have more sets. Would you like to keep them?'

'I couldn't.' Still, he had both hands in the pile now, turning cards over at random. His eyes were hungry across their surface and Shay felt an immediate need to make him happy. *They have so little.*

'What if I were to keep them here then, with you? You'd be doing me a favour.'

'Oh. That would be ... It would be so kind.' Even as he spoke, he couldn't take his eyes from the cards and his gaze flickered across them, flames on paper. He turned over three in quick succession and reflexively Shay read them.

Five of Cups. Five of Wands. Three of Swords: Jealousy. Strife. Loss.

Afterwards, outside again, the cold had come down hard. Shay and Alouette stood under the eaves where girls still waited, ratty in the drizzle. Drivers brought carriages around, rattling across the cobbles, and a stream of men leapt onto running boards and called out destinations: dicing houses, taverns, bowling alleys. Alouette had picked up more boxes on the way out and she was unsteady under their weight.

'That was kind, back there with Trussell,' she said. 'They will be his prize possession, I know. You really don't need them?'

Shay shook her head. 'They're a toy.' Usually she left any mention of her home life at the city gates, but Alouette, with her explosions and powders and lightning at her fingertips, made her feel ordinary. 'Real fortunes can only be told out in the wild, among the birds.' She gestured eastwards. Alouette would love Birdland, Shay was sure. The temple her people had built there to house and worship birds was as spectacular as anything conjured on the Blackfriars stage.

She looked around them. There was a gleam of rain on carriage lacquer and the smell of perfume. Brass door handles and musicians playing exit music. Money everywhere. She would be late home but tuppence in her pocket would soften her father's anger. She kept her voice light. 'So, do I get paid?'

Alouette's minute eyebrow raise was a sign, thought Shay. She was well-off enough that talk of getting paid was vulgar. She pulled her collar higher. 'Yes, of course, I suppose. Speak with Forster tomorrow and he'll sort you out. I think Nonesuch said tuppence.'

She looked ready to leave but something in Shay's voice must have caught on her, or maybe she noticed the thinness of Shay's shirt against the chill. 'I could pay you myself and sort out the details tomorrow?'

Shay's hand was out, wet with rain, in a moment.

4

A RAINSTORM BROKE AT six bells as the city drained home. Shay kept a hand on the pennies in her pocket as she walked south to the sound of drunks singing and the rainwater rushing through the streets. She made herself unremarkable – hands in pockets and as heedless of the other walkers as any man – and trod lightly until she was at Buttolphe Wharf. She waited in the shadows as passengers stepped from the murk onto the sodden boards of the wharf. A scrappy mist was rising and the lights of Southwark brightened and dimmed across the river. Faraway fires illuminated the last bear-baiting of the day. London never rested. To her left, the roar of the bridge's waterwheel cut through the fog, and to her right, she could just make out the windmills of Horsleydown. Constant motion. Shay squatted in the lee of a wall; there was no sign of her father's boat yet.

Above her the skeleton of a new tower rose from the remains of a monastery, and workmen cried out to each other, some in English, some in Flemish. The monks' cells had already been converted into houses and now the stones of the outer walls were being reshaped into a tower that would add twenty more rooms. Every day brought more buildings to the city. Houses grew new storeys and roads sprouted whole districts. Slums shot up like mushrooms around the gates. They said in the six months it took to draw a map of the city it was already hopelessly out of date. Wind and water and fire and stone: London consumed them all. It harnessed them and drove onward, as much a river as a city.

Shay listened to the river's whisper, storm drain gurgle, and the hushed conversations of waiting oarsmen. If it hadn't been for the cries of the passengers – 'Westward ho!' or 'Oars, oars' – she might have slept. The crowd thinned and those left were either hushed by the mist or stupefied with drink.

Bells rang twice while she waited. Lonan was late. The water was as grey as woodsmoke and lanterns were lit in the distance. Then, finally, a familiar prow peeled itself out of the mist. Its white paint looked grey in the gloom and the beak was invisible, but Shay knew the curve of it. She gave a low whistle which was echoed back to her. She levered herself from her hiding place and shook some feeling back into her feet. Careful steps over the wet boards and then – too late – she froze. Three men, gentlemen by the cut of their clothes, stood talking at the water's edge. She hadn't heard them arrive so they must have walked along the foreshore; there was a gaming house a few streets over.

'Oars. For fuck's sake, oars,' yelled one, out across the river. As if in answer, the white boat glided out of the mist but the gentlemen were staring upstream. Shay kept to the shadows and tiptoed onto the wharf. She shuffled to the edge of the boards and caught the rope that she knew would be thrown from the boat. As quietly as possible she wrapped the rope around the iron ring. Her father stood with one foot on the boat and one on the wharf to pull the craft closer. He didn't say a word. The boat had barely grazed the wharf before she was reaching for the rope but then a boot stepped lightly on her fingers. A gentle pressure, but enough to let her know not to move.

'What's this?' The man pulled back his boot and squatted down, placing his hand over Shay's. Again, he did it gently, as if about to give bad news. He called out to the boatman. 'Did you not hear me call "oars"?' His eyes scanned Shay. They were sharp; he wasn't as drunk as she'd hoped.

A voice from the water, her father playing up his feebleness. 'I did, sir. But this isn't much of a boat for a fine crowd such as you. It's a squeeze for three farmers, let alone three gentlemen. I thought I would take this young lady across and you might take a wherry. There are plenty out on the water still. Cushioned they are, and covered over. Some might even have a tot of rum to keep out the chill.'

'Young lady, you say?' The man pushed back Shay's cap. Whatever he saw there didn't surprise him. 'Well, I think we can decide whether your boat provides the diversions we require. And we could always make a detour to drop off this young lady on our way.'

Shay stiffened. The best outcome was that she got in the boat alone. The next best was that the men took the boat and she slept here. The five of them in the boat together would be the very worst thing that could

28

happen. A terrifying, adult decision: if she were to struggle, was he more or less likely to take the boat? Her father hesitated and then dropped to his knees. She saw the stiffness in his legs and how uncomfortably he folded himself up. He pulled a lantern close to his face and opened his eyes wide. Two marbled orbs, speckled and deep, like curdled milk. Pupils hidden somewhere within like fish under Thames ice. He rolled them left and right; funny, if you weren't trusting your life to him.

'As you say, sirs. Perhaps you will be kind enough to let me know of any smaller obstacles, the larger I sense well enough.'

A hoot of laughter rang out from one of the man's companions. 'Oh-ho, I didn't think the journey home would be the most dangerous part of tonight. Only you could choose a slut who looks like a prentice boy and a blind ferryman.'

The man looked from Shay to her father, and then back to his companions. He removed his hand from hers and, watching all the time, shoved her, hand on arse, into the boat. Then with the same bored air he kicked the boat away from the wharf. The rope rushed through her hands and the mist swallowed the figures in an instant. His cry came again from the shore: 'Oars, oars. Westward ho and for God's sake, oars.'

Shay collapsed back into the boat, making it rock. 'I'm sorry, Father,' she said, 'I thought the wharf was empty.'

His back was to her. 'No, it was my mistake too. I heard voices but I thought they were east of the wharf. It's this fog.'

Shay began to row while her father steered with a single long oar. He stood tall, sniffing at the air and reading the vibrations from the water. He read the tides better than anyone else on the river and Shay marvelled at the subtlety of his movements. They cut across the river, heading for the south bank where traffic was quieter. He kept up a series of low, bubbling whistles and got back an occasional call. About fifty yards across, a voice swaddled in mist said, 'That you, Lonan?'

'It is. I've not seen you all night, John. You empty?'

'I am. Been out to Westminster but I'm looking for one more fare before I head home.' The man was invisible but Shay could hear the rhythm of oars keeping the boat still.

'There are three gentlemen on Buttolphe Wharf. Rich enough and heading west.'

Shay heard no warning in her father's voice but the unseen voice laughed. 'But?'

29

'They've been gaming and I'm not sure their sport is over for the night.'

A silence as her father's words hung on the air.

'Thank you, Lonan. It's too late in the day for games, I'll try elsewhere, I think.'

South towards the riverbank. The bridge was a word on the tip of your tongue: close but elusive. Sleeping swans appeared and were lost in the mist. The boat came within a yard of a cob with his beak tucked between his wings and Shay saw a thin eye open and close. 'The birds are gods,' she whispered. South of the river belonged to animals. Lonan brought them close enough to Southwark to hear the bleat of sheep. Some unfortunate countryman had arrived after the bridge had closed and would be sleeping in the warm heart of his flock tonight. Guard dogs barked in the better riverfront properties while geese hissed in the poorer. East, downriver: bull cries and the snuffle and roar of bears. Tomorrow's entertainment proclaiming its existence, perhaps for the final time.

Lonan said, 'You're late tonight – I've been by a couple of times. We'll only just make the Murmuration.' Shay knew that he was trying to keep reproach from his voice.

She said, 'I ended up with a new job. An odd kind of thing but it pays tuppence. I'll put my back into it and we'll be there before the starlings.' Her father leant into the rudder, moving the boat fractionally away from the bank. Spiky tangles of coots' nests clumped under overhanging roots.

'Did you see any birds on your travels?' he asked.

She wouldn't mention the bird shop because he'd worry. Instead, she told him about the pair of peregrines that she'd seen near Gray's Inn Road. Her heart had leapt when she saw them, not so much for her, but to be able to tell her father later. Peregrines were old favourites of his, and rare near the city now that it was noisy and overhung by smoke. She said, 'Carts coming from the north were driving voles out into the fields and the peregrines hunted for hours.' She wished she could express the way the bird had transformed in front of her, its transition from a hanging thing into a twist of violence, barrelling down, rotating and accelerating until the talons snapped forward, the bird scuffing onto the ground and coming away with something limp in its claws.

'They're faster than death, you know?' said Lonan, edging the boat towards a rush of tide. Shay had heard him say this many, many times, but could always stand to hear it again.

'The fastest we men can go here on earth is on horseback. Up to thirty miles in an hour. The only men who've been faster than that were those falling to their death.' His laugh was a creak of oars. 'It's true, the fastest men were those on their way to die. To reach fifty miles in an hour you'd have to fling yourself from a cliff. But your peregrines today. Sixty miles! Sixty miles in an hour! Faster even than death.'

He sniffed at the air. They were east of the city now and Southwark's meat and smoke and ale and sewer were being replaced by country odours. Shay rowed harder until she could feel the sweat cool on her skin.

Later, Shay thought that she should have kept talking about the birds. Lonan manoeuvred them around the eddies of Placentia Palace's sea gate and once they were back on still water his voice had changed. 'Remember diving here when we were courting, love? We swam right under those barges.'

Shay stopped rowing. It wasn't unusual for Lonan's memory to become unmoored when they were back at home. At times he would talk to her as if she were Ava, her mother, dead these eleven years. Normally, when it happened, she gently reminded him, in the voice you might use with a dog, 'Mother's gone, Father. It's me, Shay, your daughter.' And usually that was enough. He would grumble and fiddle but he would use her name carefully from then on. Usually. Sometimes though, however dangerous it might be, she said nothing when he went into this kind of reverie. She had so little of her mother left: her tortoiseshell comb, her sewing things and these moments. They were the only times that Lonan spoke of her and in those fragile, tender seconds it was as if her mother came silently to sit alongside them. She envied nothing of her father's life except this: he had moments when he was with Ava again. But now wasn't the time for that. Not on the swan-boat where a tantrum would put them both in freezing water. She said, as plainly as she could manage, 'I'm Shay, your daughter. Ava's not here, Father,' and he was silent for a long while after that.

East again with the river racing, a tidal tug that doubled her strength. At Wapping, unspeaking, Lonan guided them deeper into the centre of the Thames. The Wapping gallows were reserved for pirates and their corpses hung low above the water until the tides had drowned them three times over. She hated to see it: bodies so bruise-purple and bloated that they squeezed like sausage meat from their clothes. Gulls would set about them in furious flurries, with beaks wet from digging deep for the juiciest prizes, and miles further on you'd still see the piles of feathers stained red with blood.

There was still a semicircle of sun in the west as the nets of Birdland came into view. Dusk meant the Murmuration: the vast flock of starlings that roosted on the marsh. As twilight fell they performed a whirling aerial display, a display from which Shay, like her mother before her, was supposed to divine some kind of meaning. She squinted out over the marsh. There was no sign of the birds yet but a raggle-taggle procession of people snaked out between the nets and the marsh's lone tree. Wings of hair silhouetted against the grey as the adults led; babble and scurry of the younger ones scattering lugworms for the crows. They moved at the pace of the slowest: men on sticks, women bent double. It looked like the whole Birdland community was there. They'd started without her.

They tied up the boat as daylight faded. Normally the path home to Birdland would be illuminated with a zigzag of torches, but they'd not been lit tonight. That was no problem for Lonan. He led the way across the most solid parts of the marsh where their feet only sank an inch into the spongy surface. Occasionally, in the distance, a plume of marsh gas spouted, treating the dusk to the kind of deep, cold blue that you'd imagine only the sky could provide. Shay sensed Birdland off to their left. The faintest of glows circumscribed the outline of the empty homes.

They caught up with the rest of the Aviscultans just yards before they reached the tree, and Shay slid in at the front of the line, trying to give the impression of arriving exactly on time. 'The birds are gods,' she said automatically, and won a volley of 'And the gods are birds' from the fledglings. An elderly man took her father's arm and the pair disappeared back into the column of people. Shay ignored the thinness of the crowd. This was all of them. In her mother's time there would have been twice the number, and *she* used to reminisce about the crowds of her own youth. The pace was slow and Shay used the time to get her mind in order. As always, she calmed herself by imagining a hawk's-eye view. Up, up, up until the parade was a charcoal arrow on a white background pointing to the bullseye of the starlings' tree. It worked its distant magic and her tension drained away.

'Here. Let's stop.' She halted the group twenty feet from the tree on a dryish patch of grass and the babble died down. She lay on her back and around her people fell gratefully to the ground. Damp grass seeped against her shoulder blades and buttocks. Her voice had sounded good. Often it wouldn't do what she wanted but today she was authoritative. The children ran around, elastic with excitement, darting to the tree and back again, while scanning the skies for the first returning bird.

Shay loved the moments just before something happened. It was the same hush that had fallen as the curtain was drawn back at Blackfriars. A hundred sets of eyes on the heavens as a single bird appeared, a lone pencil mark on a paper sky. Then a couple more, then a trickle, then a river, and then, like a cloudburst, thousands of birds turned the sky illegible, too many to count, too many to see, even; the numbers pinned and shrunk you. The sky boiled until, with a grace that even now left Shay breathless, the birds became a single entity.

What were they? They were the shape of candle smoke or that twist of stars that lights clear nights. They were black silk. Patterns dissolved seamlessly into one another as they took on a form that was older than the earth itself, from an age before men's straight lines. The flock flexed like a muscle and she felt its torsion and bulge, the way it stretched away.

Shay tried to inhabit her mother's voice – words weighted to keep them from being wind-whipped across the marsh. When it had been Shay and her mother lying out here hand in hand, her mother's thumb would trace a pattern on Shay's palm – unconsciously or consciously, Shay never knew. Years later she still felt its absence, like the first time she lost a tooth. Tongue exploring that fresh loss, her body a foreign country.

She made a fist and watched her tribe. A hundred humans huddled in thrall to ten thousand cavorting starlings. Even the little ones – the fledglings – who had cooed and cheered and gasped at the display were now breathless on their backs. She wished that this was enough. To lie damp under the sky and shrink in awe at the oldest of languages. Why did people have to know what it meant?

What she wanted to say was that it looked like London, with its beauty and wildness and the way it changed while staying the same. It had the city's graceful panic and heart-flutter joy. And, like London, to see the flock was to be part of it, there were no bystanders. But there were unspoken rules about what the Murmuration was allowed to reveal. Even the future has its traditions.

Would she ever have the gleam that had lit her mother's eyes on these occasions? She doubted it, but Shay doubted everything. Every eye watched her – needful, thirsty – and she took a deep breath. How had Nonesuch done it? She waited seconds longer than she normally would have done and sharpened the edges of her voice.

'Did we all see a candle and a wick?' A question. Shay loved the way that her mother had led you to the doorway of revelation and then invited you to step through, it made the Murmuration a gift rather than a lesson.

'Did we see bright flames that danced in the wind, and at their heart the silent fuel?'

The weight of it all. Rainclouds bearing down and black figures sullen and sodden under a dome of rain. Everyone had agreed in those rudderless days after her mother's death, when morning came too soon and sleep too late, that Shay had the sight like no one else, but she dared not admit that her visions had always been partly play-acting; a way to feel closer to her mother.

'A candle and wick,' she said. A pause to let the others see it too. 'The world is made of flames.' Her mind was blank and the birds twisted like twine. Her hands were, and always would be, empty.

'We are the wick. All will burn but only we will survive.'

Later on, back at their house, people came by. Other Aviscultans who'd travelled down for the Murmuration, who brought news from Leeds and Gwent and Cornwall and Wexford. They had the same quiet gift for anonymity that Shay had cultivated. Nothing in their beliefs was illegal but these were suspicious times and no one with any sense drew attention to their differences. They were uniformly small and quiet and endlessly deferential towards Shay. She tried to play with the children – it seemed only days ago that she was one of them herself – but the fledglings were rigid with politeness. They brought food. Once it would have been treats: crystallised ginger from the Royal Exchange or genuine French brandy, but this year it was staples. The Johnsons had brought barley, and there was a bag of turnips, still caked in mud, hanging by the front door. Shay hadn't had to ask for these things. Lonan's skin hung down like old clothes and the river had already frozen twice this year. Every iced-over day meant no money for the boatmen. Shay mingled among the strangers and left half of her dinner unfinished; Lonan could have it tomorrow and she could eat at the theatre. One single afternoon there and already she was planning her return to the Blackfriars. Why did she always want to be wherever she wasn't? In the city, with the smoke and the shit and the grabbing hands and the way money was always just around the corner, but never this corner, well, it made her yearn for a horizon and enough air to swallow her cries. But back in Birdland she was hemmed in by the scale of the place. Today she would swap this sky and marsh for a wooden box in front of a stage and a world unfolding from a painted mouth.

'Do the honours, Shay?' Colm held out a razor and strop.

The girl sat with her back to Shay, her shoulders hunching as Colm rubbed ox fat into what was left of her hair. It had been cut without care, ready for the shaving, and the girl fitted the name fledgling better than most today. Shay knelt and whispered in her ear, 'It won't take a moment.' The girl sat very still. She looked composed but her muscles were taut under the soft fuzz of her neck, and she flinched when Shay laid a hand on her. The girl was one of the flock of youngsters who followed her on her rounds every morning. Her mother would have known the girl's name and would have had a pocketful of sunflower seeds ready to press into her hand. Shay knelt and took the girl by the shoulders.

'What's your name?'

'Chahine.' An old name, Arabian, from back in Aviscultan history before they were windblown all over Europe. Too big a name for a fledgling somehow, like a child dressing in a grown-up's clothes.

'Do you want to see my tattoo first, Chahine?' The tiniest of nods. The girl parted the stubble on Shay's crown to look at the bird pictured beneath.

'Nice,' she said tentatively.

Shay stayed on her knees. 'I had it done two years ago now and it hardly hurt at all. What have you chosen for yours?'

The girl continued playing with Shay's hair. 'A goshawk,' she whispered.

35

'Oh.' Shay's surprise was genuine. Girls tended to choose peacocks or parrots. Usually it was just the boys who went for the hunters. 'Such a fierce little fledgling.' She gave the girl's ear a playful tweak.

The girl wriggled and grinned. 'I want to do the Murmuration when you're gone. I *have* to be a lone bird.'

Shay looked around to make sure no one else was listening and kept her voice low. 'When I'm gone?'

Her readings had never been as popular as her mother's but as far as she knew the Murmuration was a job for life. She hadn't asked for the role; it had been handed to her, along with her mother's things. The girl bowed her head and Shay held the razor poised, ready to shave.

'I just meant if you weren't around,' she said with her head down. 'If you went away or something.' But after that she couldn't look Shay in the eyes.

A starless night and an empty belly. Theirs was the only house with the ladder still down. Shay stamped her feet at the bottom as Lonan climbed and then she followed, placing her hands where his had melted the skin of frost from the rungs. Inside it was bitterly cold, with a thin tang of river water. She lit a candle while her father oriented himself. He touched his glass, his pouch, his needlework, until, satisfied, he collapsed back into the chair.

'A fire?' asked Shay. In previous years they lit a daily fire as soon as autumn arrived but money was scarce now. Cold pooled in the corners of the room and the furniture stored winter right at its core.

'I'm not sure it's worth it. I'll be asleep in a quarter-hour,' Lonan said, his breath white in the candlelight. Shay was relieved, and saw that there were only two scrawny logs in the basket anyway. She should have bought firewood in town today. If she'd taken one more message, then she would have had enough money to fill the wood basket and end the charade that it was somehow still autumn. But London swept the memories and responsibilities of this place clean out of her. Once she was in the city, Birdland – her home, the place she was born, her family – became something out of a story to her.

'Tomorrow then, I'll make it cosy for you,' she said. Since Lonan had lost his sight, his emotions floated to the surface more easily. His smile was brief and luminous and, as always, it stuck a needle in her. To be so loved shouldn't be such a burden. She tried to warm her hands in her pockets and found the twist of paper. 'Hey, I got you something.' She knelt in front of him and unfurled the thick wrapper. He followed the rustling with a tilt of the head and she held it under his nose. The colour was so much like amber that you expected to see an insect trapped inside, beneath its grit of sugar.

His nostrils twitched. 'Like a peach. No, peach and orange.' She touched it to his lips and he opened wide like a baby bird. He waited with it on his tongue, then closed his mouth and worked it around. Again, the pinprick of guilt; the depths of relish he found in a taste were glorious and shaming. He chewed, moving it from cheek to cheek. 'I really don't know. It's delicious though.'

'It's called an apricot,' she said.

The wind was low but still the movements of the nets transmitted vibrations through the fabric of the house. Shay slept curled around the spar that ran through the room, a conduit between the sky and the ground, and let its familiar tremors soothe her.

5

THE COLD WOKE HER. It snuffled under the blankets and in between her clothes, nagging at her skin. *Get up.* She moved as quietly as she could; quickly enough to pump some blood into her numbed toes but slowly enough not to wake her father. Two sticks of firewood and no breakfast. She'd leave the last of the bread for Lonan's lunch but that was all there was until she returned. She used the wood to boil some water. It took forever in the cold so she sat on the step and looked out over Birdland while she waited.

The huge dome of nets stretched away across the marshes, over six hundred feet, larger than St Paul's Church, as the Aviscultans liked to boast. Even in her doorway far from the centre Shay could hear its dawn chorus washing the air clean. She sat for longer than usual, letting it sweep across her. The chorus rolled and tumbled like surf, with song overwriting song until it became one voice. One containing all, all containing one. How could city folk be content with their church bells and dirges while this sweet, chittering anarchy was loose in the air every morning?

A whack on her behind. 'Stop letting the warmth out.' Lonan's voice was clotted with sleep. He turned back into the room and she watched him move automatically around the space. Mornings were usually the worst; the past inundated him as he slept. Shay imagined memories falling like rain into his dreams. She saw vast sheets of the past tear from the sky and sweep his bed out into a sea of remembrance. Sometimes he woke and didn't know where he was, as if his bed had washed up on some mountaintop. Those days were the worst; the pair lived twenty feet in the air and Lonan's bones were as brittle as a sparrow's. Shay would talk and talk with his hand in hers, thumb stroking his palm as she spoke their life back into existence, putting names to the formless things that eluded him. *Shay. Birdland. The nets. Kettle. Stove.* Over and over until the night's fog had burnt away.

He fell back into his chair, his mouth opening and closing dumbly as his hands reached for something only he could see. Shay knelt to stroke the back of his hand, making little sparrow calls to scare away the night's terrors. He gaped and shook and then calmed. A weak hand reached around her wrist. His skin was as soft as dock leaves now.

'It's all right, Father. It's Shay. Shay. Your *daughter*. Ava's daughter.' A flash of sunlight raced across his face at the mention of Ava's name.

'It's Shay. Listen, I know I said I'd stay home this week but some work has come up in the city.' She dared not mention the theatre but there was a white lie that she had been saving for a day like this. 'I thought this might be the time to go and tend to Lord Eltham's falcon. Devana – remember her? Remember the weeks we spent training her?'

The unconscious eloquence of his face betrayed him. Everything fell like a sack of grain dumped on the wharf-side. His words were neutral though.

'If you think that it's wise.'

After some tea he was more alert, mischievous even. He sat on the edge of the bed and fumbled for his sunflower seeds. Casually he flicked a couple in the air and caught them in his mouth like a gull. It was a trick from the days before his eyes clouded. She shook her head at him, pointlessly, and was halfway to asking if there was any jam left when she stopped. If there were then he would have offered.

He sipped at his tea and his blank eyes flitted back and forth. She didn't want to leave while he was still halfway between worlds so she coaxed his infuriating limbs into his clothes and he sat up a little straighter. His face's weather brightened. '*Devana*. That falcon. Now there's a bird, *there's* a bird. I saw her take a fawn once, easy as picking up this cup.' He lifted his mug and tea slopped over one side.

Shay said, 'I know. I know. I sometimes see her above the royal hunting grounds and she's looking *strong*. It's been a while since I was there, so I thought it was time to polish up her hood and gyres, maybe mend a feather or two.'

Not much of a lie; she would have to go to Lord Eltham's soon enough, and unspoken was the fee: a sovereign every three-month was a fortune these days.

'I'll take you in. There's no ice today.' He put the tea down with a bump and levered himself surprisingly nimbly out of his chair. His clothes were askew and Shay looked away. White skin, white hair, white eyes.

'No!' It came out louder than she'd wanted. 'Lord Eltham might not see me for a day or two and it's up four flights of stairs.'

He nodded, seriously. 'All right. All right, I suppose. You can handle it, love.'

A hiccup of joy rose in her. When had he last called her 'love'? She guided him back into his chair, chirruping softly.

'You can handle it. You know what to do.' His eyes were on the ceiling and he gripped the chair's arms. Then he sat upright. 'Of course, really the girl should do it but I don't know what to do with her, Ava. She doesn't have the … the … patience. She turns up late, she mumbles her way through the Murmuration and then she disappears off to the city for days at a time. *Birds* know where she goes.'

Even in the cold Shay's cheeks burned. Lonan sipped at his tea and made a face. 'I don't know what we'll do with her.' He moved his head like a bird's, trying to sniff her out. 'Ava? Ava, my love? Are you still there?'

Silently Shay climbed down the ladder.

Most of Birdland was up and awake. Leaden smoke rose from chimneys and ladders were down beneath every doorway. The nets were thick with frost and they gleamed like a filigreed bowl thrown over the marsh. Two boys with rods over their shoulders picked their way towards the river, pretending to push each other off the path. Someone was up, undoing the nets already. Shay waved and recognised Colm from his sweep of arm.

She took the rope bridge across to the nets. Its sway was as familiar as a song and she strolled through the morning light, in the air but not of it. The nets spread for half a mile, encasing Birdland's drab hexagon of marshland. Shay knew them as a part of her, like two hands cupped over her life. At the edges the supports were little more than staffs driven deep into the ground, holding up the finest of the nets: twine knotted into squares too small for even wrens to pass through. But Shay headed for the centre, instantly picking up a following of the younger children who pretended their route through hillocks and mud pools only coincidentally followed directly beneath Shay. Some mornings she'd slow until the fledglings milled around her for the rest of the journey, but today she was in a hurry. Near the centre the supports grew from saplings to masts, angled away from the middle. Their tops were holed and grooved to allow the thicker ropes to pass through, a spider's web with hexagons of rope thicker than your arm encasing smaller hexagons, each one patterned with thin nets.

And birds. Everywhere birds. The sound hit you first: vast waterfalls of birdsong, overspilling like a treasure hoard. On first hearing it was a thick braid of noise but as your ears grew accustomed you picked out individual songs. The padded ruffles of wood pigeons and the stream of wren song. Sparrows bickering across the music-box tunes of the great tit. Blackbirds moaned and there was something human to their tone, as if they might break into speech if they so wanted. There were complex helices of melody, surely too ornate for one delicate throat to produce. Cheeps and burbles, warlike caws, lovers' coos, flutters and warbles. Flutes, whole orchestras of them, bassoons, hand drums and viola screech. And then, when the air was too full, bursting with song, you raised your eyes to see a sky *seething* with birds. Unconstrained by human patterns, their paths were crazy, crazed, cracked.

Shay threw her shoulders back, inhaled and let it envelop her. Everything was airborne and nothing had any weight. She gazed up at the kingdom: the automatic writing of birds' paths, the avian orchestra tuning up, the sky alive. Behind her the gaggle of children did the same.

She hung fat-balls as she went and scattered seed into the upturned seashells that protruded from every tree trunk. Bacon rashers and Thames lugworms and scraps and seeds. Anything they could scavenge from that wasteful, extravagant city upstream or dig up on their own doorstep. For the first time that day she threw off the spell of the theatre and properly looked around her. She gestured down at the children on the ground below.

'Sing for me,' she said. Faces gazed up, expectant but close-mouthed.

She mocked a sigh. 'I have to do everything myself, do I? All right, I see, where to start?' A history song, perhaps, one that even the little ones would know. She aimed her voice down towards them and started to sing. 'We wandered from the east lands, no home of our own.'

Instantly the fledglings echoed her: *from the east, from the east.*

'Banished and harried and ever windblown.'

She raised her flattened palm to her mouth and the children, giggling, did the same. They blew imaginary seeds as she sang on.

41

'Windblown like seeds across the land and the sea.'

The sea, oh the sea, sang the children.

'But then came the falcon to guide us safely.'

The children raised their arms to the heavens.

'Where birds go we follow, we sleep where they roost.

And honour with shelter, protection and food.'

Some of the younger fledglings mimed birds pecking at grain.

'Their flights are our footpaths, their songs are our words.

The birds are our gods and—' She let the fledglings shout out the last line like the answer to a question at school: *The gods are birds!*

Shay could see Colm smile, even though he was a level above her. As the children collapsed in laughter he shouted down to her, 'Come and see me before you leave.'

She walked the rope bridges, feeling clumsy among the whirl of wings. Sparrows darted around her, eyes on her pail of food. Children's laughter and birdsong; it wiped away the morning's fog.

Colm waited at the very top of the nets for Shay to finish her rounds, his face turned up to catch the light. He had a stillness to him that Shay had only ever seen with Aviscultans. A sparrow landed happily on his arm, pecked experimentally at some seed dust, worried at a tail-feather and then flew off. He didn't notice. Still looking skywards, he asked, 'Busy day yesterday?'

'Six bells. Some problems with the crossing.'

She hadn't thought of it since: those black eyes and a boot on her hand. The blitheness of it.

'Lonan picked you up.' A statement. But weighted.

'Yes, he likes to. Says he can't sleep otherwise.'

Colm was her father's age. 'He sleeps fine, Shay, you know that.'

She said nothing. She started to untie the topknot at the very apex of the nets. Usually Colm hardly spoke, so this breaking of his silence meant something.

'It's too much to ask of him, Shay.' He didn't look at her.

'I don't ask.' Shay could hear the edge of whine in her own voice.

'You know what I mean. You're not a child any more. Doing nothing is doing something.'

'What do you suggest, that I tell him not to come? He would turn up anyway. Or he'd forget that I told him not to.'

'Not if you said you had a ride arranged. Not if you borrowed his swan-boat. Not if you told him you were staying in the city.' He untwisted a tie. 'There are a hundred ways, Shay. And I shouldn't have to tell you that.'

He hauled back the top net, lifting it over the struts to frame a perfect hexagon of sky. Birdland was open to the heavens. A couple of nearby pigeons flew out and perched on the ropes. Colm scattered seed around the entrance and talked, seemingly to the birds. 'We need you here. That's every day this week you've been in the city. It can't only be us old men running things.' He gestured at the gaggle of fledglings. Shay saw the girl with the goshawk tattoo and waved. All the children waved back.

Colm said, 'We're losing too many fledglings to the city. They don't follow me like they do with you. They won't help out with Ellis or Crow, or any of them.' He was quiet but Shay knew there was more. And still some ticking part of her mind was calculating how soon the Long Ferry might arrive.

'And what about the next time there's a Murmuration?' The fact that he had to ask showed that he doubted her, and it made Shay ache.

'I'll make sure I get word of it. I will be here.'

'Be here to lead us? Not just among us?'

Shay nodded. She sensed that he wasn't convinced but Colm wasn't a man for arguments. They sat and watched the nets for a while. Gulls left, drawn away by the heat and the river smell. Pigeons arrived for easy pickings. Two finches loitered around the entrance – in and out, in and out – as if unsure of their plans. Time stood still until city bells rang again, a pretty sound at this distance, and wordlessly the pair of them hauled the top net closed. The fledglings had headed on to their lessons and Shay climbed down through the heedless birds to the path to the jetty.

The marsh was flat and open with a horizon like a freehand pencil line. Shay was the tallest thing for furlongs, at least until the mast of the Long Ferry appeared, right on time, cleaving the last of the mist. As she walked, guilt and relief marched in lockstep alongside her. Lonan needed a village of care. He needed a cook, a seer, a provider, a priest, a nursemaid and, most troublingly now that the cards of his memory were so thoroughly shuffled, a wife. The only roles that Shay knew how to play were useless to him. She was daughter, messenger, roof-runner, thief. Here, in their little room in the fog, she was nothing.

6

CURLEWS AND JACKDAWS, OARSPLASH and sailwhip: the Thames was as busy as any city street. Shay leant her elbows over the side of the ferry and watched the marshes melt away. Gulls called overhead. In minutes London began to rise around her like a stage set; life's scenery was hauled upright. Streets like canyons and buildings tall as cliffs. The ferry began to race now, like a horse nearing its stable, and they plunged deeper into the traffic until the river was blanketed with so many boats that Shay felt that she could step from one to another all the way to the shore. The boats performed an intricate dance, birdlike in the way that they criss-crossed but never collided. Waves clapped a greeting on the side of the ferry and the buildings grew taller still, engulfing her until the boat was dipped into a vast, friendly cauldron of noise. London. She loved it.

The previous night Nonesuch had promised to meet her from the ferry but Shay supposed he was just being gallant in front of his friends. So her heart gave a little kick – a horse let out of its stables – when she saw him waiting there on the wharf. He was deep in conversation with a florid tub of a man who dabbed constantly at the sweat on his neck, even though there was still ice on the darker fringes of the river. As the ferry glided up to the jetty, Shay saw them embrace and the fat man limp away. Nonesuch turned to offer her a hand down but she shot him a look – *messenger-boy not flapper-girl, remember* – so he stood, arms crossed, and watched her disembark.

He sounded amused. 'Well, good morning, young blade.'

She doffed her cap. 'Blade.' The ferryman's eyes were curious on the pair of them.

They walked along the waterfront with the morning sunlight sending their shadows rushing out in front of them. Shay loved the way the city stretched and creaked into life. Prentices yawned, arm in arm and surely late already, dodging the spray from sailors washing down the decks. Gangs of gulls patrolled on the lookout for country folk who didn't know to shield their bread, and maids bustled like pigeons, repeating shopping lists under their breath.

'Who was your friend? The fat fellow,' Shay asked.

Nonesuch shrugged ostentatiously. 'Never saw him before in my life. He was just resting there. I make a point of impersonating somebody new every day, it keeps me on my toes.' He popped onto tiptoes and threw a one-two of punches into the air. 'It means I have to talk to a *lot* of strangers.' He said it as if it were some intolerable burden imposed on him, rather than a game of his own making.

They cut along Thames Street, perpendicular to the river, where it was quieter. Shay caught glimpses of ships between the houses as they walked: brief forests of swaying masts. 'So who were you today?'

'I was a French sailor who had missed his voyage home. After one night ashore among the perfidious English I'd been robbed, conned, beaten and drugged. I was trying to hire a fast boat to catch up with my ship before I was stuck here, *pour toujours.*'

He didn't look much like a French sailor. He was wearing an over-sized white shirt with a panel that had SATURNALIA NOW stitched across it. Shay laughed. 'Did he believe you?'

Nonesuch pulled a shilling from his pocket and winked. The slope of New Fish Street pulled them riverwards: London's tide always going out. They skirted the traffic that snarled around the entrance to the bridge and made for the deeper wharves where the ocean ships docked. Ships from Norway and Barbary and unnamed islands. Onshore there was a sweet, filthy smell of river mud and a saltwater tang from the ships themselves. Something was tossed from a deck and birds thrashed against the water in pursuit. Everywhere a creak like new shoe leather.

'And how was *your* show?' Shay had told him more than she'd planned yesterday. He'd heard about the Murmuration and the fortune-telling, the slow decline of her community. She was normally stingy with details of Birdland – you never knew who might be listening – but the Blackfriars Theatre's air of smoke and shadows leant itself to confession. Still, knowing that she'd talked so much about herself gave her an oddly naked feeling and she pulled her jacket tighter around her.

45

'It's not really a show. It's …' She couldn't think what it was. Maybe it wasn't that different to the theatre, after all. 'It went all right, but it was as if I was making it up as I went along.'

Wind whipped at sails like sporadic applause and they walked without talking for a while.

'I'd like to see it,' he said finally. 'The Murmuration, I mean. Though I doubt it could be as magical as I imagine.' He shook something off. 'I mean, what is?' He was quiet again as they skirted a patch of ice. 'Do you think your mother really saw the future?'

It was a question that Shay often asked herself. 'I don't know. Maybe there's some way of seeing things that I don't understand yet. I wish I could spend one minute in her mind. Just to see how it felt when it was happening.'

Already Shay loved the way Nonesuch listened to her. Whatever she said, he considered, seriously. He said, 'Ah, but then you'd be her, rather than you.' Wordlessly he took her hand and they walked beneath the bristling shadows of ships. They passed the hulk of the spice warehouse and for yards the air smelled of Christmas Day.

Here the ships were as big as churches, wedges of stern sending shadow spires across the foreshore. Warships were tied up together in a row, presenting mouth upon mouth of waiting cannon, gaping like baby birds. A troop of schoolboys, dawdling, wrote the ships' names down in notebooks and compared lists. Nonesuch hurried them along, reading off the ships' names – *Dreadnought, The Santa Ignatius, The Seahorse* – with such pride that Shay wondered quite how much schooling he'd had.

He asked, 'Isn't it odd, keeping your gods in nets? It's like locking up Saint Paul in the Tower.'

She checked his face for malice, or worse, pity, but his interest looked genuine. 'We open the nets back up every morning after feeding. And so many come back every day that it can't *feel* like captivity to them. Think of it as a church. Jesus isn't trapped in the chapel, is he? He's worshipped there.' A strange guilt swept her. Was that a heretical thing to say?

Nonesuch stole a glance to see if they were being overheard. 'Who knows? Perhaps if he weren't nailed to the cross, he'd want to be out in the streets too.' He was quiet for a moment. 'So how do they tell you how to behave?'

46

Shay tried to place each step in her argument, like she had so many times, like stones across a river. 'They're not those kinds of gods, Nonesuch.'

He jiggled the coins in his pocket. His stance said, *go on.*

'Our gods are ...' She'd never found the right words to capture the churn of feelings that Birdland sparked in her. 'They're ... heedless. And they're unknowable.' The next sentence she only said in her head. *Just like yours.* 'But they are beautiful and free. If you watch them, if you really *see* them, it's to know that there is another world.'

'But doesn't that just make them proof of God? Rather than the ... embodiment?' He said the last word with care, as if he were trying it out.

'Maybe,' Shay said. Even that much doubt would have drawn gasps back at Birdland. 'But they're so different from the insects and rocks and the flowers and the water.' She struggled for a Christian analogy. 'Think of them as angels.'

The paucity of language infuriated Shay. How to express the audacity of a magpie's tail-feathers or the cruelty of an eagle's beak? What words could capture a hummingbird's unlikeliness, or cage a hawk's talons? Grace. Awe. Love. Just words like leaky containers, slopping their meaning out with every movement. Words were down here with Shay in the mud.

She threw her head back in frustration and saw a snow-white cupid's bow of gull-wings arrow past. It was everything she'd said, but made flesh, and she laughed at the sheer joy of it.

Nonesuch followed her gaze and smiled. 'Of course, it does mean that your gods eat worms.'

He stopped a few paces further on and turned to her, made faceless by the sun behind him. 'I could show you what *I* believe in, if you're game. If you come to the theatre with me.'

Shay was unused to mirrors. Lonan had no need for them, obviously, and as for herself, she spent more time concealing her appearance than examining it. It meant she had to concentrate on holding her own gaze while Nonesuch painted a character across her. He hung shells from her hair and ears, and swiped a swallow-wing of black paint thick around her eyes. Beneath them he smudged two hearts of blusher, like she'd been pinched. Black oil combed into her long hair at the sides, which was then swept back, dried and slicked down like the ears of a hissing cat, covering her scalp tattoo. He smeared a white paste that smelled of beef fat across her lips. It was slippery and sticky and strands lengthened and broke when she spoke. A scornful face appeared, her but not her, and she thought *oh, here's another way to hide.* Out in London's streets there were eyes – men's eyes – that could pierce her disguise of caps and rags, but this painted shield would bounce such sharp gazes back at them. The old Shay was gone. She stuck her tongue out and was surprised to see her reflection do the same.

Then the outfit. Nonesuch pulled things from the costume room and held them up against her. He settled on a simple, high-necked gown in a bruisy purple and then draped her with necklace after necklace, from delicate chokers to mayoral medals, until she rattled like a gun cart if she turned her head. Even here, behind closed doors, Shay could feel the weight of attention the costume would draw. She was simultaneously vulnerable and powerful. The colour worried her most of all; purple was a regal hue, banned for all but the fanciest ladies and gentlemen, and there were places in the city where she could be arrested simply for wearing it, but Nonesuch was unconcerned. He stepped into the shadows to better examine his work and then said, almost to himself, 'Right. Yes. Let's see what kind of trouble we can get in, shall we?'

'Make way. You there, pull across.' Nonesuch steered traffic out of Shay's path while he scattered petals into the mud at her feet. She made sure to step on every single one; it seemed important, somehow. She concentrated on the smell of roses and fresh dung rather than watching the hundred faces turned her way. Still she felt them like a kind of pulsing heat. They stared from windows and shopfronts, they stopped their carts and gawped. The crowd flowed around her, attention coming in waves, and she looked up and away from them, nose in the air as she read the omens in the birds above: a rook, on the wing, and two magpies beak-deep in roof thatch. That meant danger and guile, one of her mother's favourite readings.

'What am I supposed to *be?*' she whispered to Nonesuch as he led her east into the quieter streets in the shadow of the city walls.

Nonesuch blinked away winter sunshine. 'I've no idea. Yet.'

They stopped somewhere just north of the gate, in a grubby, ramshackle area too poor to have featured in Shay's messengering. Nonesuch seemed to know where they were going though. He pointed her towards a gap between two low sheds, no wider than a handcart, and took her hand. She lifted the hem of her gown to follow him into the mire. A sunless alley with moss growing on all sides and at the end a swinging tavern sign hanging off its hinges: a skew-whiff magpie stared out at her. *One for sorrow*, a voice said in her head, as she followed Nonesuch inside.

'Gentlemen, sportsmen, gamblers.' Nonesuch's voice was brittle in this unadorned box of a room. Shay felt the bite of gravel on her feet and the ooze of mud between her toes. 'I have found a treasure.'

He pushed Shay forward with the toe of his boot and she came stumbling into the candlelight. She kept her gaze aimed up above the shadowy ring of drinkers.

'I found it down by the docks, shivering under a boat cover. Runaway from a ship I suppose. Skittish as a fawn but with the kick of a mule. Not from these parts, obviously, and it doesn't seem to speak any English. I was on my way to see Doctor Dee on the chance that there might be some kind of reward, but, knowing that the denizens of The Magpie love a wager, I made a detour.' The room was quiet now. 'A shilling buys you a guess. Where in the world does our little enigma hail from? Closest gets the pot, minus, of course, the most meagre of cuts for the banker.' He made a curt bow.

Coins clattered across the table and in moments men surrounded Shay. Ale-breathed, muddy-handed men. They examined her, proprietorially; grubby hands on her hem, tugging at her earrings; biting the stage jewellery. A man tried to part her lips to look at her teeth and Shay couldn't help herself; she growled, deep from the back of her throat, and won a wary retreat. Her real self crouched inside the outfit, hidden, knife between its teeth, ready to pounce. Men tried her with French and then Latin. She said nothing. Then languages that she'd never heard before. A man whispered in her ear, 'If you don't speak English then you won't mind me saying that I'd like to fuck that pretty mouth.' He whipped round to watch her eyes and she concentrated on staying blank. He smiled. 'Is that a yes?'

'Enough,' barked Nonesuch. 'Bets please.'

'Persian,' came a voice from the back. 'I've seen that make-up on east-ern whores. She'll be some shah's plaything. Keep her for yourself, I would. She'll know a trick or two.'

Nonesuch repeated it back. 'The man in blue says Persian.'

A voice from the crowd: 'She's never from Persia. Not wearing purple. Only the Venetians let ordinary folks wear purple. She'll be from the canals; an actress or painter or some such.' The guesses flooded in. She was Scottish or Siamese. Moorish or Malaccan. One man, the youngest of them all, said she might be a flapper-girl but he was shouted down.

'Don't waste your shilling. Flappers are as dowdy as dormice.'

Nonesuch swept the coins into a purse. 'I'll take her to Mortlake then. Dee'll know what she is, even if he has to slit her open to find out.' With another push of the boot he drove Shay back out into the sunlight.

Back on Broad Street Nonesuch tossed the bag of coins from hand to hand. 'You were *perfect*. Everyone loves a mystery. Did you notice how they all see what they wanted to see? The lovelorn saw a whore, the ambitious a princess.' He pulled out six coins. 'Here's your cut. Not bad for a part without a single line.'

She hadn't spoken during the whole thing and the paste on her lips cracked when she opened her mouth. 'You're not coming back with their winnings?'

'Pfft! They weren't even close. Anyway, they're drinking at ten bells on a work day. Those aren't men who expect good things to happen to them.'

Shay tugged her hem higher. The streets were gummed with people and the air around the gates was thick with insects. Everything here – the filth, the poverty, the city walls – made her yearn for open spaces. She took the money and said, 'Thank you. But we go back my way. Over the rooftops.'

Nonesuch trotted happily behind her, still clinking his coins.

7

A ND JUST LIKE THAT, their routine was set. For ten days straight, every morning by nine bells Shay was in costume and made up, her stomach churning as Nonesuch decided on their roles. She was a nun in Newgate, a whore in Horsleydown. On Thursday Nonesuch told a gang of prentices that Shay was a servant girl who'd killed the master who'd tried to bed her, so they spirited her away to a St Albans church on the back of a cart under a mountain of beetroots. Shay had never been north of London before and it was two hours later that Nonesuch finally arrived, lazy on horseback, already laughing at the state of her.

The mornings were his, but the afternoons were all hers. She took Nonesuch on her rounds of messages and showed him a hidden, windblown city. Shay flew across London with a frantic grace, arriving breathless and bruised at the back doors of grand houses with her hands tucked behind her back to hide her nails. From west to east and north to south carrying fine letters sealed with wax the colours of cream and cherries. When Nonesuch could keep up, they scrambled and leapt and sweated together, seemingly the only two people alive in a rooftop world crowned with clouds. She read his fortune in the paths of birds – always drama, always adventure – and they drank rainwater from the crevices in gargoyles. And when he couldn't keep up any more then she'd release him back to the centre of her new world: the Blackfriars Theatre.

The days stretched and yawned to accommodate all of the theatre's wonders. There were seven performances in those first ten days and nothing had ever seemed so right. It felt right to be a pair of eyes watching the stage while the flame-lit room rotated around her. It felt right for audience noise to wash over her like waves on pebbles. And it felt right to chase words across the page with a finger – beautiful words like birds of paradise among the London pigeons. She rolled the rarer ones around her mouth – *Byzantine. Perspicacious. Diabolic* – ten-letter spells, worlds in miniature.

But what felt most right of all was watching Nonesuch from the shadows and being led down his secret alleyways. Three different plays a week meant three very different roles, but to Shay his was one long performance. It was a recurring dream that ran night after night without ever fully revealing its meaning. Fragments glimmered darkly back at her: Nonesuch weeping down the aisle in a torn wedding gown, as hand after hand involuntarily reached for him from the audience, some in aid, some in desire. The Moor's trumpet blaring an atonal noise through a battle scene then sliding, imperceptibly casually, into a funereal melody at the exact moment that Alouette dropped a sheet of scarlet glass in front of the lantern: *crack* and the stage was bathed in old blood. It might not be real but the emotions it churned in her were. Joy. Love. Terror. One scene returned to her time and again – Trussell playing Nonesuch's reflection. Behind a sheet of glass he mirrored the movements of Nonesuch's child-queen as she made herself up for an assignation, an assignation that the audience already knew would mean her death. It began as comedy really, the two boys' actions so exactly matched as to have the audience breathless with laughter, but then Trussell's face as Nonesuch departed, a reflection left alone behind the glass, that look of abjection and awful realisation: it had her weeping in a way she hadn't since her mother's death. There was fear there too. Every time that Nonesuch ventured into the audience Shay worried for him. Only she could see the looks that he provoked, looks that the wearers thought were shrouded by the darkness: envy, thirst, hatred.

8

A SATURDAY MORNING WITH skies bell-bright and high-ceilinged. Shay woke in the dappled dark of the dovecote atop Brewers' Hall. She'd missed the Long Ferry back to Birdland the night before, after one too many curtain calls, and the dove house had long been a haven for her. There was a soupy thickness to its air, part feather-dust, part ale-malt, and the drowsy conversation of dove calls was as homely to her as a fire in the grate. A Saturday: for once she resolved to spend a morning on her own. She could deliver her messages and let Nonesuch wonder where she was. Brewers' Hall to Newgate, Newgate to Fetter Lane, Fetter Lane to Stangate Stairs; she stayed aloft for as long as possible, willing the Blackfriars Boys to be missing her the way that she already missed them, and when she finally levered herself down into that familiar street, she found the theatre in turmoil.

The auditorium swelled with the heightened air pressure of impend-ing panic. Boys were clucking over lines and stitching and unstitching costumes. Every corner smelled of fresh flowers and new candles. Nonesuch was nowhere to be seen but Trussell stood upon the stage where he was painting the backdrop in great sloppy waves of umber paint. She watched him for a while as an image of a raging inferno unfolded. When he finally stood back to examine his work she hopped up next to him. 'What's going on?' she asked.

His voice was giddy with excitement. 'Evans turned up this morn-ing with some new play he expects us to perform tonight, *Lucifer in Limehouse*. We need new sets and costumes and everything. Tonight's an *opening night*.' He said the final two words like he was announcing a royal birth. He turned his back on the painting. 'There's a boy copying out scripts down in the dorm, see if he has a copy for you yet.'

As she lowered herself back into the auditorium Trussell said, 'Could you stay away from Nonesuch until four bells?' She must have looked stricken because he added, 'He has hundreds of lines to learn and I'm trying to keep him out of the way of distractions. Could you see who else you might help, and be ready to do a *lot* of prompting tonight.' His hands were red from fingertip to elbow but he wore a dizzy grin. He doffed his cap. 'I apologise for my performance in advance.'

Shay let herself be seconded to any task that needed doing. She was passed from tiring room to stage and from auditorium to the costume store. By four bells everything slowed and she snuck away to watch the opening-night crowd arrive from the rooftop. The street was jammed with carriages – fine, mirror-shined carriages with crests in scarlet and azure. Coachmen rolled out rush mats for their passengers, the men's boots spotless and the women's fur slippers dry as the day they were made. Street boys tried to keep the traffic moving – *park your carriage for penny, a penny more to watch it* – but these gentlefolk didn't like their entrances rushed. They stopped, ostentatiously, to chat with other arrivals and made sure that the waiting crowd caught every inch of their outfits. The stage-door girls hung back under the eaves but still, whenever an unaccompanied gentleman arrived, there was a chorus of '*sir, sir*'s. Once inside, the crowd glittered. The women were more ornamental than the theatre itself with their domed farthingales and cushioned bodices. They swept in like ships with attendants for tugboats, rearranging and primping and lifting their peacock-tail trains over the grimy seating. The men were dark and combustible and keen to get involved, shouting advice and slapping arses. It was Alouette who'd taught her that what happened on stage wasn't the only performance going on in the theatre; the audience watched each other as keenly as the actors. The gasp from the crowd that went up when Mapesbury and the visiting Duke of Guise arrived together, and then huddled, heads almost touching, in the most expensive box, announced their alliance more clearly than any public notice would have done. Wives chided husbands by attending alone; fathers draped daughters in diamond dowries. A skilled social expert could see who was on the rise and who out of favour with a glance at the seating plan.

'Forget parliament,' said Alouette, half scornful, half proud. 'Court and the Blackfriars are where London really *happens*.'

It was the first time that Shay hadn't been in the tiring room as Nonesuch dressed and did his make-up, so when his Lucifer stepped onto the stage he caught her by surprise. He wore street clothes and Alouette lit him in a dull white light. He played Lucifer as bored and restless, like one of the gamblers from The Magpie. Londoners, he explained, were too easy to corrupt and he yearned for a real challenge. So he'd renounced his powers for a month, and come to earth as the humblest creature one could imagine: 'An actor, for shame. Lower than a whore. Lower even than a lawyer.' His task was to corrupt the incorruptible – nuns, penitents, princes – with no more magic than the power of his words.

He stuck more closely to the script than usual, though he peppered the play with topical asides and veiled insults aimed at members of the audience. Some were so barbed (and so filthy) that Shay was surprised that their targets didn't leap up and run him through right there and then, but Alouette whispered, 'It's a great honour to be included. Like your head on a spike, but less painful.'

The play was funnier than most she'd seen, but it was crueller too. Nonesuch delighted at every soul that he turned from the path of righteousness and, from the looks of glee that shone out from the crowd, most of the audience did too. But at the denouement, when Lucifer finally persuaded the flower-girl to steal from her employer, warring emotions skirmished across his face. Pleasure was mixed with pity at her downfall. Triumph and regret battled during her execution, and, like weather, his moods infected the watchers. There was already discreet weeping in Act II and, by the final scenes, sobs and whimpers were louder accompaniment than the musicians. When the company took their bow Alouette's lanterns illuminated streaked make-up and surreptitious dabbing of kerchiefs.

It was nearly an hour before the audience fully emptied and Shay and Alouette sat in the box under the stage and talked. Shay still couldn't get a handle on Alouette. Her conversation was tidal: she got swept up in enthusiasms, grasping Shay's wrist with wide eyes and mouth and then, catching herself, ebbing back into silence as if she'd somehow been tricked. If the talk turned to pyrotechnics or printing or portable clocks then she sprang back into life, and her words tumbled over one another. But then she would slap a hand across her mouth and retreat into quiet.

Finally there was silence, bar a jangle of spurs. From their hiding place they saw two pairs of legs cross the stage. Velvet hose tucked into leather boots, topped by scraps of conversation – *Evans says the latest is finer still* – and for a moment the room was filled with light as the stage doors were flung open.

Shay asked, 'Where are *they* going?'

It wasn't the way back to the dormitory and she could hear a low ripple of conversation from deeper in the building. Alouette caught the look and when she spoke it was with a gentleness that hadn't been there before. 'Backstage. Nonesuch will be there for a while. There's entertaining to be done.'

'Entertaining?' she said.

Alouette's mouth was tight. 'Those types? The *gentlemen*? They don't feel that they have had their money's worth until they've seen something that the rest haven't. Call it access or closeness or something.' Her face stayed flat but she watched Shay to make sure she understood. Shay wasn't certain that she did.

Alouette sighed. 'For those boys, the night's work has just begun.' She shut her props box with a crack. 'We can go and watch, but only for a while.'

Shay nodded, and followed her across the stage. With her finger to her lips Alouette guided them into the backstage room, which was now transformed. It was lit with lanterns of every colour and in the centre amber lights turned two toga-clad boys into bronze statues. The back of the room was lit in blues and greens, and a deep-water gentleman bent to tie the boots of a bilious-looking lady. The Blackfriars Boys appeared reduced in here, underfed and beardless, all elbows and knees. Only Blank, the Moorish musician, looked as if he belonged in the company. He played trumpet softy in the corner and the younger boys kept as close to him as possible.

'We're not here.' Alouette was at Shay's side, pulling her into the shadows. Rainbow lights jewelled their path.

'That suits me,' Shay said, shrinking into an alcove, 'but why?'

Alouette's eyes skim-read her. 'This is a shop window. Unless you want to be merchandise ...' She didn't finish the sentence.

Nonesuch stood in a nearby corner between two men in black leather. Alouette whispered, 'That walking codpiece is Lord Mapesbury. And the other is our boss.'

Evans. Henry Evans. Though he was the man paying her two pennies a day, Shay only knew of him through gossip. Theatre owner, friend of the Queen, with a foot in court and a foot in the gutter. Rider of black horses with black plumes and bits and chains reputed to be solid silver (not that anyone would dare steal them). He surrounded himself with a retinue of wastrel younger sons with bad tempers and worse debts, who were vicious with strangers and craven with him.

He was tall but curiously put together, as if he'd been assembled from leftovers. His shoulder-length grey hair had been stained inexpertly with blueberries, giving him the look of an old, piebald horse. Round shoulders, round belly, and long arms that hung down. Muscle gone to fat, black gone to grey, hair on his knuckles but not on his crown. His eyes were busy though. He took in the room in quick side-glances and then returned to focusing on Mapesbury and Nonesuch. They were close enough for Shay to catch the conversation.

'I heard it closed after three performances. People left before the late-comers had even arrived. We made more selling oysters last night than they did in tickets.'

Mapesbury sounded disinterested. 'Good. I don't care for clowns. Fools, I can see for free.'

Evans heard some kind of invitation in this dismissal. 'Of course, you're right. Leave the comedy for the country folk. The city is for magic.' His arm brushed Mapesbury's lightly. 'We have a private show on that very topic, eh Nonesuch?'

Nonesuch became animated, as if his strings had been pulled. 'We have. Ovid's *Transformations*. Boys become asses, gods become men, birds turn into beautiful women.'

Mapesbury had shopkeepers' eyes. 'Which of these birds …' an arm took in the room behind him '… is in line for such a transformation?'

There was eagerness in Nonesuch's voice for the first time. 'Trussell has been taking the lead. The lad playing the costermonger tonight. He sings, he dances and he speaks very well.'

Mapesbury's boredom came down like a portcullis and Evans butted in. 'But of course, the part was written for Lord Nonesuch here. The Queen herself was entranced by his performance.'

'It's been seen at court?'

'A private masque. Extremely select crowd. *Trusted*.'

Mapesbury looked around the room. 'It's hardly new then, is it? Maybe some other time.' He gestured to a man in the corner. 'Bring the carriage round.'

When they were alone Evans' face displayed nothing amiss, but he reached out to grip Nonesuch's arm at the elbow – then twisted and pulled him close. 'Fucking Trussell? No one wants to see Trussell transformed into a maiden. He's barely palatable as a boy. God's teeth, are you stupid or just bored of working?'

Nonesuch's shoulder sank as Evans twisted. 'He's good. I've been tutoring him myself. You'd be surprised.'

Nails dug deep into his arm. Nonesuch twisted, yelping, towards the floor. Evans' fingers bulged around his rings as he said, 'I don't want to be surprised. I want to be paid.'

A nobleman in a plumed hat passed by and made an elaborate bow as he left. The briefest of smiles left Evans' face as the man disappeared. 'And, speaking of surprises. The script is the script. It's not a damned suggestion.'

Nonesuch shook his head and then stopped abruptly. 'The playwright repeats himself. There has to be some variety.'

Evans' face twisted. 'Wear a different fucking frock then. The speech about the riches of Russia isn't optional. Curton paid a fortune for those lines. He needs backers for his adventure there. Get something straight: you're not an artist, you're an errand boy.'

He let go and regarded Nonesuch from head to toe. 'You've got a beard coming in too. How old are you now, thirty?'

'I'm fifteen. You know that.'

'I could have sworn you were older. You look it. Time for an adult theatre, maybe? I hear The Curtain is looking for someone.'

Nonesuch shrunk into himself. 'I'm happy here, Evans. We're sold out for nearly a week. People come to see me.'

'For now. And anyway, do you know how much I make from this place? After the rent and the Master of the Revels and free tickets for every fucking court favourite and the bellows and firebugs and fucking mushrooms for your fat Flanders sow skulking there in the corner' – Alouette dropped her head – 'and the playwrights and the cleaners and—' He threw his hands up in despair. 'Not as much as you'd think. Certainly not enough to lose any sleep over sending you back to your *snooty* family with a penny in your pocket and a boot up your arse. So,' he grabbed Nonesuch again, between his legs, 'why don't you go out and sell some private shows? Because *that's* where your money comes from.'

'Come on,' said Alouette, under her breath. 'We're not helping.'

Outside Alouette turned her collar up against the rain. She shivered and her veins looked blue with cold, but she made no move to go. Shay dared not think about staying in London for another night but for now something kept her within the theatre's orbit. Alouette rarely looked at her directly but now she did; cool duck-egg eyes under bovine lashes. 'Go home, Shay. Two shows tomorrow. Don't worry about Nonesuch. He's a big boy.'

But she didn't sound convinced.

9

BACK TO BIRDLAND VIA a Thames scattered with stars. Back to that misty dome of nets, while the sight of Evans' fingers digging into white flesh replayed in her mind. Black rings, filthy nails and Nonesuch twisting like a wick beneath that grip.

She stayed in Birdland for no time at all. Lonan was asleep when she arrived and he was asleep when she left again, but at least now there was eightpence under his pillow and firewood in the basket. She walked alone to fill the seed-cups before sunrise, but even the first inklings of the dawn chorus couldn't quell the voice in her head. *Are you stupid or just bored?* Evans' hand between Nonesuch's legs. Fox eyes and a voice like broken glass. She left a note under Colm's door; he could read it to her father later: 'Finally today I'll get to Eltham House to groom Devana. I'll remember you to her. There's jam on the table.'

Dawn was a whispered promise on the horizon as she rowed back towards the city. She wore the clothes from last night and the theatre's smell had walked with her all through Birdland. The same old stars reflected in the same old river and black nails puckered pale skin every time she closed her eyes.

0

10

T HE LAYERS OF STAFF that populated Eltham House were as
numerous and closely packed as an onion's. Once Shay had peeled
away a bell boy and discarded an under footman or two, she still hadn't
penetrated much beyond the surface of the house. She was patient. She
showed her credentials, such as she had, to a footman, wilted beneath
the stare of a terrifying butler, and waited as the message was passed on:
The Aviscultan is here to tend to the falcon.

She was passed like a baton from butler to lady's maid, from lady's
maid to secretary, and then on to other, more opaque staff deeper within
the house. They deposited her in a room that was larger than her home in
Birdland, surrounded by biblical scenes painted onto silk wall coverings.
She was awed by a room so palpably used for nothing more than storing waiting strays like herself. The clockwork of the house ran around
her, unseen but heard via footsteps, doors opening and closing, and the
bass rumble of all-male conversation. She was examining the painting
of the seven deadly sins and trying to work out which figure was glut-
tony and which was greed, when the same massive butler returned and
announced that she was expected on the roof.

Up they went together through floors that narrowed and became
shabbier as they rose. Through the servants' quarters, past damp uniforms
drying over clothes lines, into rooms littered with broken furniture and
a lifeless maid draped across a tiny bed with her thumb in her mouth.
Past a room full of beds pushed so closely together as to make a kind of
second floor, and into another with a tin bath steaming over a fire. It was
busy and warm and drab and homely. At the house's apex was a final set
of steps: doll's-house slats of bare wood.

'I know my way from here,' said Shay and the butler unbuttoned his
first smile of the day. He handed her a minuscule brass key and said,

'Leave it with Cook once you're finished. You may ask for one slice of the cherry cake.'

Clear, clean air and fresh lick of wind. Devana's mews sat in the corner of the rooftop. It was ornately ornamental in the style of an oriental pagoda and more care had been taken over its construction than with anything else above the first floor. She gave a falcon-call but no movement came from within the mews. She smiled. 'I have to come to you, do I, Your Majesty?'

She pulled a stool around and unrolled her tool bag. Devana stood at the very end of her perch, pointedly looking the other way. Even in stillness everything about her flowed. Smudged black feathers streamed back from eyes like a starless night. A cloudy, grey hook of beak atop a white chest, white wings and a triangle of white tail that was shot through with grey, arrowed feathers. Her plumage was snow on a furrowed field. She stretched out her wings and then tucked them away.

The falconry gear hung from bare nails inside the door. Shay found it unfathomable that it was left visible like this. The jesses were imperial purple with snow-white stitching and a splash of rubies around the handle. Devana's bells were made of solid brass. Her anklets of lilac suede. And the hood itself was an extraordinary thing made from an outrageous purple leather, as soft as rabbits' ears, and grained with a pattern so subtle that it took a fingertip to read. The stitching was white and gold: feathered patterns surrounding the opals that were the hood's unseeing eyes. It was her mother's work. Nothing back at Birdland ever showed Shay this side of her: extravagant and fanciful. Birdland was home to her mother, but only here on the rooftops did Shay see Ava. Shay wished that she'd known *this* woman.

She unfurled her tool roll and made soft chirrups deep in her throat. Devana looked away. Shay worked linseed oil into the grain of the leather, using the end of a twist of soft linen. Vinegar freed the light sleeping inside the gems. She unpacked replacement feathers for the headpiece. The spray of boisterous grey crane feathers was still good, but others at the back had lost lozenge-shaped chunks. She'd use ptarmigan feathers as replacements. They were the white and black of wave-break. She knew that other makers would have used something tropical – the azure from a bee-eater's throat or the scarlet of the tailorbird – but Shay thought that was emasculating to both falcons and their prey. White, grey and black: life and death shades.

The falcon sidestepped across her perch and locked her eyes onto Shay. Shay looked at the floor. Everything would be done without the merest moment of eye contact. Never, even for an instant, did she look into those blackwater eyes. Shay understood what it meant for a bird like Devana to be looked at. It was threat and promise and challenge all wrapped up together. And the bird's gaze meant danger too. When a falcon latches her eyes on prey then that's the end of the business, not the beginning. The brutal geometries of the prey-bird, the diving velocities and wind-sheer calibrations, the veer and tumble, the shaping of wing and tail into a single, terrible arrow, and then the gorgeous, inevitable snap of neck or back: all this was negotiated in the moment that those eyes met yours.

'How are you?' she said. 'You look well. Sharp of eye, beak and claw, as Father would say. You remember me, don't you? Maybe not the voice but the shape of me.' She tried to replicate her father's huge gentleness. She worked, with her hands where her mother's had been, her feet where her father had stood, and talked. She reached a gloved hand into the mews and tried Devana with a piece of rabbit, fresh this morning from the marshes. The bird's scorn was palpable; she looked away, out over the city.

'My, but we've gotten fancy. Too good for coney are we? I suppose I should have brought you some swan.'

Devana swivelled her gaze back Shay's way as if she understood, and Shay dropped her eyes like a bride.

How many days and nights had she spent up here? She was on this rooftop the day that Devana arrived. It was one of those wind-scoured, bleached-out days after Ava's death. The fledgling was a mewling, open-mouthed scrap of a thing then, torn from her Arctic home, as frail as a fawn and as vicious as a wolf.

'You break a horse,' her father told her, 'but you make a falcon.' Shay and Devana learnt the tricks and techniques of the falconer's art up there on the rooftop together: the jesses and lures, the widening spirals of the leashes. But technique only got you so far. The bulk of the training was just time and patience and in those shipwrecked days Shay had plenty of both. They leaned into each other's helplessness, doing little more than being there, at the same time. They dozed together, they sheltered from the rain together, and they even ate together. Rabbit and suckling pig, lobster and mouse. 'A taste for me, a taste for you.' These were long weeks of advance and retreat, closeness and tantrum. Perch to arm. Arm to glove. Glove to hand. Until one spring morning Devana took a strip of cooked coney right from Shay's mouth with the freckled feathers of her crest ruffling under Shay's loving breath.

She missed it here. Birdland was where she lived but this was where she'd grown up. Her first paid work, her first real freedom. First love too, her and Devana wrapped around each other like teenage sweethearts. But Devana's destiny was clearer than Shay's. On her first hunt with Lord Eltham the falcon killed a heron, on the second she took down a swan. That marked the end of Shay's days on the rooftops; Devana would now kill for whoever wore the glove.

She tarried over the work. The theatre needed her at four bells but until then she was content to sit and talk. She told the falcon about Alouette's smoke bombs and the fledgling's tattoo. Gossip and news. And she talked about Nonesuch, and as she talked, his myriad faces slid across one another for her and she saw him complete and whole for the first time. And all the while Devana drowned those memories in her inexorable eyes.

When she was done, Shay made her way down through the maze of rooms to the kitchen. She liked kitchens. She and her father were adrift on a motherless, wifeless ocean and neither had progressed much beyond bread and meat, so to sit on an upturned saucepan, her hair damp with steam, and be fed was some kind of heaven. She drank in the aromas of four dishes each at differing stages of readiness. Sharp darts of apple and clove, the unctuousness of browning goose skin one delicious inch from burning, the fresh dung of boiling eggs, and under it all the homeliness of fresh bread. She was still waiting for her cherry cake when the butler reappeared. He beckoned her with a plump finger.

An anteroom; another appendix of a space. The wastefulness of it made Shay feel breathless. The butler aimed his words towards the ceiling. 'Lord Eltham says that he was unaware that your father was no longer present at the sessions. And, on account of your father's mastery and your …' he stumbled '… youth, he is reducing your wage to sixpence.' He didn't meet her eye.

Sixpence. A halving of their fee and not enough to cover even three days' outgoings. She sheathed her anger. 'I do the job at least as well as my father did. I've been caring for Devana since she was a fledgling. Tell me one single way in which your service has declined and I will rectify it for free.'

She knew it was hopeless. The butler had started with 'Lord Eltham says …' which meant that what followed was a sentence rather than an accusation, but the iniquity pulled the words out of her. Her fists were balled and she stood on tiptoe.

'The issue isn't the work, it's the worker. The rate we paid was for a master falconer, as befits a man of Lord Eltham's standing.'

'My work is masterful.' Shay was rigid with anger. 'Find a falconer who says he can do what I do and I'll take him on.'

There was a new layer of ice across his voice now. 'If he knew that it was you who'd been here, alone, for the last two years, he would have asked for those payments back too. Leave it alone, boy.'

She knew the tone; he was preparing to lose his patience with her. If she snapped back then he would have better justification for kicking her out.

'What's your name?' Shay's shoulders trembled with the effort of appearing unruffled. Still, the question had sounded less threatening in her mind. She wasn't sure why knowing his name would make a difference but the situation was so insubstantial: two strangers in a room that wasn't a room, negotiating on behalf of other, more solid beings. In the East End the cheapest houses were topped with roofs of bundled straw and sometimes they buckled under her weight. That was the fragility she felt now.

'My name is Carver. And this conversation is at an end. Take the sixpence and be grateful that you've chiselled so much from us over the last two years.' Surprisingly, it was the 'us' rather than the 'chiselled' which finished her. She slapped the coin from his hand, making sure not to watch where it flew, and stepped from the room.

Outside she simmered with anger. A cockfight had just finished and it disgorged men flushed with money, blood and drink. They blocked the traffic with voices rising as the bout was picked over and recreated. A toad of a man, wet with sweat, demonstrated some avian deathblow to his friends and caught Shay across the cheek with a stray arm. She prodded a receding shoulder. 'Oi, fighting cock, watch your wings.'

He spun around and, along the line of his colleagues, hands went to knife handles. He looked her up and down, and then visibly made up his mind about something. He reached into a pocket, pulled out a greying handkerchief and wiped it across his brow. Then he turned his back on her and walked on. The pressure built in her again. The enormity of the money-pit that she had dug wiped everything else from her mind. She climbed, hand over hand, up the side of a garden wall, fingertips complaining at the gaps in the brittle mortar, and then threw herself on top. It was a short jump to grab the eaves and then swing back and forth until she could hook a toe over the opposite eaves. She pulled the bow of her back to thrust herself up and onto the roof and without looking down or back she aimed herself towards the moon, dreamlike in the afternoon, and started to run.

An hour later she lay, sweat-drenched and shaking, in the shadow of Devana's mews. She had run with a fevered carelessness, throwing herself onto roofs like they were feather beds. She had scuffed, tripped, broken and hip-charged, clung, pirouetted, scrabbled and slipped, until her hands were gloved in soot and blood and she was back on the roof of Eltham House. What she couldn't bear was the thought that the butler now thought this was about money; she would have cared for Devana even if she'd had to pay.

Devana shuffled herself to the edge of her perch and eyed Shay patiently. A connoisseur of damage, the bird monitored the wreckage with proprietary interest.

Her father's voice was as much part of this place as the tiles. A question from years ago. 'How do you think a falcon recognises prey, Shay?' His thick fingers pressed lovingly into Devana's neck feathers, eliciting a girlish flutter.

'I suppose its size. Maybe the shape and colour?'

He shook his head. 'All she sees is what fears her. Whatever runs, that's prey.'

'So, what am I?' she asked the bird. Everything she needed to know was in Devana's perfunctory once-over. Professional eyes catalogued vein-flutter and bone strength. She tasted the blood in the air and the sweat on the brow. Shay had to laugh. 'Prey, huh?' The bird scratched at some itch deep in her belly feathers while Shay packed the hood, leads and gloves into her pocket. There was an invisible thread that ran between them, she thought. They were two motherless things with eyes only for each other, despite Lord Eltham's ownership papers, or maybe because of them. Shay took a last look across a skyline turning dark as wine, untied Devana's leash and shooed the bird out of the mews onto the roof. She locked up the mews with the little brass key and then hauled herself, whistling, over the side of the building.

She sensed, rather than saw, Devana's escape. A shuffle of feathers and a flash of snowy wing. An angel ascending. Shay blew a kiss at the sky and headed west towards the theatre. At least one of them was free.

S HE DIDN'T BOTHER WITH the front door of the theatre but
instead jackknifed herself through an open window and padded
down through the gallery. The place was humdrum during the day; the
candles were burned down to nubs and her feet crunched on discarded
oyster shells. Down, down, into the dormitory. The hutchy smell of boys
from even outside the door: sweat and ale and worse. It was so quiet that
she assumed no one was home but she opened the door to find most of
the troupe up and semi-dressed. There was the stilted hush of a church
service; heads turned towards her and then away. Only Trussell got up
from his bed. With a finger to his lips he led her over to the corner.
Shafts of daylight turned his face serious.

'You'll have to be quiet, they had a private performance last night.'

'Nonesuch did?' Shay asked.

'Him, and Pykman and Pavey.'

Shay had seen Pykman and Pavey around. They were pale and timid
and thin as snakes. They didn't have speaking parts and were relegated
to moping around in the background in the cheaper costumes.

'What play? The Cleopatra?'

Trussell's downturned eyes were a warning. 'The private masques tend
to be more … improvised than that.' He looked her in the eyes for the
first time. 'More … um … audience-led.'

She made her way over to Nonesuch's bunk. His was the top one,
draped on all sides with a greying Turkish rug. She pushed a flap aside
and climbed in next to him. Where the rug had worn thin it let through
a mottled, mossy light, and Nonesuch was a fallen statue overgrown
with lichen. A tick of pulse at his neck was the only sign that he was
alive. His make-up was in ruins: black streaks ran from his eyes to his
chin and there was dried blood at the corner of his mouth. Shay pulled

close and wrapped her arms around him. The carpet dulled the noise of the rooms outside.

They lay that way for long minutes and then Shay began to talk. She poured out the story of Devana and the butler and everything that had happened, not caring if the boys outside could hear her. It took half an hour to tell the tale and when she was done, and had wiped her eyes on the bedsheets, Nonesuch still hadn't moved. Maybe he'd been asleep after all. She'd taken his stillness for attention but his breath stayed flat and even. She didn't care: talking about Devana had relit the anger in her. She straightened out a stray curl as his ribs rose and fell under her touch.

His voice wasn't sleepy though, when it came. He said, 'However little we have, still they want it.'

She nodded and stroked his hair. The blood under her nails might have been hers, might have been his.

He rolled over to face her. His lips were a bleary red. 'It's not enough that they have more than us. So much more than us. They want us to have *nothing*.' Her hands moved in his hair and then under the sheets. Ribs, hips, ridge of scar.

'They ruin us over and over again and then they despise us for our poverty.'

His eyes were pondwater flat. 'Last night, or this morning I guess, Pykman and I are dressed up as fucking Helen and Clytemnestra, not that any of those fat perverts would know the names. They're full of French brandy and swan meat and have *suggestions* for how the action should unfold.' Unthinkingly his hand went to touch a bruise on his cheekbone. He slipped into his gentleman's drawl. '"*You do this and then he does that. Then the three of you together.*"' There were marks around his wrists, pink as gums, which Shay couldn't look at.

'Did you know that Evans keeps every penny of the private performance fees? The gentlemen may tip if "the performance is exceptional", but otherwise we're merely another course at the feast.'

Their breaths had reached a kind of shared rhythm. He brought his hands to her face. 'Do you know what they can't take from us? Our voices.'

After a moment he said, 'Picture this. A black ship with black sails torn to tatters, leaning hard into the wind.' He brushed her hair back in the shape of a wave. 'There are stars above and reflected stars

69

dancing on the surrounding waves. Belowdecks a child is hunched into a corner of a cupboard, clutching a seashell so tightly that we see the beginnings of a cut.' He squeezed her fist. 'She sings to herself in a voice designed to go no further than her lips, even though the ship is as empty as a fresh grave. Then she stops dead, to listen ...'

No sound but the movements of the dorm. Shay said, 'Listen to what?'

Nonesuch waited. 'I don't know. Anything. But you see her?'

Shay did. Could see her still. 'Of course.'

'Her clothes?'

'Yes.'

'Describe them.'

She closed her eyes. 'They're too young for her. Doll's clothes. With unnecessary frills and buckles. They're singed at the hem.'

'And her hair?'

'Cut with a knife. It's as uneven as a St Giles stitching.'

He smiled at that. 'The ship. That curve of spray springing from the bow like a bridal train? You see that?'

'Yes, yes, yes.'

'I made that. In this moment. We made it with our voices. We made it out of nothing.'

He lit his pipe and gestured her close. Lips grazing hers as he exhaled. Shay letting the moist smoke fill her up.

'We made it and sent it deeper than that smoke. Right ... to ... our ... bones.' He sounded dejected at the very idea of it. 'A black ship. A living girl. A *sea*. Evans couldn't do that with ten thousand pounds to spend.' He pulled on his pipe again and his voice turned matter of fact. 'We need our own theatre. A free theatre, made out of words. A world that we can breathe in.'

Her hands on his bony buttocks and their shared breath stale and sweet. The question was implicit and she whispered into the whirlpool of his ear.

'I'm in.'

He kissed her on the forehead and resumed his stage voice. 'On the ship the girl wipes a trickle of blood across her dress and then climbs the stairs, singing. A note of her song punctuates every step.'

Shay could hear it: *la – thud – la – thud – la.*

12

S HAY WOKE IN THE little bunk, draped across a sleeping Nonesuch, content in a thick air of mixed sweats. She propped herself onto an elbow to listen to the theatre's version of the dawn chorus – the sounds of sixteen boys waking. Already she could pick out individual songs. That was the scratch of Trussell's pencil, those breaths were Clifton doing his exercises. The rumble of conversation would be Pykman and Pavey retelling their dreams. Ordinary, workaday noises from a place that already felt like home. Shay had only known the Blackfriars Boys for two weeks but they had taken to her with that particular fierceness of the motherless. What had she become to those boys with the city's grime in every seam and under every nail? She was not quite boy but not quite girl. They addressed her as one of them: older lads called her 'boy' or 'blade', the younger ones even 'sir'. They ordered her the same ales, discussed the same whores, and made sure to include her in any teasing about height or lack of brawn. And when, in the lazy hammock of hours suspended between the matinee and evening shows, they passed around Trussell's charcoal nudes, they gave her the same quarter-hour of solitude in the curtained-off back room. But she was different from them too. Each of those fourteen days that she'd stayed at the theatre had brought her a new role. She was news-bringer, message-taker and repository of tragically tiny secrets. Every begrimed adolescent problem found its way to her ear, even though there was little she could do to help. She wiped tears and noses, ignored erections, and read lines with them, over and over, until she hardly needed the script for her prompting. Some boys brought her letters home to be delivered, copied, or even written for them and she saw the fathoms of pain that lurked beneath their bland words: 'I have five lines in *Cupid & Psyche* so I think that I am still needed here,' or 'Does Snowy pine for me? Please reply although I know you are busy, please, please, please.' Hopeless, spindly words that Shay knew that they would never share with the other boys. Too young to be a mother to them but too worldly to be a sister, she was, she realised in a rush of blood and excitement, a friend. That was a new thing for her. Even the word itself was exotic: a windblown jungle bird. A *friend*. There in the bunk she practised saying it until it didn't feel lumpen in her mouth. 'My friend Trussell.' 'Do you know my friend Alouette?' 'Oh, a friend gave it to me.'

Nonesuch's voice came scratchy from under the covers. 'You remember what we talked about last night?'

She slid a hand under the sheet, into his warmth, and stroked at his elbow. What she could see of his arm was garlanded with bruises. 'Of course I remember.'

With his head still buried beneath the covers he shook her hand, like an adult might. 'Good, today we'll go and see Blank for costumes. Tomorrow we write.'

An hour later and the pair sat on Broken Wharf in the shadow of a greening hulk of vessel that was moored tight to the bank.

'What's wrong with it?' asked Shay. The ship was ill-shaped and somehow encrusted. The gunwales were fringed in a deep green and the sails hung in grubby tatters. It leant away from the shore as if repulsed by dry land.

Nonesuch reached out and stroked the side of the ship. 'This old girl is as ill-starred as they come. She's been many things – warship, coal hauler and ferry among them – but when its crew scooped Blank right out of the water and sold him as a pearl diver, well that's when she was a slave ship. Didn't last long though – some English expedition that was sent to discover rare plants and animals for the Queen needed an inconspicuous ship to send their booty home in. Guess who they chose?' He patted the hull like it was a pet. 'Blank finagled his way back on board but the English must have picked up more than just animals because once they hit open water the crew started dropping like flies. When the ship finally limped into London she was called *The Albatross* and there were six crew left, all a-huddle in the crow's nest, Blank among them. There are about a thousand different legal claims on her ownership, so until the courts sort it out, this is where Blank lives. Here with those rare plants running wild across the boards. He swears there's a jaguar loose belowdecks too, but that might just be a story to deter thieves.'

He whistled up the gangway to where a sailor sat carving a pattern into a hunk of driftwood. It looked casual but it was a neat way to have your knife drawn without looking threatening and Shay tucked this knowledge away. The sailor didn't look up but said, 'Who will aboard?'

Nonesuch leaned on a hip. 'Four hours in a tavern, drinking on my slate, and you don't remember my name? I'd heard that sailors weren't the cleverest, but—'

The man still didn't look up but there was a curl of laughter in his voice. 'Ah, yes, but that was a lad called Lord Nonesuch, or so he told me. But a day later I was up in Blackfriars for the theatre and there he was again, calling himself Faustus. Day after that he was a girl, or so I hear. I'm under strict instructions to let up no more than two people. With you it might be a hundred.'

Nonesuch laughed. 'It's just me and my friend today.'

The sailor considered them. 'Seems fair. Blank's up the mast. He's not been down all day.'

Nonesuch made a face and led Shay aboard. The deck listed at a nauseous angle and everything was overgrown with vegetation. Vines burst from hatches and clambered for the freedom of the gunwales where they spilled, uproariously, down the sides. Flowers sprang from cannon and rope stores; a rotting lifeboat carried a cargo of plate-sized yellow blooms. Shay walked across a carpet of moss and grass, as softly hillocked as old graves. Everywhere was strange and foreign. Palms sprouted dense orange spikes while fruit rotted in piles beneath a lopsided tree.

'How did it get so wild so quickly?' she asked.

Nonesuch said, 'When they were quarantined here the crew emptied out the seeds and brought the trees up top. They ate what they could and threatened to burn the rest down unless they were freed. We're facing south here and it's rained every day for a month. These plants are eating the ship alive.'

Shay looked up at the mast. Climbers coiled green shoots around the crumbling wood and even the sails hung heavy with moss.

Nonesuch stood at the base and shouted up, 'Blank. Old pal. We've come a-visiting. Come on down.'

The voice that called back was distant but certain. 'No, come up.'

'Blank! Old, old friend. There's two of us and one of you. It makes more sense for you to come down.'

No reply. Shay looked out over the stern of the ship. Clouds scribbled rain across the horizon. Nonesuch cursed. 'Looks like we're climbing.' He hauled himself onto the mossy rope ladder. 'Damn … stupid … place … to live.'

Once they were higher than the rooftops he quietened, and his breaths came more quickly. The crow's nest swelled above them. It had been extended with bare boards that hung out over the sides and the last few feet were tricky because the rope ladder sloped backwards to reach the entrance. For a moment Shay found herself hanging out over the deck with her eyes fixed on the clouds above.

She hauled herself behind Nonesuch into a tiny room where bright canvas walls were splashed with colour. Blank sat in a patch of sunlight. He wore a tricorne hat and a jacket with a swing to its tails: too smart for this place. Brass buttons glinted and jangled as he leant forward and stretched out a hand to Nonesuch. 'Hello, flotsam,' he said.

Nonesuch was still out of breath. 'Hello, jetsam.' He nodded. 'And this is Shay.'

Even on her knees Shay made a bow. Something in the tenor of Blank's voice made her feel out of place: a serving girl in a dining room.

He returned the bow with a smile. 'Grubby knees but pretty manners, you're already an improvement on Lord Nonesuch's usuals. I've seen you backstage at the theatre, haven't I? I trust Alouette is taking care of you.' He spoke with a careful, precise accent, each word like a stone being dropped in a pool. She nodded, and caught him studying her tattoo and wings of hair. With his naval costume and jangle of decorations Blank was more conspicuous even than her. She lowered her head and could only hear his sigh of pleasure. 'A rare bird indeed,' he whispered.

She had no time to return the compliment; Nonesuch was instantly up, pacing and talking. He must not have slept at all because since yesterday he had refined and expanded his plans. He talked to Blank about a theatre of the streets with impromptu plays in taverns and abandoned places, for an audience so involved that you wouldn't be able to tell who was acting and who was spectating. The room was too small to contain him and, as he talked on, scheme tumbled over scheme and new shoots of ideas sprung up in every corner. Shay let the tide of words wash over her as she examined the crow's nest. It had been vertiginously extended up and out with open sides wrapped in a thick, creamy fabric. Three walls were embroidered with a detailed picture of a tropical island in the most un-English of colours. Sapphire waves lapped onyx shores while garnets and rubies hung from emerald fruit trees. A canary-diamond sun warmed aquamarine skies. Amid the wash of voices and the sway of the boat Shay felt like a bird looking down on this fantastical island. She was so caught up in its details that she didn't notice that the Nonesuch and Blank had stopped talking. Blank was watching her, mildly.

'May I?' he said, tapping her on the shoulder. Shay nodded, unsure of what she was agreeing to. He came closer and touched her elbows and hips. Then he turned her side on, like a figure on a coin. Cool fingers at her neck.

'We'll need costumes,' said Nonesuch, seeing her confusion. 'And Blank is the very devil with needle and thread. Clothes and tattoos. He's a master on the trumpet too. And he can sail, and dive and swim. Thank God he's such a rotten actor or we could never be friends.'

Blank measured her by touch alone, turning her this way and that, and Shay couldn't shake the feeling that she'd been seen naked. In minutes he was sewing away, working without watching his hands. He said, 'Come, Shay, sit by me. How do you like my home?'

She didn't have to think about that. 'I love it. High places. It's a little like flying, isn't it?'

His smile was quick. 'I suppose so.' He lit a saucerful of dried herbs and the room filled with a foreign scent, heavy and floral and gritty with spice.

Remnants of the theatre's stock were piled up here and there. A stack of Alouette's smoke bombs in little straw packages stood in one corner, beneath a cardboard moon sitting half-painted against the mast. A vast scarlet kite that had been flown from the theatre roof before performances of *St George and the Dragon* glowered out at her. Clothes hung in the corner: stage outfits, here for repair or cleaning. Shay stroked each of them in turn, relishing the feel of lace and silk, fabrics she'd never even touched before coming to Blackfriars. A month ago, that's all these costumes would have been to her – pretty things – but after days spent with Nonesuch everything she touched turned into a story. Each costume was a world in miniature. In a script those tweeds would indicate a country gentleman dressed up for a day in the city: beard and boots and an eye-watering codpiece. She pulled on the jacket. It fitted her well enough and instantly she felt the character flesh out inside her, priggish and pugnacious; she stuck out her chin and pawed at the ground like a show horse. The black silk and veil would look good on Nonesuch; just his pretty eyes showing. What character would wear that black dress? A widow, but not a grieving one. The roles started to stroll, hand in hand, through her thoughts: a little pug of a man up in London for the cockfights, eagerly showing off his latest conquest.

The cockfights. That set her thinking. She interrupted the boys' rapid conversation. 'Blank, would it be all right to borrow these two costumes for the afternoon?'

Nonesuch's head to one side, like a dog's. Blank guarding a smile.

She pulled on the hose and tugged the codpiece into place. A bandolier hung across a rail and she threw it over her shoulder. The smoke bombs fitted into the bandolier's pouches as if they were made for it. Nonesuch raised an eyebrow.

'Just for show,' she said. 'Why should you always be the one that people fear?'

But the scene unrolled in front of her like a script and she knew well enough that some stories have their own momentum. Somewhere inside her head the smoke bombs whispered to her that they had a role to play too. She placed the veil over Nonesuch's head and deepened her voice.

'Come on, sweetheart,' she said, 'I'm taking you out.'

13

T HEY MADE AN ODD pair, the stocky, military squire and the slinky widow, but any reluctance the carriage drivers might have had over their bruises and bandoliers was trumped by a bulging purse. The traffic was jammed south of the river, and it would have been quicker to walk, but Shay wanted to be seen arriving in style. They crawled through Southwark's streets and sound poured from every doorway: cries, laughter, animal noises. The traffic was at walking pace by the cockfighting ring but still Shay made the driver pull up right by the entrance, blocking the street in both directions. She willed herself into character and the weight of the tweeds and the ridiculous codpiece helped. She helped Nonesuch down – flash of ankle, red lips beneath the veil – and even his hands felt somehow softer than usual. She scanned the skies for Devana and there she was, slanted against a bank of wind, claws tucked away ready for some errant prey to break cover. A good omen; Shay tipped her hat.

She could feel it as they walked in. Fear. Animal fear. Shit and blood and sweat and something else: the taste of biting down on metal. Fear rang out across the whole room. She concentrated on the crowd rather than the game cocks but still slivers of the fight reached her. There was a frantic scratching and an explosion of red off to her right. The rising slaps of useless wings against the air. And a crowd noise that you heard nowhere else: low moans and laughter and breath pulled back hard against teeth and the lowing of disappointment mixed with the caw of victory. It swirled into a waterwheel roar that threatened to lift her up and then drown her. She froze and Nonesuch discreetly took her arm. 'You can do this,' he whispered. 'Remember, it's not fear that you feel, it's anger.'

There was a thick fug in the air. Bloodied feathers fell like snow, buffeted by spittle and ale-breath as the crowd howled. The front row was all prentices with wet palms and clenched fists who wore their blood-spatter like soldiers. A tier back the gentlemen lounged. She recognised Gilmour. His cockerels were reputedly the best in London and she'd hoped he might be here. She pulled Nonesuch close. 'He's here. I knew it. Where do you think they keep the birds before the fight?'

Nonesuch's eyes flickered around the room. 'There's a door over there at the side. But even dressed like this I'm not sure they'd let us back there.' He took a purse from inside his skirt. 'This is stage money so don't let him see it properly, but he'll love the weight of it.' He tossed it from hand to hand. 'Tell him ... tell him your lady wants a fighting cock and she'll pay whatever is necessary. With a bit of luck, you might walk out of here with it under your arm.'

He shoved her out into the crowd before she could complain and they pushed through the throng in the calm between bouts. Benches turned into stairs as the crowd milled. The boards were slick with sweat. Gilmour sat among his men. He was rigid and wet-lipped, drying his hands on his breeches.

Shay prepared her voice and baked it hard in her mind. She thought back to the gentleman on the wharf and the heavy boredom of his tone. 'Gilmour. Lady here wants a fighting cock and I'm told you're the man.' Her tone suggested she cared little whether Gilmour was the man or not.

He didn't take his eyes from the pit. A red curl of feather landed on his upper lip and it quivered with each breath. 'Come by the shop like everyone else does. My boys will sort her out.'

'The lady wants one of these birds. Blood riles the blood, if you know what I mean.' She jangled the purse in front of him and for the first time he looked up at them. He automatically priced their clothes, located their accents, and calculated the trouble they might cause.

'See my man on the door down there? Tell him to show you Prince Troynovant. It'll cost you a guinea, mind. He's a killer, that one.'

Without looking away from the cockpit he reached out and encircled Nonesuch's wrist. 'And if killers are what the lady likes then I can always oblige.'

A shout went up from the front row and Shay stared at the feather trembling on Gilmour's lip. Below them two cockerels were being tossed into the ring.

'Now piss off,' said Gilmour. 'I'm working.'

They made their way through two tiers of roaring spectators to the side of the building where it was ill lit and dusty. A youth slouched by the door, watching the fight. Shay said, 'Your boss is selling us Prince Troynovant. Show us now.'

He opened the door with one eye still on the bout and hovered at the entrance. The cock pen was hotter still than the arena. Square cages were stacked on top of one another in teetering piles and cocks pecked blindly at their neighbours. Wingbeats churned the dank air; Shay thought she might retch. The youth dragged a cage across the ground and said, 'This is him.'

Shay had to look away from the crude, rusty scars where wattle and comb had been removed. The bird had been so hacked and stitched and streamlined that he resembled a feathered knife. Long silver spurs like metal thorns hung from his ankles.

'Vicious little fucker. The pretty ones always are, eh?' He nudged Shay with an elbow.

Again she let the gentleman from the wharf inhabit her. 'Speak to me that way again and I'll whip you from here to the river. Wait outside.'

The youth didn't look particularly chastened, but he did lope for the door. As it opened he winked at Nonesuch. 'Enjoy yourself, miss.'

When he was gone Nonesuch pushed back his veil. 'Lord knows what he thinks we're going to do in here. What's the plan? Pass off a stage guinea on the boy and walk out of here with Prince under our arm?'

The bird regarded them hopefully from its cage. Shay was trying hard to hold back her bile.

'All of them,' she whispered.

'What?'

'We need to take all of them.'

Nonesuch shook his head. 'How? If we go through the arena they'll fucking hang us.'

A roar from behind the door shook the room and the candles rattled in their holders. Shay looked around them. 'How did they get them in here? Not through the crowd. There must be another way in.'

She pushed aside the cages that were stacked against the outer wall. 'Block the door.'

Nonesuch dragged a bench over in front of the door while Shay searched the main wall. Two-thirds of the way around she found what she was looking for: low double doors. They were shut tight but there was a tool of her father's that she always kept on her: a peacock quill with a flattened end, and she tried it in the lock. No joy; the metal was furry with rust and the quill jigged uselessly in the keyhole.

The youth's voice came from outside. 'Make yourself decent, I'm coming in.' The door slapped against the bench and he tried again. 'Can you move away from the door?'

Nonesuch gestured to another bench. 'If we take one side each, we could use that to ram the doors.'

They took an edge each and ran the bench at the outside exit. The doors must have been warrened with woodworm because they shattered on impact and shafts of autumn sun scrambled across the floor. Instantly the birds flapped against their bars. Shay tried to drag a cage out through the hole in the wall, but the cockerel pecked blindly at her. His beak had been sharpened to a point and it drew a thin line of blood. She whipped her hand away.

'Like this,' said Nonesuch. He lay on his back and kicked the cage across the floor. Noises grew behind the blocked door and he kicked harder. Shay joined him, sending cages tumbling on their way, end over end, with the cocks a furious blur at their centres. They were heavier than they looked and, by the time all had been pushed out into the street, Shay and Nonesuch were wet with sweat. For one moment they lay there as a snow of feathers fell around them and then Shay scrambled through the hole and out into the street. Nonesuch turned back and wedged his shoulder against the door back into the arena.

Everything in Southwark was a show, whether paid for or not. Out on Pike Street passers-by stopped to watch Shay struggle with the clasps. Even at the very moment of their freedom the birds fixated on her fingers and every cage she undid came at a cost to her hands. Blood trickled down her forearms and dropped in spatter patterns at her feet. *The birds are gods*, she reminded herself, helplessly.

What had she expected once they were free? Cockerels weren't great flyers, but they had enough speed and lift to at least get themselves away from the street. But instead they shook themselves down like prize fighters and then attacked whichever bird was closest. In moments the street was a battleground; it was hard to tell where one bird started and the next ended. Spurs glinted in the sun, plunged, and then came back up, red with blood to their hilts. Heads hammered into flesh, sewing threads of red across white bodies while forty wings beat a dust storm around them.

'Stop. Run.' Shay threw herself into the tumult, her trousers torn, as she split up tangles and kicked birds to the side of the road. Her face was wet with tears, her ankles sodden with blood. 'Run, for God's sake.' Some stumbled away, unsteady and bloodied, while others lay in broken piles at her feet. The noise was incredible: a keening wail, whether of pain or triumph it was impossible to tell. They died down there in the dirt and piss and bones while all the time a huge, empty sky hung above them. Skirmishes continued around her as women cowered under shop awnings with their skirts wrapped tight around their legs.

A pulse of fury rose up in her chest. She pushed through the gawpers back to the front entrance to the cockpit. The guards eyed her with alarm – the torn clothes and freckles of blood. She stood tall. 'All the fighting cocks are loose around the corner. Hundreds of pounds' worth. There's going to be a riot.'

As soon as the guards' footsteps echoed around the corner Shay swung the bolt across to lock the main doors. Then up, using the bolt as a foothold, levering herself onto the architrave. Windows ringed the first floor, now closed against the sun. She edged around to the nearest one and forced the shutters open. Down below a bout had finished; men exchanged money and slapped backs. Someone swept what was left of a losing bird into a sack.

She was maybe fifteen feet up and she could see every inch of the arena. 'Fighting cocks,' she yelled. No response. Her face warmed with anger. 'Stage voice,' she told herself.

'Fighting cocks!' This time faces turned towards her and she fought the urge to duck out of sight. She made herself meet Gilmour's gaze. Now would he recognise her?

'So, you big men enjoy a fight to the death?'

It was curiously quiet. A hundred or so faces looked up at her and in the main their expressions were of amusement. She took one of Alouette's smoke bombs from her bag, waggled it at the men and then lit the fuse on a wall-torch. It fizzed and then caught. They were listening now.

'All the doors are barred. The only way out is the loading entrance in the cock pen.'

Heads swivelled to the rear of the room. She heard someone try the door below her.

'In five minutes, this place will be burned to the ground. Only the strong will survive.'

She lobbed the bomb towards the front door. She wanted to bottleneck the whole crowd, force them out through the back, to see how they liked it. The missile wrote a line of black through the air, bounced, broke, and then coughed out smoke. There was a moment of incomprehension and then a furious moan – almost sexual – before men clambered towards the pen.

'Run, little chickens, run.' The next bomb landed in the cockpit and spun around ineffectually, but the one after that spat smoke through the air and a pancake of grey dust settled over everything. She could hardly see the men now, but she could hear their progress. Coughs, screams, clashing of swords and splintering of wood. She set off another bomb and then crab-walked around the building's exterior to look down on the exit from the cock pen. Gentlemen crawled through the broken door, bloodied and begrimed, and the whole side wall began to shake. Muffled from within came the cry *one ... two ... three* ... There was an ominous, weary creak and the whole side wall came crashing down in slow motion. Men fell coughing to the floor and were then trampled by the next wave. All had swords drawn, and many already hobbled. Shay threw her final bomb, turned on her heels, and set off across the rooftops. Sun and tears in her eyes and the churn of the cockfight still there when she closed them. Blood-stained feathers and the taste of metal.

She was back just minutes before curtain-up and she found the theatre in uproar. Trussell paced the entranceway, so absorbed in his own troubles that he didn't take in her dishevelment. He wore a hurried mask of make-up and a too-large gold tunic.

He grabbed her shoulders. 'Were you with Nonesuch? Where the hell is he? I've never played Cleopatra before.' He let go of her and kept up a circuit by the door, muttering lines under his breath.

Shay looked behind her. 'He's not here yet? He left Southwark before me.' He might not be as fast as her across the rooftops but it had been a half-hour – plenty of time to get from Southwark to the theatre. Her stomach fluttered at the memory of the street: the blood and smoke and violence.

A bell rang inside the theatre and Trussell shook his head. 'He's not been back all day. Can you wait here for him? I'm not on until the third scene. Alouette could prompt.' Behind her, pigeons scattered before the noise of a speeding carriage. Trussell's hand went to his mouth. 'Oh hell, Evans is here too. He'll fire us both if this performance goes badly.'

Final latecomers trickled inside as the bell rang for a second time, leaving the street oddly quiet. Shay picked dried blood from her fingers and begged the birds for Nonesuch to appear. She looked up and saw the familiar sight of Devana bisecting the sky. She whistled with two fingers and whispered, 'Where *is* he, girl?'

As if in response, a cart barrelled around the corner at such speed that two wheels left the ground. With a yelp Nonesuch half jumped, half fell from its back. He brushed himself down; his shoes were in his hand. He was trying to keep from smiling but couldn't help himself.

'Did you forget something?' He was flushed but uninjured. 'Once you took to the roofs, there was only one stranger left to blame. It's taken me a whole quarter-hour to lose them. Then the owner of that carriage wanted a fare for hiding me that I wasn't prepared to pay.'

He put on his shoes and took her arm. 'Seriously though, that was madness. I thought the bombs were for show – you might have killed those men.'

Shay laughed with relief. 'It was *smoke*. The worst they'll suffer is a bit of a cough.'

They slipped inside on tiptoe and around the back of the audience without once looking at the action on stage. Backs of heads and no laughter. Down into the tiring room where Nonesuch started to strip out of his widow's silks. 'It was beautiful though. I've never seen men like that so scared.'

They could hear the introductory soliloquy. Those footsteps would be Trussell pacing the wings. Nonesuch cocked an ear to the performance, naked bar his veil. He pushed the door closed. 'Plenty of time.' He took Shay's hands and pinned them above her head. Her knuckles scuffed against the bricks and she locked her eyes on to his. He pushed back his veil and his kiss was harder than usual. She tasted smoke on his lips and his hands were urgent on her buttons. His veil slipped and he laughed.

'How long until scene three? It'll do Trussell good to sweat a little.'

Later, Shay wondered whether Nonesuch had somehow timed it that way. Her clothes falling to the floor just as the audience gasped at Caesar's arrival; the tense hush as he entered her, the sounds of sword-fighting as his rhythm built. Their first time – first proper time – was punctuated and driven on by a crowd of unknowing gentlemen only inches away. And finally, as he slipped from her, and they fell, laughing, to the floor, the scene on stage reached its denouement. They lay breathless and bruised with their hands still in each other's hair, as the room shook to round after round of frenzied applause.

14

SHAY SLEPT IN HER cockfight outfit that night, curled up in tattered tweeds and a ruff that smelled of smoke. The empty bandolier slung over her shoulder was somehow more threatening than a loaded one would have been. She slept through six bells and slept through the boys' waking too. Slept through Nonesuch leaving, still marooned in dreams where she rode on the thermals of a London on fire. Smoke trailed from her wings and her talons were silver thorns.

A hand woke her. A hand on her arse, shaking her hesitantly. Once she'd finally thrown off the dream and opened the flaps, Trussell was waiting, apologetic in the empty dorm. 'Sorry, I didn't mean to touch you ... there. I couldn't tell which end was which.' He reddened and looked at his feet; Shay suppressed a smile.

Trussell was awkward with everyone. On stage they gave him the clownish parts because he was bound to trip or belch or forget his lines; it was better to pretend that it was part of the act. And his confusion at his own clumsiness had the audience howling. But at first this general awkwardness had hidden from Shay the fact that he was even more awkward around her. He stood, nose twitching, shifting his weight from foot to foot. It appeared his speech was over.

She coaxed. 'So, why did you wake me, Trussell? Is something wrong?'

'Yes, sorry. Pavey went for a drink after the show last night and he said there were men in The Blue Boar buying drinks. They were asking after a tattooed girl with spikes of hair. Asking who might know how to make smoke bombs too.' He lapsed into silence again.

She'd spoken to Gilmour last night. Looked him right in the eyes without even a pinch of recognition. What had changed?

'Did anyone mention my name?'

'Pavey doesn't think so but he was too scared to get close. You know that no one here would say a thing, right? I've been around every one of them and they all know to say they've never met anyone like you.'

So they hadn't been to the theatre yet, which was good. But they knew what she looked like, which was bad. At some point that would lead them to Birdland. Eight bells; she could be there and back before the afternoon's performance.

She stood at the front of the Long Ferry like a figurehead and let the spray scour London from her until she was pink and raw and small again. As they rounded the last bend before Birdland a bubble of excitement rose in her: her father's swan-boat was moored on the jetty. Rings of mud covered its sides so it must have been at least a week since it had been used. As she disembarked, she stroked its head for luck; its beak, once an oily black, had been worn to grey, and she made a mental note to repaint it while she was here. Another thing on her list. Paint the boat, build a fire, mend Lonan's clothes. Her chores coming home to roost. She repeated the list in her mind like a mantra and she was so caught up in the words that she almost missed the warning call. It was two short crow caws in succession, so expertly done that at first she didn't recognise them as made by a human. It was only when the caws repeated that she stopped. A call that even the fledglings knew. *One means come, two means stay.*

She was still two hundred yards from Birdland, but somebody working high in the nets might have seen her. It would do no harm to wait and see. She sat on a tussock and an invisible bittern boomed away somewhere as a figure hurried from the nets. She raised a hand in greeting as she recognised Colm but he waved her back, pointing towards the jetty. She picked her way through the sodden marshland and sat in the back of the swan-boat. Gulls wheeled overhead and she took a hunk of bread from her bag and amused herself by throwing pieces high in the air and watching their acrobatics.

Colm was talking even before he stepped onto the jetty.

'Men were here.' He said it without reproach, the way he might point out an interesting bird in the nets. 'Londoners, with what looked like bloody wolves on leashes.'

'Looking for me.' It started as a question, but what else would they be here for?

'Yes. Looking for you.'

Tattoos and spikes of hair. Any impecunious drinker would have told the men to try Birdland.

'When?'

'Yesterday night. But they promised they'd be back. Threatened, I should say.'

'What did you tell them?'

'I told the truth. That we never see you any more. That you stay in London most nights but we have no idea where.'

Shay looked back at the city. She'd never thought what happened there would affect Birdland, they'd always been different worlds.

'We told them that you weren't ever coming back, but they asked to see your father.'

The idea of Gilmour's men in her father's room made Shay feel sick. They were too big, too clumsy for that fragile space. She pictured Lonan's birdlike wrists and ankles, his mouth opening and closing.

'And, of course, he got confused. He told them that he'd seen you a day ago and that you came every week for the Murmuration. I tried to explain to the men that his memory was gone but I don't think they believed me. There's every chance they'll be back today.'

The gulls had given up on her. They floated, watchfully, on the river.

'I want to see him. I'll explain.'

'I don't think that's wise, Shay. You have to understand that we've had to tell him over and over again that you're not coming back. I won't have those men up there again. I had to stop him taking the swan-boat into London. For now, Chahine is staying in his room, teaching him what to say if they come back.'

'Chahine? The goshawk girl? What has she got to do with anything?'

'We needed someone to step in for the Murmuration. The flock is huge and everyone here is spooked. She's doing all right, she's a quick study.' He ran a hand through his hair. 'It's probably temporary, but you can't be here, at least until this business is over. If Lonan tells them that you're back in Birdland, then they'll never leave us alone.'

He looked over his shoulder and Shay remembered the crow call. 'Why did you sound a warning? Why didn't you just come out to meet me?'

'Shay. Shay.' He dropped his eyes. 'Some people think it would have been better to hand you over to the Londoners and be done with it.'

'Which people?'

'A few. No one important. But it might not be as safe here as you think.'

Chahine. She'd shivered and shaken all through her tattooing but hadn't cried once.

Colm's face cracked for the first time. 'They killed all the *doves*, Shay.'

The gulls watched with interest as Shay emptied her bag of gifts onto the jetty. First the candied ginger in twists of brown paper and five silver pennies. She found that she didn't care that someone else had read the Murmuration, but she ached at the idea of another's hand being the first thing Lonan reached for in the morning.

She took out a miraculous, ripe apricot. A painted wooden box filled with tea from India. It pained her that someone else would pilot him to the shore from his nightmares. His name would be on someone else's lips.

Walnuts in their shells and a posy of wilting lilies. Someone else would guide his hands around his tea. Someone else would brush his wild hair flat. Her little pile of treasures looked tawdry under Birdland's brutal sky and even if Colm told her father who the gifts were from, it would be gone from his memory in a moment. She visualised the flash of pleasure across his face; that would have to be enough. 'I'll have to take the boat,' she said, and Colm nodded.

He helped her push off, the boat listing to one side with only her in it. He waited on the jetty, his hand shielding his eyes. She called after him, 'Tell father that there are a pair of breeding peregrines nesting in the spire of St Paul's.' She'd heard them the day before, squabbling like an old couple.

The tide tugged the boat towards the city and Colm shrank with each second. When she was ten yards out, she shouted to him, 'Tell him they're faster than death.' Then she rested her head against the smooth wood and let the tide take them for a while. Gulls followed for the first mile, but gave up when they realised that her hands were empty.

15

I T WAS THE FIRST thing that Shay saw as she disembarked onto
Broken Wharf. She hardly recognised herself at first. The poster bore
a crudely drawn portrait – the subject was cross-eyed and leering – but
the twin tufts of hair and scribble of tattoo could only really be her. She
stared at it for a moment before thinking to read the text below. It read:

FLAPPER SHAY

WANTED

DESTRUCTION OF PROPERTY – ARSON – INJURY

She looked around her. Collars were up and hands were in pockets; the
cold had everyone scurrying. She tore down the poster and crumpled
it into her bag. As she walked, it felt as if everyone were looking at her
and she pulled her cap down lower. Two minutes later she saw another
poster. It was in a shopfront and there was no way she could get at it. She
crossed to the other side of the road and kept her eyes lowered. A few
yards on there were three in a row, glued to a tavern wall. WANTED
WANTED WANTED. She tore at the corners but they were glued
fast so she ripped strips from the eyes and hair and then looked for an
escape route – she couldn't bear being at street level any more. There was
a ladder propped against the wall of Barkley's Inn and she climbed it, up
onto a peaked roof. Cracked tiles made it as treacherous as ice up there,
but at least there were no more posters, and it was an easy route north
across the rooftops to the theatre.

   To her surprise, four figures waited on the theatre roof. Blank and
Trussell looked sick, Nonesuch amused, and Alouette furious; she had a
pile of torn-off WANTED posters at her feet. Nonesuch slow-clapped
as Shay pulled herself up over the ledge, and said, 'Destruction and
arson? I am *wildly* jealous. Though I'd sue over the portrait. I'm going to

petition Gilmour to have Trussell do a more flattering one. You know it reflects on me too.' He gave her a wink but then reached out a hand to clasp hers. 'I'm sorry. I don't know how he worked out it was you under that beard.'

Alouette butted in. 'I took down a few but they're going up faster than I can get to them. Gilmour's men are pasting them all over town. Of course, it doesn't mention his name anywhere but the street kids will know who is after you.' She smoothed out one of the posters and stared at it. 'We were talking before you got here. One of us can be with you at all times. Nonesuch can pick you up in the morning, I'll stay with you while you're at the theatre, and Blank's offered you a cot on his boat. We'll draw up a rota for the rest of the company.'

Shay's heart swayed; she could barely hear what Alouette was saying. They would protect her. But more than that, it hadn't occurred to them not to. Not once, she thought, had anyone loved her as much as she loved them and she ached to be able to show them a similar kindness. Blank had been quiet until then but now he spoke up. 'I actually have an idea about how I might fix this.' He held up his hands against the others' questions. 'It will need some organising. I'll need Alouette and Trussell and a couple of hours off. You might have to do tonight's performance without me.'

Once he'd left none of them was inclined to go back downstairs. Nonesuch paced the roof's edge and then sat back down to undo a cloth that was wrapped around four cooked piglets, lacquered with fat, which a stage-door girl had brought for him that morning. The four of them sat in silence and ate until they were stupefied and greasy, with bones scattered around them, like hawks in an eyrie.

'Four whole hogs. That poor mare will get a flogging if she's found out. I hope that you at least gave her tickets for tonight.' Alouette had eaten less than the others, only picking at the whitest meat. She leaned back to catch the sunlight and a faint down glowed on her arms and face.

Nonesuch said, 'I couldn't even if I had wanted to. We're sold out for weeks.'

Trussell was buried deep in a second carcass, gnawing away with the kind of concentration that Shay had only seen in those who'd gone properly hungry before. When even he lay back with his hands across his swollen belly, there were still two glistening carcasses left.

'What a waste,' said Alouette. 'Shall I give them to the boys downstairs?'

Just a day ago Shay could have taken one home for her father. It would have been a rare treat. There was someone else though.

'Could I have one?' she asked.

'Of course. Take the pair if you want.'

'No, one's fine. Watch ...'

She scanned the sky. Swifts hunted insects and pigeons bunched and flitted from rooftop to rooftop. Crows pulled moss from tiles. And, a whole realm above, the hunters played. Falcons. Three ... No, four. A pair was corralling some rooftop rodent to its doom. And among them, leaning against the wind like a thug leaning on a carriage door, there was Devana. Shay brushed herself down, stood, and cupped her hands around her mouth. Her first attempt was little more than a croak, but the second was better and it sent the crows barrelling away in alarm. She had everyone's attention now. One last call.

Devana circled. A tilt of the head and her spiral tightened a degree, but she made no attempt to descend.

'Don't make me beg,' Shay laughed. The others watched, unsure of what was happening. She tried the cry again and Devana made two more circuits. Lazy. Nowhere to be. Then there was the merest wing-tuck and the bird fell into a long, banked curve, growing rapidly like a horse-cart coming too fast towards you. Shay stood and raised her arm and Devana didn't make the slightest adjustment to her path – she arrived in silence, with wings braked against the air, and both talons took Shay's forearm at once. Contemptuous eyes swept across the rooftop. The familiar weight of her; lighter than she looked, but stronger too.

'Don't look her in the eye,' she whispered. Devana's presence was, as ever, a miracle. She made herself comfortable on Shay's arm and gave one last stretch of wings – *behold the bird!* – before she settled in to groom.

Nonesuch couldn't take his eyes off her. 'Oh my saints, she is beautiful.'

Without taking his gaze from the falcon, Trussell reached for his paper and pencil, and, with his mouth opening and closing like a fish's, he began to sketch. For a split-second, Devana focused on the pencil nib – that scratch like mouse-claws – and then went back to her feathers, satisfied that it was nothing she need kill just yet. Shay held up a piglet leg. Instantly Devana had it in her beak. She tossed her head left, right, left before gulping at the flesh. Shay revolved the bone and the bird did the same thing again. She tilted her head to one side and picked a precise strip of flesh from the bone. With a flourish she threw it into the air, caught it in her beak and swallowed it whole. Her eyes latched immediately back on to the meat.

'Show-off,' whispered Shay. Twice Devana rolled her gaze around them, twice more she tore and swallowed, and then, with a gentle squeeze of claw, she let Shay know that she was done. She folded her wings into a soft 'M' and, without warning, she was gone; three ponderous, thoughtful wingbeats as she dipped below the eaves and then up over the city.

'Keep watching.' There were other birds of prey up there, but none moved quite the way Devana did. There was a hint of the theatrical in her cliff-edge dives and vertical turns. 'See? See how you'll recognise her.'

Nonesuch nodded. 'She's like an assassin.' Devana curled again and disappeared below the line of buildings.

It was as if they'd all held their breath. Nonesuch and Alouette were full of questions – 'When did you learn to ...' 'Does she always come ...' – as Shay tried to tell the story of her and Devana. How she'd known the falcon as a fledgling when it was just a riot of feathers and gaping mouth. How they'd grown together, explored together; feral kids with London laid out beneath them. And how, when she pictured herself, it was through Devana's eyes: a rodent figure running across the carpet of the city. When the other two were done with their questions Shay went to sit beside Trussell. His drawing was a sketch of Devana's head. A gleam of eye under heavy lids, a river of feather tips and a beak sketched in three sharp lines. A liquid knife. He kept his voice low with his eyes on the drawing as he said, 'Now I understand, Shay. *That's* what you worship.'

The afternoon's performance was sloppy and nervous. Pavey stood in for Trussell and Nonesuch's Doctor Faustus prowled the front of the stage, only inches from the prompter's box, worried that with the others gone there was no one to keep an eye on Shay. But Shay felt untouchable. Devana above her and her friends all around her. Nonesuch kept his performance casual but he made one of the more loving speeches directly into the gloom that surrounded her. She blew him a silent kiss. Even the curtain call was brief. Nonesuch and Pavey took a single bow each and they were wiping the make-up off before the applause had died down. Usually she hung back when he left the theatre, leaving him to flirt with the stage-door crowd, but tonight he took her arm and guided her out alongside him.

Out into the dusk. Candles just being lit and farmers driving unsold livestock back towards the gates. At every step, Shay expected the sound of a carriage or the howl of the wolfdogs. They walked north up Blackfriars towards the city walls. The crowd blocked Shay's view but Nonesuch was up on tiptoe. 'Shit,' he whispered. 'They didn't get rid of the posters. I actually think there might be *more*.' They pushed through the crowd to find posters papered across virtually every inch of the wall, plastered in sloppy groups, edges peeling from slapdash gluing. They shone a milky white in the dusk like mushrooms that had just sprouted. Shay felt sick. Worse, she felt surrounded. There was no escape from them. The columns that guarded Ludgate's route out of the city fluttered with hundreds more.

Nonesuch wrapped an arm around her. 'I don't understand what Blank has been doing all day.'

Shay kept her eyes on the ground. The day's detritus was ground into the mud at her feet.

'Oh wait. Look though,' said Nonesuch. He pulled Shay into the shadow of the wall where there was a spray of bills. The top one was a lively caricature of Nonesuch in which he was all curls and eyebrows. Beneath it, in the same hand as her wanted poster, stood the words:

LORD NONESUCH

WANTED

DEVILRY – HEARTBREAK – SEDITION

Shay laughed out loud. The next wall sported a gang of sour-faced Alouettes that read:

FLANDERS ALOUETTE

WANTED

MAGICK – WHORING – ENCHANTMENT

Then two lone Blanks, rakish under a tricorne hat, with a list of crimes that included embezzlement and thievery. And across the bottom, a bold message in thick black letters. A message that adorned all the other posters, even the few Flapper Shays that still remained.

WELCOME TO THE GHOST THEATRE
SECRET LOCATION
COMING SOON

Now everywhere that they walked, from the walls of St Paul's Church to the river, the four faces stared back at them. The Flapper Shay posters were lost in a blizzard of words. Nonesuch was almost running with the excitement of it all. 'The Ghost Theatre ... Welcome to the *Ghost Theatre* ... I like it. Blank must have thought of the name. Alouette doesn't have the imagination.'

He stopped outside Cole Abbey and took Shay by the hands. The faces of their friends looked down on them from the church walls. He said, 'It's happening. We have to do this now. It's beginning.'

Churches had the best handholds: gargoyles and crenellations and architraves and waterspouts. Nonesuch bent her over. 'Help me up.' Up, swinging with laughter. Racing each other up the walls until they were hand in hand on the rooftop looking out over half the city. He raised her hand like a winning boxer and bellowed up into the sky, 'We are the Ghost Theatre.'

16

Nonesuch, alouette, blank and Trussell. Acting, lights, music and sets – fire, air, water and earth. The four of them were the knot at the centre of the theatre's tangle, and every thread led to them. And deeper down, pulled tightest of all, was the secret of the Ghost Theatre. What was it to be? Nonesuch wanted stories, real stories, stories without gods and demons and sorcerers, where people 'just like you and me' lived, laughed and died. A first rule: no scripts, just tales dragged up from their dark places. It meant that their rooftop rehearsals sounded like confessionals – 'Tell me how it felt,' 'What did they do to you?' – as they each told stories that had never seen the light of day before. When Shay was among them she felt elevated, when she spoke they listened. But whenever she had a rare moment to herself she was overtaken by a fear of becoming ordinary to them – she worried that she would exhaust her scant reserves of novelty. She set a rule: no more than two nights in a row in Nonesuch's bunk: she would not become a fixture. Even with Gilmour looking for her she was freer than any boy at the Blackfriars and they both envied and celebrated her for it. So, she still ran messages in the mornings, returning with gossip and the chilly air of the rooftops, to spice the stew of the dormitory. And on the coldest nights she slept at Blank's, under piles of costumes in fur and cashmere, stupefied by both the slow tick of the ship and the smouldering spice bundles that warmed every corner. Blank himself kept erratic hours. He was in and out at all times of night and day, silent in the daylight but garrulous in his sleep. The pair fell into a largely mute, comfortable friendship that was blessed relief after the tumult of the dormitory. But in the main, when she wasn't at Blackfriars, she slept on the roof of Eltham House. She curled around the furnace of the chimneys, which never seemed to cool, what with the last roastings of dinner and the first bakings of the morning being so close together in a house that size.

Devana took much coaxing down the first time Shay slept there, circling, lower and then away, time and again, a caution unusual in a bird now accustomed to doing exactly as she pleased. Her mews stood cold and locked, and the chimney was a good ten yards away, but still she eyed her former home like it was some predator. Their courtly dance took an hour, and it was only when Shay blanked the bird, and curled herself catlike around the brickwork, that Devana landed with a sound gentler than snowfall.

How many nights did the pair spend there? Enough that Devana's talons wore grooves into the handrail where she always perched, looking haughtily down over Shay. Enough nights that Shay had time to polish and mend all of her jesses so Devana wore lilac leather in the skies, like a knight with his lady's handkerchief. Enough nights that Shay recited every one of her Ghost Theatre lines to the bird, her haughty incomprehension lessening the stage fright somehow.

How Shay loved the noises Devana made as she groomed. Those oily complaints and smothered caws, the rounded riffle of her tail folding and the scritch of beak under wing. They worked like a sleeping draught on her but when she woke Devana was always gone – like Blank was always gone, like her mother, too – and it was the smell of the first loaves baking a hundred feet below that woke her and drove her out onto the rooftops.

It was on one of those post-Devana walks, feeling stiff and cold and spurned, that Shay found what she'd been looking for. A place for her and Nonesuch, somewhere away from the claustrophobia of the dorm, where for once he would have only one pair of eyes on him. She'd been searching for one of those grand houses whose owners decamped to a country home in the months when London stewed in its soup of smoke and sweat, grand enough to have the kind of expanse of bedchamber that she wanted for them but not so grand that a skeleton staff would be left to tend to the place. One caught her eye. Ivy Bridge House, directly en route between Westminster and Newgate, a path often beneath her feet. Three days in a row she passed it and saw no sign of movement. A high-up, end window showed her pale linen and pale wood and a four-poster bed as fussily white as a wedding dress. The security thinned as the storeys rose; on ground level there were arm-thick bars over mullioned windows, forests of locks and grates and fences and spikes. But by the fourth floor it took her an eye-blink to force a roof-hatch and she spent an entire morning walking the rooms like a ghost, listening to her footsteps shrink and grow huge as she scoured the kitchen for leftovers.

She brought Nonesuch the very next day, fresh from rehearsals, with him in a cloak and scholar's hat and her in her blackout suit. In through the hatch and then quietly to the bedroom, the pair of them suddenly shy, gentle as cats, shuffling around the four-poster with eyes sliding from each other, hands reaching for hands. In the end the bed was too soft, too forgiving for anything but sleep so instead they fucked on the floor. He positioned her gravely – *there and there, a little bit lower* – with her on her knees as his cloak enveloped them and they giggled, playing like kids under a sheet fort. It was good. Quick. Uncomfortable but not painful. With his hands he moved her, repositioned her. Showed her what he wanted in the way he did with his words on stage. From behind, holding her like you might a sheep about to be sheared. Then again, him on a chair, her astride him, better this time though a row of family portraits scowled down on her until she stuck out her tongue at them, closed her eyes and stayed that way until he was done.

No watching eyes and no chatter of boys through that ratty old rug. It felt like another first time. After, as she cooled and dried, she looked at her nails and her feet and thought about all the places he'd touched. She wanted to paint them on her from head to toe. Those spots where he lingered. Her clavicle and the dimples of her back, her neck from shoulder to ear, the softest skin of her inner thigh. She imagined tattooing them black, each time, until she was a statue in jet.

Nonesuch woke to the three bells, looking stupidly, uncomplicatedly happy.

'We have an hour,' she said. She wanted to explore. The house or him, either would do.

He kissed her on the spot on her scalp where the sparrow's beak came to a point and whispered, 'How would it be if you were to leave me here, just for a half-hour?'

She tried to hide her confusion. Was this part of it? Some universally acknowledged male need that a flapper-girl had never been educated about?

He stroked her neck. 'How often are you alone, Shay? Without another person in sight?'

She thought about it. When she rowed herself to work. Out on the marshes. There were broader rooftops out east where she was the only figure for miles. 'Sometimes. Not a lot.'

He talked into her ear. 'I can't remember the last time. When I was a kid, I guess, lost in the woods. To be in a room. On my own and not a word of chatter. It would be something …'

It was hours later that he returned to the theatre, but he brought something for her. Something he'd found in a jewellery box stuffed half-way up the chimney. He said, 'People always think they're being clever hiding things there, but they'd be better off leaving them out on the dressing table, that's the last place I'd bother to look.'

It was a skull earing. Coral maybe, painted in black with a kind of dark jauntiness.

All through the winter it was the same. Shay would find them an empty place and they'd make love in whatever costumes they were already wearing. And then she would leave, alone and dazed across the rooftops, and him alone too, spreadeagled across some snowy, forbidden bed. Every time he brought trinkets home to the theatre, so many that their bunk – *their* bunk, it thrilled her to say it – rattled as they moved around inside. Necklaces and bracelets and medals and knives. Cameos and pearls and lace and velvet. It ought, she thought later, to have made her feel bought, every coupling coming with a present. But instead, it made her feel like a treasure. She was just one of the hundred beautiful things that shone and rang and glinted from the bare brown boards of that subterranean bunk.

Act II

17

S HAY DIDN'T START TO sing until she'd been stabbed through the chest.

She came crashing down the stairs. Her jacket caught on a hangnail that spun her around and threw her to the floor. The ox carcasses hung in neat rows, marbled pink in the reflected glow of the ice blocks. She crawled across the floor and threw open the skylight out to the street but it was gridded with thick iron bars. She tugged at them as footsteps circled above her head. No alternative exits and nowhere obvious to hide. Above her the footsteps paused and then got louder. With a grimace she climbed up and crawled inside the largest of the carcasses. The meat was stiff with cold but its chest had been split and pinned back so she was able to squeeze inside like a pupa in a cocoon. From her roost within the ribcage she tugged at the slit in the belly and drew the meat around her like a cloak. Her feet scrabbled for purchase on the frozen rungs of rib and she held herself rigid. There was little light in the cellar and the men upstairs couldn't be sure that she'd come this way so she slowed her breathing as the carcasses creaked on their chains. They made slow revolutions in some unseen draught.

The men, when they came, were careful. Low voices and a single torch. They did a circuit of the room, passing just inches from her, and she tried not to exhale; her breath would show white in the icehouse air. The carcass revolved ponderously and she saw a sliver of the room: four men in black leather with swords drawn, not speaking. She watched their feet through curtains of flesh.

A voice: 'This skylight's been opened.'

One of the men spread his hand between the bars. 'She's a skinny bitch, but not that thin, surely?'

There was no answer. 'Do you think she could have gone out the back, then?'

'I don't see how but she's not here, is she?'

Silence. What were they doing? Shay couldn't see, but the Ghost Theatre audience could. They saw the look on one man's face as he noted that the floor-rushes had been disturbed. They watched him follow the path from door to skylight to that one particular carcass. And they saw fingers on lips and men with soft steps. A mimed count to three and then blades were drawn and thrust all the way through the ox in a single movement. Four blades in, four blades out. And then …

Slow drip of blood, fresh blood now, onto the rushes below. A creaking of chains, held breath and ice cracking. And then a body, as bloodied and quiet as a stillborn, fell and landed on its knees.

Silence again, then the blood-stained head rose and the dead girl began to sing.

The place went wild.

Four hours earlier, when the Ghost Theatre troupe crossed the river, Southwark had been alive with crowds. A bright, shirtsleeve-warm Sunday had appeared out of nowhere and the city was playing truant. Queues snaked outside every tavern and the streets crunched underfoot as a mix of crushed shells – nut and oyster both – pockmarked the dirt. They had to wait a quarter-hour to see the heads on display at the southern entrance of the bridge. Shay couldn't look, but Nonesuch examined each one with relish, and spent a long time in front of one in particular. 'Lord Carlyte,' he said, to no one in particular. 'He used to come to the Blackfriars.' He took a comb from his pocket and carefully restyled the hair, trying it this way and that, until Alouette moved him on.

Shay kept quiet. In her tunic, cap and hose she looked as blankly male as she ever managed and the drunken prentices didn't even register her presence. Still, it was Southwark – here, as the saying had it, every pot has a lid, though not in the charmingly romantic way that her father used the expression.

There were no Blackfriars performances on a Sunday so they had all morning to check out the venue for the first Ghost Theatre show. But this play needed none of their usual props or tricks so after running through the sightlines and checking the entrances they were left with hours to kill. Nonesuch had plans. 'First an ale at The Cross Keys, then lobster at Ginty's and then to the bear pit to touch Sackerson for luck.'

Sackerson: undefeated, indefatigable, unbowed but much-bloodied champion of the bear pit. Nine feet of muscle with breath like a charnel house and paws the size of bellows. Those paws had clawed, batted, scratched, torn, teased and twisted whole packs of dogs, wolves and, in one much-storied evening, lions back to their constituent parts. Sackerson was the fever-dream of London's youth: pure power and anger, caged but unbowed. He was a recurring obsession of the Blackfriars Boys, who invoked his spirit the way gentlemen might talk of their lord. Trussell charged a half-penny for his heroic drawings of the bear, pitted not against dogs but instead rampant against sheriffs, theatre owners and schoolmasters. If a man had wronged a Blackfriars Boy, then he could, for the price of an ale, be pictorially reduced to a puddle of blood by the sainted animal.

The bear pit was a squat, windowless building that brooded over the Southwark skyline like a storm cloud. Nonesuch paid a shilling for each of them to get ten minutes in Sackerson's pen; a touch of his paw was supposed to bring courage.

'C'mon in.' Nonesuch's pupils were blank black discs in the gloom of the pen; he looked frantic and blind. Even in the dark Sackerson's presence was overwhelming – the bear gave off an odour so thick as to make you swoon: sweat, musk, sodden straw, and the foundry smell of fresh blood. Shay was tiny amid the glut of the atmosphere. Well-deep breaths echoed as the bear shuffled sideways and the boards beneath her feet dipped towards his corner. He was big, too big for the room, too big for people, even. Shay was close enough to make out his features and she couldn't see those paws without sensing the fragility of her bones. It would take the smallest of effort for him to snap her, to crush her. She stepped towards him despite herself. The bear smelled sweeter up close, clotted and overripe: cherries on the turn, meat on the hook. His fur was the deep grey of charred wood but it was matted a glossy black in patches. Mud and blood, and not all of it from the dogs. Shay stepped closer into the weight of him. The floor dipped and creaked as her breath stirred a patch of fur on his belly. She shrank in proximity to so much power and so much pain. Heat poured off him and Shay wanted nothing more than to plunge into that fur and be swallowed by the warmth.

'Careful, they don't chain him in here. And if he were to get angry ...'
Nonesuch's voice was urgent, 'well, no one's opening that door for us.'

Hot breath raked Shay's skull as Sackerson bent over to smell her.
She let that delicate, leathery nose explore her. Then, without warning,
he flopped back inelegantly, setting the whole pen shaking. He ended
up on his arse with his hind legs splayed out in front of him and he
began to lick at his wounds. He cleaned the darker patches, occasionally gnawing at some tangle, and all the while he kept up a rumble of
yawns, grumbles and deep vibrations in his belly. As he sat that way,
like a weary toddler, Shay was struck that, of course, he'd once been a
cub, with boisterous siblings who'd scrabbled with him down hillsides.
He'd had a mother who'd carried him by the scruff of his neck, cuffed
him and licked down stray tufts of hair and, yes, cleaned his wounds for
him. Tears formed before she knew why and she moved closer, between
those huge hind legs, and Sackerson abandoned the claw on which he'd
been chewing. Doleful eyes, vigilant ears. A shoulder wound at Shay's
eye level pulsed with a black heat. She saw what she first thought was
a knuckle of exposed bone but, as she came closer, she realised it was a
tooth set amid bloody flesh. Sackerson twisted his body and the tooth
shifted. He gave an offhand grunt which was more of a throb through
the floor than a noise.

'Where's he from?' Shay asked.

'Schwarzwald, in Germany.' Nonesuch sounded nervous. 'It snows
nine months a year and the forest is so thick you can walk a month
without seeing the sun. It took twenty men took to bring him here.'

Shay saw a sea of pine-treetops. White sky, white snow and trees that
never dried out. German forests meant woodpeckers and linnets, turtle
doves and ravens. So what would sound like home to Sackerson? She
wetted her lips and tried a dove call. It was the aural embodiment of
the soft grey at a pigeon's neck and it was surprisingly hard work: throat
and belly had to move together. She tried again and Sackerson's ears
sprang up doggishly. Shay cooed once more and it bloomed inside her,
the sound of snow falling from firs. The bear let out a questioning moan,
gentle and lost, and she moved closer still with her throat vibrating. She
laid a hand on the bear's wound: it was warm and wet and it throbbed
with pain. She pressed herself against the blood-beat and battle-twitch
of ancient muscle and she sought out the tooth. Her dove-coo was a tiny
thing against his gallon draughts of breath. She twisted and pulled the

tooth out in one movement while keeping her body hard against his. The fang was the length of her hand, gnarled like old trees and stained the yellow of pus. She held it out for the bear to see but he was back to worrying at that broken claw. The wound blossomed with fresh blood.

Back out in the sunlight she kept her hand wrapped around the tooth. They wound their way back through Southwark crowds that were, if anything, rowdier now. Prentices had been drinking since the morning and the executions were over. Her stomach jolted as they arrived at the tavern; there was a queue outside and a crowd inside, all waiting for them.

The upstairs room was filled with loose groups spread across the bare floor. The play needed no stage but that meant there was nothing to focus on and the crowd churned. People shouted across the room and carried clutches of chinking ale-jugs under chins. Fifty people now, sixty. The space cloyed with the drying sweat of post-work revelry, as voices were raised over others and soon there was a roar like the wash of a great ship. So. Many. Faces. Shay looked at them one by one – great rosy slabs with mouths agape for talk and beer and unchewed hunks of bread – and the enormity of the evening squatted in the pit of her stomach. Soon every one of these faces would be turned towards her. They would want something from her and she was certain that she didn't have what they wanted. What *did* they want? Fear hunched and turned in her gut – a dog settling in for the night – and the room sweated around her. She needed air.

Through the crowd and out into the cold of the alley. Evening air slapped her across the cheeks. She stood with hands on her knees and breathed in the frost, relishing its scratch against her throat. Somewhere high above her a bird rolled a black ball across the starlight and her heart reached for it. She imagined herself up there in the wind-roar and snow-seeds, looking down on a girl in an alley who meant nothing at all. It helped.

A hand on her shoulder made her start. 'All right?' Nonesuch was framed against the door, another black bird against the light. He didn't wait for her answer. 'Needed a piss.'

He walked a couple of paces and then pissed noisily against a door. Steam and his off-key whistle and a sharp smell like marsh water.

'All right?' he asked again as he buttoned himself up.

'I don't think I can do this.' Saying it gave the fear teeth.

'I know.' His voice was blank. Not angry but not compassionate either.

'You know that I can't do it?' She hadn't considered that he might offer her a way out.

'I know how it feels.' He lit his pipe and she caught the long lines of his face drawn tight. His eyes were hidden doorways. 'All those people. All those eyes. They want *so much*. Your body is telling you to run to the furthest corner of the world and to curl up and hide there.' He turned to face her. He tapped his bottom teeth against the top ones unconsciously.

'Yes.' So he understood. There would be an escape.

Wordlessly he took her hand and slid it inside his shirt. His heart juddered so hard that his ribs rattled. If Shay had thought that finding Nonesuch in the same boat might help, she was wrong. He puffed on his pipe. 'I feel that way too. Like my skeleton wants to run back to Blackfriars, pulling me behind it.'

'So what do we *do*?'

Nonesuch tipped out the last of the tobacco and extinguished the tiny amber stars with a boot-tip. 'We just do it. We're going to feel, right up until the moment that we start speaking, that there's no way we can do this, but remember, all we have to do is to stay here.' His eyes searched hers. 'Stay. Your wax might burn out but your wick will remain. You won't think you can do it at the start. You won't think you can do it while you're doing it. And next time?' He pressed her hand against his chest. 'It'll be harder still.'

A rush of light and a voice from behind them: 'Nonesuch, it's time.'

The other three stood in the doorway and Nonesuch gestured them into a huddle. They stood, arms around one another's shoulders, heads so close that their icy breaths became one. Blank squeezed her hand, and the feeling was joy and fear in such perfect balance that she almost laughed.

Nonesuch said, 'I know that all we have is our words, but we are going to *build* something with them tonight.' The ring shook with nodded heads. 'Most of the people here have never seen a play that's not about gods and kings, hell, some of them have never even seen a play.' He looked around the circle, making sure all eyes met. Shay wished she could stay there forever, her friends' breath in her mouth, their arms around her.

'Keep it truthful,' Nonesuch said. 'Keep it beautiful, and tomorrow these people will feel like heroes, and we five will have something that can never be taken from us.' His nails dug into Shay's palm. A last flicker of eyes around the circle and then the seriousness lifted from him. He stood tall, pulled his hat down low and said, 'Right. Let's start a fire.'

The play was simple enough: the four of them had robbed a shop (Gilmour's bird shop; a hat-tip to her) but they'd been caught in the act. They were scattered and set upon by Gilmour and his men. Nonesuch had made it back to the meeting point, this very back room, while Shay and Alouette and Blank were still being pursued. And while Nonesuch waited for his friends, he talked.

There was no raising of the curtain or dimming of the lights. Instead a butter-soft trumpet note, alien in the wash of noise, cut through, and Nonesuch said, 'I lost the thugs on the corner of Knight Ryder Street. I went left and they went right, following the others. I've always been lucky that way.' He knelt and drew a long oblong in chalk on the floor around him: a stage. Instinctively the crowd stepped back.

He talked ruefully, as much to his ale as to the crowd, recounting the plans they'd had and the mistakes they'd made. Hearing him talk made Shay's stomach lurch like the moment that horses get a carriage moving. He spoke in a pure London accent, slurred and playful, words running together and wrapped around the kind of slang that Shay recognised from overheard ale-house conversations. Boys were blades, girls were sheaths and every little piece of backslang had the younger watchers hooting. He sounded winded, almost beaten, and far from the heroic figure that he usually played. But the audience were rapt. He got his first real laugh about two minutes in, a nervous, should-we-find-this-funny ripple, and then they came regularly. Every face was angled his way. Eyes shone. Mouths were closed. What was that look, that collective look they wore? She couldn't describe it exactly, but it was a kind of surrender.

'And then Blank stuck him. Only a nick across the ear but you know that bleeds like a pig. And you know a penny's worth of noble blood costs the likes of us a sovereign.'

That was Blank's cue. He threw open the side door and a moment later he was outside in the cold night air. The crowd surged after him.

Now the alley was lit with lanterns and Blank waited at one end on another chalk outline. He whispered his lines, quiet and desperate. The crowd shushed one another to hear and then shushed the shushers. He said that Gilmour's men were upon him and this was the end. He said he had secrets that he'd never told and if no human ears could hear them then he would tell them to the night. With mounting horror Shay recognised that, whatever Nonesuch had said, Blank could really act. His fear and sorrow painted the backdrop. You fancied you could hear the barking of dogs and the cries of the encircling men.

Shouts came from the other end of the alley and Blank looked around him. Still trapped. The crowd parted to let four boys in black leather through. Hisses rained down and Shay marvelled at the faces in the audience. Genuine anger, genuine fear. The men were on him in seconds, clubs rising and falling with Blank unseen beneath them. It took a whole minute. A minute where the crowd held its breath and then the men were gone, with arms around one another and sweat on their brows.

Before the audience could applaud Nonesuch called out, 'And what of my friend, Flanders Alouette?' He hurried back inside and climbed the stairs. The crowd followed him. Alouette's scene took place on the roof so Shay sat in the now-deserted tavern and tried to breathe. She followed the action upstairs through muffled noises. Running footsteps, laughter. A collective gasp. A thud and just the edges of a song.

And then they were coming back down and it was her turn. A flood rose in her. Something viscous and hot that swelled up into her throat. Her cue was a funeral drumbeat from Blank. Nonesuch crouched in front of her with the chalk and he drew a curve from her feet, around and behind her. A heart. Carefully he withdrew, not looking at her, and faces turned. The weight of the audience's attention was a physical thing. She lurched forward and there was a moment when she thought – no, she knew – there was no way she could do this.

Her line: *I knew he'd be the death of me.* The words sat there like the horizon. *I knew. I knew. The death of me.* Faces like a wall. *I knew he'd be the death of me.*

The line died on the way out of her mouth. Stubbed its toe and limped into the room. She repeated it and the rest of her lines piled up in front of her, carts running into the back of each other. She rushed at the parts she could remember and others pulled up before their fences. The wall of faces lost its rapture and her chest throbbed with shame; she was ruining the others' hard work. And then the actors playing Gilmour's men entered. Their cries – 'Over there. I see the bitch' – had the crowd craning their necks and Shay dropped to her knees and crawled into the throng. Action was easier than talking. Across a floor sticky with beer, rush-ends cutting at her palms, but unseen hands guiding her towards the steps. The crowd coalesced around her and a cry went up: 'To the icehouse!' Shielded on all sides she made it to the trapdoor. Hands pulled it open for her and pushed her through. She half fell, half climbed down into the cool of the ice room. The huge blocks gave off a ghostly glow, as if lit from within, and carcasses hung in a neat square. She looked around her for somewhere to hide, even though the whole point was that there wasn't anywhere. Earlier, in rehearsal, climbing inside the ox's body had felt claustrophobic, now it was a relief.

When the men finally surrounded her, she ran through the checklist: squeeze the blood-bladder, flour across the face and hide the evidence at the back of the carcass. Harder than it sounded, hanging jammed inside an ox. She watched the men's feet and saw the blades slide in on either side of her. Squeeze, smear, hide. Once done, she let herself fall forward and hit the ground with a crash, less elegantly than in rehearsal. She landed on an elbow and the jab of pain made her cry out. Stupid, stupid Shay. She was supposed to be dead. She lay on the floor where she could feel the audience rather than see them. What now? The song.

Not one of them had wanted to sing but Nonesuch had been insistent. 'Stage plays need approval from the Master of the Revels but musical performances don't. A song or two might save our skin.'

Her mouth wouldn't work. *He'll be the death of me*, she thought. Her heart raced but she felt light, hollow-boned, and suddenly her vision lurched. She rose like smoke. Up, up, up until she was looking down on herself. A girl, dressed as a boy, sprawled on the floor. She watched her mouth open and close as the view pulled back, the audience like stones on a beach as she raised her arms and the clouds drew around her …

And then she was upstairs with hands on her back and voices shiny in her ears. At first she thought that the prentices had grabbed her for a beating and she shrunk from the touches. But no, they were slapping her back. Men howled victory at her. They were drunk, she was a treasure and everyone was much too close and much too loud. She waited until they were done with her and then ducked out into the alley where the swollen moon was framed between overhanging eaves and rats scuttled in the shadows. Rain had washed the street to mud but at least the air smelt fresh. She breathed in deeply and bathed herself in moonlight. Only the smear of mud across her knees and the ache in her elbow told her that it had really happened.

Again the oblong of light. Trussell came blinking into the alley and a smile broke his face as he saw her. He pulled a pouch from his bag and then patted his pockets. 'Tobacco?' he asked.

'If you have spare,' she said.

He lit and fanned his pipe and then took her shoulders like he might shake her. 'Are you all right? That was extraordinary.'

She checked herself over. Her face still burned and her arm hurt. 'What happened? I don't remember.'

'Why didn't you say you could sing like that? What even was it? It wasn't the song from rehearsals.'

'I don't know.' Her throat was sore.

'You really don't remember?' He couldn't take his hands off her. 'You were good.' He sounded surprised.

'Really?' True, Trussell was always doggedly complimentary towards her, but she still ached to hear that she hadn't let the others down.

'Really. When you started, I thought you were going to lose them, after y'know …' He made a vague gesture. 'But your singing just reeled them in.'

Pride. Praise. A drunken feeling. 'How? What did I do?'

'It's hard to describe. I wish I could replicate it. It started like a song but then it seemed to shake apart. It was almost birdsong, and then almost prophecy. Can you really not remember? You were cooing like a wood pigeon. Then you sang that we were all birds. You told us that from now on our feet would never touch the sullen earth. People were crying. Tough old men, weeping.' He spoke with the awed whisper that the Blackfriars Boys reserved for the natural order of things being overturned. 'They wept like girls.'

He took her hands in his. He was shaking even though the night wasn't that cold. He said, 'Shay, could I—' but he stopped as someone materialised through the side door. Blank listed to one side and his jacket hung open. He raised his trumpet and blew a ragged fanfare; he was hopelessly drunk. 'You should have warned me!' He sounded elated as he complained. 'I caught some of the melody by halfway. I played something but I'm not sure it helped.' He planted a kiss on her cheek. Stubble-rub like old brick and a rotten smell of strong wine. 'Come inside, you two. It's opening night.'

It was an hour before Nonesuch found them. He was propped up against a young baroness and his arm around her looked like it might have more to do with support than lechery.

'There she fucking *is*.' He gave a mock bow, his hat falling from his head but neatly caught before it touched the mud. Maybe he was less drunk than he appeared. 'You, my darling flapper. Are. The darkest of horses. You're a midnight black stallion in a coal cellar. A fucking funeral horse in mourning rags on a starlit night.' He snuffled. 'You're that dark.' He shook himself free from the girl and pulled Shay over to Alouette and Blank and Trussell. All were surrounded with admirers but Nonesuch told them, 'Piss off for a bit, my lovers, would you? Company meeting.'

Five heads together in the cold, steamy breath co-mingling and shoulders touching. 'That. Was. Something.' His hand tightened on Shay's shoulder, his hair was on her hair. 'It was ... it was ...' Then he slid, almost gracefully, onto the alley floor.

A maze of a night. Two more taverns. Different rooms drowned in the same sea of noise, and stragglers lost along the way. Quiet in the streets and then raucous behind closed doors in places that only Nonesuch knew. They called in on a card game in a bakery that was already heating the ovens for the morning, and Nonesuch lost a hatful of coins to two slumming gentlemen, who then paid him straight back to do his impersonation of the Queen. On to a shipboard going-away party for sailors set to leave in the morning, boys who were just-shaved and raw in fresh white uniforms. They drank with a grim purposefulness and tattooed each other inexpertly and made wills and drank again and begged Shay for kisses, and more, that she didn't feel she could decline because they were so young and so bright. She danced and ignored the parade of adolescent groins ground against her and only slapped away the most egregious hand-wanderings. And Nonesuch spun at the centre of the night, the still point of a whirlpool. In those moments when she lost sight of him she just watched the crowd rotate and waited for a glimpse of its centre. She knew that when the dawn wiped the shadowy glamour from the scene she would circle and drain and find herself in his bunk, in his arms, with her nose in his curls, curls like miniature whirlpools themselves, and the two of them would be the centre of the city, and everything would slow and revolve around them.

The night would have been perfect for one of those cautionary tales about the licentiousness of London life that she and the other fledglings had heard, rapt with fear (and secret delight) from the older Aviscultans. It was an evening of drunkenness to the point of oblivion, lewd songs that woke lawful citizens long past curfew, and a celebration of excess. Spilt wine, discarded food. Shilling bets and tuppence tobacco. But actually experiencing it, deep in the swirl of the night, Shay found it gloriously innocent, just the froth and chatter of children alive, for the first time, to their voices and the chance of using them. Until, with even the hardiest revellers beginning to slump, Nonesuch dragged the four players and an eddy of followers back along the Thames to 'the last, the final, I promise ... the ultimate drink of the night.'

On board Blank's ship the warm rot of vegetation and blazing braziers gave it a tropical air, even as the boys' breath turned to ice-smoke in front of them. Lads rolled a greening barrel up from belowdecks and Shay, though already more thick-headedly drunk than she'd ever been, queued up laughing with the others for her chance to lie on her back and take a huge spluttering gulp from the gushing spigot. And as a corona of dawn bloomed on the horizon, like the first stirrings of a hangover, a mist began to roll in from the river. It came as a slow, glutinous ocean, as smoothly *right* for the moment as if Nonesuch had stage-managed it. (Could he have done? Shay imagined him conjuring it somehow with a casual stage direction: *Enter, stage left: the fog*). Without needing to be told, boys started climbing the rigging. Up, up they went, Shay following, climbing above the gathering whiteness, until the rigging was strung with youths. They were suspended there in their joy and drunkenness, swinging from one hand with a jug in the other, heads pointed at the heavens as the mist thickened and rose and roiled – ankle-deep, thigh-deep – so up they went again, until they hung like stars themselves, looking out and down over a landscape of cloud, with London softly blotted and only the tallest of landmarks peeking, toylike, from between the banks of fog. Sound came with intense clarity and seemingly from all around, and it took Shay a moment to realise that the voice in her head was coming from an Italian boy hanging just inches from her.

He said, 'Did you hear? We are birds.'

He smelled of hair oil and sweat, and the wonder poked through in his voice just as the spire of St Paul's poked up through the fog. 'Did you hear, did you hear?'

His hand was around her wrist, but his eyes were untethered. He leaned out, out over the abyss, and spoke loudly enough for every boy to hear.

'We are *birds*,' he said. 'And our feet will nevermore touch the sullen earth.'

18

'OF COURSE, THE RIVER is the best cure for a hangover.' Alouette didn't bother to hide her laughter.

Shay had hoped she'd hidden how sick she felt; Alouette appeared entirely unaffected by the previous evening's drinking. They sat in the back of a tilt-boat with their knees touching, astride a low wooden bench that had been rubbed to a sheen by thousands of behinds. The Thames frothed around them, the brown of weak tea, scarred by a hundred over-lapping wakes. It was as loud as the streets here. Barks of laughter and gull cries, church bells and the ubiquitous thunder of the waterwheels. A wherry passed so close that a youth in a blue cap could lean over and drop his apple core laughingly into Alouette's lap. She examined it for a second and then lobbed it back at him.

'Are you feeling all right? We could have gone to see Dee another day, but I thought the river air might sober you up a bit.'

Shay nodded carefully. 'I'm fine. Well, I will be fine.' The air did make her feel a little less queasy. 'Why doesn't Dee come to the theatre?'

Alouette laughed. 'Because he is on call for the Queen night and day. And, like all of them in her inner circle, he simply *has* to be ready to go at any time. He frets that the second he steps out of Mortlake she'll need an angelic reading to decide something vital, like what to have for dinner. And if he's not there, there are plenty that would replace him.'

Shay nodded, she didn't mind. A boat trip, Alouette to herself and an actual magician: all were wonders. She'd heard John Dee's name spoken at the theatre, always with a quiet awe. Much of their stage-craft came from his Mortlake laboratory. Intricate packages arrived by Hackney carriage: handmade wooden boxes that sat on individual cushions like princesses, stuffed with straw to protect the machinery and explosives inside. Dragons made with curved strips of willow and coloured paper so thin that you could see through to the other side, coarse black gloves with fingertips that spouted fire at the tug of a string. And there were rumours of far more elaborate effects that were reserved for the Queen's private performances. Nonesuch claimed to have seen a full sea battle erupt on the moat at Flemings Hall. Cannons fired, sails burned and, he swore on his family's life, you could hear the cries of the sailors on board, all the more terrible for their childish pitch.

'Did you go to any of the masques? For the Queen?'

Alouette nodded. 'A couple, but Evans and Dee keep those nights pretty close to their chests. They spend weeks on the script and effects, all huddled away in his house. Nothing is left to chance. You know how angry Evans was when Nonesuch altered the Cleopatra speech? That is *nothing* compared to what happens at a royal masque. Dee believes there are magical combinations of words, like spells, which he hides in the texts, and even Nonesuch has to learn it word for word. It's the only time I've seen him study.'

'And what kind of masques does the Queen like?'

Alouette considered the question. 'Same as the rest of them, really. Cruelty and happy endings. Things that only go together in fiction.'

Traffic thinned as they headed north and the river bifurcated into rich and poor lanes. The fishing boats were little more than rafts while the boats from Westminster and Lambeth were like floating houses. She saw palisades and cabins, trumpeters and squires; on one a full garden, replete with pear trees swollen with fruit, swayed in the breeze. It took Shay a while to realise what it reminded her of, but once the idea was born it itched at her: it was theatre. In east London and the City you got what you saw. Faces, landscapes, doorways: all were open. But west London was scenery. They passed a house on the north bank in towering red brick, illustrated with ornate curls of flowers and birds, prettier than any painting. Fruit trees were trimmed to perfect spheres, hedges became lions and bears as you came closer. The life going on behind that scenery was unimaginable. Shay would never walk the corridors concealed there, never eat the nectarines and passion fruits from the orchard. She would never see the musicians who were playing the harpsichord tune that spiralled from an open window. She trailed her hand in the water, relishing the cold and the pressure, and imagined herself as someone else.

Alouette waited until the river was quieter and then asked, 'Did you hear what happened last night, after our performance?'

Shay said, 'Not a thing.'

'There was some violence. Some looting. That audience was all riled up. Apparently they smashed up Gilmour's shop. *And* a couple of its neighbours.'

'For real?' The idea worried and excited Shay in equal measure.

'For real,' she said. 'You could hear it streets away. Lads with hammers chanting, "We are birds." Nonesuch is telling everyone you prophesised it.'

The jetty was dark and slick with algae. Dead leaves had gathered in the downstream corners and Shay smelt the thick clot of decay. Ancient elms with knuckled branches sunk the house in shadows and even at midday candles burned in every window. The boatman wanted a whole shilling to wait and, after some unsuccessful negotiations, Alouette paid it. 'Every fucker out in Mortlake has their own boat. If we don't keep the pilot here, then we'll have to swim back.'

The garden looked abandoned and flowers rotted where they grew. Snails ran riot and the path was slippery with silvery trails. Water dripped from every overhang: eaves, sills, cornices. They stood in the porch looking back at the river through a curtain of droplets, and Alouette shivered to herself.

Inside was better though. A bell-pull summoned a bewigged servant who led them through a suite of comfortable rooms with fires burning in every grate. All were unoccupied but they had an air of anticipation, as if the owner was expected back at any moment. The servant led them deep into the house and then down a long passageway lined with books. At the end double doors opened out into a vast, stone-floored room, suffused with a dim green light. The walls and ceiling were glass, Shay realised, but so mottled with algae that they looked like some miraculous stone lit from within. The light was thick and glutinous, and the air was as warm as a midden in midsummer. Dee stood with his back to them, hunched over something. Alouette went to speak but he simply raised a warning hand and went back to what he was doing. Alouette rolled her eyes.

Shay looked around, trying to capture the scene to tell Nonesuch later. On the left hand side of the room the algae had been rubbed away, leaving a smeared circle of light in the centre of each pane. The sickly light bathed a wooden rack festooned with hanging things. At first Shay thought they were spools of cotton but when she stepped closer she saw row upon row of cocoons. The top row were furred in white and on each subsequent tier the pupae were darker and harder; the bottom row was as gappy as a drunkard's teeth. Some had hatched, shards of cases hanging limply from the rack; some looked ready: brittle and swollen. As Alouette waited beside her, tapping her toe with frustration, Shay saw the rightmost one shiver. She knelt down and the pupa twitched and spilt along its joins. Moist, feathery blackness poked through, questing for the light. Shay couldn't watch, it was too intimate. She turned back to face the room. The corner in which she stood was as wild as a jungle and plants leapt from pots on every surface. Thick fingers of green and white split the peat. There were herbs that she recognised and many more that she didn't. A single orchid, smaller than her thumb, grew lonely in an expanse of earth.

'Watch,' whispered Alouette as she poked the tip of her pencil in between two bizarre leaves bordered by fronds like eyelashes. The leaves snapped together and the fronds interlaced as if in prayer. Alouette's grin was infectious. She began to silently point things out. A huge butterfly the colour of a sunflower slowly clapped its wings, exposing a pair of fake eyes. Then Dee gave a grunt and turned to them.

'Alouette, always a pleasure.' He was thin and crop-haired which had the effect of making him look like an animated skull. You could see the contours of his bones beneath his skin. The hollows under the cheekbones and at the temples were sunken and shadowed, and his veins were plain in his forehead and neck; he looked almost flayed. His eyes darted and narrowed and hunted and caught.

'If this ...' Dee rolled a pupa in his palm, 'can become that,' he gestured to the butterfly trembling on the glass, 'then how much easier should it be to turn lead into gold?' Lines crowded his face: around the eyes, deep into the brow, channels of disappointment around the mouth, and Shay knew the words weren't really intended for them.

'Nature must be persuaded to give up her secrets. She must be *seduced*.' On the final word he turned to Shay. 'And what is this?'

He stepped forward and directed Shay into a patch of light. His hands were slender but his grip was as sure as a hawk's. Those mobile eyes catalogued every inch of her. He reached both hands into her hair and parted it at the centre. He peered at the thin line of exposed skull.

'Why, an Aviscultan.' He sounded delighted. 'The birds are gods and—'

'The gods are birds,' Shay replied automatically.

'Wonderful. I will have questions for you later. But first, Alouette. How are the little ships working?'

'Excellent. We had two not go off at all, and one burst into flames in its box, but the rest have worked just as planned. That scene is the talk of the coffeehouses. Lord Henrick claims that he saw tiny homunculi with torches on board so now *everyone* wants tickets.'

Dee pouted. 'Idiots. Give them a miracle and they turn it into an impossibility.' With that he tired of theatre talk and turned back to Shay. Men had looked at her as intently as him before, yes, but with other ends in mind. She felt pinned and mounted.

'Sit, boy, sit.' He gestured to a long table and sat opposite her. He looked her over again. Fingers like skeletal spiders, shaping the air.

'An Aviscultan. And a young one too. You are skilled in divination via flocks of birds, yes?' The hands mirrored each other, weaving unconsciously. Shay nodded.

'And through entrails and offerings too?'

'Never.' His attention smothered her and she felt herself rolling towards the heft of it. 'We cause no harm to birds. Ever.'

Two bony fingers pointed in unison, nail-tips crescented with who-knows-what magical earths. 'But you do commune with them? You've learnt the secrets of birdsong?'

She shook her head. These were the same breathless rumours that Shay had heard all her life. Flappers could talk to eagles and bend them to their bidding. Flappers could persuade magpies to share their loot. A hungry look stole into Dee's eyes. He placed his thumbs together and spread his fingers into wings. His eyes shone as he made the wings beat and reach for the ceiling. Even with his eyes obscured the whole tilt of his body asked the question.

She sighed. 'No, of course not. Even children know that's not true.'

Dee had something to show her. He guided them towards a darker corner of the room. Shay had never seen a space so cluttered before; how would it feel to own so many things? As the light dimmed Alouette took her by the elbow and moved her to the right. She whispered, 'Listen. Just follow me and don't look to your left.'

'Don't look at what?'

Alouette's voice was urgent. 'Just don't. Please.'

It was impossible, of course. The moment that she was safely past, she felt she could reward herself with a quick backwards glance. A mistake. The wall was decorated with a display of Chinese fans, pinned at each corner. Then she looked more closely and realised the sprays of oily green and blue were no fans. Peacocks. Nailed, quite dead, to the wall, with their bellies plucked and slit in the shape of an X. Tubular, worm-white workings were exposed to the air. Shay stopped and threw up in her mouth, and then gulped it back down. Alouette hurried her along, but she was rigid with disgust. Dee looked over his shoulder and took in her gaze.

'Pliny the Elder says that in the Indies the peacock eats lead and shits gold. I've been trying to find the methods they employ.'

Shay was a statue. The peacocks' innards were translucent tubes dotted with lumpen swellings.

'How is the experiment progressing?' Alouette's voice was a finger trap, gentle and binding.

'Inconclusively,' said Dee, turning back down the room.

Alouette's fingers dug into Shay's elbow as they walked between two tables lined with glass jars. Shay fought the urge to sweep them all off just for the sound it would make. Her mouth tasted of vomit and the room smelled of shit. Dee stood by a door with a hole cut in it at waist height, which was covered from the inside with a black cloth. He knelt with a creak like old bellows and poked his head through.

Alouette aimed a pantomime kick at his backside and mouthed 'Sorry,' at Shay. Amid the nausea Shay prickled with pride. Her friend had recognised her pain; better still, she had gone through it with her. She took Alouette's hand and squeezed.

Dee pulled his head out with his few remaining strands of hair smeared slantwise across his face like seaweed. 'They're doing well. See.'

Alouette parted the cloth onto a square of black. She pushed Shay to her knees. 'Look through here. It's worth it, I promise.' Shay poked her head into the abyss. Inside was the black of a moonless midnight but then, like stars emerging, pinpricks of light started to appear. She blinked them away. They remained; some grew and some moved. She focused on where the floor should be and made out soft bulbous shapes, of sizes she couldn't calculate without reference points, lit from within by a hazy light. Pale, pale blue, a colour that she didn't have a name for. The shapes stretched away like a stunted forest.

'What am I looking at?' she asked.

'Be patient,' said Dee.

She willed that unclenching of the pupils that she adored watching in Devana – sword-point to musket-mouth in a breath – and the air above the forest burst with random squiggles of light, the same almost-blue as the forest. It was like London and its birds rewritten in ghost-light. She tried to judge the scale. It could be five feet or five miles and the nausea of the other room returned.

'You live out on the marshes?' This was Dee again, his voice sharp-elbowed.

'Yes, me and my father.'

'I was there once for the ceremony with the starlings. The susurration.'

'The Murmuration.'

'Yes. Exactly. Extraordinary. Personally, I believe the patterns they make are part of an angelic language long forgotten by men. I've written liberally on the subject. But the seer there was skilled. Very skilled indeed.'

Shay tried to stand and her head hit the frame.

'Don't move yet,' said Alouette. 'Just a minute more.'

The landscape in front of her began to glow. It was a room, bigger still than the laboratory, that was blanketed in mushrooms which shone with a sickly, pale light. A ghost forest. And the air, she now saw, was a shifting starscape of lights moving like birds.

'The seer,' Shay wrung her voice of any excitement, 'was she called Ava?'

'I believe so. Striking woman. Tall, calm. She knew other realms, you could see that in her. She read those birds as surely as you or I might read a book.'

Her comb, the feel of her hand and Devana's hood: that was all Shay had of her mother. She was desperate for other memories.

A hand tugged her belt and she was back, blinking, in the room.

'What did you see?' asked Dee, as if it weren't his experiment she'd been examining, as if his own world was a mystery.

'A dead city. And ghost birds.' Shay fancied she could still smell the peacock's insides.

Dee nodded, like she'd revealed something, and Alouette said 'The forest is made up of foxfire.'

Shay shook her head.

'They're mushrooms that grow on dead logs and glow. Originally *faux*-fire, probably. Those were honey mushrooms, from Moldavia. And the birds are Polish fireflies. The miners there take them underground in jars. You can harvest their light.' She looked pointedly at Dee and he turned his mouth down.

'One can harvest their light at great cost in both time and manpower.' He turned to Shay. 'That entire city yielded, in the past month, this little fruit.' He took a bottle from the workbench, stoppered and black.

'It may get easier soon though. I hear tell of the same thing in the forests near Carlisle.'

Shay swallowed her impatience and anger. 'That was my mother, Ava, who you saw. She was the scryer.'

Dee's attention redoubled. 'And do you have her gifts? Wait. Are you the child from last night?'

Shay was confused. 'Last night?'

'The Ghost Theatre.'

Alouette butted in. 'You know about that already? This one hasn't even slept off the hangover yet.'

Again, his hands went to Shay's face. 'Of course I know of it. If a child speaks in tongues and causes a riot then people tell me. It's within my *sphere of interest*. I've had four messages about it already today.' He moved Shay's head from side to side and then took a quill and paper from a side table. 'Tell me what you said at the end of the performance. The prophecy, please.'

'He can't remember.' Alouette sounded like she was enjoying herself.

'The drink? Or maybe you were in an invocatory trance. Did anyone in the audience transcribe it?'

Shay said, 'I'm sorry. It happened so quickly. I was supposed to sing but at the moment I opened my mouth I felt myself rising up—'

'Yes, yes, yes. A divine viewpoint. The seventh sphere perhaps.' Dee's quill-tip raced across the page. 'Did you find yourself in the presence of others? Winged beings?'

She made herself look at the peacocks. She would give him no more. 'I don't remember anything after opening my mouth. The next thing I knew, it was later and the show was over.'

Dee stood and circled the room. 'Idiots. Idiots everywhere. Can't see what's in front of their faces.' He circled back and grabbed Shay by the wrist. 'When is your next performance?'

'I don't know. We were waiting to see the reaction to the first show. Soon, I'd warrant.'

Dee rummaged in his purse and handed Alouette a coin. 'A guinea to the person who can transcribe whatever he says next time he's in that state. And wait.' He went back to his paper and wrote out seven short phrases in Latin. Shay had no idea what they meant.

'Give these to your butterfly friends, Lord Nonesuch and little Trussell. Tell them there's no pay for the masque unless I hear them spoken.'

Shay wanted to ask more about her mother but Dee turned his back on them. Alouette mimed a throat-slitting gesture at Shay – *we're done* – and they left the way they'd arrived.

Despite the shilling, the boatman hadn't waited.

19

AUTUMN TURNED TO WINTER and the leaves that clogged the riverbanks burned and burnished and then turned black. Cartwheel tracks froze and melted and froze over again until the streets were riven with ruts. Crows and jackdaws grew squabblesome over the scant booty, and the rooftops were treacherous but oh-so-pretty. Shay twisted her messenger routes so that they always took in the Blackfriars Theatre, just to feel its roof under her feet. Her footsteps were messages to whoever might be awake below.

Tap, tap, tap, I miss you, said her feet on the roofboards. *Tap, tap, tap; do you miss me too?*

On the evenings that she wasn't with Devana, Shay stayed at the theatre, and every night she heard the boys crying for their mothers. Weeping that was passed along like beacons on hillsides, like wolfpack howlings. Always for the mothers, Shay noticed, never for their fathers. Not during night, the heart's domain.

Nights were when Shay took to the river too. She left gifts for Lonan on the Birdland jetty like so much bird seed. Did they get to him? However hard she tried to keep her home solid in her mind, it was turning into a place of mists and moonlight. London breathed out and blew it away.

And what happened to Nonesuch and her? They became a double act, playing scene after scene in their private places. Shay lived for those hours in abandoned houses where they hid to map each other out. Her fingers tracing the contours of a new land: his cities and his outlying islands, his main roads and uncharted territory. He was Magellan, circumnavigating her from toenail to hair-tip and back again. By night she was his swan – beneath him, pale and extravagant – and by day his magpie, stealing pretty things for him. And above and beyond and around them something was growing: the Ghost Theatre. The five of them played shows on the backs of carts and in burnt-out chapels. Shay sang in cellars and attics and never remembered a word that she said. And then, as winter bit, Nonesuch led a hundred followers, singing, up through Cripplegate to the wilderness of Tenter Ground, where twenty open coffins were lined up, and inside, twenty white faces stared blindly at the clouds.

Alouette was the first to sit up and talk:

It was my mistress who forgot the cherries so muggins here has to brave St Giles, still in her uniform, which is something I swore I'd never do again, but it was either that or a beating and the master enjoys those a little too much, and halfway across Whitecross Street comes a carriage where no carriage should be and I hardly have time to shout before the front wheel hits my shoulder and I'm on the ground and I look down at my broken arm, and it was my mistress who forgot the cherries so ...

Further along a boy's voice started up:

... they said the Irish would be glad to see us and like fools we believed them and we even waved at the soldiers on the beach, and it was the first time I ever saw muskets, lined up like pins in a pincushion, and us boys fell in our hundreds, most dead before we hit the water, but I was only wounded so under I went and the sea was red with blood and when I broke the surface for air they fired again, over and over, until I couldn't breathe and I almost welcomed the shot that went through my eye and they said the Irish would be glad to see us ...

Different voices with stories of different lengths that piled up like stones until they were the sound of an endless landslide. Shay's character joined in last of all, repeating her lines in a rush of breath with Blank's trumpet a savage bird overhead.

... they said come with me your mistress is sick and deep down I knew it wasn't true but what can you do when they are four and you are one and they are rich and you are poor and even as I was dying, right there in the alley, I saw my new kerchief stomped into the dirt and I thought that's a shame that's a shame, and they said come with me ...

She rushed at it like a child's prayer until some sandpaper song rose up through her, unbidden, dragging her heart along with it, and she looked down on herself, one coffin among many, her mouth moving but no sound, and the crowd surging like a waterfall and then ...

... who knows how much later, she woke in the back of a cart, sodden with sweat and stung with cuts, asking, 'What did I do? What did I say? Who was I this time?'

20

A SUNDAY AFTERNOON AND the Blackfriars troupe were supposed to be rehearsing but an unexpected spell of sunshine left them beached and languorous on the theatre roof. There was something post-coital in the mood. Trussell chewed on a chicken leg while Alouette lay with her head on Blank's lap as he mended a seam on her jacket. They all had their ailments from a Ghost Theatre show the night before. Shay was bruised at her knees and elbows; linen piles had broken her fall as planned but still it was a two-storey fall for maximum spectacle. Nonesuch was a mess. His blackened hair had run, leaving purple stains at his hairline, and his clothes were ragged. It didn't stop him from pacing the perimeter of the roof, talking.

'I really thought they might kill me. When you jumped? They *bayed*. Like animals. All of them lost in it. Two prentices had me by the ankles and shoulders, ready to toss me off the building.'

Shay shook her head.

'I hated to do it, but I was shouting, "It's a play, it's just a play." I had to swear that you weren't dead before they would let me down.'

He did another circuit, and then his brow furrowed as the skylight swung open. It crashed back onto the roof and an unseen voice said, 'Oh, for God's sake.' A face popped out, wet with sweat and puce with fury. 'What the fuck are you lot doing up here? I don't climb stairs for anyone. Certainly not for you insects.'

Evans hauled himself up through the gap and then caught his breath slumped against the skylight. As he mopped his brow with a grubby kerchief, Shay backed behind the chimney; she wasn't sure why. He was pink and plump and those heavy rings cut into his podgy fingers.

'Well, isn't this the motliest of crews?' He hooked a finger at Nonesuch and Trussell. 'You two are supposed to be rehearsing and Christ knows you need it.' He looked at Alouette. 'And I don't know where *you're* supposed to be but I'm certain it's not on my fucking roof stuffing your fat Flanders face.' He mopped his brow again. 'And ... who do we have here, playing the world's worst game of hide-and-seek? Is it? It is. Little Miss Boy-in-the-streets, Girl-in-the-sheets. Out of your nest you come, I need to speak to you too.'

Nonesuch stepped forward. 'Evans, this is Shay.'

Evans waved him away. 'I know who she is, Dee told me all about her. I believe I'm even paying her.' He took Shay by the wrist and moved her to the centre of the roof. His eyes read every inch of her face. 'Is that right?'

Shay nodded, suddenly shy.

He jiggled the coins in his pocket. 'Two pennies a day for sitting there watching your lover tit about. I'm not getting much for my invest-ment, am I? Maybe it's time that you did some actual work.'

He stretched his arms wide to incorporate the four of them. 'Right, to business. I am having an event at my new house on Saturday. The great and the good will be there so I need the small and the shit to entertain them. Trussell and Nonesuch, you'll be serving drinks and dressing up.'

Nonesuch asked, 'Is this a proper masque? Or will we be nothing but glorified serving boys?'

Evans grinned. 'You won't even be glorified. No, it won't be a masque because I want people to circulate. So we'll dress you up in a toga and make sure your arse is hanging out. You too, Trussell, so no more fucking chicken for you this week.' He looked down at the carcass and balefully pulled a leg off. 'Now you, Flanders. Get back to Dee's and get those fucking fireflies we paid so much for. Stock up on fireworks too, you know what the Queen likes.'

'The Queen will be there?' Nonesuch couldn't help himself.

'Probably. Possibly.' He stood in front of Shay. 'And you. Flapper-girl. You're doing your act.'

They all turned towards Shay. Alouette said, 'She's a prompter. It's not much in the way of entertainment.'

Evans stretched. The rooftop wasn't made for a frame like his. 'I'm talking about her *act*. The singing. The soothsaying. From your little plays?' His voice was thick with sarcasm and Nonesuch looked as nonplussed as Shay had ever seen him.

'Oh ho. Did you think I didn't know? Nonesuch, you couldn't buy a pie without someone telling me what the filling was. You couldn't have a wank without me knowing who you were thinking about. Dee tells me that this little flapper has been telling fortunes for a bunch of penny groundlings and now she's going to do it for the quality.'

Even thinking about it sent a shiver through Shay. How could she explain? 'I can't ... it doesn't simply happen.' The words were out of her mouth before she knew it.

Evans gave her a dead look and his sarcasm reappeared. 'Oh, I'm sorry, I didn't realise. Well, if you can't then you can't. That's fine, little one. All we can do is try our best and if it doesn't work out then I'm sure people will understand.' He took a bite of the chicken. 'And then I'll personally throw you off this roof.'

It was as if she'd been slapped. Was it possible to have stage fright days before the event? Nonesuch stepped forward with his palms up. 'The thing is, Evans, it's as if she goes into a trance. She doesn't know what she's going to say or sing before she does it. It can be a bit ...' he reached for the word '... apocalyptic. The moon on fire. Armies of eagles. That kind of thing. It might not be appropriate for the Queen.'

Evans pinched his nose. 'Christ. Well, now I know how to answer my friends when they ask, "Do the actors just make it up as they go along?"' He looked impossibly weary. 'Right. So, Nonesuch and Trussell, be at mine for six bells on Friday. Flanders, head out to Mortlake and bring our flying friends back here for tomorrow afternoon. And you, Little Miss Neither-one-thing-nor-the-other, are fired. Get your things and fuck off back to the marshes.'

'You *can't*.' Nonesuch and Trussell said it in unison.

'Can. Will. Did. She gets tuppence a day so that you two don't have to bother learning your lines? If she has no other skills then she's over-paid already.' The rooftop was silent bar an incongruous wood pigeon. Shay could feel a heat rising in her, like the moment before a song wiped her out.

'The cards,' said Trussell.

Evans tilted his head. 'What?'

'I made you special cards, Shay. They were to be for your birthday but they're pretty much finished.'

'Cards?' Evans asked.

'Cards for ...' Trussell searched for the word that might unlock the situation '... predestination.'

Evans made a ho-hum gesture. 'Card-reading? It's all a bit village fair. I suppose it might work with a costume and everything, let me see these cards.'

The box was wood, studded with red stones. Stage gems – there was a drawer of them in the prop cupboard. Shay slid the lid off and removed the pack. They were thick, red-backed cards with a picture on each one: suits of ravens, sparrows, hawks and magpies. They were beautiful. One bird to a card, sketched in ink and then overpainted. The portraits burst from the page; each bird captured in movement. The hawk was frozen as it grasped prey, great wings balanced on the point of the talons. A raven perched and pecked at a bone, the wren peeked from its nest. She didn't have time to check all the Major Arcana, but she could guess most of the cards from their form. The two swans with their necks entwined must be the Lovers, a flamingo with its legs crossed into the shape of a number four resembled the Hanged Man. She took a breath and placed three cards in a line between her and Evans.

'You can tell fortunes with these?' He looked dubious, and Shay risked a glance of gratitude at Trussell; the pictures were the birds of her childhood, of Birdland, and she had no idea how he'd known her so well.

She turned the first over. The Eight of Sparrows. It showed birds fleeing and a man turning away: disappointment. 'Yes.' Her heart beat high in her chest. 'Yes, I can.'

'IS IT *ALL* GLASS?' Shay kept stumbling because she couldn't keep her eyes from the building that shone ahead of them. The streets were rutted hard with ice; a ploughed field would have been gentler underfoot. Alouette and Trussell had stopped, open-mouthed; only Nonesuch seemed unsurprised by the apparition.

'Every wall is etched Venetian glass,' he said. 'Over thirty panes apparently. Each one costs more than a Shoreditch house. And the whole thing is built in the shape of a letter E, just in case Her Majesty pops by. There is a wooden ground floor so that Evans can sleep and eat in peace. And, of course, the servants' quarters are tucked away out of sight. But the rest is just as you see it.'

It floated on the night air, drawing them closer. And they weren't the only ones. The street was thronged with gawkers, faces all tilted the same way and lit by the same strange light. Already chestnut sellers and whores, always alive to a crowd, plied their trade.

'Who would live that way?' It didn't square with Shay's view of Evans. He was vain, sure, but this looked unbearable.

'No one. It's not really for living. It's a queen trap. The country lords have their fireworks and banquets, Evans has this. Even if she only visits for an hour, it'll do wonders for his status.'

They came closer. There was movement behind the glass windows; each one was an individual room. Torches blazed inside and the etchings and mouldings that patterned the glass turned the firelight into something geometric. They trapped the light in etched stars and coats of arms, in mirror patterns and rainbow bursts. Inside the rooms stood figures who, even at this distance, were clearly gentlemen: drinking, talking, dancing and circulating, each huge window a new scene. A chubby man kissed the hand of a woman so tall that even when curtseying she looked down on him. Two young bloods played a game, getting servants to toss fruit towards them. The took it in turns to slice the missiles in two before they found their target. As Shay watched, one caught a peach on the tip of his dagger and bit into it with relish. Lit from within and caged in reflections, they looked like living paintings.

Nonesuch took them down a side street and by the time the building glowed back into view the personnel had changed. A man in black poured wine into the mouth of a kneeling girl, pulling the spout further and further from her. When the liquid finally spilled from her mouth a cheer went up, audible even in the street, and money changed hands. It was too much to take in, like watching ten plays at once.

They reached the house just as a gentleman arrived on horseback with his men in a V behind him. He leapt to the ground and pages wordlessly took the reins.

'He won't let anyone wait at the door. No horses, no carriages. It *untidies* the place.' Nonesuch's voice was half scorn, half admiration. 'There are stables and parking around the back.' They stood at the building's base, soaked in rainbow light, as carriages unloaded nobleman upon nobleman and the air rang with raucous greetings. A set of double doors wide enough to drive a carriage through stood open onto a set of polished stairs. Two of Evans' men stood at the entrance.

'You lot.' One of the men pointed at them. 'Back entrance, with the staff. And you're late.'

Nonesuch mock bowed, making sure his face was caught in the blaze of lights. 'Sorry to lower the tone. *Capisco.*' He added, under his breath, 'Next time I'm coming through the front door.'

They entered into the barely contained panic of a kitchen at breaking point. Boys with trays of food, girls pinning hems, steam, smoke and sweat. A damp-haired cook shouted, 'Shoes and hose off. Oh, for fuck's sake.' The latter was aimed at Shay and her filthy, bare feet: ash-soled and streaked with dried mud, every little crease filled in with black. The cook pushed a grimy bowl of water in Shay's direction. 'Try and get the worst of it off.'

'Who are you?' The cook was spattered in flour and sugar. 'Don't tell me, the entertainment?' She didn't wait for an answer. 'Sit there, keep quiet and do not touch a thing.'

They squatted against the rear wall and watched the hysteria unfurl. A team of cooks worked on sugar sculptures. There were palaces, castles and even a simulacrum of Evans' glass house, all of which were whipped away by serving boys even as the finishing touches were applied. Someone called out, 'Get them upstairs before they melt. Faster.'

Two turnspit-dogs ran inside wooden wheels suspended from the ceiling. Occasionally, one or the other barked, whether in pain or exhilaration Shay couldn't tell. Where did they think they were going? What did they think they were doing? She pushed closer to Nonesuch to avoid a string of drool that fell from the closest dog's maw. In the corner two seamstresses worked on a serving girl's outfit, pinning the hem provocatively high. Shay tried to give the girl a rueful grin, but she turned away, damp eyed.

Trussell dug an elbow in her side. 'Look at that.' Three girls were launching delicate sugar-work galleons onto the lake-surface of a brimming punchbowl. The little boats shivered and righted, ghostly white against the deep plum of the punch. Once they'd settled down, the serving men took the handles of the vast silver bowl and hoisted it onto their shoulders.

Shay didn't see Evans enter. One minute he wasn't there and the next he was leaning against the doorjamb, scanning the throng, reaching without looking to pluck a sweetmeat from a passing tray. His shirt was a liquid canary silk, bright as sunflower petals, but there was already a stain on the lapel, and it strained at the waist. His cream hose bunched at the knee. He ate the sweetmeat without chewing and reached out to Nonesuch, turning his face towards the light. Dirty nails and rings on every finger; Shay smelt duck fat and lilacs. He stood aside to let the men with the punch bowl struggle past and then clapped his fat hands together. 'Players, get over here. I have costumes.'

Behind Evans stood a man in rough linens with a bucket of golden liquid. Nonesuch eyed it suspiciously. 'Gold paint? We're doing a *tableau*? Christ, Evans, what is this, 1590? I thought I could do my Faust. Or one of the Henrys, that's always popular with the monarchy.'

Evans' voice was loud enough for the whole kitchen to hear. 'Well, you thought wrong. Your tendency to attempt to improve upon the agreed script means you are not to have a speaking part around our sovereign. In fact ...' He watched Nonesuch's mutinous face and then picked an apple up from the table. He polished it on his hose and then tossed it to the lounging man. 'Daltrey, paint this up too and then stick it in his mouth. He can be ... who was the girl with the golden apple?'

Daltrey looked blank.

'Eris,' said Alouette, hiding a smile.

'Eris, right. Nonesuch, you're Eris. That means Trussell can be Paris. If Paris was a short-arse with rabbit teeth. And Frenchie here with her classical knowledge gets to be Aphrodite for a night.'

Alouette's mouth hung open. 'I'm not an actress. I'm here to do the pyrotechnics. I have it all set up.'

'And a lovely job you did too. My man says he's rarely seen finer.' He gave her a sharp look which she immediately returned. 'But this is when the adults take over. Time for the little ones to say their prayers and shut up for a bit.'

Alouette didn't change her stance.

'Christ. Try to understand. You three are a tiny part of tonight. I do not want you talking or acting or setting off firecrackers in front of the bloody Queen. You are strictly,' he threw his arms wide, 'decorative. I want you naked, painted gold and holding a plate of fucking—' He looked around the room. 'What are we serving for starters, Cook?'

She was bent double over an oven. 'Coxcomb stuffed with turmeric leaves and sweetmeats.' Evans sighed, 'I want you holding a plate of fucking coxcombs. Now can you manage that, or do I have to recruit more street children who might show an inch of gratitude?'

When the pair finally quietened, Evans took out a package. 'And where's our flapper? Hiding behind Nonesuch as ever. Out you come.'

Shay stepped forward and he handed her a package in tissue paper. Something slight and slippery. 'Get changed, let's see what we're working with.'

'Here?' She looked around at the cooks and the serving boys and the maids and the dogs.

'No, in my private changing room. Of course here, you little wretch. No one's going to be watching. Do you imagine there's anyone here who actually wants to see you naked?'

They changed in silence. Trussell and Nonesuch wore linen pouches tied with string, Alouette the same but with a band of cloth for her chest. She smoothed it down self-consciously to cover as much as possible. Somehow, the idea that others were watching Nonesuch's naked body, a thing she'd come to think of as her own personal treasure, upset Shay more than the prospect of her own embarrassment. Her own costume was different from theirs. It lay on the table under thin paper, midnight blue and roughly patterned. She untied it carefully. Oil-slick iridescence and a fantail of colour; Shay's heart leapt and then plummeted. The skirt was made from magpie feathers. And not the black-and-white ones, but instead those from the tail, the exact colour of the sky's last moment before night. She pushed a wad of nausea down. There must be a hundred feathers. A hundred feathers meant a hundred dead birds. She stripped, quickly, as close to the wall as possible, trying to hide her taped-down breasts. Still, she felt the pressure of eyes upon her.

The dress fitted perfectly. Again her heart jumped and then dived as the beauty of it gave way to the realisation that someone had studied her closely enough to know her shape that well. She hoped it was Blank. Once she had wiggled into the dress she turned back to the room. Nonesuch and Alouette and Trussell were lined up, arms aloft, as Daltrey sloshed gold paint over them.

'Careful, for fuck's sake.' Evans was supervising. 'The paint costs more than you do.'

He caught sight of Shay watching. 'Come on then, let the dogs see the rabbit.'

She walked into the room. There was something unreadable in Alouette's eyes. Nonesuch and Trussell looked away.

'It'll have to do, I suppose. It doesn't do anything for me but hopefully not all my guests have such ... discernment.'

Even Shay heard Nonesuch's snort. Without looking up, Evans said to the painter, 'Apple,' and Nonesuch's smirk disappeared. 'Open wide.'

Shay eyed the bucket of paint cautiously. It had grown a thick, brown skin on top.

Evans followed her eyes. 'Not for you, little flapper. We have other plans for you today. Sit.'

He positioned her on a stool and drew a razor from his pocket. The bustle of the kitchen continued but the room's attention settled on Shay. You could be seen without being watched, that she knew. Evans sat in front of her and sharpened the razor on a strop. His voice was low, meant for her alone. 'So, you're a flapper, yes?'

Shay sought out Nonesuch's eyes but they were saying nothing. 'I'm an Aviscultan, yes. It's ... it's not a crime.'

He sighed. 'I didn't say it was. There are lots of bad things that aren't crimes, though.' He looked up and caught the fear in her eyes. 'For Christ's sake. No one cares that your gods lay eggs. This is London, not the countryside; plenty worship stranger than you. I'm just checking that you have the tattoo.'

The *slap slap slap* of the razor on the strop was the loudest thing in the kitchen now. Shay nodded.

'Hot water and soap, for God's sake.' The last was aimed at the broad back of the cook, who straightened up and brought him a bowl of water from the stove. Evans dissolved the soap, his smile disappearing behind a wall of steam. 'Right, let's see what we have under this stubble then.'

Fat fingers, thick rings. He held her by the chin as he worked, tilting her head with a gentle pressure. What did he see? Shay worked hard at becoming whatever people saw in her. A boy. A messenger. Nothing to worry about. But Evans didn't really see her, she decided. He saw the use of her, like a tool. She met his eyes and looked at him properly for the first time. Lines folded around his eyes and deltas of wrinkles radiated from their edges. Deep ruts ran from eyebrow to hairline, bisecting the furrows of his forehead at an angle. Under his eyes a cross-hatching of soft patterns crumpled his skin. He placed his palm on the back of her head and she felt the scrape of razor against her scalp. He washed the soap off as he went, gentle with a cloth, a sensation so shockingly intimate that she had to cross her legs harder. He knew what he was doing. He left the sides, just as her mother once would have done, as two wings of hair that would have to be thickened and shaped with the soap. Once he was done, he stood back to examine her tattoo, turning her head this way and that. Even in the warmth of the kitchen her scalp was cold.

He sighed again. 'I would have preferred something more warlike really, something *mystical*. An eagle would mean we had a good stage name for you. Or a phoenix-bird.' He brushed off a stray soap bubble. 'Oh well.' He turned her chair around so that she faced the throng and he put on his master-of-ceremonies voice.

'Ladies and gentlemen, I give you ...' he beat a drumroll on the table. 'The fucking *Sparrow*.'

A squadron of serving girls left with platters on their shoulders. Alouette and Nonesuch fumed from behind gold paint. But Evans was still focused on Shay. He scooted closer. 'It's an improvement. Now you look like a Bedlam patient, which adds just a frisson of danger. But it's not enough.' He lowered his voice so only Shay could hear. 'Hunter or prey?' He tilted his head as he looked at her. Shay held his gaze but said nothing. He sighed. 'Silence means prey, little one.'

'Both then.'

He looked genuinely disappointed. 'There is no both. You don't get to be everything in this life.'

'Magpies are both. Kill their own, get killed by their own. Foxes too.'

He looked away, uninterested. 'True, true. But you're not a fucking magpie, whatever your barmy relatives might think. You call yourself a man, and men choose.'

Shay screwed up something inside her. 'Hunter,' she said, with the voice she saved for stage.

'Perhaps. Not yet.' Something in his look shot an arrow in her. 'But you have potential. Say it again.'

She steeled herself. 'Hunter. I'm a hunter.' Then, suddenly, more quietly, 'A sparrowhawk.'

He nodded. 'That's something to work with, at least.' He fumbled in his pocket and said, 'Hand.'

It took her a moment. She reached her hand out to him. Her nails were long with tips blackened with London grime. He took a greasy leather case from his pocket and unrolled it to show a gleam of metal. Knives, picks, files, like a locksmith. Her heart leapt. What might he try to unpick in her? He removed a file and twisted her hand upright in supplication. 'Don't move.'

His face was womanly as he worked, sharpening each of her nails to a point, turning her fingers towards the light. Somewhere nearby a servant sang a lullaby and the domesticity of the atmosphere disconcerted her. He was surprisingly deft. He scraped the dirt from under each tip and made adjustments. Then he unstoppered a little glass bottle and painted her nails a glossy black, the colour and sheen of his carriage.

He blew on them. Bad breath and a tremble in her stomach. 'There. Try them.'

She now had sharp daggers of nail, more claw than talon. She held them up to the light and then, gingerly, dug them into her arm. Evans laughed. 'Some hunter. I give you a weapon and you use it on yourself.'

She reached her hand to his cheek and his eyes flickered for the briefest moment. Black eyes like a bird's but red at the edges, as if he never slept. Shay searched them for a sign – *yes, no, don't, please* – but there was nothing there; night sky, still water. With care she dug and dragged, unblinking, until five beautiful beads of blood blossomed under her claws. A second, an eternity. Gently he took her hand and wiped it on her cheek. Black eyes of well water and dead wood. When he dropped her hand, she went to wipe the blood away from her face but he said, 'No, leave it.'

Daltrey rushed over. 'She's here,' he said in Evans' ear, and the whole room stilled.

'Really? You're certain?'

'The harbingers arrived while you were working. Her carriage is outside.'

'Who is there to greet her? Just Palmer? Oh Christ.' He breathed against the back of his hand, grimaced and took a bite of an apple. 'I'll be there in a jiffy.' He turned back to the room. 'You three, take a tray each, second floor, three empty plinths, you can't miss them.'

He wiped the blood from his cheek. 'And, sparrow girl? There's a perch on the top floor. You'll have to find your own way.'

'A perch?'

'Yes, a fucking perch.' He looked at the four of them. 'Jesus, what I have to work with.' He clapped two short gunshots. '*Go*. And if you mess this up, I'm sending you all on a tour of Scotland.' He pointed at Nonesuch, stupefied with a golden apple in his mouth. 'And you'll be playing Edward II.'

They followed Daltrey up wooden steps, and the noise of the party swelled in front of them. Alouette picked at her costume, trying to cover herself, but instead just flaked gold paint in her wake. Nonesuch was grim-faced. At the top of the steps Daltrey showed them towards the ballroom and then opened a door out into the night for Shay.

'Take the outside steps and then come back inside on the next storey, you'll be in one of the arms of the "E". The back stairs on your right lead up to the maze and then your room is above that. It's getting pretty wild in the ballroom and I wouldn't put a wager on you making it upstairs in one piece. Not in that dress.' He shook his head at something and then lowered his voice. 'I saw you at the icehouse, you and the others. It was great. It was like I was part of something for the first time.' Shay didn't know how to respond. She had still not become accustomed to the idea that she lived, visible and responsible, in other people's minds. Daltrey shook his head again and then headed back down the stairs, leaving her out in the cold on a rough wooden platform. It was somehow obscene to be outside in such a costume. She climbed the stairs quickly. Another floor up and lines of light showed around a low-level wooden door. She pressed her ear against it and heard the party within. She shivered again, though not just through cold. The streets below were quiet and she let out a quick falcon-call. The immediate response from above made her feel less alone. She pushed the door and entered.

It was too much, stepping through that door. Out into a starburst of music and heat and laughter and colour. The room was drenched in light; it leapt from crystal glass, arrowed across the room to flirt with a diamond brooch, returned, prismed, rainbowed and reflected between mirrors until the air was afire. The mezzanine was so spangled with light that it took Shay a while to glimpse the people there. Gentlemen all, gentlemen and ladies dressed far more finely than Shay had ever seen, even at the theatre. These were costumes like architecture: concoctions of wire and padding and ruffles and cinching, with detailed construction plans and dedicated teams of workmen. Ruffs like cartwheels and farthingales like rowing boats. Moments came and went. A wig pushed back level. A hand on an arse. Trays of sugar mice, spent matches. For a moment, the noise and light pinned her to the wall but then she forced herself to move on. She hugged the near wall, skirting drunken couples, and made for a set of internal steps that stood, unlit, in the corner. Waves of sound crashed against the glass walls. She pulled herself up and around the corner until the light and sound died down and she could make her way up to a quieter storey. Glass steps, glass walls. Her feet left ghostly footprints which evaporated in moments.

She was in one of the arms of the E and someone climbed the stairs in the adjacent arm, parallel to her. Only ten feet away but silent. She looked across idly and he seemed to sense that he was being watched. He turned to face her through the glass walls. Gilmour.

Looking back, Shay was shocked at how fast he reacted. He was behind and below her but immediately upon seeing her face he started to bound upwards, three steps at a time. She saw him loom and cursed her slowness. Like Devana, he would be upon his prey almost before it realised it was being stalked.

Up or down? The ballroom promised safety in numbers but she'd still have to make her way to the top of the house at some point. Up then. She flew up the glass stairs, feet squeaking, and burst out into a glass corridor. More steps, a half-stair and then the ground disappeared under her. She stopped and grabbed at the wall. Held herself there for a second. It wasn't an abyss, after all, merely a polished glass floor. There was a framework of pale wood, she now saw, holding it in place. The sound of steps from behind propelled her on towards a crossroads. Three ways to go as the slap of footsteps got louder.

Straight on. The floor and ceiling were glass and she had to ignore her mind telling her that the world was giving way beneath her. A T-junction. The left was mirrored, the right all glass. Left might be towards Gilmour but she'd be hidden by the mirrored walls. She shuffled that way and then stood, silently, between reflections stretching off into infinity.

Slap, slap, slap of footsteps and then a curse. Close but not closing in. She kept still. Three Gilmours crossed the end of the corridor. Were all reflections or was one the real thing? She couldn't tell. Her first instinct was to flee in the opposite direction, but she waited. 'Don't be prey,' she told herself. She pressed her claws against her temples. No, follow his route. He wouldn't go back over old ground and he wouldn't expect her to be behind him. She kept low and made for where she'd seen him. She walked slowly, letting her footprints fade behind her. It made her feel erased.

A figure appeared and she stopped. The figure did too. Just her reflection. She took in her pink scalp, her black talons. At the junction where Gilmour had turned right she carefully stuck her head around. Her half-face, one wing of hair and a raised eyebrow retreated, in ever-smaller versions, all the way to the horizon. The footsteps sounded further away.

What had Daltrey said? Her room was a floor up from here and she hadn't seen any stairs yet. She walked as lightly as possible. Every squeak and footstep echoed and her breath sounded oddly loud. She hadn't seen an upper room from the street so it was probably tucked away at the centre. It was hard to get her bearings among the mirrors but she thought that the middle of this floor would be to her right. She took a passageway with a mirrored floor and every few feet there was a clear-glass panel and shards of the party below refracted and reflected around her. She saw gloves and trays, laughing mouths, the sparkle of torches, jewellery and flowers. A lamb turned slowly on a spit. Once she caught sight of Trussell, crouched and moving, his mouth forming words, but all she could hear was heels on glass and the creak of the building. She took a right into a corridor with no roof. She looked up into the sky and said a prayer to the invisible nightbirds. 'The gods are birds and the birds are gods.' Quiet now. Footsteps, but not Gilmour's. These were heels, two pairs. She moved their way and when she turned a corner she found herself face to face with two women. Sisters, she took them for, in white taffeta and white wigs. Their farthingales were so wide that their dresses brushed the walls and they had to walk in single file. They squealed in unison at the sight of her and she put her fingers to her lips.

'Quiet, please. Have you seen a staircase up? To a room with a perch?'

The elder looked at her with distaste. 'Don't tell us to be quiet, not dressed like that.' She pulled out a handkerchief and put it to her mouth. 'What are you supposed to be, anyway?'

Silence and then the sound of footsteps. Nearer now and closing in. It sounded like he was behind the women. Shay turned tail and ran back the way she'd come. This time she turned right into the long, mirrored corridor. She'd taken five steps when Gilmour stepped out, maybe five yards in front of her, but facing the other way. Shay crouched and stilled her breath. She could see his broad back, his hands on hips. Then he turned. Again, the speed of his reaction shocked her. He was a big man, but he was on his toes and running at her in a moment. She scrabbled around and headed back. Her feet were damp with sweat, and she slipped on the glass. He was close. She heard his footsteps and then a crash that shook the floor beneath her. She risked a look behind. Gilmour was on the floor and a patch of blood smeared across a glass wall that had blocked his path. He shook himself like a dog and droplets of blood spattered the glass.

She went left. Laughter came from over her shoulder. She padded down the passage with hands outstretched in front of her; she didn't want to hit an unseen glass wall the way Gilmour had. Her bearings were off but if she could get back to a roofless section then the moon might give her an idea of east and west. Another passage ran parallel to hers and she saw movement. A door opened in the other corridor and Gilmour stepped out. His face was bloodied and his nose looked broken. He faced her with just glass between them. A head taller than her. His mouth moved but she couldn't hear his words. She stayed still. Both corridors were yards long. If the passages met then she would be caught. She darted right. Gilmour followed. She stopped. She turned back and Gilmour copied her, padding like a cat. He let out a howl and the glass shook. She stopped and so did he. Could she wait him out? She could hear laughing voices but it was hard to judge distances here. He howled again and she had an urge to stick her tongue out at him. Back and forth they paced, like mirror images. 'Don't be prey, don't be prey,' she told herself, but her legs shook with fear. Gilmour looked left and right and then threw himself at the glass. The whole room shook and the wooden frame creaked. He picked himself up and tried again. The support at the top splintered and the glass cracked. Shay didn't wait for a third time; she took off like a rabbit, with her feet skidding on the floor. She'd gone ten yards before she heard the crash and the floor shook. She went left and left again, trying to keep out of view. Left a third time into a room of mirrors where the two sisters stood, pulling faces. They were reflected back in myriad ways: skinny, plump, wavy, corseted into an hourglass. Shay couldn't see another exit.

Footsteps, fast. Close, closer and then stopping. A curse and then away, off to the left.

'It's a dead end,' said the older sister. 'You have to go back. Really, this is so tiresome.' Shay held a finger to her lips again. Bad idea. The lady gave her a look. 'I told you, I will not. Find us the exit and take us there.' The footsteps started up again, coming back this way.

Calculations. She was a rabbit in the field just as the hawk's cold shadow came over it. She had to be quick. In an instant Shay was on tiptoe with her sharpened nails against the woman's jugular. She whispered, 'I've already killed once with these nails today, don't be the second. You're going to walk back the way you came. And if anyone asks if you've seen me then you send them the other way.' The woman's eyes widened, and Shay thought she might faint. 'Do you know the way out?'

The woman shook her head, but her sister said, 'We don't, but we saw the stairs you wanted. Up to the top room.'

Again Shay used her stage voice. 'The jugular isn't the only vein that can kill. You know what they use on pigs? To drain their blood?'

Another tiny headshake.

'The vein in the thigh. It gushes like a fountain.' In one movement she pulled up the woman's voluminous skirt to reveal a domed lattice framework sturdier than a Whitechapel cottage. She slipped under. In a low crouch under the back hoop there was just enough room to squat and hopefully walk. She raked her fingernails against the woman's thigh and a quiver convulsed the flesh. She dug her nails in just enough to pucker the flesh.

'Walk,' she ordered. 'To the stairs.'

She had to slow the woman down twice with a prick of nails. 'Not so fast,' she hissed. Her thighs already burned from the effort of squatting and walking and keeping pressure on the woman's thigh. It was humid under there, humid and close and her bare feet stuck to the floor with sweat. They went right, with her legs on fire, and then walked back the way she'd come. She built a rhythm; two little shuffling steps for every one of the woman's, and it got easier.

Then they stopped. A man's voice. 'Have you seen a serving girl? Shaved head, blue dress?'

The woman's flesh shivered on Shay's nail-point. Too late, she wondered if they were signalling silently to the man. A shake came from above her but no words, and then the sister said, 'We did. Horrid little creature. If you go back that way, then you can see the blood.'

The woman turned to let Gilmour past and Shay almost fell. She grabbed the woman's leg and heard her gasp. The tips of Gilmour's shoes showed under the hem as he squeezed past. 'Thank you, ladies.'

Slowly they stepped on. The sisters didn't talk. Her thighs ached, her knees ached. It took ten minutes to find the staircase. They stopped and then the front of the dress rose like a curtain. The sister's face appeared.

'We're here, I think.'

Shay slid out with the glass floor cold against her skin and rolled onto her back. Two faces looked down. They were in a narrow glass passage with a wooden platform in front of a glass box. A playbill was posted on the wall.

FLAPPER SHAY

CARDS

FORTUNES

FUTURE SONGS

Shay rubbed some life back into her thighs and the sisters looked on curiously. 'Are you the bird girl? From those underground plays?'

Shay nodded, still winded, and the woman brought her face closer. 'Can you tell us our fortunes?'

Shay groaned. 'I can tell you I'll have vultures peck at your livers for eternity if you tell that man where I went.' The women shrieked, half in terror, half in glee, and scuttled away down the corridor.

Heels on glass. Far-off laughter. Shaky starlight. Shay stretched out and wished she could lie there forever. If Gilmour found her, she was done for, but heading back downstairs would be more dangerous still. She might be safer in the glass box though. She hauled herself to her feet and dusted herself down. She'd lost a feather or two and the fabric was soaked in sweat.

At the centre of the room stood a glass box which had been minutely etched with avian scenes. Birds tumbled and fell and curled around themselves so that beaks met tails. A peacock fan prismed light in a rainbow stain across the floor. She stepped inside and her skin was striped in coloured light. The perch sat in the corner like something from a fairy-tale stage set: a log, complete with moss and dew, wrapped all around with daisy chains. She climbed up onto it and squatted. It was ridiculous but at least she'd be hidden from anyone outside. The dress chafed as she watched rainbows flicker and lengthen across the floor. Where was that moving light coming from? She looked up and gasped. A glass ceiling gave out onto the night, but it was somehow lit with a hundred dancing stars. She stood on tiptoe to look more closely. There, trapped between two sheets of glass, fireflies swirled through a thin layer of air. They gave off a soft, flickering light like a dying fire.

Ten minutes passed. Then twenty. Twice people read the playbill and pressed their noses up against the glass, but they didn't enter. Shay lay on her back and watched the fireflies write foreign phrases across the night. Party noises came and went: bursts of braying laughter and breaking glass. Her knees ached, her feet ached. She imagined the tableaux below and how it would feel to be on display in front of all those people. Still better than being here. She rapped her toes on the floor. *Tap, tap, tap* means I miss you. *Tap, tap, tap;* do you miss me too? Not that they would hear, but she felt better for knowing that they were close. She'd read the cards for everyone in the dorm the evening before to reacquaint herself with the meanings. Alouette was haughty but then delighted when she drew the Empress; Nonesuch claimed that he could predict the cards before Shay turned them over and when, on the fourth go, he was right, he retired, crowing, to his bunk. Trussell drew the Lovers three times in a row and reddened and stuttered as the whole troupe teased him about his secret beau. Knowing they were here in the building with her, even floors below and unable to move, calmed her a little.

She heard Elizabeth before she saw her. Not the woman herself but the cloak of whispers that preceded her, like the first signs of rain. Moments later, the Queen swept in like a ship. She was smaller than Shay expected, with neat features and thin hands. Her dress was scarlet brocade stitched all over with a pattern of laurel leaves. A short cloak of white fur and a waistcoat in cushioned purple with a pearl in every dimple. Every inch was littered with careless, priceless gems, all in colours only the Queen and the birds could afford. A lacy ruff framed that extraordinary face – grimy white mask the colour of day-old milk. Around her eyes and mouth her make-up was as cracked as a riverbed in high summer. But behind that broken crockery something watched. Still, black eyes and thin lips. Men filed in behind her – pages, advisors, gentlemen – taking up the space until she was swallowed in the mass. The air turned liquid with scent and breath and whispers.

She tutted, which had the effect of silencing them. Shay avoided her eyes and curtseyed. She wasn't supposed to speak until spoken to but the Queen was silent. She didn't glance at Shay's dress or the perch. Instead, her eyes flickered over Shay's face. Eyes, hairline, mouth, chin. It was the same feeling as when Blank measured her. She kept quiet until Elizabeth said to the gentlemen behind her, 'Leave us alone.'

The room began to empty, not without many a backwards glance, until it was Shay, the Queen and a trio of gentlemen, each with a sword the length of Shay's arm. The Queen's voice was a raised eyebrow. 'This is hardly alone.'

The closest, a man in green leathers and an extravagant moustache, said, 'For Your Majesty's safety ...' and trailed off.

'*Tchh.* What's she going to do, peck me to death? I'll take my chances.'

They didn't go far. Figures crowded the glass walls. No one was gauche enough to stare but they kept up a slow perambulation around the perimeter. Mouths moving in conversation but eyes only for Shay and the Queen.

In silence Elizabeth sat down on the stool. Her dress pooled around her and she looked imprisoned within it. She looked Shay over again. 'Show me your hands.'

Shay had kept her talons tucked away but Elizabeth's eyes were everywhere. She reached out a hand and the Queen touched the pads of her fingertips against the points. 'That's neat. There's no room to draw a longsword in here anyway. Still they insist on wearing them. Men and their weapons.' She looked weary and Shay wondered how much her outfit weighed. 'Blood under your nails too, bird girl. Should I be concerned after all?'

Was there a hint of humour in her question? Shay dared not assume so. 'No, Your Majesty. It was … self-inflicted.'

A silence.

'And your head.'

Shay nodded and brought her brow down. Fingers brushed the outline of her tattoo. 'Sparrow-girl. Pretty work but some might call it blasphemy.' Shay held her breath.

'Well, at least you're not a Catholic.' She placed her hand back over Shay's. 'You live with your people, the Aviscultans?' Shay nodded.

'Not being Christians in these times.' She shook her head. 'That's a hard path.'

'We don't mean anyone any harm, Your Majesty. And we are as loyal as any Christian.'

'No harm? Maybe to a certain bird-seller?' Shay dropped her eyes to the floor. The hand on her chin was soft, but forceful. 'You can't afford enemies, little one. You don't have the *resources*. Still …' Elizabeth looked over her shoulder at her courtiers. 'It's four flights up to your nest. What do you have to recompense my aching feet?'

Shay kept her head down and said nothing. The Queen read the play-bill. 'The Sparrow: sings like a bird, tells fortunes like a Vestal. One of each?' Shay sat on the floor and pulled a table of etched glass between them. She fanned Trussell's cards.

'You don't need to touch me?' Elizabeth's voice was bright in the room's brittle air. 'To feel my energy?' She had falcon eyes, quick enough to peek into the future. *Careful now*, Shay told herself.

'It's not necessary,' she said, but she reached her hand out and laid it flat on the table. Elizabeth peeled off a white glove, dropped it on the floor, and laid her hand on Shay's. It was as light as a fledgling's. The slow circuit continued around them; eyes through the glass, eyes reflected. Shay shuffled the cards, hoping the tremble in her hands wasn't too noticeable.

'Keep a question in mind but don't tell me.' It sounded too much like an order. 'Your Majesty,' she added.

She handed the pack back. 'Cut, please.'

The Queen cut the cards, then, unasked, cut them again. 'You can call me Elizabeth while the door is closed. I can't remember the last time somebody did.' Shay didn't think that she could; it was best not to call her anything at all.

'If I could take my hand back.' She counted out the cards and laid three face down.

'I'm here because Dee speaks highly of you, bird-girl. Though, he believed that you were a boy so I'm not sure I should trust his judgement. He is always telling me that everything is either useful or ornamental.'

Shay nodded noncommittally.

'He's certainly no ornament so I suppose he must be useful. Evans too. What about me, child?'

Shay was still deciding which was less insulting when Elizabeth continued. 'A useful ornament perhaps. And you?'

'I strive for usefulness. I'm not sure whether I succeed.' She turned over the first card. The Swift. Elizabeth raised an eyebrow and Shay saw flakes of make-up crinkle at the corners of her eye.

She said, 'It means nothing on its own. It's the combination that matters.' She turned over another: the Falcon. The third was the Swallow. Not too bad. Shay had already been worrying how she would find a suitably regal explanation for a wren, or even, God forbid, a sparrow. The way Trussell had drawn them, the Swift and Swallow curved in towards the Falcon, who was an arrow pointing towards the ground, talons outstretched in glorious anticipation. 'Speed and power. Your Majesty combines both. Agility and grace. Truly auspicious.'

Elizabeth looked bored. Outside the watchers craned over one another's shoulders to see the cards. 'Ornament, ornament, ornament. Do you think I need flattery? Flattery is to me what shit is to you. I step over piles of it every day. Useful, remember.'

'Swifts and swallows sleep on the wing, eat on the wing, fuck on the wing.' She blushed as she spoke. 'They die on the wing too, and drop like stones when they're done. They have useless legs and useless claws. They are speeding, voracious mouths. Faster even than the sun. They see the summer before it's born and feel the night while it's still light. Plus the falcon. Small, but pure, unashamed death. The beauty of death. The terror of it.' Shay was talking from another script now, one she didn't remember learning.

Elizabeth's eyes licked at her like tongues. 'Better. But it's still only information. Make it a tool, sparrow-girl. Sharpen it.'

The words overtook her mind. 'Use speed and violence. Unleash a death that doesn't rest until it's burnt up. Strike before your enemies see you unsheathe. Never rest, never wait, never consider.'

When Elizabeth's laugh came, it was as if another person had entered the room – someone younger, more carefree.

'"Never consider." Oh, how they would love that. How many people do you think consider my decisions? In fact, change that. How many *men* do you think consider my decisions before they are made?' She pondered the question as if it had been Shay asking. 'Maybe a hundred? Fifty at least. Fifty for a decision about the menu for dinner or which jewels to wear. A hundred for anything important. "Never consider."'

Shay shuddered. Elizabeth was death, sat there in fur and jewels. Shay dug deep for her mother. The weight of her. Words she'd heard lightly thrown a decade ago came back. 'I'm only a weathervane. You know what I'm showing you.'

There was the longest silence then. Elizabeth's eyes softened and after a while she reached for Shay's hand again. 'I see. I see. Too much to expect that you'd wield the axe as well as showing me the necks.' She burst into a peal of laughter, genuine, tavern-style laughter. 'Thank you, weathervane.'

There was an uneasy silence. Faces crowded the windows, bisected by the bird etchings. Was she done, maybe? Had she made it through?

'Dee says that you know an older magic?' Elizabeth's questions all had trapdoors in them.

Shay tried to pick her words. 'He is too kind. I read the movements of birds. Or at least I try to.'

Elizabeth waved the idea away. 'And your songs? Dee believes they contain a secret language.'

'I don't know, Your Majesty. When I sing I lose myself. I don't know what I am saying.'

Elizabeth nodded but there was a hunger in her eyes now. 'Sing for me, sparrow-girl.'

'I … I'm not sure I can. It's not something I can command.'

'But it's something *I* can command, no? You are as loyal as any Christian, remember. Sing for me.'

147

Nothing in her scant repertoire was fitting for a queen. Nonesuch's songs ranged from the profane to the seditious and the tunes she knew from Birdland were for children. There was a song from the Cleopatra play, though, that she must have heard twenty times. She thought she could recall the words. She shut her eyes and started to sing.

'All crowns are crowns of thorns, all queens are queens of night …'

The glass had the curious effect of amplifying and multiplying every note. Phrases thickened and slurred, and the echoes came before she'd sung the note.

'All hearts are made to break, all wings are made for flight.'

Wait, those weren't the words. But the tune rose like water. To her chest, to her throat, to her closed, closed eyes, until she was under, swept out into open ocean until … until …

… she woke curled up in a ball with her hands hugging her bare knees. She scratched at her scalp and felt the sharpness of her nails. The room was so strange: the woodland perch, the grey lines of the bird etchings. She looked up to orient herself. No stars. Only one firefly remained alive, batting helplessly against the glass. The others were dead, turned to stains against the sky. Her thighs and shoulders ached like sunburn and there was a taste of blood in her mouth.

'Hello?' she said. Nothing.

She made her way out, past greying mirrors and dull glass. Ashes and vomit smeared the floors; twice she had to step over prone figures. The maze was easier in the dark, though she kept coming across wild reflections of herself hanging illuminated in the air. At one corner she was face to face with a magnified doppelgänger, pale and ragged and wide-eyed. She reached out to touch her face and a tremor ran through her as her nails touched the cool glass. Down through the shipwreck of the party. Broken glass and partridge bones. She was halfway to curtsey-ing at a lady sprawled in a corner when she realised it was a discarded dress, kept semi-upright by its stays and corset. She giggled and bowed instead. 'M'lady.'

Cleaners mopped at the floor in the ballroom, singing a work song softly to one another. She skirted back the way she'd come. Even the kitchen was quiet. The cook was sprawled dead drunk across the serving table while the turnspit-dogs slept in the corner. Shay took a sugar ship from a discarded tray and broke off the mast, sucking on it as she left. Only the guards were still awake, and their eyes followed her back all the way down St Anne's Lane. Was it four bells already? As dark as it ever got, anyway. The moon was a grey smudge behind clouds and there wasn't enough light to risk the rooftops. Instead, she picked carefully through the streets, guided every now and then by some night-owl whose candle still burned in an upstairs window. It was so quiet that she could hear snores from within the meaner houses. She tried a falcon call. No reply.

Further west the streets grew busy. The sky glowed fiery over Whitehall, meaning whole teams of people must be up and working by lamplight. The frantic hoofbeats of outriders racing along the main thoroughfares drove her into the back streets. Something was happening. On any other night she would have found herself a vantage point and watched to see what unfolded. She caught glimpses of messengers and soldiers and that meant just the kind of gossip from the outside world that would have the boys in the dorm agog. But she didn't trust the roofs with the quiver in her aching limbs, and she had a need like hunger to see the others. She kept to back alleys, letting the lights from Cheapside and Knightrider Street send her shadow scurrying across the walls.

Someone had left the hatch from the street to the theatre unlocked. Nonesuch, hopefully. She slid through and tiptoed down to the dormitory, into the yawns and sleep-mutters of home. She found her way by touch to their bunk, but it was cold and empty inside. No matter, she was asleep in moments.

22

I T WAS TRUSSELL WHO woke her, his hands on her shoulders. A bell clanged upstairs and Shay forced her eyes open.

'Evans is here,' Trussell said. 'That's him ringing the bell. Get dressed.'

The empty space in the bunk beside her seemed significant. Trussell followed her eyes and nodded. 'There was an ... an incident last night,' he said.

The ground was giving way beneath her. 'Nonesuch?'

Trussell nodded. 'While we were in our tableau, Lord Exeter hung his coat up on Nonesuch. Who, of course, tore it to shreds and returned it, saying he'd done him a favour. One of them would have ended up dead if Evans hadn't broken it up. So Nonesuch was sent away in disgrace but I don't think it's about that. He wants to see you.'

'Where is Nonesuch now?'

Trussell blew out his cheeks. 'Who knows? Licking his wounds somewhere. Or someone else's. Please, it's a bad idea to keep Evans waiting.'

She got changed in the bunk. The sparrow dress had moulted during the night and a ring of midnight feathers outlined where she'd slept. Trussell waited outside and Alouette scuttled behind him but otherwise the dormitory was empty. They climbed the stairs in silence to find Evans sitting cross-legged on the toadstool from *Arcadia*. He wore the same clothes as the night before and he stank of booze. He watched them climb onto the stage and rang the bell one last time.

'Ah, Trussell, if it isn't the Plinth Regent. I hear you were spectacularly adequate last night.' He put the bell down and smiled at Alouette. 'And you brought London's most ill-tempered Aphrodite with you. Excellent. Don't pout, Flanders. Lord Surrey told me that if you need any help scrubbing gold paint from hard-to-reach places then he's game; it appears some men *like* their goddesses surly and fat-arsed.'

He clapped slowly. 'But there she is, the real star of last night's show. She may have almost given me a heart attack but she came through in the end.' He reached out a hand to Shay. 'You little beauty. Ask me where I was at midnight.'

Shay said, 'Where were you at midnight, sir?'

'None of your fucking business.' He grinned to himself. 'Sorry, force of habit. At midnight, my tiny, feathered fantasist, I was sat upon the Royal Barge, drinking a private nightcap with Her Majesty. Who is quite smitten with a certain bird-girl. Which is good news for you and even better news for me because now the rest of the court all want their fortunes told by the Sparrow. I've had six messengers here already this morning trying to book a session. We may have to build a roost for you up on the roof somewhere.'

'What did I do?' asked Shay.

Evans reached for her hand and touched her nail-tips. 'So you really don't remember? I thought maybe that was part of your act.' He stroked the back of her hand. 'You read the Queen's cards and then she commanded you to sing.'

'I remember that. But I can't recall anything after the start of the song.'

Evans sat back against the toadstool and let out a satisfied belch. 'Well, you started off pretty conventionally. You sang a verse of the Cleopatra song, but quite quickly the lyrics started to ripen. I'm sure the original had more *regal visages* and far fewer *blood-dripp'd moons*. It got quite graphic. Quite *physical*. And then you were on your knees with your claws in her hands and you were singing like a bird.' He looked at her closely. 'I don't mean that as a metaphor. You sounded like a bird. A whole flock of them in fact, crows, at a guess. Even from outside the glass it was fairly terrifying, so God only knows what it was like in there. Elizabeth's men had their swords drawn and I was ready to slit your throat myself if it came to that. You kept up the dawn chorus until the very walls were shaking and then you slumped to the floor.'

Shay's shoulder twinged at the thought of it.

'So you're lying there, dead or whatever, and the walls are still ringing. The Queen looks thoughtful for a bit and then throws her cloak over you and gets into a huddle with her advisors. I had no idea whether they were discussing the insult against her in my house or whether she had found your performance useful in some way. Anyway, they yammered away, and an hour later me and the Queen are sharing a brandy on the Royal Barge and laughing it up like drinking buddies. Oh, and Gilmour? Won't bother you for a while. She properly told him off.'

Alouette was grinning at the story, but Evans said, 'There's something else.' He turned to Alouette and Trussell. 'You two, bugger off. I want a private word with our bird-girl.'

Shay had never been alone with Evans before. He appraised her and she held her head high. He said, 'I assume that you haven't heard what happened this morning. All over the city.'

The soldiers. The horses. The glow over Whitehall. She shook her head.

'Around midnight, a squadron of soldiers left Westminster. They swept up through the county picking off Catholics as they went, without stopping to sleep or eat. Usually as soon as the first recusant is nabbed the others get word and go into hiding. Not this time. I hear there are prisoners in chains all the way to Colchester. And apparently, they're still going.'

'Because of what I said?'

'What do you think? It would be quite a coincidence. And anyway ...' His smile turned rueful. 'I heard that the soldiers all chalked an emblem on their shoulders: a swift.'

'It couldn't be because of me.'

'You made a choice last night, Shay. You chose hunter over prey, and I have to admit I had my doubts. But here you are, half a day later, with your first kill. How does it feel?'

It felt nauseous. '*She* picked the cards and *she* decided what they meant to her. She gave the orders. I was just the vessel.'

Evans' smile was an invitation to conspiracy. He sang, 'Unleash a death that never sleeps,' and she remembered the taste of those words in her mouth. Visions flickered – rabbits haring for their warren, swords swung at heads, Birdland ablaze – and the bile rose in her throat.

'I said what I thought she wanted to hear. I didn't think anyone would get hurt.'

The five neat scabs on his cheekbone were pink around the edges. He reached a hand out to hold her wrist and said, 'That's theatre, Shay.'

23

A FTER IT WAS OVER Shay saw the kidnap happen again, in snatches like lightning strikes. Evans and his men and his horses, all in black. Spurs dug into flanks, hunting cries and the Blackfriars Boys whispering, 'There'll be a new boy in the dorm tonight.'

She'd gone up onto the rooftops to watch the sport. The men working like sheepdogs, herding a group of schoolboys away from the throng and into the quieter back streets. Children running, hands on caps. Men laughing.

Evans one-handed at a gallop, plucking the boy he wanted with a studied ease, cuffing his ear even as he rode on. Shay saw a pair of bare legs kicking at the air and then all was silence. The only sign that anything had occurred was a school cap trodden into the mud.

She had chores to do before she could see the new boy. Alouette needed a hand mending the bellows and once that was done Shay rebuttoned a frock coat for Blank. And when there was nothing meaningful left to do, she dusted and cleaned, just happy to be part of the clockwork of the Blackfriars. Now she was halfway competent at the theatre work, Shay realised that the first jobs she'd been tasked with here came more from pity than necessity, the way her mother used to have her carry the seed-pouches during the Murmuration, but she was a quick study and had the Aviscultan way with a needle and thread.

It was nearly dusk before she had time to visit the dorm. The new boy lay face down in a corner bed and wept, quietly but steadily, into his bedsheet. Shay watched his thin shoulders rise and fall. He was barefoot and he kicked out like a girl. Younger than he'd seemed from the rooftops; thirteen, maybe. She felt the immediate kinship of the lonely. Normal dorm life went on around them. Pavey was stitching a sleeve back on to a jerkin, his tongue poking out in frustration, while two boys mimed a sword fight with sticks. Over and over they fought, the same pattern of thrust and parry, spin and crouch, until it became something of a dance. Nonesuch squatted on the edge of his bunk and gave her a solemn wave. He was in the same clothes he'd worn to Evans' and he pulled on a spluttering pipe. Shay wanted to go to him, but the sight of the new boy tugged at her. She couldn't bear to see the dorm revolve around the still point of his weeping. She sat next to him, the thin cot creaking under their combined weights, but Nonesuch wagged a finger at her. He slid down to join them.

'I was just going to talk to him,' she said. 'I know what it is to be new here.'

He laid a hand on her shoulder. 'You can't, Shay. You'll say the wrong thing.'

'I only want to tell him that however hard it is, everything will work out in the end.' She wanted to say more, that there were deep wells of friendship here, oceans of love.

'Like I said,' said Nonesuch. 'The wrong thing. Everything won't work out. Not if he doesn't stop crying. He has maybe two days to impress Evans.' He took Shay's wrist. 'Understand it's not guaranteed that we'll keep him, and Evans has much worse places to work than the Blackfriars Theatre up his sleeve.'

He stood and kicked the bed frame. 'Up. And stop crying. It won't help.'

The boy wiped a sleeve across his nose and his shoulders shook helplessly.

Nonesuch sighed. 'You have to adjust. Now.' He clicked his fingers, and the boy watched his hand.

Nonesuch put a thumb under the boy's chin and tilted his head up. His voice wasn't unkind. 'This is it now. Here. Us. There is nothing else.'

The boy still didn't look at him, but he nodded.

'And no one is coming for you.' The boy went to contradict him but Nonesuch shushed him. 'I've been here four years, longer than anyone else. I've seen boys come and go, high-born and low. And every single one has said, "They'll come for me," and every single one has been wrong.'

The room was quiet now. The sword fight continued but the boys listened in to the conversation.

'Say it after me. No one is coming for me.'

The boy nodded but said nothing.

'Not enough. Say it.'

'No one is coming for me.' He had a pretty voice: delicate, well spoken. 'And no one will *ever* come for me.'

'Nonesuch ... please,' Shay whispered, but he held up a hand.

'I mean it. Ignore Shay. Everyone here was once where you are now. Most everyone here thought they wouldn't stay. But look at us.' The room was quiet and every face was turned towards the two of them.

'No one will ever come for me?' The boy turned the statement into a question, but at least he'd said it unprompted.

Nonesuch nodded and then grinned. 'It's not *such* a bad life. You can rise late, smoke all day and drink for free. And all the girls love a player.' A tatty cheer ran around the room, and he took the boy's hand. 'Come on, let's get you a script.'

That night in the bunk as their two bodies moved silently against each other, Shay whispered, 'Where did you go to last night? I was worried.'

His voice had a shrug in it. 'Just drinking. The taverns outside the gates are less fussy about curfew. I thought it best to keep out of Evans' sight but your little ... performance last night seems to have mellowed him.' He hadn't asked her anything about her audience with the Queen. She was bursting to talk about it – he was the one person she knew who might understand the feelings it had stirred in her – but she dared not mention the previous night until he did. He stared at the ceiling. 'You know that new boy is a warning to me, don't you?'

She didn't. She hadn't thought. But she'd seen the sideways looks of the boys as the extra cot was lowered down into the dorm. Did he really want to talk about it? She thought not.

So instead she asked, 'Will you tell me how you got here, Nonesuch? I know more about the new boy's journey than yours.'

He stroked her hair, and said nothing. Then he sighed, long and low, and said, 'I was born upstairs on the stage four years ago. I came out walking and talking like a miracle. There was nothing before, nothing. All right?'

In two minutes he was asleep.

24

I F LONDON IS A body, then gossip is its blood. News of Shay's performance poured like rainwater through the streets. It trickled from every eave and ran like piss through the ruts in the roads. A story like hers spread faster than plague and grew more virulent with every telling.

A creature half-bird, half-boy told the Queen where to find every traitor in the land.

She sang a song that left listeners lovestruck and cracked every window for miles.

She was a siren, she was a soothsayer, she was death itself.

Evans moved her into a high room at the Blackfriars with country scenes painted across the walls and a stage throne, hastily repainted with cavorting sparrows, for her perch. Day and night a queue of gentlemen and noblewomen snaked down two flights of stairs even while the auditorium downstairs was only half full. They came, bare-headed and reverent, and knelt even after Shay said they needn't. Bright eyes watched those hands with nails like dagger-tips as they dealt the bird cards. Shay couldn't keep track: twenty readings a day and money falling like rain.

The Tower, Two of Hawks, Ace of Ravens: high places, loss and influence.

It was as if London could only bear one of them to succeed. As quickly as Shay's audience grew, Nonesuch's fell. Three new plays in a row failed to catch the city's attention and those nights where boys were carted off after the show for some private masque grew more frequent. Often when Shay finally returned to the bunk, hoarse and numb-brained, Nonesuch was already asleep with his stage make-up smearing the sheets.

What Evans knew of the Ghost Theatre performances Shay wasn't sure. He never mentioned them but time after time, just as she was getting ready to rehearse, he would produce some lovelorn duchess with urgent questions and a fat purse, and Shay would be stuck on her perch as Nonesuch cursed and waited and stamped around on the roof above her; Ghost Theatre shows went from weekly to fortnightly to monthly.

King of Magpies, Justice, Eight of Hawks: control, mastery and punishment.

Elizabeth's Black Swifts tore a strip from the map of England, leaving prisoners (and worse) in their wake. People said that they never slept. People said that they could see in the dark. People said that Shay controlled them through birdsong.

Knight of Magpies, Queen of Magpies, the Hanged Man: ambition, determination, suspense.

Most days Shay could rein her talents in and ride them like a broken horse. Then the money came easily, and she sent fortunes home to a Birdland that was becoming a dream to her. Somewhere, sometime, someone else was reading the Murmuration, agape under a tundra of sky, while Shay sang like a caged bird for painted lords and ladies. Someone else was feeding Lonan, their hand in his, in the same way that Shay grasped Nonesuch's ankle as he slept. She tried to hide from this knowledge, tried to smother it under piles of coins. But when she looked at herself – through the make-up and talons and silk costumes and silk shoes – she knew she couldn't go home. Thoughts of Birdland made her gifts buck and bolt. Three times now she'd walked out of a reading without warning and thrown herself across the city's skyline with Devana a joyous compass above her. She ran until her nails were blunt and her feet were raw. Evans whined about refunds but what could he do? He needed her. It was the real first power Shay had ever had, and she polished that idea in her pocket. Each morning he fussed over washing and shaving her. He made her swear loyalty even as he dressed her in ever more elaborate costumes. And all the while Shay just watched him through Devana's eyes.

Sometimes it was just the two of them preparing for a morning reading. Sound of razor on strop and file on nails. A dead theatre and faint birdsong. Evans taking her hand like a lover might, as she studied the throb of blood at his throat. Cruel, cruel nails, and Devana whispering in her ear, 'Not yet.'

25

Tobacco and honeysuckle and a hangnail of moon.
Butterflies the size of hands convulsing in a stream of brandy. And
for accompaniment the sickly snap of leather on flesh. It had been a
terrible mistake for Shay to have followed the boys here.

Nonesuch had always been meticulous in keeping the details of the
private masques from her, but she'd learnt to read the signs and this
evening, when all the clues added up, she resolved to follow him. For
Shay, loving someone meant sharing their pain, even if the sharing
didn't lessen that pain, even if it doubled it. Today's signs: Nonesuch's
closed-door conversations with Alouette, which dwindled into silence
as Shay entered; Blank spending hours on costumes that fitted no play
in their repertoire; Pavey's red eyes and close-bitten nails. Shay had
seen this all before and she knew that Evans' black carriage would
be next, arriving unannounced to wait out the back without even
unhitching the horses.

From her hiding place on the theatre's roof she couldn't see exactly
who got into the carriage, but she knew in her bones that Nonesuch was
among them. The black sheen of the carriage roof was easy to spot in the
moonlight, and she followed its route through west London, watching
the vehicle scatter crowds like birds. And she wasn't the only one in
pursuit. Somewhere far above, Devana, drawn from her nighttime roost
by the promise of a hunt, was stalking her as she stalked the boys.

Shay guessed that Whitehall Palace would be their destination long
before the building's lights began to burnish the skies. There, in the
heart of London's body politic, all was fire and noise. The carriage raced
on, through the open courtyards, through the hawkers and petition-
ers, and Shay followed the sight of crowds parting like a ship's wake.
They skirted the closed spaces of the palace buildings and Shay followed

across a pitted, lunar landscape of old plaster and leaning chimneys. As the carriage slowed, Shay hung back a little, because the site of the masque was obvious enough.

The courtyard shone a gemstone green amid the sooty roofs and lightless squares of the palace interior. A garden. Not only a garden but somehow a spring garden; too bright and fresh and bold to exist in this stony winter. Braziers blazed in the corners, turning the air tropical and throwing shadows across the walls. Shay kept to all fours and got as close as she dared. She spread herself like a spider across an incongruous rose-woven pergola and tried to work out how much of the scene below was real and how much was Alouette's handiwork. The fruit trees looked natural enough, though it was too wintery for those blossoms that fluttered in an unseen breeze, and she remembered Blank taking delivery of a bolt of snow-white silk earlier in the week. A stream flowed where no stream should be, whispering and too dark, so that must be a creation, but the statues, with their marble bodies shadowed in moss, looked as if they had stood there for decades. As she slowed her breathing, there came a noise like steam escaping, and a shivering river of white rushed out from two arrow-slit windows. Butterflies, in their hundreds, were buffeted by the warm air until a few settled breathless on the trees, wings wheezing like lungs. She wished Devana was with her to watch their manic spread, but the pergola was practically at ground level and Whitehall was still busy; Devana hated to land anywhere that it might be hard to take off from.

There was the *scritch* of a bolt being pulled back, and four gentlemen entered the garden. Shay didn't recognise them but she knew the type from the Blackfriars' private boxes: fur-lined capes and stomachs the size of ale barrels. There was a moment's stillness, and then the sound of footsteps and shouts of delight. The men discovered that the pears hanging from the fruit trees were actually concoctions of roast beef and gold leaf. The river flowed with brandy. Butterflies clung to their clothes like stage-door girls. But still something seemed unnatural to Shay, even within this artificial oasis. She scanned the scene again as the gentlemen strolled and called to each other, voices authoritarian even in their pleasure, voices that were used to directing men and things. There. A movement. Shay looked closer and saw one of the statues – a nymph in flowing robe and sandals – shiver. Shay knew a tremor of fear when she saw one. She crawled forward for a better view. It was Pavey, caked in make-up so thick and grainy that he looked for all the world like stone. He shook again and a dark stain spread across the crotch of his robe.

A voice from off to her right: 'Welcome to the Garden of Arcadia.' The statue of Pan was facing away from her, but she'd know that voice anywhere. Shay was embarrassed that she hadn't recognised him, even under his layers of plaster and lichen – how had she missed those eyes, that knotty torso?

'This is a garden of wonders where nothing is as it seems, and everything is permitted.' Nonesuch moved oddly, with a rigidity that made him appear jointed only at the waist and shoulder, and his head stayed chillingly still, but his voice was full of humour. Among the men's chatter and the susurration of wind, Shay only caught snatches of what he was saying – *part girl, part animal, driven mad by godly desires* – while the gentlemen sat cross-legged like schoolgirls at his feet. When he stepped, stiff-legged, from the podium, with his plaster codpiece bouncing comically in front of him, the men followed him through the leaves. The other statues revolved to watch them and with a shock she realised that the faun was Trussell; even under the ears and muzzle she recognised those wet eyes. The shepherdess was a boy she didn't know though. Younger, she thought, with wrists and neck looking doubly fragile in their plaster sheaths.

Shay had made a study of men, of course. You couldn't disappear among them without knowing their ways. So she'd always kept sly eyes on every street-stall serenader and three-ale braggart for badges of masculinity that she might wear later. But there was one male trick which she'd never mastered: that ability to change state in a sliver of a moment: from love to hate, from calm to violence. There was some hidden astrology of cues and provocations that remained opaque to her. So it was, in the garden. One moment the gentlemen were following Nonesuch through the masque with the skittish enthusiasm of children, dipping cups in the stream or freezing in wonder as butterflies landed on their outstretched palms, but then, with no catalyst that Shay could see, they changed. Like a thousand birds becoming a single flock, they went from boys to men to animals.

The transformation was instant and brutal. A belt raised and brought down three times. Fingers dug into flesh, puckered skin giving the lie to the illusion of stone. Trussell on his knees, the shepherdess on his knees. Hands pulling hair and cracking plaster as the men worked with all the intentness of labourers. There were no smiles or laughter now, but just the concentration of serious men doing an arduous task. The statues were positioned and moved, captured and discarded. And among them, one minute one of the boys and the next working alongside the gentlemen, Nonesuch played both hunter and prey. He directed the action but then was thrown to the floor. He moved Trussell and the shepherdess into an obscene tableau and stood back to admire his handiwork. Shay remembered his hands on her in rehearsal – *you go there and he goes there* – as he made sure that the sightlines worked.

Then, Shay felt a pain like a knife-blade. Devana landed silently on her shoulder and it was fortunate that the men's noises drowned out her cry. The bird was quiet as night, but those talons dug deep in an instant, and when she squeezed, it left Shay breathless. Devana settled herself, and for a moment Shay could pretend that the garden was a stage set, scenery in gold and white and green, facing a midnight auditorium, and she and Devana were mere spectators. It was almost peaceful. But then a gentleman bent Nonesuch over a bench and took a huge, roaring mouthful of brandy, dark liquid spilling down his cheeks until he wiped his face and took off his belt. More sounds of men's exertion and stifled cries. A hundred dead butterflies scumming the stream.

What was it that Devana saw in Nonesuch's eyes as the gentleman grabbed him around the neck – a lamb about to be sheared – and forced his head up and back? Did she understand those eyes that sparked like flint into hatred before something in them died and they became stone again? Another ecstatic squeeze of claw and Devana called out in the voice that she reserved for the killing moment – abrasive, inhuman, triumphal. The cry was loud enough to make Nonesuch look up, and for a moment Shay's eyes met his, and then she was up and running. Blindly careering backwards with Devana wheeling away in alarm, her wings clumsy in the confines of the palace. Shay scrambled noisily across the boards, not caring who might hear below, racing and leaping, the only thing she really knew how to do, trying to outrun her own thoughts, colliding with walls and chimneys, relishing the ache of it. Away, away, until she popped like a cork out into lonely west London streets, for once not caring whether Devana was tracking her from above. Back, up, down, east, a mile at least, blood on her soles as she threw herself across chasms, along gutters and down thatched slopes, winded and weeping as she vaulted through the theatre window and down into the dorm where everyone was still awake, but everyone knew not to ask.

She lay there, not sleeping, through the dead hours until Nonesuch returned. He was miraculously clean. There was no trace of plaster on him, but his skin was as raw as a plucked chicken, and they never spoke of that night, not even a word.

From then on Nonesuch was consumed by the Ghost Theatre. There would be two shows a week, three if he had time, taking place in the dead hours between the end of the Blackfriars performances and sleep. Now he dispensed with props, dispensed with rehearsals even. Instead, he acted out stories that ordinary people brought to him. A sailor boy with two black eyes like stagnant pools whispered the tale of his punishments into Nonesuch's hungry ears and twenty-four hours later Nonesuch stood on the gangplank of *The Albatross*, inching out into the black, repeating the boy's story as a hundred pairs of ears strained to hear him over the noise of waves.

There was none of the Blackfriars' elegant language now, but a London drawl and tavern tang that drew bigger and bigger crowds. These new shows terrified Shay, looking out over so many faces, faces that knew her although she didn't know them. Street kids and prentices and flower-girls and Moors. Southwark Geese and gypsies and gallowsbirds and thieves.

Now Nonesuch was known from palace to poorhouse. If they walked London's richer streets together, sometimes Shay played a game, hanging back far enough that no one would know they were together. Hungry heads turned to watch his back after he'd passed, and once they were certain they were unseen, both men and women stared at him the same way: a brittle, acquisitive look, as if they were picking fruit from a stall. To these people he was available, yours to watch for a sixpence, yours to own for who knows how little more. Frank, mercenary gazes combined lust and disgust in equal measures. A flash of imagery – Gilmour's caged lovebird and her with the hook in its door. The thought of Nonesuch trapped in one of these lustful, hateful looks unsettled her so much that she ran to catch him up and cling safely to his arm.

In the poor streets it was less complicated. There they loved him and wanted to show it. He was magnetic, gathering a train of boys and girls behind him, like ducklings, and from every street corner came a gift.

They would return to the Blackfriars with bags of food and notes and clothes and tobacco, and the other boys would fall on the booty like dogs.

Even the lovelorn notes that were pressed damply into Nonesuch's hand at the stage door could become a show. One message, whose author Shay was never able to discover, had caught Nonesuch's attention. It was in a painstakingly fragile hand – every letter as shaky and separate as the stage-door girls themselves – and it covered five straight sheets. The Ghost Theatre show that evening was simply Nonesuch reading the note aloud in a tavern, still in his work clothes but his voice somehow recognisably a girl's, riven with pre-emptive apology, words like steps on a midnight staircase, while around him Shay and Trussell and Blank bayed hunting songs full of bonhomie and violence. As they sang, they drowned out his story and the crowd moaned, desperate to hear the girl's words, but the troupe sang louder, shouting almost, drowning him like a rat in a barrel, and Shay puffed out her chest and bellowed until, as always, a cold tide swept up through her and the next thing she knew Trussell was shaking her awake back in the dorm. She no longer even asked what had happened.

26

THEY CLIMBED DOWN THE side of the building into a quiet
courtyard where Nonesuch stood with his hands on his knees
and his chest heaving. Shay had found them a grand house out by
Leadenhall Market, which the owners had left empty for the season,
but the bedroom was such a haven of quiet softnesses that they'd both
overslept. Across the rooftops Shay could be back in fifteen minutes,
but Nonesuch tagged along, rather than risking the traffic, and she'd
taunted him that he might not be able to keep up. By St Sythes Lane
he shone with sweat and at St Mary-le-Bow his breath came in torn
lungfuls. They could have walked the last mile at ground level, of
course, but Shay wasn't letting Nonesuch off the hook unless he asked.
And he didn't ask. So she took them on another run across sodden
thatch and chipped tile, and another set of leaps that seemed to widen
as they tired.

'You need a while to catch your breath, old man? It wouldn't do
for your public to see you panting like a stag at bay.' Still bent double,
Nonesuch waved her on, out into the clamour of the street.

A knot of people obscured the theatre doors. Two Hackney cabs
waited with their horses blinkered; someone had sent servants ahead
to reserve the best seats. A group of six girls, all pointedly not speaking to
one another, tried to look as if they weren't just hanging around. They
were still here for Nonesuch, even as his audiences dwindled. But
behind them stood a more meagre group: Shay's supporters. It still
surprised and worried her that such a band of people could exist. They
were smaller and quieter than the girls who waited for Nonesuch. Street
boys and street girls, mute and often crippled, with hopeless, thatchy
hair and old-man wheezes. They darted out to touch her like fish going
for insects on the water's surface. Fingers rubbing her hem, a hand on

her knees. Every day she tried talking to them and every day they said nothing. Just dart and peck with their eyes in the dirt.

'Hello,' she said, as she always did. 'Hello. Hello.'

She pushed open the doors. The theatre was just a black rectangle against the winter sun but, before she could step inside, a hand grabbed her shoulder and spun her around. 'Where the hell have you been? You had readings at twelve bells and at two. I had to send Pavey on in a flapper wig.' Evans shook his head. 'I own twenty businesses in this city and this is the only one where people don't do as they're told.' His voice carried; Shay was being made a public example of, and it stung. 'Ungrateful little goose-fucker. Do you think I don't know about your eightpence in tips yesterday? You should be down on your knees thanking me – if it weren't for me you'd be back in Birdland, worshipping ducks and eating dirt. Do you realise that you've not once ever said thank you for all I've given you, flapper?'

It came out before she could stop it. 'Don't call me that.' Her face was red and she shored herself up against tears. Everyone was watching: the girls, her fans, the grooms and the prentices.

Evans nodded, his hands still resting on her shoulders. Close enough to smell the meat on his breath. He said, 'Flapper. Chicken-fucker. Worm-eater. I'll call you what I want, I own you.'

The words landed like slaps. They were schoolyard insults, the kind of thing she used to hear from older kids, but they set her mouth moving before her mind could catch up. 'There are names for people like you, too. Lard-bloat, bald-head, boy-stealer, *thief*.'

His face didn't alter. In fact, so placid was his expression that it took Shay a moment to realise what had changed. His thumbs were digging into the gaps beneath her collarbone while he kept a tight hold on her shoulders. The pain followed the realisation. She twisted to try to get out of his grip, but he tightened and pushed her towards the ground. Too late she got a sense of the power behind his flab. Two of his men watched hungrily from beside the Hackney cabs. He twisted her shoulder, forcing her head to one side, and brought his mouth close to her ear.

'You call me a thief?' His voice was light, not unpleasant.

'It was a joke, a stupid joke,' she mumbled.

'Evans, stop.' Nonesuch stood amid the gaggle of girls.

Evans didn't turn around. 'Lord Nonesuch. There's another ungrateful wastrel. Have we had a busy morning?'

165

Nonesuch said, 'We need to get inside, Evans. I have make-up and costume to do. Shay was going to help me with that.'

Evans laughed. 'You're playing the goddess Diana. I doubt this plain little thing knows much about making you look more feminine.' He dug his thumb hard into Shay's shoulder. 'Anyway, we are having an instructive discussion. Our friend here thinks that I steal boys. Now, who might have given her that idea?'

Nonesuch's shoulders sagged. 'She didn't mean it, Evans.'

He considered the statement. 'That wasn't really my question though, was it?' He turned back to Shay.

'Why don't you tell everyone exactly which boys I might have *stolen*?' He dug his nails in deeper and Shay let out a yelp. Fat fingers and black rings. Sweat and meat. She should shut up, she knew, but so many people were watching.

'Trussell,' she whispered.

Evans pulled her upright and brushed down her shoulders. Her little knot of fans watched from the corner, and she stood a little taller for them. 'Trussell,' she said. 'You plucked him off the street like a fat peach. Pavey. I heard that you led him through the alleys like a market goose.' She caught Nonesuch's eye, but his face was blank. '*Lord* Nonesuch. Taken from a family who loved him, and kept him, and miss him still.'

Evans took a step back. She had surprised him. 'So our sparrow chooses today to be a hawk? What a lot we've seen, haven't we?'

He patted himself down and checked his pockets for something he didn't find. 'Trussell. Pretty little Trussell. I never wanted him at all. Don't you find him a bit slow? All that *weeping*. He misses his family, he misses his dog.' He gave a shudder. 'Altogether too much like hard work. But unfortunately someone did want him. Your old friend the Queen did, little sparrow. She'd heard him sing at St Paul's Church one year so I got my orders. *Master Trussell is wanted for the court revels.* Not yet but once he's all trained up. Which in his case took forever.' He looked Shay full in the face. 'Is it stealing if the Queen orders it? If she orders you to procure for her what she already owns? I'll tell you that one for nothing. It. Is. Not.'

Nonesuch went to take Shay's arm but Evans brushed him away.

'Now, Pavey. I can see how that one looks. Legally, I'm sure there's a case that could be made that I stole him. But then I stole him from the gallows. He was an hour from having his neck snapped when I picked him up.' He looked over his shoulder at his men. 'What was his crime again?'

An older man laughed. 'Pavey? He stole the Christmas Box. The one for all of Seething Lane. There was a pretty penny in it too, by all accounts. He'd hidden it under his bed.'

Evans shook his head. 'The Christmas Box for his own fucking street. Lord, but that lad is an idiot. It took money, and influence, and some long, long words to remove the noose from *that* neck. And yes, we led him down the street like an animal because he had to be seen to be punished. That procession probably saved his life. If I stole him, then it was in the way Joseph of Arimathea stole Christ.' He gave another harmless smile.

'She understands, Evans, she's sorry.' Nonesuch's hands were raised in supplication.

Evans was quiet for a long moment. He looked at Nonesuch and took a step back. A look passed between them, some male thing, and Shay thought that perhaps he was about to let them go. Then he said, 'Nonesuch, though, that's a choker. Ripped from the bosom of his loving family by an uncaring theatre-owner. Now that *is* harder to defend, yes?'

Shay looked across at Nonesuch, but his eyes were fixed on the ground. She'd never seen him so meek, and her stomach lurched.

'Tell me, fledgling, about Nonesuch's family. I expect that they're noble?'

Knots in her belly. 'I don't know.'

'But they're gentlemen at least? That elegant face and that pretty voice. Even the name. *Nonesuch*.' He said it with relish. 'There's a Nonesuch House on the bridge. Four fucking storeys of noblemen. Surely one of them must be the distraught pater.'

Shay had been robbed once. Even before she heard the footsteps and the snick of a blade, something animal inside her told her danger was coming. She didn't know in what form, but it wouldn't be good.

'A gentleman, yes.' The girls looked at Evans. His men looked at Evans. Shay looked at Evans. He called over to the carriage again. 'Dunn, get me the books from four years back.' The man unbuckled a bag from the rear horse and its tail flicked at him.

'What day, Nonesuch?'

Nonesuch wouldn't look up. Evans reached a long arm out to pull his chin up until their eyes met.

'What day did we meet, son? I know that you know. Don't make me search.'

'January the twelfth.' His voice as small as pebbles.

'That's right, January. Ice on the Thames, if I remember. Chestnut sellers doing a trade.' He paged through a leather-bound book, stopping occasionally to wet his fingertips. 'Here. Expenses for January the twelfth. Candles, eight pence. Snuff, one shilling. That's expensive. Maybe there was a pouch or two for you in there too, Dunn, eh?' Dunn laughed obligingly. 'Feed for the horses. Water and ... here we are. Boy: sixpence.'

He kept his hand under Nonesuch's chin. 'Boy. Doesn't say a name. I probably didn't think it mattered. Now, who do you think that boy was?'

Nonesuch took shallow breaths. His hand was on his hip, inches from the handle of his knife. When he spoke, it was with a timidity that Shay didn't think he had in him. 'Evans. Please. We don't need to do this.'

His voice was private, Evans' was for the public. 'Who was the boy who cost sixpence?'

'Me.'

'That's right. You. Cheaper than a box of candles, which seems about right, for all the trouble you cause.'

He turned back to Shay. 'I didn't have to steal or pluck or flatter to get this ripe peach. It fell right in my hand. His mother and father couldn't wait to get rid of him. And, what a surprise, the price they wanted was exactly enough for a bottle of brandy. What kind of people do you think they were, boy-in-the-streets?'

Shay would have given everything she owned to make him stop there and then.

'Let me tell you. They were no more gentlemen than you, little sparrow. And you're no kind of gentleman at all.'

Evans rested his hands paternally on her shoulders. Tails swished and flies buzzed. Nonesuch had shrunk into himself. It might be over. Evans looked bored as he said, 'His mother offered herself first, of course, I'll say that for her. Same price as the boy but only for an hour. Still, she wasn't worth half that.'

If Nonesuch hadn't made the sound that he did – an anguished, animal bellow – then who knows how it might have ended. He was on Evans' back in two steps and he dug those slender fingers into his face, clawing for purchase: eyes, mouth, ears. Shay saw bared teeth and a throat convulsed with sobs. Evans stumbled, tottering from leg to leg, trying to throw the weight off him, and then Nonesuch buried his teeth into the back of his neck with a nauseous, liquid sound. Evans reeled around, elbows flailing, but Nonesuch clung on like a monkey. He whirled back the other way and the crowd was shocked still for a moment; the only noise was of Evans staggering across the cobbles like a baited bear. He twisted an arm back and shook but Nonesuch just gripped tighter. Then Shay saw a thin arm in red velvet reaching down, searching for something. Nonesuch, going blindly for his knife.

'Nonesuch, no,' she said. If he used the knife, then that would be the end of him, she knew. One step and she was slapping his hand away, another and she was grabbing at his elbow. Evans spun around to try to reach him and she caught their fight in glimpses. Fingers tearing at clumps of hair. A bloodied mouth open, then biting down. An elbow driven back into a belly. Their cries intermingled: slaughterhouse sounds.

She tugged again, ducking an elbow, and Nonesuch pulled back, stronger than she would have imagined, but at the same time Evans whirled and she kept hold of his shirt. It tore from collar to tails but it brought Nonesuch down too, landing with a dull thud on the cobbles. The street turned curiously quiet; the only sounds were two men breathing hard and wind through the spires.

Evans' hand went to the back of his neck, and it came away sodden red. Shay stood between the two of them and raised her hands. Enough time for Nonesuch to scrabble, wide-eyed, up from his knees. She didn't turn but could hear him run: a child's feet on cobbles and then the rush of boots as Evans' men realised what was happening. She planted herself in front of Evans and opened her mouth to placate him.

He skittled her across the street with a sweep of arm and she came down hard on her elbow and then on her skull. Teeth jarred together and when she tried to straighten up, her arm gave way beneath her. Cold, wet cobbles and a cushion of horse dung. She tried again with the other arm but she couldn't see much. Evans and his men were gone. Finally, she stood and made for the alley from where they'd arrived; she could get to a better vantage point from there. She levered herself up onto the outhouse and then climbed one-handed onto the roof. Her elbow panged with pain but it wasn't broken. From the roof the streets were laid out like a map beneath her. The river lay at the bottom of the hill; he'd probably turn left there because the open courtyards of Bridewell were to the right, and that would be too exposed. So she cut left, over the buckling lead roof of St Andrew by the Wardrobe, to the corner of the street. Beneath her Evans and his men fanned out at walking pace, one to each street, but there was no sign of Nonesuch. He'd been too fast.

27

Bruises bloomed under shay's collarbone and her elbow was swollen like an egg. Something clicked, troublingly, every time she moved her neck. Tonight's performance would still go on, surely – Evans didn't do cancellations – but that lead part had always been Nonesuch's. Church bells rang off to the east and Shay realised with a jolt it was only an hour until show time. She sat in the shadows of the theatre roof and watched the street below. A river of people flowed towards the Blackfriars: Dutchmen with Holland's Leaguer whores in five-guinea hats and young gallants in packs, smoking whichever tobacco was most fashionable this month. Evans' men came and went but there was no sign of the man himself.

A noise: feet on plaster and hard breaths. Two arms appeared and then Nonesuch dragged himself up onto the roof. His face was red with sweat and his hair was lank. He scooted over and she wordlessly put an arm around him. She could sense the beat of his heart and the tremble in his arms.

'Are they going ahead with the show?' he asked.

'I'm not sure, but the doors are open. Who takes your part if you're … ill?'

'Trussell, perhaps. He's rehearsed the role before. He'll be lost without his prompter, though.'

His eyes shone like wet paint and the pair stared out at a sky fading from blush to bruise. In that pose, with his shoulders slumped, he looked like a child. The skin over his left eye was split and had turned the purple of rosehips. Shay pushed the side of her foot against his.

'We were all out looking for you.' It sounded more accusatory than she'd planned.

'You could have just waited here. I have nowhere else to go.'

They watched the sky's colours drain without speaking.

'Why didn't you tell me about your parents?' Shay asked. 'I don't care that you're not a lord. I might even have liked you more. You know how I feel about gentlemen.'

He looked at her properly for the first time. 'I didn't call myself that to be liked, Shay. I needed the name's power: *Lord* Nonesuch. A title opens doors, and wallets, and legs. Evans was right behind the idea too, in the beginning; there's nothing like a posh boy in a dress to bring in a certain kind of punter. All he had to do was lie. If he treated me like a fallen gentleman, then I *was* a gentleman, whatever my true birth. There are plenty of poor-born men who have made enough money to wipe out parents even humbler than mine. No, the name was all that mattered. A name like a spell.'

Lights were appearing in the neighbouring houses. A glow like fireflies scattered across windows and stars peeked through the velvet away to the east.

'Do you know how the Queen transforms you from a man into a knight?' he said. 'Seven words: I declare thee the Lord of Wherever. Seven words and a man is raised up above all others. Names are their power, Shay, with swords in reserve. Nothing more than that.'

He pulled his foot away and Shay realised, with a feeling like missing a step, that he might be angry with her.

She wanted to keep his mind from the performance that would soon unfurl downstairs. She asked, 'So, who are you really?'

The sky smeared from one impossible colour to another. He pulled closer so that his lips were inches from her ear. 'My name is Gully.'

Immediately there came the far-off cry of a tern.

'Well, it was. I suppose it still is. The place I was born was some farm halfway between nowhere and nothing and I can't imagine that my parents bothered to register my birth.'

He picked at a flake of mascara that had clumped on the tip of his eyelash and said, 'My father was a sin-eater and my mother was a drunk. Actually, my father was a drunk too, but he had to fit it in around his work. My mother could dedicate herself full-time to drinking.'

'What's a sin-eater?' asked Shay. It sounded like something from a storybook.

He stretched his arms as if the memory were hunching him up. 'It's the kind of occupation that could only exist in the back of beyond. Country people think that a dead man's sins can be transferred to another person and that way the deceased might still get into heaven. And guess who would receive all those evils?'

'A sin-eater?'

He nodded. 'My father would be called out whenever some notorious local wrongdoer had died. A proper sinner, mind, he wouldn't get on his horse for anything less than manslaughter. The three of us would ride into some crumb of a village and then he'd squat there by the coffin on this stupid little stool that he took with him. And the family would bring him a crust of bread and a jug of ale; the idea was that when he ate and drank, he'd be taking on all the sins of the deceased.' He shook his head. 'Idiots, the lot of them. He was the one who called me Gully. My mother just called me Boy. Local children called me names. Gully-in-the-dirt. Mud-boy. Gully-from-nowhere.'

Shay thought *Gully: like a gull. Brash, wheedling, cocky. Gully: a drain, a washing away of things.*

'And because we needed a fresh supply of dying sinners every month, we were always moving to new towns. Some unknown place where I was still skinny and red-haired and plain, and my parents were still ridiculous. Three things that are targets for inventive children. But that wasn't why they hated me. They hated me because I was unloved.'

The word hung there, a cloth on a line.

He shook his head. 'Children can always tell.'

From the street came a cry – 'Doors!' – and dual thuds of the entrance being closed up. Three floors down, Trussell would be starting the soliloquy. Shay wanted to keep him talking. 'Tell me how you became Nonesuch, then.'

At first, she thought he hadn't heard. He sat, alert, listening for the audience below, but then he was back into his stage voice. 'Evans didn't ask my name, the day that he bought me. He and his men had arrived unannounced, like a rainstorm, all on horses whose coats shone like leather.'

The rooftop was his theatre now, and the sunset his scenery.

'He stood at the gibbet because that was the closest thing to a stage that we had.' Nonesuch drew himself up and thickened his voice to do Evans. 'Boys who can sing, line up here.'

'But there weren't many takers; the cleverer parents hid them-selves and their children away. They didn't like the look of Evans' mob: those much-used scabbards, the facial scars. Just three boys were brave enough or stupid enough to step forward. The first was a pale boy, a hair short of an albino, twitchy-thin like a weasel. He started to tell them what he was called but Evans brushed him off. "I need a voice, not a name." The boy sang well enough, bit of gusto, a game attempt at the high notes but Evans waved him away before the first refrain.'

Shay could picture it so clearly. The wind across the thatch and the bare legs on the gibbet.

'A lad called Burns was up next, but he didn't even get to open his mouth. Evans sent him packing. The boy looked disappointed, silly goose. That told me something though. Whatever they said, they were after something more than just a singer. The third boy, oh Lord. He was even younger, with his cap in his hand, and he moved like the gibbet was on fire. On the command he opened his mouth and then … nothing. A man prodded him with his sword and the crowd laughed as he pissed himself. A waste of Evans' time.'

He stepped up onto the edge of the roof and spoke out into the street. 'And then there was a hand on my shoulder and waist.' He placed his hands in those places.

'My mother was a big woman, with arms like hams. She shoved me, blinking, out towards the men and said, "This 'un sings like a bird."

'I said, "Aye. A crow," and that got a laugh.'

He shook his head again, answering some question that Shay hadn't asked. 'I wonder what Evans saw there that day. I look for it sometimes in the mirror. But maybe you can't see it in yourself, whatever it is. Anyway, his interest was immediate. He placed a hand on my head and turned me round, looking for God-knows-what, and then he guided me up the steps.'

He stopped to cock an ear at some sound below.

'So, my first time on a stage was a gibbet. Fair enough. I died that day and I'll die again.'

He pulled himself upright. 'He ordered me to sing, so I sang.'

Shay hadn't heard him sing before. He had a precise, colourless tone.

'Oh, the city folk come in their hose of gold,
With their noses in the air and their brass so bold,
Send 'em back with a boot up their arse,
Send 'em all back with a boot up their arse.'

174

He wore the faintest of smiles. 'It didn't get the response I was used to. No cries of *more*, no laughter, no one even joined in on the refrain. The crowd stayed silent, and Evans gave me a final up-and-down look. Then he told his men to toss me in the back of the cart with the geese.'

Doors opened far below them, letting out a bubble of noise. A group of gentlemen took turns pissing in the alleyway round the side. 'Interval,' said Nonesuch.

'His men didn't ask my name either. I lay in darkness on the straw with the bleats of geese for company and a crack in the side to watch the journey through. Hours of trees and then finally the city being born around us. Muddy little villages and dusty encampments. Washerwomen by black pools and the sails of tenter grounds like beached ships. Into Southwark where it was bright as day at eight bells. Torches on every corner and the roads like silk. London Bridge was blocked that night, it was slower than walking. I remember that two men in leather gloves walked a camel, a real life camel, past us and behind them I saw this building with a stone on its lintel: NONESUCH HOUSE, 1543. Such a nice word to roll around your mouth.'

A wave of laughter rolled up from the theatre and Nonesuch made a sour face.

'After the bridge the horsemen were keener with the whips and the horses sensed home. We ended up here at Blackfriars, not that I knew it at the time, and one of the men walked me through the dead theatre. That was my first time on an actual stage, that feel of a church and the smell of a tavern. Down steps into a basement full of boys. Twenty faces – not hostile yet, but ready to be. My captor pushed me forward and said, "New boy." Someone asked, "Does it have a name?"'

The night, and the theatre, were quiet now.

'Doesn't matter who they might be, twenty faces is an audience. I waited, I sighed and then I pulled a pipe from my pocket. "Call me Nonesuch," I said.'

A ripple of applause rose from below.

'End of Act II,' Nonesuch said. 'Trussell must have nailed the murder.' He stood on the edge of the roof: a black figure against a black sky. 'In a week I had my first speaking part, in a month my first lead. There were boys here who were pretty and there were boys who could sing. A few were pretty *and* could sing. But not one of them could lie. When you've had a knife to your throat and five seconds to explain why you have a gentleman's pocket watch under your bed,' he looked out into the gloom, 'then playing Cleopatra, child-queen of a continent and lover of the Caesars is an easy one.'

They sat in silence for a while. 'There are other companies,' she said. 'Adult companies.'

His response was immediate. 'What do you imagine they think of boys like me?'

The animosity between the boys' companies and the adult troupes was obvious enough. Shakespeare sniped at Evans, Lord Strange mocked the St Paul's Boys. But Shay thought of it as that gentlemanly competition that rich men played at, the way boys played with toy soldiers. She had never considered that Nonesuch or Trussell or the others might be combatants too.

'I don't know,' she said.

'They think, and this is a direct quote, that I audition well enough. A little flouncy but nothing that can't be beaten out of me. But they would prefer a player who'd spent his apprenticeship learning lines rather than sitting on some gentleman's lap.'

Shay knew she was concentrating on the wrong part of what he'd said, but she couldn't help herself. 'You've auditioned elsewhere?'

He looked more despairing now than when he'd arrived. 'Of course I have. We all have. It's not like we can do anything else. We're already in the Tower, we're just waiting for the executioner's knock.'

Shay felt sick. This new world had only just appeared, was it to leave as quickly as it had come?

'And you, Shay?' Gentle, now, his voice. A worry in it.

'What?'

'You understand that this will come to you too?'

She didn't. She hadn't. At least until he said that, and then, of course, it was plainly true.

'You're not Evans' first fortune-teller. You won't be his last. What happens when the next sensation hits London and you're not his ticket to the Queen any more? How do you think he'll treat you?'

Her stomach lurched; all the digs that she'd made at Evans, and the fury he must be storing up.

'Who'll protect you from Gilmour? Who'll protect you from the families of those taken by your Black Swifts? Or, come to that, if opinion turns against them, who'll protect you from Elizabeth?'

She waited for him to say that *he* would, that he had a plan. But in silhouette he looked slight as a sapling. Tiny, and tired; just a boy.

'The Ghost Theatre,' he said, firmly. 'It's the future. My future, at least.'

He knelt and took Shay's hands in his. 'The thing is, Shay, the stage is the only place where anything makes sense. Out there,' he flung his arms wide, 'is arbitrary. Heroes die and the good suffer.' He stamped his foot on the theatre roof. 'This, here, is where truth lives. Outside everything is dead and nothing can breathe and nothing can grow. Words are stillborn. But here ...'

He stood with one foot thrust forward, like he did for heroic roles, and he spoke to the clouds. 'We are kings.'

He clicked his fingers and a wisp of smoke rose from below; the stage-door lanterns must have been extinguished.

'The real world has nothing for us. Its scenery is flat. The lines are nonsense. The costumes are drab.'

He let out a long sigh.

'Shay, we'll die out there.'

28

T HE NEW YEAR BROUGHT the plague; it and the Ghost Theatre were the only shows in town. The plague opened on Crooked Lane and by the end of the month every second house was boarded over and nearby residents were packing their valuables and shoeing their horses.

The Ghost Theatre countered with a midnight performance atop the London Bridge waterwheel. Nonesuch was chased by men in black leather up to the apex, where he dived, like a kingfisher, into the void below. Afterwards, a gang of prentices torched ships from Buttolphe Wharf to Costumehouse until it looked as if the very river was in flames.

February came and the plague turned Billingsgate into a ghost town. Langbourn, Candlestick, and Dowgate wards fell soon after. A royal trip to Norfolk was surreptitiously brought forward a month and, once Elizabeth was gone, the rich drained from the city as quickly as the poor had. The queues outside Shay's room dwindled until she was lucky to tell two fortunes a day.

The Ghost Theatre gave the plague a run for its money though. In March they set up a mock gallows at Tyburn and charged a penny to hang straw men dressed in any costume you chose. Laughing boys executed lords and slave-owners, politicians and priests. (Nonesuch took all of their pennies for himself, and Alouette, Blank and Shay looked the other way. Who knew where he stayed now – they at least still had roofs over their heads.)

The plague went west and the plague went north, rushing through the poorer streets like floodwater. Each day another theatre or tavern closed. Actors begged on street corners while ale soured in cellars.

With time on her hands, Shay escaped aloft, like a swallow. She stayed on the roofs, ate there, slept there sometimes, only coming down to tell fortunes. Her world was in high places, Nonesuch's was in low ones. He squatted in abandoned plague houses, swathed in smoke and bad ideas.

The pair mostly met on stage now – *oh, who are we supposed to be today?* – and Nonesuch wrote parts for her in which she betrayed him time and time again. Their fights and kisses, their fears and furies, all took place under the gaze of a hundred strangers, with burning buildings as their consummation.

There were only two shows in town. The Ghost Theatre had the drama, but the plague had the numbers. London would fall to one of them.

29

S HAY AND NONESUCH WALKED through Queenhithe streets that were as deserted as country lanes, between houses that faced each other over a sea of mist, and when far-off church bells rang, Shay pictured the buildings as stricken boats adrift. The pair were together at street level for the first time in months – in plague days, no one was chasing them, not when it might mean burning fever and buboes at the armpit, so they could sashay down the centre of Trinity Lane like two gallants at St Paul's. She would never dare say it but Shay found London beautiful in times of plague. She loved the fires that burned on every corner, as mountains of infected clothes and bedding blazed, adding a layer of smoke to the haze. From a distance they were ghostly will-o'-the-wisps, but as you neared you heard them pop as fleas and ticks sizzled and died. The pyres threw handfuls of bright embers up into the air, which fell later as a black snow. Nonesuch guided her across the lane. They were ten steps behind two plague doctors in floor-length black cloaks and beaked metal masks. Nonesuch followed a trail of gruff grey smoke that came from the burning herbs – camphor and cloves, laudanum and rose petals – in their metal beaks. The doctors' cloaks brushed the floor, making them appear to glide over the rutted ground, and Shay and Nonesuch drifted in the wake of the burning petals and the tapping of their canes. Tap *tap* tap *tap* tap *tap*. They looked mythical in the dreamy air.

Bells rang again, miles away. A reminder that in the richer parts of the city life went on as before. But here the only street noise was the posters flapping from nearby plague houses. The richer buildings had signs reading MAY GOD FORGIVE OUR SOULS, while the poorer simply sported a red X, warning enough to give them a wide berth. They passed a threadbare house that had a crude cross daubed a mere foot from the ground and Shay shivered at the thought of how young you would have to be to only reach so high – five, six? A frantic barking came from behind the door and she stopped, torn. Instantly, claws scratched at the door, setting it shaking, but Nonesuch tugged her along. 'Keep up, we're only really safe in the wake of those quacks, you know that.'

She scurried after him, watching her step. Without horses stomping and pissing all day long, the roadway was as hard as cobblestones. Nonesuch said, 'The plague is a great opportunity for you, you know? All the other theatres are closing. The King's Men have gone up north somewhere. The Curtain has plague houses on both sides, so, even if the players turn up, the punters don't. It doesn't matter if London is quiet. The Blackfriars is the only game in town.'

He pulled his blade from its sheath and ran through some moves, carving shapes into the mist. He turned to face Shay with one hand held behind his back. 'They have left London to the brave ...' he touched the knife-tip to his chest and made a bow, 'and the foolish.' In a moment, the blade was at the tip of her throat. She swatted him away.

The plague doctors turned right, snuffed out by the mist, and Shay and Nonesuch turned left. It was like waking from a dream. The west of London was busy still and the mist was starting to burn off. Nonesuch pointed at a cart-man who was nodding sleepily in rhythm with his horses' hoofbeats, and whispered, 'C'mon.' He lifted Shay up onto the rear of the cart and then swivelled up himself. The boards shifted under their weight, but the driver didn't turn. Nonesuch whispered, 'Our own carriage.'

Shay kicked her feet in the air and watched the city rush by like water. Shop tables were piled high with hosiery and vegetables, cold slabs of meat and bolts of fabric. Prentices yawned in doorways, stepping aside for women in headscarves, in ruffs, in sables. Carts thundered while horsemen wove in and out of the slower traffic. Signs creaked in their brackets and buckets were emptied from third-floor windows. It made Shay feel tiny, the sheer weight of it; how could one street contain so much? And this street was only one of hundreds. A mad whirl of men and animals and colours and sound braided until it became some hybrid beast of legend: a thousand-headed monster with a roar that could deafen and plumage that blinded. Shay thrilled with ownership. My city. My people. It all seemed glorious, even the reek and sweat, the slime and stone.

'Wake up, dopey.' Nonesuch prodded her as they neared the junction for the theatre and they jumped off together, the cart-man only now noticing them, but his complaints were lost forever amid London's blood-roar. There were no girls by the stage door. No carriages making deliveries and the cobbles hadn't been washed down. Nonesuch kissed her on the top of her head and said, 'See you later. Don't do anything that I would.'

He was halfway around the corner when Shay called him back. The theatre doorhandles were tied with rope and there was a letter on cream paper nailed above them. It flapped in the wind like the plague posters, but this was written in a dense, curvaceous hand. Shay spied the signature of the Master of the Revels and knew what was coming. Nonesuch read over her shoulder and she told him, 'You shouldn't have tempted fate. We're closing too, apparently. There was outbreak on Creed Lane.'

That was only two streets away. She read on. 'It says indefinitely.'

Her stomach dropped away. She'd relied on prompting and card-reading after losing Lord Eltham's. Now all she was left with was her messenger work and, with half the city quarantined, the competition had grown fierce. Kids half her age were running errands for bread money. A pang of guilt – others had it worse. What could a Blackfriars Boy do in the city without theatre? The pair stood for a while in the entrance with her head resting on Nonesuch's shoulder, unsure of what to do next. And then a voice called from overhead.

'Well, if it isn't the recently unemployed.' A face hung upside down from a window. Greasy swoop of black hair and broken veins: Evans.

He looked at them, unblinking, and the silence lengthened. Then he said, 'Come on up, both of you. I might be able to save you from the poorhouse.'

Only now did Shay realise how run-down the theatre had become in the preceding months. The air was musty and props and costumes lay around in piles. There was none of the air of anticipation that usually overhung the place. As they climbed unlit stairs, Shay watched Nonesuch's face. He wore a look of grim determination.

'Have you spoken to Evans since … that day?' she asked. Nonesuch shook his head. Their footsteps echoed in unison up through the stairwell and there was an outdoor chill to the air. *Tap, tap, tap,* like steps up to a gallows. They found Evans in the attic room where Shay usually did her readings. At some point, the roof had leaked and her woodland scenes had filthy tidemarks halfway up their fabric. Everywhere smelled of the marshes. Evans slouched in the bird-throne and sipped from a flask of brandy. 'So, welcome to the *real* ghost theatre. The audiences are dead, but the rent is real. How's your little troupe? Still passing the hat around like beggar-boys?' He was talking directly to Shay and his eyes never flickered towards Nonesuch.

But it was Nonesuch who replied. 'It's doing better than this place. No one can lock our doors.'

Evans shook his head. 'We'll see. They're closing the taverns and tightening the curfew. Let's see how generous your audiences are when they don't have a drink inside them. And you know the Master of the Revels will be taking a particular interest in your little geese now that he doesn't have me and the others to soak any more. Expect him to be very interested next time you do a show.'

Shay had already worried about that. The Master had had bigger fish to fry than them up until now. She asked him, 'So, what will you do now that the Blackfriars is closed?'

Evans stretched. He smelled of booze and sweat. 'Go to the country and wait the plague out. Shoot some deer and fuck the wife. Or vice versa. More importantly, what are you two going to do?'

He still pointedly only looked at Shay, and she could tell that it emboldened Nonesuch. He stepped in front of Evans and said, 'Why do you care? I thought we weren't of interest to you any more?'

'You're not, but I've had an offer to send the Blackfriars Boys out on tour. There's no plague up north yet and all they have for culture is clowns and puppets. It's possible that a couple of London plays and some actors they've heard of might make a packet.'

Nonesuch feigned indifference, but his unconscious foot-tapping gave him away. 'Well, that's nice for you. I'm sure Trussell and Pavey will be able to handle running a whole troupe.'

Evans laughed. 'Trussell got lost last week picking up costumes from Whitechapel. And Pavey managed to fall off a donkey and break an arm. We're talking about a wooden stage donkey, mind you. I don't think they'd make it half a mile outside the gates before they were robbed or murdered, or both. And anyway, though I hate to say it, we could do with a name to pull in the country crowds.'

Nonesuch preened. 'I do have my admirers outside the city. Some sheath still sends me fresh wood pigeons every week from Kent.'

The look on Evans' face was pure delight. 'Well, that's lovely for you, but I was rather thinking about the Sparrow. She'd be quite a draw up north.'

Shay was barely used to being recognised in London. She kept quiet as Evans spoke.

'It's a bit less sophisticated outside the walls.' He looked at Nonesuch. 'You are going to hate it. But a bird-girl who tells fortunes and speaks in tongues? Maybe. It helps that no one is quite sure what she has in her trousers, and she knows the Queen. Now that might shift a ticket or two.' He laughed again. 'Don't pout, Nonesuch. I'm sure that in the bigger cities they'll want whatever was hot in London. Give them your Lucifer or do the *Chronicles*. But once you get to the deep countryside it's going to be all bird calls and trances.'

He spoke as if it were already decided, and Shay felt the pull of it. All of them together again and no looking over shoulders. She imagined nights sleeping under horse-carts and starlit performances and weeks of Nonesuch bored and well-fed in her arms. Lonan and Birdland would be miles away, making her absence a necessity rather than a choice. She kept her enthusiasm hidden, though.

'Why would we need you?' she asked. 'We can tour on our own. Nonesuch knows whole plays off by heart.'

Evans turned back to her. 'Be my guest. All you need is costumes and scripts for the rest of the players. Oh, and contacts in the theatres. Carriage drivers. Horses. Provisions and water. Maps. Oh, and then there's this.' He produced a piece of paper from inside his jacket. 'The Queen's Warrant. Remember I own you two.' He pushed himself upright. 'Give me ten pounds and it's all yours. You can even keep the profits. I'm not chasing you halfway across the country for a couple of shillings a week.'

Ten pounds was an impossible sum and Shay cursed herself for getting carried away. But Nonesuch didn't hesitate. He reached out a hand and said, 'It's a deal. Give me two days.'

30

THOSE WHO MOVE TO London from elsewhere cling tightest to the city. And the further afield they come from, the fiercer the attraction. Devana had been hatched on some bleak Arctic tundra and she was now the most committed of Londoners, so Shay's heart sang at the sight of the bird's silhouette, hanging above the boat, shadowing her path out towards Birdland. Devana glided disdainfully high, as if keeping the city safe within view, and Shay willed her to descend, desperate for some companionship on this trip. If she'd known that Devana might follow her beyond the city walls, then she would have brought meat. Instead, she chirruped and called to guide the bird down, circuits of long, low ellipses, until she materialised on the prow of the rowing boat, examining the river with distaste.

'I don't have anything for you, girl,' she said. 'Just me.'

Devana stretched her wings against the breeze and went back to staring murderously at the water. Something in the wavelets was spooking her prey senses. Shay risked a glance at those night-sky eyes.

'Nonesuch is performing for Lord Mapesbury tonight, girl.' She stressed the name as if Devana might recognise it. Lord knows everyone else did. Boys crossed themselves at his very mention, and even Evans was grim-faced if he came up in conversation. When Shay had finally admitted to Alouette that she'd spied on the private masque, her only response had been, 'At least it wasn't one of Mapesbury's.'

'Yes, he's performing tonight. And tomorrow we'll have ten pounds.'

Don't connect those two things, she told herself. Was it better to know what Nonesuch would have to do, or not? The question was moot, really; he had been silent as he prepared in the crow's nest, lost somewhere behind his eyes as Blank measured and dressed and painted him. Just the three of them knew where he was going; it was the only way to keep the fee from disappearing into other people's pockets. Once he was dressed and gone, Shay and Blank watched Nonesuch from their eyrie. A small figure disappearing into the maw of the carriage, turned side-on to protect his glistening wings but not looking back. Then Blank set about getting dead drunk, drinking with a kind of dedicated desperation until he passed out on a pile of costumes. It would be better to know, she decided. Anything would be preferable to the images that appeared when she closed her eyes: blood and teeth and huge hands on slender wrists. She was a child afraid of the dark and every shadow became a monster.

She turned her mind back to Devana. 'You're never usually out this late,' she said. 'And it's too dark to hunt, anyway. Will you wait on the boat while I deliver these?' She held up the bag and Devana watched it side-on. 'No meat, sorry. Just sweet things.'

Vast snowbanks of cloud scattered the moonlight above her. The Birdland torches were all gone, rotted to stumps in places, but the ground was firm. She saw no sign of guards and barely a house had a light on; still, she circled the long way around just in case. Their house had been lowered to the floor. That must mean that Lonan couldn't manage the climb any more. Ten small rungs. She closed her eyes against a memory of him carrying her up them, one-handed on the ladder, swinging her, then pretending to drop her, and, just as her stomach lurched, catching her by the wrist.

He was so thin. His hair wild like frosted grass. She hid gifts in places where she thought that he would find them, but visitors to the room might not. A dried apricot tucked into his shoe. A tiny jade dove under his meat-knife. Coins in every crack, candies in every crevice. Back on the boat, she'd told Devana, incurious on the prow, 'He won't know that they're from me, but he will know that someone is thinking of him. Every single day.'

A strand of hair lay across his face and, as she brushed it behind his ear, he stirred. Eyes closed, he shook his head three times – no, no, no – and then reached out a hand. She took it in hers. Fragile as twigs. Let him think she was Ava, what did she care? She stroked a recalcitrant tuft of hair, and he shook his head again. She dredged her mother's voice up from the depths, 'Shh now, darling, back to sleep.' Is that how they spoke to each other, adults? He relaxed, opened blank eyes that searched for something, and then lay back. 'Thank you, mother,' he whispered, and in moments he was asleep again.

Devana had found her way into the nets while Shay was saying good-bye. She was waiting again on the prow but now feathers fluttered in her beak. Blood on her talons and a whole, perfect white wing lying torn off at her feet.

'Oh, girl,' Shay sighed. Red blood, white flesh, the snap of bone and sinew.

Nonesuch.

Act III

31

B ACK WHEN THE BLACKFRIARS Boys were playing *Lucifer in Limehouse*, there was a scene that Shay loved. Nonesuch's Lucifer wrapped his cloak around a flower-girl – a bird under his wing – and in an instant she disappeared. Shay knew it was a stage trick, indeed she had helped prepare the trapdoor, but still the dark grace of it gave her chills. And now London vanished in the same way. One moment they were rattling through the outskirts with the whole troupe hysterical from the constant motion and the hilarious peasants, and then, without warning, the forest wrapped its cloak around the carts and something opened up beneath them.

If Shay had ever imagined the deep woods before, she would have pictured them as fresh and green and ripe with life. But now she discovered that they were a realm of death and rot. The horses' hooves stirred a mulch of black leaves and dead insects and rotten logs that crumbled like embers. What did live there was pale and eyeless: worms writhing towards some hidden home, and sickly mushrooms. Worst of all, no birds. They appeared even more suspicious of this skyless realm than Shay. Time slowed in that mud-thick air, and it made her breathe more shallowly, fearful of invisible tendrils coiling themselves down through her lungs, dissolving into her blood and then sprouting from her city-stained fingertips.

'If you took ten steps off the path, you'd be lost forever,' said Nonesuch, pulling his hood over his head.

For those first weeks, they were a roaming Blackfriars Theatre, with prop carts and tailors and boys with only a couple of lines in a whole play. They played in petty, one-dimensional towns that Southwark could have swallowed whole. When the town gates opened, you could see all the way down the main streets to the back wall. The taverns combined city prices with country food, and the crowds wanted to see last season's London shows (and then complained that they weren't as shocking as they'd been promised). The audiences were creakingly old too; they grumbled and fidgeted and pissed where they stood. The occasional well-born daughter would be allowed to watch, flanked tightly by her parents, as she fumed in some approximation of last year's Venice fashions. The whores, according to the older boys, charged for what you could get for free in London and drew the line at anything worth paying for.

One joy broke the boredom though. On a south-coast ride they hit open farmland where the tracks were little more than flattened grass and Shay saw prey-birds gather. They used the carts the way hunters used beaters: to flush prey out into the open. The cartwheels thundered and Shay saw a bird, high above, peel off, tuck in its wings and fall. It was down in a finger-click and it took a vole one-clawed. *Snap* and it was away in a single propulsive arch of wings. And then the falcon casually tossed the prey out in front of it. Even at a distance, Shay saw the creature's writhing, its final convulsive seconds in this strange airborne world before the beak came down like a curtain and the drama was done. She knew that bird; it was Devana. Her homesickness vanished. Devana *was* London to her: its style and violence, and all the time the bird watched over her, Shay felt as carelessly safe as she had in her childhood bed.

That night, before they made camp, Shay bought a rabbit from a passing poacher. It cost a day's profit but there was nothing else to spend it on out here. She staked the body on the roof of the cart and when she woke in the morning it was gone.

Dover, Winchester, Bath. In and out like locusts for one performance per town; after that the place was sucked dry and they wouldn't be able to return. Days of rain and nights of stars, as the shows got smaller and the taverns got worse. Once they'd exhausted the bigger towns, the troupe began to shed its Blackfriars skin. They left useless props and mouldering costumes by the roadside, sold the carts, sold the swords. Boys seeped away too, lost to uncomplicated country girls and farm work. Gone like ghosts, the only sign they'd been there a pair of boots by a rooming-house door or one horse unsaddled in the stables. Soon they became the Ghost Theatre again in all but name. Shay, Nonesuch, Alouette, Blank, Trussell and a couple of the more determinedly urban boys who huddled at the dead centre of their campsites and asked every day for news of the plague's retreat.

Nonesuch wrote, rehearsed and discarded whole plays while lolling on horseback. Love scenes in the saddle and one-handed sword fights. Not that they needed new plays. Most nights he veered from the scripts the moment he was bored, and in the country he was always bored. He started what was supposed to be a version of *Abelard and Heloise* with the words, 'Yesterday I awoke to discover I had become a bird ...' In these moods only Trussell would try to keep up with him and Nonesuch dragged him through labyrinthine two-handers with tales growing taller and taller. The crowd roared at their bird impressions and nonsense stories.

In a muddy village on the road to Oswestry, Nonesuch extemporised a whole play out of thin air. Two pairs of lovers were transformed by love potions. Shay and Trussell and Blank and Alouette were coupled and parted, entwined and divided in every conceivable pairing. Dandelion seeds in their hair, grass stains on their knees. Shay was washed away by the drama's liquid logic and the words moved her like a chess piece from body to body and mouth to mouth. Trussell's tongue in her ear and Alouette's hand on her breast. Afterwards, she and Nonesuch lay alone in their tent as if it had happened to someone else.

Wild as birds, the troupe criss-crossed an England alive with rumours. They weren't the only wanderers, it seemed. The signs of Elizabeth's Black Swifts were everywhere. Gibbets so fresh that their wood was still green and sappy hung with corpses that flapped like flags under the onslaught of crows. And there were other, less explicable traces too. Twice they came across burning enclosures where smouldering fences cast a battleground pall for miles. The second was crowned with a tattered banner that read: NO MASTERS, NO FENCES, NO REST.

'What does it mean?' Shay asked everyone. But the boys had no idea and the locals scuttled away at the question. The burning places scared Shay. She'd proudly learnt London's code and knew in her bones where was safe and where was dangerous; where she would be invisible and where she stood out; and where a girl, however well disguised, should never walk alone. But here danger struck as randomly as lightning.

England's interior was a wild, landmarkless place, as arbitrary as the marshes, and liable to burst into flame without warning.

Summer slouched into autumn. Dead skies opened up above them and the tips of things turned brown like burnt paper. Birds prepared for the winter assiduously, making Shay fret about the weeks to come. Devana followed often but visited rarely. She flitted in on wings of snow with her beak blood-black in the moonlight and took Shay's pitiful offerings with a sniff.

They climbed the ladder of England, mimicking winter's slow arrival as the land turned grey and bare and hard. The towns now were on no map and had no name. Hamlets. Villages. Encampments. Now the company acted without props or staging. A length of rope was enough to divide actors and audience. Swords were cardboard and crowns were fashioned from leaves. Everything was conveyed by the body. Here, they loved Trussell's pratfalls, both inadvertent and deliberate. They watched Nonesuch in a dazed silence and Shay could never tell whether it bespoke scorn or awe.

Brecknock was nothing more than a ring of houses that cowered from the surrounding forest where the troupe ate acorn stew for dinner and shooed sheep from their stage-to-be. Nonesuch, awake before show time for once, spent an hour with the village children and Shay watched him squat and chat and ruffle hair. Once he was done, the children left in twos and threes, whispering happily to each other. She knew better than to ask what he was planning but something was afoot. With only minutes to go until show time, he pulled her aside. 'Do you know "Every Lost Lamb?"' he asked.

She nodded. A lullaby: everyone knew it. 'What's my cue?' she asked. 'You'll know when.'

No costume or props. Nonesuch squatted on the wet grass and said, 'I lived near here once. Maybe five miles away. I can't remember the village's name, it may have been too poor to have one.' Someone in the front row laughed. 'I didn't live there for long. Three months, maybe. Enough to yearn for the excitement of Brecknock, anyway.' More laughter.

'My father was a sin-eater,' he said, and a man near the back crossed himself, 'but times were slow. There weren't enough sinners dying in Brecknock. My childhood hunger was your fault. You Welsh are too clean-living to keep a sin-eater in the manner to which he'd become accustomed. "If only he was a London sin-eater," I used to think. "Then his belly would be full of murders and mine would be full of meat.'" He got another easy laugh for that.

'So, no sins, and of course we had no land. So we foraged.' Noises of sympathy came from the crowd. 'One day we were picking mushrooms. Well, I was picking mushrooms. My parents lasted about a quarter-hour before the tavern called. The best spots had already been picked clean because my parents weren't ones for early starts, so I had to go a little deeper into the forest.'

He leaned forward. 'You all know how it swallows you up, out there. Even ten yards from the edge of the forest you're in another world, like Jonah in the whale. Mushrooms prefer the damp and the dark, so that's where I started. Looking for the black and sodden places, anywhere that you would usually avoid. I was just a little boy, y'know? In those cloth shoes with no heels that get wet through in a minute. But I had a good sense for where you might find mushrooms, it was a kind of gift.' His voice thinned. 'Dappled light on wet leaves, the smell of rot and the drip of water. Listen and look, and there they would be.' As he talked, his hands made shapes in the air.

Shay was there. She saw ragged white phalluses pushing aside a carpet of leaves.

'I picked hundreds. My basket was so full that I needed both hands to carry it.' His voice was now boyishly high, spiced with a pinch of pride. 'And then, of course, I looked up and I was lost. Hours had passed and I was deep in the forest, all alone.'

A child in the crowd gasped and the vision in Shay's mind darkened. Now the treetops rose into a night sky and the undergrowth crowded around her. No air and no birds.

'At first, I tried to retrace my steps but God knows where I'd come from. I shouted and cried.' He crossed his hands over his chest now, like a child in his bed. 'I knew that the sensible thing to do was to wait, but …' His voice was tiny now. 'I didn't think anyone would come to look for me.'

Involuntarily, Shay looked up to see if Devana was there. Nonesuch said, 'So, I walked in as straight a line as I could manage.' He raised his hand into the air as a signpost. 'Straight as an arrow and everything rotting and crumbling beneath my feet.'

The girl in the front row said, 'So, what happened?'

He took her hand. 'Oh, they came and found me eventually. I wasn't even that far from the village.' He gave her hand a squeeze. 'Even then, I was six, maybe seven, I was so surprised that they bothered looking for me.'

His laugh was a harsh punctuation. 'They probably needed the basket back.' When he started talking again, it was in a voice that Shay hadn't heard from him before. It was flat and featureless: a fen of a voice. 'I sometimes think that boy is still walking. Beneath those ancient trees. In the minutes before sleep, or straight after a show, or in the back of a boat, I see him. Deep in the forest and deeper with every step. But this time no one is coming to get him.'

He cleared his mouth and started to sing. 'Every lost lamb will find a path ...'

Shay joined in on the second line. An octave up with some space between them. It was one of those shallow melodies that rose and fell in easy intervals, worn like the dip in old stairs. Their voices followed each other but never met. She saw the pair of them running across the rooftops on that first day. Then a cry went up from the crowd.

The children of the village stepped out of the forest from every direction, each with a basket of mushrooms, each singing. At first their songs were separate, in different keys and different rhythms, but as the circle tightened they came together into one voice. One joyous voice singing 'Every Lost Lamb' until they collapsed, proud and giggling, onto the stage. They smothered Nonesuch under a mountain of laughter, and the song faded to rags, and then all Shay could hear was the noise of the hat jangling with coin after coin after coin.

That evening, in the tent, Shay straddled and pinned him. 'How much of that was true? Did you really live here?'

He tried to push her off and failed. His face was a blank piece of paper. 'I don't know. Probably. It all looks the same here.'

She couldn't see his eyes in the dark. Her hands gripped his wrists. Her lips on his brow.

She said, 'If you are ever lost again, I will find you. I will search and I will never stop looking for you.'

32

THE NEXT DAY, THEY lost the last Blackfriars Boy. Pavey had met a girl in Hereford and then pined all the way through Wales, so none of them were surprised to wake to find one tent with its sides open and a note fluttering on the front. Pavey could read well enough, but he couldn't write, so he'd pinned a battered page from a script to the canvas. It read: 'Jezebel exits stage right – night falls.'

So they were five again: Alouette, Blank, Nonesuch, Shay and Trussell, the Ghost Theatre on horseback. That day they rode for hours without seeing a soul, but fresh signs of devastation preceded them everywhere they went. The roads were fringed with blackened, smouldering stumps where mile upon mile of hawthorn hedge had been set alight. Shay's arms ached from holding the reins tight – the horses shied at the smoke and the crackling of embers. At a bleak country crossroads a teetering bonfire churned with smoke and turned the sky to dusk. The troupe rode warily past smoking fenceposts that were piled head-high. In the valley beyond, livestock had been set free and a herd of cows sat unmoving across the road until Alouette scared them off with a firecracker.

They came to a village green that had been scythed as short as a beard. Smoke rose from the east. The five sprawled around a cook-pot with just wood pigeon calls and river burble to break their various silences. It was enough, though, thought Shay, it was more than enough. She lay in Alouette's lap and let her braid dandelions into her hair. Scritch of nails like a cat grooming.

'You know that gibbet we passed a couple of miles back? Do you think we could drag it here?' A low moan came from the others; this was one of Nonesuch's *ideas*. Only Alouette took the bait.

'I don't see why not. Borrow an ox-cart. Two men to tip it on its side. The lane was fairly wide. What's the plan?'

Nonesuch stood. 'Me, centre stage …'

('What a surprise,' whispered Trussell).

'With my neck in a noose.' He mimed it, cocking his head to one side. 'A hangman next to me.'

Trussell raised a hand. 'Respectfully, I'd very much like to volunteer for that role.' He brushed grass from his hair and put on a country accent. 'Less mouth, more neck, sonny.'

Nonesuch waved him away. 'It's got to look realistic, so I'd rather not have the clumsiest man I know holding the other end of the rope. Alouette can do it.'

He wheeled around, facing Trussell like a boxer. 'I've been arrested for …'

'Sedition?' said Blank.

'Sumptuary?' suggested Alouette.

'Sodomy,' said Trussell.

Nonesuch rolled his eyes.

'Stealing cattle?' said Shay.

'Stealing cattle, thank you, Shay.' He blew her a kiss.

Blank propped himself up on his elbows. 'I see it. The audience is a jury.'

'Yes, yes.' Nonesuch was almost dancing now.

Trussell circled him, saying, 'I produce evidence: witnesses, blood-stains, cuts of meat.'

Nonesuch raised an invisible sword. 'I parry. My good name, my unblemished character.'

They all scoffed at that. Alouette said, 'I'll be a local – that way I can sow doubt. There have been thieves in the area. Strange tribes are afoot.'

Trussell raised his hand. 'I tighten the noose; just enough breath for one last speech.'

Nonesuch bowed. 'In which I plead my innocence for the final time. I beg and entreat, even through the tightening rope. When I convince them of my innocence, the audience carry me out of there on their shoulders.'

'Only if you convince,' said Trussell. 'What if *I* win?' He watched Nonesuch dance around the fire.

Nonesuch threw himself back onto the ground. 'Trussell, the day I can't sway a crowd of ignorant peasants is the day you can hang me for real.'

The silence rushed back to cover them. Shay dozed. Alouette read. Trussell drew. It was Nonesuch who broke the spell again.

'Where *is* everyone?' It was already past four bells and usually by now village children would be milling around, but there was no sound bar the birds.

Nonesuch took Trussell's pencil from him and gave him a handful of coins. 'Go into the village. Buy an ale or two and show off the quality of your costume. Tell them that the Sparrow will be singing as well.'

Shay hid a smile. The further they rode from London, the more of a draw she became. North of Oxford, the audiences didn't care about the plays that had made the Blackfriars Boys' name, but a soothsaying half-girl, half-bird was worth a penny or two. Nonesuch had resisted at first. She hadn't even been mentioned on the original playbills, but as the weather turned and the trees thinned her name appeared, then rose, and then topped the page. *Sparrow, that's the Sparrow, she advises the Queen:* that's what she heard when she climbed on stage. But she was content to play the parts Nonesuch created for her and be gawped at – only now did she realise how much the weeks of fortune-telling had drained her. Now she sang only when she wanted, and the trances felt more gift than burden.

An hour of nothing and then Trussell was back, wet-mouthed and smelling of ale. He said, 'They've all gone to Cockaigne.' Crumbs clung to his jacket.

'The magical city of Cockaigne?' The icing of scorn on Nonesuch's voice was the one that he reserved for the most rural of beliefs. 'It's supposed to be in Europe somewhere, isn't it? If there really were a city of endless treasure on the outskirts of Ulverton, then I think we might have heard of it.' He stared around, as if daring the city to materialise in front of them.

Trussell sighed. 'Obviously I know it's a myth, I'm just telling you what they told me. Cockaigne rises for one night only.' He put on his yokel accent again. 'I'd rather see a city of wonders than a bunch of Londoners in dresses.' He scratched himself. 'Anyway, they're not coming, not a single one of them.'

Cockaigne: Shay had heard the name, but no picture came to mind. Alouette would know, though. The shows out here in the sticks had no need for props and Alouette was relegated to a supporting player.

She spent her days collecting specimens: poisonous mushrooms that would kill in less time than it took to draw breath; herbs to stoke ardour, or to quell it; animal blood that made the drinker invincible. In Bury she finally found a source of Dee's foxfire, those glowing mushrooms that grew on rotting wood. Now, when she rode, her saddlebags clinked with the bottles of the luminous liquid that she painstakingly distilled over campfires every night. In Herefordshire the troupe had come across the remnants of a massacre; men's skeletons lay where they'd fallen, not long stripped of flesh by the crows. Most of the players averted their eyes, but Alouette dived in, scraping any shred of moss that had grown on the skulls. It cost her a crown – an enormous sum – to send the skull-moss back to Doctor Dee by horse messenger, but three days later a rider appeared with two guineas and a sealed letter for her.

Shay found her lying on her bedroll, surrounded by jars and boxes. She scowled when she heard what Shay had come to ask. 'Cockaigne? It's a children's story. Hang on.' She took a book from the chest and read. '"In the city of Cockaigne, roast pigs carve slices from their own backs for you to eat, and grilled rabbits leap happily into your mouth. The rivers are made of wine, the sun always shines and legs are …"' she snapped the book closed '… always open.'

Shay laughed. 'Well, get your best dress on – we're visiting it tonight.'

You could see it from miles away. High golden walls shimmered in the night air, and as the troupe grew closer, the glimmer resolved into the shape of a fiery castle. It rose from the hilltop, haloed with blazing torches that threw the surrounding fields into darkness. A relentless one-*two*-three, one-*two*-three drumbeat drew a stream of villagers up a torchlit path. The troupe mixed in with the throng, swept up by the carnival atmosphere. The queue ran hundreds of yards down the slope – a slap in the face after the Ghost Theatre's thinning audiences.

Nonesuch squinted at the end of the line, far enough down the hill that the lights of Cockaigne hardly reached it.

'Fuck this for a game of soldiers. Come on.' He set his face at its most contemptuous. At the entrance, two sweating drummers, stripped to the waist, worked feverishly as lads took pennies from the newcomers. Nonesuch walked past them and made for a figure in the shadows. The man was tall, maybe six foot, in muddy hose and shirt that would have shamed a farmer, but he wore silver at his ears and neck, great shining lumps of it.

Nonesuch said, 'We're the Ghost Theatre. Touring from London. We thought we'd take a look at your show.'

The man moved his stool round into the light but said nothing.

'I'm Lord Nonesuch.' He held out a hand and the man engulfed it in his own. Dirt under his nails, dirt in the creases.

A slow voice, riverine. 'Jagger. The Jagger.'

'It's quite a stage set you have here. Do you erect it every night?'

The man sighed. 'There's a queue.'

'I'm aware of that. I was hoping that, as fellow showmen ...'

'Fellow showmen. From London.' He considered it and then called over to the lads on the gate. 'These five? Charge them double.' He looked back at Nonesuch. 'And there's still a queue.'

Nonesuch's hand went to his blade and Shay was ready to pull him back, but Trussell stepped between them. He said, 'We have the Sparrow with us too.'

The Jagger tilted his head and pulled a torch from the wall. Shay drew back from its heat as he examined her. 'So, the rumours are true. People have been asking after you, offering money. Saying the Queen would like you back in your nest.' He brought the torch closer. 'You really a flapper, girl? Or maybe you take country folk for halfwits?'

She removed her cap and rifled her hand through her hair to show hints of her tattoo and The Jagger laughed. 'All right, then. You four can go in for free, right now. His Lordship still pays double.' He executed a mock bow to Nonesuch and retreated back into the shadows.

Inside was a golden maze. Crowds sang and shouted and churned the mud underfoot. The troupe wandered, part of the crowd, buoyed by the laughter and noise. An alehouse sported eight identical barrels as big as horse-carts, and it was so busy that the taps were jammed open, barmen dipping tankards under the flow. Serving maids walked by with steaming meat on trays and passers-by took what they wanted.

'It's just a set. And not a particularly good one, at that,' said Nonesuch, and he was right – up close it looked tawdry in its simplicity. The walls were wooden board, not even a hand thick, covered in a rough, reflective paper that tossed the torchlight in a hundred directions. But he had gasped along with the rest of them when they'd first seen the lambent city and the crowds were as wild and numerous as those at any London fair. Every golden wall was punctuated with a series of open hatches and people queued up to see whatever was hidden inside. Shay found an unoccupied slot and poked her head through. Dim lights illuminated a figure lying in a rope circle. Something white, with the body of a horse, but a man's torso and head, which stretched and yawned and talked into the gloom. She tugged at Nonesuch's arm and made him look too. He laughed. 'See how *he* moves but the body doesn't? I can't say that I'd like to spend my evenings waist deep in half a dead horse, but it's a living, I suppose.'

Back into the fray. Tents of soothsayers and boxers, fire-breathers lighting up the night and living statues on every corner. A tightrope transected the main square and two tumblers endlessly cartwheeled and leapt past each other overhead. They were close enough that Shay could see their minute feet adjustments and feel the beads of falling sweat.

Everything was free. Children picked the whitest meat from chicken legs and discarded the rest in the dirt while adults poured brandy into their ale and swallowed the lot in hungry draughts. You couldn't go ten steps without a leaflet being pushed into your hand. Some were for shows – SEE THE MERMAN DIVE or THE ROOM THAT RAINS WINE – but others were political tracts. While Shay and Trussell ran wild like children, stuffing themselves with pig trotters and playing quoits, Alouette sat and read to herself.

'They're Commoners,' she said, when Shay had to rest. 'Remember the burnt hedges and fences that we've been seeing? That was their work. They tear down the enclosures and return the land to the commons.'

Through a mouthful of food, Trussell said, 'So, they are good people, right? They're supporting the peasantry.' His cheeks were wet with fat.

Alouette shook her head. 'Good people? Probably. Criminals, certainly.'

A drumbeat started up and Trussell pulled the others towards the noise. They turned a corner into another golden square where girls in milkmaid costumes toted pails of ale that they tipped into any upturned mouth. Again, hatches were cut into the walls. Shay watched each and every one of them. At first Nonesuch explained and demystified – he showed her how the gypsy fortune-teller might have known about Trussell's errant father, he claimed that the tame lion was, in reality, a shaved mastiff – but after a while, the sheer weight of spectacle silenced even him. They walked and walked, and he took it all in with magpie eyes. By eight bells, he wore the same look that he had when he and Shay browsed in the Royal Exchange: hunger and scorn combined.

They sat for a while by a huge bonfire, which was Cockaigne's bullseye. Overhead, a banner with the slogan NO FENCES – NO LANDLORDS – NO REST was buffeted by the waves of heat. Children played, running, laughing, in and out of the fire's warmth. Over and over they returned to a stall holding shelves of corn dollies, all dressed in London fashions, ready to be thrown onto the pyre. It made Shay shiver: the children's destructive glee and the sizzle of lace and cotton.

'How do they afford it all?' she asked. She was crushed by the weight of people and the heat and noise. 'I know the crowds are big but it was only pennies to get in.'

Nonesuch had obviously been thinking the same thing. 'I'm sure they take a cut on the gambling. And, maybe—' He grabbed Shay's arm. 'Look.'

The lad was still a child, with a busy, haunted face and hair tied back like the other Cockaigne employees. He talked to himself as he slipped between revellers and, as Shay watched, his hand dipped quickly, like a cat's tongue, into pockets and bags. One step, a pocket; another step, another pocket. Shay admired the sheer artistry; it was beautifully done. They watched the boy's path through the crowd and when he drew close Nonesuch turned to face Shay. 'Talk to me for a moment and don't look at the boy.' He put his hands on his hips so that his jacket pocket gaped open. Shay babbled and kept her eyes on Nonesuch's face. One second longer and it would have been too late. The boy was alongside them for the briefest of moments. Nonesuch thrust his hand backwards and caught the boy at the elbow. The boy ducked and twisted, but Nonesuch spun around and grabbed his other arm too.

'It's not really the done thing to rob the punters, you know.' Nonesuch used his stage voice, loud enough to interest the people around them. 'It's frowned upon by the better sort. The worse sort too, really.' The boy looked blandly at him and then whistled, two short notes. Nothing. He kept his eyes on the ground as Nonesuch held him tight. Then the crowd parted and The Jagger was pushing through. He took in the scene: Nonesuch's white knuckles and the crowd's expectant faces. He turned to them.

'Ladies and gentlemen.' He had the kind of voice that demanded silence. 'If you would all check your pockets, you will find that some of you have been blessed.'

Heads went down and then laughter rippled through the crowd. One by one, hands reached for the sky, many of them grasping gold coins.

Now The Jagger laughed too. 'They're Spanish half-angels, liberated from a shipwreck and redistributed to you good people by my boy here.' The lad gave a curt nod. 'See, we have riches within us that we don't yet know. London takes your pounds and spends them on palaces, we take your pennies and we give you the world. Remember that when their tax men come.' He tossed a handful of the gold coins into the crowd. 'Spend them how you see fit.' As a cheer went up, he removed Nonesuch's hand from the boy's elbow and leant in closely. His words were meant for Nonesuch, but he looked at Shay as he spoke.

'Not all shows are the same, little one.'

Nonesuch was quieter after that. They walked, dazed and drunk as the night wound down around them. The ground was a quagmire of ale and bones and trodden-in pamphlets, and already the braver rats darted out of corners to eat. Men staggered and were dragged through the mud; girls and boys disappeared into the darker corners. Blank left them, saying he'd seen enough, and Nonesuch disappeared soon after; one moment he was there, the next he was gone. So Shay and Trussell and Alouette walked, watching performances in silence and groaning with belly-ache; Shay hadn't eaten so much in years. In a muddied square, two men wrestled in a raised ring. One wore gentlemanly silks, the other a farmhand's smock. The crowd booed the gentleman mercilessly and cheered every blow the yokel landed. Trussell watched for a while and then said, 'I thought Blank had left?'

A familiar tricorne hat and a broad back in naval blue. He was watching some unseen show through a hatch. Shay tugged at his sleeve and said, 'Why are you still here?'

He pulled his head back. He was wide-eyed. 'I stopped for a moment to see this. Look.'

Shay and Alouette took the hatches either side of him. A tank of water, stained blue by stage lanterns, stood upon a platform. A wooden frame towered overhead and men with slicked-back hair worked on it.

Shay whispered, 'What are we looking at?' and Blank said, 'Wait, they're about to start it up again.'

The lights dimmed and the men carried something behind the tank. It was heavy enough that their progress up the wooden ladder was slow, and Shay heard the strain in their 'One, two, three, go!'

A triangle of turquoise like a falcon's tail was lowered into the water. It was followed by a curve of iridescent scales the same oily blue-black as a peacock's feathers. The tail beat once and then the torso was submerged too. A broad back, human, crosshatched with scars and muscles, like an acrobat's. The merman's neck was fringed with three slits on either side, which fluttered in the water. And finally, a head of curly black hair.

'I know him.'

Shay had to pull back to watch Blank's face. He was rapt with attention. The merman floated upright in the blue and blinked. Shay fancied she could see thin strings at his armpits holding him in place, but he looked so real. He beat a slow rhythm and then somersaulted with his tail caressing the glass. A fat bubble of air escaped his mouth. The men touched a torch to the surface of the water, and it erupted in flame. People gasped from every corner of the show.

Alouette whispered, 'The water is burning. It's Greek fire. Dee would die if he saw this.'

But Shay didn't care about the fire; she couldn't take her eyes off the merman. 'Who is he?' she asked.

Blank grabbed Shay's hand. 'His name is Malik. I dived with him many times. He's from my island but I thought he died years ago.'

'Is he real?'

'Of course he is.' Blank shook his head. 'Oh. You mean does he really have a tail and gills. No, of course not.'

The merman hung in the blue, hardly blinking, his tail like a watch hand.

'It's beautiful.' Shay felt the time weigh on her. Another bubble of air escaped his lips as he tumbled in place. She forced herself to breathe. 'How long can he stay in the water?'

'Three minutes maybe. This is already longer than I ever managed.'

Shay breathed hard, willing her breath into his lungs. Her chest hurt at the idea of it. The merman twirled, a curl of smoke, and his shoulder blades came together like wings. He sank towards the bottom of the tank. Above him the flames raged noisily.

Shay ached all over. 'Let him out. It's too long.'

He spun so that he could be seen from every side. The flames grasped for the sky above and then, without warning, a blanket was thrown over the top and the scene descended back into night. There was a collective exhalation of breath. Shay realised how many hatches there were and how many people had been watching. She slumped as if she was beached. 'That was too much.'

Shay had never seen Blank ruffled before. He ran along the wooden perimeter, searching for a way through to the tank. 'Come on, we have to get backstage.' Nonesuch was still nowhere to be seen but Shay didn't dare leave Blank in this state. The warren of streets had no obvious exits so the four of them circled the walls looking for ways through to the stages. It was Trussell who spotted a Commoner pressing on a patch of bare board which slid aside to let him through. They waited a moment and then followed. A hole in the wood, barely finger-width, had a taut string hung behind it. Blank hooked his thumb around it, pulled, and the whole panel revolved open. Alouette nodded in appreciation. 'Oh, that's nicely made.'

Inside was like coming home. The plain backs of wooden scenery and the smell of sawdust and paint were so familiar. Midgets and fire-breathers rushed by, stage-hands and barmaids dragged their stalls behind them. Blank stopped a small boy to ask after the merman and the boy sighed and gently took his hand, leading the four of them deeper into the camp, to a tent pitched against the blank backs of the castle walls. A tent in a camp, in the midst of a giant wooden castle, in the middle of nowhere. The room was wide and obviously home to many performers. It smelled of camphor and damp.

The merman lay starfished on a tiny wooden cot with his tail lying still beside him. It curled like a comma on the table as a girl rubbed linseed oil into the scales. It had the exact same sheen as peacock feathers. But Blank only had eyes for the merman. He crouched alongside him so that their faces were inches from each other and for a moment Shay thought that all he had come to do was watch that face, childlike with exhaustion, but then he placed a hand on Malik's shoulder and whispered, '*Réveille*.' The word shook him awake instantly. He sat up, eyes wide, breathing like he'd just finished a race.

He and Blank embraced for a long time, not speaking, leaning into each other like they might fall. Now Blank sat across the tent from him, watching in wonder. The merman whole and talking, far more of a miracle than his act had been. His voice was slow, like Blank's, picking out words like dry spaces on the marsh.

'I was diving in Scotland in a lake. Or is it loch? It was reputedly the hiding place for some treasure, stashed in some cave ten yards underwater. We wore suits of whale skin and blubber under ice as thick as your arm. It was hard work but the pay was good. But one morning I arrived at the berth and the foremen had disappeared with all the equipment and all the money. Three years. I walked south, begging on the way. Sometimes in the northern villages they'd pay a penny to touch my hair.' He ran his fingers through tight curls.

'I came across Cockaigne at Carlisle. They were rebels then, purely political folk.' He shuddered and water dripped down his torso. 'They toured from town to town, fomenting rebellion. Anti the Queen, anti the Lords, anti the Church. Not many of them. The Jagger and a few others. Serious men. Dour men. They asked me to join them, but I told them there were already enough reasons for people to hate me.'

Blank nodded at that. He turned the tail over and stroked the oil against the grain. Scales rose in little rainbow peaks.

'He came back six months later. Same stool, same brandy, and he told me, "I've given up telling people about a better world. I'm going to show them instead."'

Malik looked around the tent. It was small but comfortable. 'When I got here, the tank was already made and the costume was at the tailor's. Cockaigne gets what Cockaigne wants. Every penny we make is shared, equally. The privy builders make the same as The Jagger.'

Shay hadn't spoken until now. 'But what *is* it?'

'It's Cockaigne. The land of milk and honey.'

'But is it a show? Or a rebellion? Are the acts here to recruit Commoners? Or are the Commoners here to protect the show?'

Malik considered it. 'I'm not sure even they know that any more. Even if they ever did. It's more like a wildfire than anything man-made – it goes its own way.'

From outside came noises that Shay knew well. Rumble of scenery and jangle of coins and everywhere the voices of working men, quarrelsome and sarcastic. The city was being packed down and they were still miles from home. Reluctantly she gestured to Blank that it was time to go.

'Stay.'

They were already halfway out of the door. Cockaigne was now just wooden panels on the back of horse-carts. Malik was up on his feet, tense as a boxer. 'All of you, stay.'

They waited in the doorway.

'Blank, you could work with me. I can only do three shows a night, together we could do six and there are always parts for actors.'

He gestured to Trussell. 'We know of the Blackfriars Boys here. Our paths almost crossed plenty of times. You and Nonesuch would have much to do.' He bowed to Alouette. 'And we have money for effects. Greek fire too. Anyway, The Jagger would take every one of your troupe, just to get the Sparrow.' The way they turned to face her, the three of them, made her heart sink.

Shay blanched. 'He knows my act?'

'Of course. Word gets around. Not as quickly as in the city but fast enough. The Jagger speaks of you often. He saw you in Bellbrooke.'

Bellbrooke: a half-forgotten hamlet, not even on the map. They'd put on an impromptu show on a patch of wet grass and she'd tranced deep, waking up with feet stained black from inkcap mushrooms.

'We share the money. No one has top billing. We're all peasants, we're all kings. We eat well, drink well.'

Leftover food covered the table in front of them. Chicken legs with plenty of meat left on them, grapes fat as eggs. But Alouette turned back to leave. 'We're only in the country temporarily. Until London is safe again.'

Malik nodded. 'Then why not make it temporary here? You see our crowds.'

'We're already our own masters.' Alouette wouldn't step back into the tent. 'Where are you going to be tomorrow?'

'No idea. We'll ride for the night, sleep for the morning, play in the evening.'

Alouette threw the words over her shoulder. 'You're not kings. You're livestock.'

They found Nonesuch sitting in the shadows at the wreckage of the entrance. His foot tapped as if there was music playing. 'Where did you go? I've been *exploring*. I take it all back. This place is extraordinary.' Stragglers stumbled down the hill in darkness. The torches had burned down and the path hung with smoke.

'Did you see the Greek fire?' Alouette had the same breathlessness that stage girls did when Nonesuch stopped to talk. 'I watched them set a tank of water ablaze.'

Nonesuch grinned. 'Oh, I did better than see it.' He pulled a quiver of arrows out of the shadows. They had an odd, gritty texture near the tip, and they smelt somehow of marsh gas.

'You didn't? How?' asked Alouette.

He touched the side of his nose. 'Wait, watch.' He notched an arrow and pulled back the bowstring. Then he dipped the arrowhead into a torch's flame. He waited until it sparked and then fired a long arc into the air. It rose, fizzing and spitting and spiralling, and then burst into a bright white flower that dripped light as it fell.

Alouette whispered, 'Oh *yes.*' As it landed it continued to burn, even as it spat on the wet ground. She grunted with satisfaction. 'Don't waste another one. Save them. If I can work out how they're made, then Dee will sweat money for us.'

She went to take them from him, but he wagged a finger. 'Get your own.'

The horses stepped gingerly in the darkness. Shay could only see Nonesuch's outline ahead of her but his voice sparkled with pleasure. 'That's what we could have been doing all this time.' His fingers were black with soot and he smelt of destruction. 'They're reshaping the whole countryside. Did you see the children? I've never seen glee like that at one of our shows.' He couldn't stay still. Time and again he dug his spurs into his horse's sides as he made a point and each time he leapt on ahead. He swiped at moths with his sword. Alouette was just as excited as he was. She was one pace behind Shay. 'Greek fire,' she said. 'Liquid flames. Do you know what it means?'

Shay didn't.

'It's … it's …' Shay had never heard her lost for words before. 'It's some fabled mixture that the Byzantines used. They could fire jets of fire from hoses on their boats. They could bottle it in grenades. Arrows dipped in the mixture would burn for hours.'

She and Nonesuch shook their heads in unison. 'Those are some clever, clever yokels.'

Riding at night always made Shay feel guilty, like she'd missed curfew and The Watch might stop here any moment. They rode slowly through invisible lanes, in and out of coppices. Warm air and the faintest of moonlight. Nonesuch and Alouette talked over each other, spurring their horses on and then pulling up.

'Set fire to the Thames and then race boats through the flames.'

'String high-wires from St Paul's and stage sword fights in the sky.'

'The Ghost Theatre written in light across the clouds.'

They trotted down an avenue of trees that leant, tenderly, towards one another. It had the feel of the arched ceiling at St Paul's. Shay smelled moonflower and, from somewhere, the scent of tobacco. Nonesuch swiped at moths with his sword. 'Take that, you feathery bastard.' For the hundredth time he slowed to let them catch up. 'Imagine that show in London. Imagine the *fear*. We've been wasting our time!' He took an arrow from his quiver and notched it to his bow. 'Fuck.' He touched the wick to his torch, and it caught instantly. Alouette barely had enough time to say, 'For God's sake, Nonesuch, don't spook the horses,' before the rocket erupted in a shower of brilliant white and shot skywards in a crazy spiral. Light like it was day. And, for the briefest moment, framed in black in front of them, three men on horseback with swords drawn.

Blank reacted first. 'Don't make a sound. Just turn around. Quietly.'

Trussell had been looking the other way. 'What? Why?'

'Tell you later. Do as I say. Quickly.'

Shay wheeled her horse around. Her eyes still hadn't adjusted from the flare, so she judged the distance by sound. The soft clop of hooves and no talking. They made it ten yards before Nonesuch reached out and laid an arm across her chest. 'Wait. I hear more men this way.' They stood for a moment and the oblivious horses started to nibble at the grass. Backstage voices. 'Where now?'

'Off the path?'

'It's wild back there. If we go that way, then a horse might break a leg.'

There was a noise, close. A scratch of flint and sudden torchlight. A face was mere inches from hers. The man was low-browed with tied-back hair, and he said, 'Worse still. *You* might break your neck.'

She reared back and torches lit around her. Four men with lanterns and swords. Ponytails and a contented air. The furthest forward spoke. 'We would like a word with the Sparrow here.' His horse pawed at the ground and Shay sensed, rather than saw, other men behind her.

'Go ahead,' she said.

'In private, if you don't mind.'

Alouette pulled her horse in front of Shay's. 'She's going nowhere with you. Come to the show tomorrow. Buy a fucking ticket.'

Four here and three on the road. But five Ghost Theatre players. Not too unequal a fight by numbers but the men had an ease about them that Shay associated with killers. She kept her voice neutral. 'Alouette is right. Come to the show tomorrow. And, of course, you don't need tickets. We'll be happy to see you.'

The men seemed content with the silence. The lead horse bent to nibble at a tuft of grass and the man pulled him upright again. 'It wasn't really a request, I'm afraid. Think of it as a requisition.'

Nonesuch slid his horse alongside Alouette's and said, 'A requisition? This a press-gang?' He smirked. 'Worse, you might call it a kind of human enclosure.'

He was pleased with the jibe, but the man seemed unconcerned. 'Whatever you choose to call it. She's necessary to us. She has a gift, and gifts must be shared.'

Nonesuch seemed happy that they were trading words rather than blows. 'Gifts are given, not taken.' He was relaxed in his saddle, but his voice was urgent.

The men laughed and put out their hands. 'Give, then.'

Nonesuch pressed his heels into the horse's flank. 'Form a line,' he whispered, and they moved into a broken rank. Nonesuch reached out his hands both ways. Shay took his left; it was cool and dry.

'We're coming through. If you stop us, then it'll be your choice.' Shay squeezed her thighs and her horse inched forward. She clung hard to Nonesuch's hand. His horse lurched and then stopped. Shay saw his heels pucker the flesh on the animal's flank. Reluctantly it stepped closer to the men and the others followed, mere inches at a time. When they were close enough that they could hear the men's breaths, Nonesuch's horse threw its head up and back. It reared but Nonesuch calmed it.

'Come on now, girl.' Another small step. Shay urged hers on too. She was near enough to smell tobacco on the men's breath. They were moving though.

Metal on metal. Three times. *Swiiiick swiiiick swiiiick.* Knife blades caught the moonlight. Trussell cried out as his horse reared and then it turned and bolted back the way they'd come. He was gone in moments.

'There's a smart boy. You'd do well to follow him.'

Shay pressed her horse on, and it snorted and pawed at the ground. Flecks of spittle formed on the black of its mouth. It was wary of squeezing through the gap between the Commoners' horses, but Shay dug her heels in. Two more paces. Nearly level with the men, close enough to reach over and pluck the hat from the nearest. Another step, saddles brushing one another, and the horses stopped again. Nonesuch was eye to eye with their leader. He said, 'Will The Jagger not mind if you bring him a dead sparrow then?'

The man nodded. 'Aye, he would, but I'm not sure that will be necessary.'

Shay had no idea what he meant until he pushed his blade deep into Nonesuch's belly with all the ceremony of handing over a message. For a moment they stared at each other and then he retracted the blade. Nonesuch looked down at his white shirt; there was just enough moonlight to see it bloom black all the way to the tails. No one moved and then Nonesuch slid, almost gracefully, from his horse. It was quiet enough that Shay heard his blood pump and drip; the air even smelled of it: iron and shit.

And then Shay felt arms around her, and she was hauled across a shoulder, and the world turned upside down. The men's horses began to trot and she was watching Alouette and Blank dwindle in the moonlight, watching them hunched over the pile of rags that was Nonesuch, watching them lay him down and press on his wound, and then the scene became a miniature as the horses started to gallop, and she could hear nothing but the hooves and the blood in her ears until they rounded a wooded corner, and suddenly everything she knew was gone.

33

T HE BIRDCAGE WAS HUGE. Six feet tall and four across; large
enough to bang against the sides of the cart in which it rode. It
was girded with wooden slats and the base was filled with something
heavy. Shay grabbed the bars and rocked back and forth but she could
barely get an edge off the ground. Her cart was in the middle of a slow
snake of vehicles that drove through the night. At one point a boy with
an eyepatch came trotting alongside to hand her a bowl of soup, a hunk
of bread and a bucket. The bucket worried her the most; obviously they
weren't stopping soon.

She rubbed at her wrists. The men had tied them and then hoisted
her on a pole over their shoulders like so much baggage. They'd ridden
in silence for miles, ignoring her writhing, and then she was pushed into
this cage and the door was locked. The fact that Cockaigne contained
such a thing – a girl-sized cage – was another terror on the pile.

The carts sped through unlit lanes and Shay fumed and paced and
spat and shouted, but the rhythm of the wheels and the convoy's indifference wore her down. Finally she lay curled like a shell for what she
promised herself would only be a minute, but the next thing she knew
it was light, and The Jagger was sat on a stool opposite her. He whittled
at an animal tooth the length of Shay's hand. She kept her eyes half
closed, but he'd seen her stir. He turned the tooth around and regarded
it. 'How is our guest?'

'I'm a captive, not a guest. Cages make captives,' she said. One
sentence from him had lit the wick of her anger.

'Maybe so,' he said, 'or maybe it's the other way round.'

'If so, then can I have the key?' she asked.

'Of course not.'

'Then I'm a captive.'

He looked unconcerned. 'Your words. If it's of any help, think of yourself as a tax.'

She didn't hide her sneer and he went on. 'I mean it. Whitehall takes from us folk. Money. Men. Food. We're just taking back a little of what the city owes.'

'So you're no better than them.'

He put down the tooth. He was quiet for a moment and then said, 'The palace that we build is open to all. Our men spend their days freeing the land that your lords enclosed. We don't keep anything for ourselves. Here you will give succour to thousands, men and women who need you far more than any London lady.'

'And what I want doesn't count?'

He tilted his head. 'It counts. If the rest of life was equal, then I would set you free. But we all must be weighed. Our audiences have had sons stolen to die in foreign wars; you'll have three meals and an armed guard. You're lucky.' He mimed a pair of scales and leant heavily to one side.

It exhausted Shay, the things men did with words. The way they used them like they were magic things. The Jagger thought calling her a tax meant he was free to lock her up. As if there were no serfdom without the word 'slave'. Men and their words was an arena in which she would never win. Action was the only thing that really touched them. She placed her face in the gap between two bars and said, 'I won't perform for you. Ever.'

He sharpened the tip of the tooth and said, 'We'll see.'

They spent a day and night travelling, Shay alone on the cart over long miles with only soup and bread and a clean bucket for company. The broth was black and oily with slivers of mushroom floating in it, and the bread was burnt hard. She ate unenthusiastically but as the food's heat surged through every inch of blood in her, the world seemed to slow and tip; clouds lowered and the road transformed to a glistening stream. She lay flat on the straw at the bottom of the cage and slept a shallow, fitful sleep. Last night repeated over and over: Nonesuch slipping from his horse and Blank's hands in his blood. Was he still moving as he slipped from her sight? She couldn't remember.

When she woke, the carts had halted under a forest canopy so thick that she couldn't tell if it was day or night. Off to one side, The Jagger talked with men she didn't recognise, their heads together over a map.

The boy with the eyepatch appeared with another bowl of the soup and he whispered, 'Watch the fire-cart behind us when we reach the enclosures. It's quite the show.'

The convoy pulled out of the woods into a geometric landscape where the countryside had been divided up into neat squares. Hawthorn hedges were a feeble imitation of the vast avenues of sycamores through which they'd ridden. Shay turned to watch the cart behind her. With a sudden jolt, plumes of flame gushed from its side, and, even though she was yards ahead, her skin shrank from the heat. Men with wet rags tied tight across their faces worked the pumps and the jets shot further. Hedgerows smouldered and then caught, and the flame stuck to them like paste. They left a fiery wake behind. Shay thumped at her bars. It was April: the hawthorns would be knotted with blackbird nests, nests that were guarded by thorns from the hawks and the falcons. Blind gummy fledglings and harried adults. She watched their homes blaze like tinder and shouted, 'Stop, wait,' until her voice gave out.

The Commoners transferred her to a barge for the last few miles and then placed her, still caged, in a daisy-strewn coppice, and Cockaigne was erected all around her. Stagehands hauled the castle walls upright on long ropes and the sound of hammering came from every direction. Men hauled her cage into a room-sized tent, through which other performers wandered. Some tried to talk to her, but most looked the other way. Shay ignored them all, anyway, compacting her anger. She wouldn't perform for them, but she couldn't stop her heart beating faster; opening nights had their own rhythms. The air tightened as final preparations were finished. Barks of laughter and urgent questions. The queue growing at the one backstage mirror. Heart-crossings and last prayers and then, somewhere unseen, the doors opened and, like the moment a bird takes flight, the wooden city sparkled into life.

A costume, her costume, lay by her side. It was a short cloak of cloth feathers in every conceivable shade of brown, from russet to near-black. Autumn plumage. Shay heard acts starting up – the anticipatory whisper of crowds and stage introductions – and then four men thrust long rods through the top of the cage and carried it out of the tent on their shoulders. Shay was hoisted through the backstage where the guts of the city hung out: empty barrels and piles of bones. A high-wire walker practised on a line drawn in the dirt. The men parted the flaps of a tent with their shoulders and deposited her on a Turkish carpet. A red velvet cloth was draped over her cage and then a man pulled up a corner to wish Shay good luck. She looked away.

The audience entered, talking under their breaths as chairs squeaked and conversations overlapped like waves. After a minute, a voice stilled the crowd. 'Ladies and Gentlemen. We have a rare treat tonight. Queens consult with her and lords hang on her every word. In London she's a thousand guineas a pop, but here, tonight, she is free. Because we are all lords in Cockaigne.'

There was a round of applause.

'Ask her the future, speak to your lost loved ones through her, ladies and gentlemen, I give you … the Sparrow.'

The cloth whipped back and the sudden light hurt her eyes. The Jagger bowed and unlocked the cage. She looked out on a tent lit with candles and a crowd of curious countryfolk. Even if she had meant to put on a show, the setting had none of the magic of the theatre. A girl, on a stage, with her dress at her feet.

Whoever speaks first loses. She'd heard Evans say that once, apropos of some business deal. She stared out and the crowd stared back. The embarrassment of it was almost enough to prick her into speech but she held her nerve. She waited. A woman pulled herself to her feet. She was stout and grey with an outdoor face and she leant on a stick to ask, 'My son went away to sea two years ago and I've not heard a single word from him. Where is he? Is he safe?' She flopped back into her seat and Shay stared out at her, unmoving. There was a mutter from the back, and someone stood and left. A man got to his feet and said, 'How will our winter be?'

Shay didn't look at him. She checked over her shoulder at The Jagger, but he was sitting whittling. When she didn't respond to the man either, more people began to leave. She turned to face the back of the tent and listened to them drain away. The noises of Cockaigne were muffled. Cheers and boos and the scratching of The Jagger's knife.

When the tent was empty, The Jagger whistled. 'All right boys, wrap it up. Next show in two hours.' He led Shay out by the elbow; it was good to get her legs moving again.

She said, 'I'll do the same again for the next show. And the next, and the next.' Cursing a petulance she couldn't keep from her voice.

'Go ahead. I'd prefer a fortune-teller to a freak show, but I'll take what I can get. They'll still queue to see the girl who advises the Queen. And they expect Londoners to be stuck-up bitches. I win either way.'

An hour and they started again. The same malodorous yokels in the same weedy candlelight, but this time she started talking before they had even taken their seats. 'I am a prisoner. I was free like you but these men kidnapped me and forced me here. In the streets of Cockaigne they preach freedom but when money is involved they are worse than the meanest London usurer. England opposes slavery but here I am, a slave.' She had their attention but there were no cries of agreement, no applause. 'This isn't an act, do you understand? I am trapped here. They caged me. Call for help. Tell the Blackfriars Boys you saw me here. Tell them to storm this place.'

It took longer for them to leave this time. They filed out when she stopped talking, filed out silently, and Shay heard a slow handclap from the back of the tent. The Jagger was at her shoulder, almost whispering. 'What little land they have has been enclosed and they die if they don't pay their tithes. These people know what slavery looks like and it's not Turkish carpets and French brandy. I look forward to our next show. You'll think of something.' He raised his voice. 'Pack it up boys, that's us done.'

And so began the Sparrow at Cockaigne. Every show meant two days travelling and one day performing. Whenever they could, the Commoners travelled by water, in a convoy of flat, unadorned barges that housed the stage set, performers and supplies. The centre boat sat low in the water and was rimmed with arrow-slits for the archers. That was where The Jagger and his retinue travelled. They kept Shay there too. Most of the time, the journeys could have been Thames pleasure cruises if it weren't for the cage. Commoners rowed drowsily under arches of trees, and Shay watched swifts and kingfishers and the herons folded up like flick knives. Once a day, The Jagger opened the cage door to lecture her on his politics. He spoke badly, with no inflection or passion. He described the way England was being parcelled up and stolen, sliced, bit by bit, back to the bone, but he could have been reciting a recipe, for all the fire in his words. Still, stretching her legs was such sweet agony that she almost looked forward to his talks. And, if she lay flat on her back, she could frame her view so that she could see only sky and birds. She knew that Trussell and Alouette and Blank were under the same sky somewhere and it soothed her. And Nonesuch? She had seen him die so many times on stage, heroic on his knees, squeezing out one last gravel-throated speech, but she'd never seen him look the way he did the night that the Commoners stabbed him: that O of a mouth and the dead weight of his fall. When she asked if there was any news of him, The Jagger whispered, 'You won't be seeing that boy again in this world.'

The days slurred and smeared and left her dreamy. Her head swam and weighty nightmares swooped upon her every evening. At first, she thought it was an effect of her captivity, but as days passed, she realised that the only moments of clarity that she had were when her belly was empty. Her diet never changed – black bread and mushroom soup, red wine and brandy – even when the rest of the crew were served something different. That meant something. She kept her eyes open for clues. One of the pots of mushrooms in the galley had a chalk bird drawn upon its side, and her soup was always made separately, under the care of the Commoners' huge, one-armed cook. Even her wine came from its own bottle. The crew were lucid enough but every night after dinner Shay's world liquified and swirled. She was either being poisoned or tamed, and she didn't know which was worse.

A fortnight into her captivity, Shay went on hunger strike.

'You must eat,' said the boy with the eyepatch, when she handed back the still-warm soup and still-cold wine. Shay ignored him. A minute later, the lieutenant sat by her, signalling with every movement how beneath him this little crisis was.

'You must eat.' The soup was congealed now, with a greying skin that made her resolve easier to keep. She only really began to worry once the younger boys crowded around her with urgent whispers. 'You must eat. Please, Sparrow, trust us. It's for the best.' But her head was clear for the first time in days, and the gnaw in her stomach was something finer than hunger.

Next afternoon the barges sailed through a coiled stretch of river where willows dipped leaf-tips in their wake and the banks swarmed with insects. At five bells the cook brought her the same black bread and black soup. Shay ignored it the way a cat would. Only now did The Jagger come to sit with her. He squatted to one side and waxed his bowstring. His bow was a double curve of trembling yew like an upper lip; it stood as tall as Shay. He grooved the wax through the string and then pushed the bowl of food back through the bars. 'Eat.'

She pushed it back until it clanged against the bars. 'It's poison. It's poison and I'm caged. Cockaigne is a prison.' The Jagger slumped back against the deck and furrowed his brow. Had she won? Could it be that easy?

Then he took his bow and notched an arrow in one motion. He raised it without looking, drew and released heedlessly, like he was throwing something away. A screech and the slap of wings on water. Shay swivelled round to watch in horror as The Jagger nodded and a boy dived into the water. The lad hauled the dying swan up on board even before its wings had stopped convulsing. Pure brilliant white and pure blood red. Colours too perfect for this grey world. The Jagger nailed the bird to the cabin door by its neck and then pinned those sheets of wing up and out like an angel's.

'Tomorrow I kill two,' he said, and took the meal away.

During the days, the Commoners were soldier ants. They tore fences up at the roots and dragged them behind for miles. Hedgerows were doused in pitch and then put to the torch. Their route was nonsensical, filled with doubling-backs and acute angles. Every burning led to the bounty on their head rising, but no one, the Commoners included, seemed to know where they'd be next. Somewhere near the Scottish border they liberated a recently enclosed valley and then the whole convoy climbed up into the foothills. For the first time, Shay saw the entirety of the wreckage they left behind. Fields of smoke and raw, red earth: a bloody bridal train.

Days of fire were followed by Cockaigne nights. The golden walls and carnival patter outside, the smell of pork and ale and vomit inside. The other performers blanked her, whether through fear or jealousy Shay couldn't tell, which left her with only the audiences to interact with. She tried everything to provoke them. She ignored them, cajoled them and insulted them. She pled and entreated but it was as if she were under glass. Whatever she did became her act. And every night they came with their sad, earnest questions, which were slowly breaking her heart.

'When will there be rain? We're boiling shoe leather for soup.'

'Will my boy survive? We've had eight children and only the girls live past two.'

'Where is my wife? Where is my son? Where is my mother? Can you take a message to them? Please. A word, a kiss.'

Slowly she saw that they were as trapped as she was. How could she answer their questions when her own loves were lost in the wind? Every bright-eyed boy in the audience was a Blackfriars ghost to her, ghosts who haunted her days rather than her nights. She listened and tried to answer but there was no succour in either of those things. So she sang and it seemed to help, if only for a moment.

Days flowed like a black river on which she floated, half-submerged, with her eyes on the clouds above. Cage, soup, carts, clouds, barge, soup, cage and then stage again. How many shows did she do? She couldn't tell – it became one long performance that she watched from a distance, and the sounds were thin echoes by the time they reached her. Children's songs torn apart by crow caws. Dressed in the autumnal costume, weeping on her knees with her head in some farmer's lap. Now the cage door stood open; some part of her was tamed, some part was wild. She answered questions with nightingale whistles and they nodded back *yes, yes, I understand*. Black soup and cups of river water, sometimes with a leaf floating in it, like a gift. A world turned on its back; the river was air and the sky was oil. There was no land, and every day was a leap from a tall building without a foothold in sight.

Her night-guard was the boy with the eyepatch. Valentyne was his name. An orphaned city boy, no older than her, who could have been a Blackfriars Boy for the way that his daylight swagger folded down into nighttime terrors. When all around them were asleep, he would talk, urgently. Memories of his mother, or his brother who was away at sea, his dog, his friends – and once, when a thunderstorm set the barge rocking, he thrust a dirty hand between the bars and held hers tight; for his benefit or hers, she couldn't tell. One night he whispered to her, 'Your beau, I hear that he's alive still,' and she had to shake her head to recall his name. Nonesuch, Birdland, Lonan: foreign words that floated away on noiseless rivers.

There was one performance where Shay couldn't stand to hear any more about loss and hunger and fear, so she sang without stopping for the entire hour. One song with one single lyric that repeated over and over, but the audience watched rapt and silent. They heard something in her that she couldn't.

One afternoon they came across a fallen tree that blocked the river, so The Jagger gave her an hour loose on the barge. The men worked at clearing their path and Shay lay on her back so that the treetops framed the sky, and she could see no men or boats – just the heavens and far-off birds writing sentences across the air. Swifts told outrageous tales while pigeons bickered. A straight-talking heron was drowned out by a gossipy V of geese. And then, like a lightning strike, a falcon took a pigeon in mid-air. White flash, flurry of feathers and the prey was gone. Joy broke through her black ice. It must be Devana, She couldn't see her marking, but only a city bird used to violence and plenty would kill with such extravagance. Shay climbed up onto the galley roof and watched the falcon bank and circle. Only then did she notice something unearthly about the bird. Devana gave off a spectral glow – the colour of illness, the colour of foxfire – that made her stand out against the dusk. Shay squinted and tried to latch her eyes onto hers, even so many yards above.

And in that instant some hourglass turned, and the world was upside down. Shay lay glued to a sky of water, gazing down into an abyss of air. The wind buffeted her wings and she laughed at the slowness of the world below. Its ridiculous earnestness. She hung and sidestepped and angled and sharpened, as if the winds themselves were under her command. She curled down the merest feather-tip, tightened an angle and became a spear aimed at the centre barge. The wind tore at her, shaping her to an arrowhead, down, down, the bullseye of the cage yawning open like a lover, and then …

She was back on sweated straw and rabbit bones with a black bile rising in her throat and the sky was a foreign country again. But some spell on her had been lifted.

She'd not seen Devana since before her capture. So she doubted the falcon had been following her. No, if Devana was near now then it meant the Blackfriars Boys were too. And if it was foxfire that illuminated her wings, then it meant Alouette was watching her somehow. Alouette and Trussell and Blank. And, hope against hope, Nonesuch too.

Hour upon hour she lay awake, seeing her situation anew through those bird-of-prey eyes, and by the time dawn broke, Shay knew how she would escape Cockaigne.

34

I N SHAY'S DREAMS DEVANA speaks. Not with the rasping cry that she uses to scare prey, but in a girl's voice. Soft and rounded like breast feathers. Full of flutter and coo. The voice says that Shay has become prey. It whispers that she's been weak. Asks how many nights Shay has spent feeling sorry for herself.

Shay tries to reply but Devana rears up with her wings a glorious reproach. *Shut up, girl.*

Devana says that men have brittle bones and thin necks. And that they all have points where they bleed until they die. Devana says all you need is fear.

Without waking, Shay starts to sharpen her nails against the cage's bars: *snick, snick.*

Devana whispers like a lover, with blood on her breath, that one either hunts or is hunted; there are no bystanders.

With eyes closed, Shay tucks her hands behind her back and smiles sweetly. She is ready …

35

VALENTYNE WAS ON GUARD and she let him tell his stories until the crew had settled down to sleep. Only once the night was quiet did she ask her question: 'Could you get me some meat?'

He said, 'You're not allowed meat, sorry. Your menu is set,' but it was clear from his voice that he was unsure why. Shay kept her face in the shadows and prepared herself. Nonesuch once taught her that the juice of an onion on a hem was all it took to make yourself cry. When she'd asked why he didn't just think of some sad memory – a moment remembering her mother was enough to set her sobbing – he'd smiled and said, 'Ah, but you need to be able to stop crying, as well.' No matter, the barge was dark enough that her tears needn't be real. She let her shoulders shake and said, 'Every day you give me nothing except black poison and then you watch and you laugh.'

His expression was hidden but she heard his concern. 'No one is laughing, least of all me. The broth is, well, it's best for you, I promise.'

'How can it be best for me when none of you will drink it?' She aimed for his raw points. 'I'm never allowed a taste of home or a memory of my family.' She threw herself to the floor. 'Never even a taste of kindness. What did you eat tonight?'

'Goose,' he whispered.

There was no point asking for scraps then. She mimed sobs.

'But there's rabbit left too,' he said. 'From yesterday.'

He was frightened and she dared not push him too hard. She said, 'I know it's dangerous for you, but I can't ask any of the others. They don't know me the way you do.' There was a story that she'd saved for this moment. She said, 'When I was little, I used to hunt rabbits with a falcon. East of the marshes where the sky and the land bleed into one. It would be just the two of us, fledglings really, in this world of giants, and I would throw that bird at the sky and watch her shrink until I was so ... nearly ... alone. She would fall like a stone, and I'd be with her, falling with her, lost with her ...' She let the silence build. 'You only feed a falcon a little taste of what they catch. That way she never knows that she doesn't need you. I always shared the kill; a little for her, a little for me. Even a caged bird deserves that.'

When he returned it was with a chunk of meat wrapped in a kerchief, and Shay felt a pang of power. With nothing more than her words she'd made someone do what she wanted. But the boy didn't hand the package over right away. Instead, he sat closer, side-on to the cage. Silently he reached inside and took her hand. He guided it inside his breeches where he was already hard. He pushed the kerchief through the bars and said, 'Tell me more about the falcon.'

Later, when it was done, Shay divided the meat in two. She ate her share without pleasure and then placed the other half on the top of the cage. If she could keep Devana following, then the bird would act as a signpost pointing to her location. Nonesuch would recognise Devana, she was sure. The troupe had spent so many mornings on the theatre roof with Devana a haughty sentinel above their heads and always Shay pointed out her unique style. She stayed awake as long as she could, but everything conspired towards sleep; the gentle rock of the boat and the warm night air were cradle-like. When she woke, the meat had attracted nothing more than flies.

That week Valentyne came every night to make their sad little transaction. Shay thought of nothing while she did it, and afterwards left half the meat on the roof of the cage. No sign of Devana. One time a water rat, bold as brass, scrambled up the bars with its nose twitching and swallowed it in one bite.

They performed near Colchester. Or maybe it was St Albans. The black soup made Shay's days slide back and forth across each other until she had no idea how long had passed. Wherever they were, it was close enough to London that she swore she could smell the smoke. She drew a crowd that would have filled Blackfriars ten times over and the need radiated off them like heat. Their questions set loose a thousand lost boys in her mind. She saw them dying in foreign mud; a hundred days to get there and thirty seconds to die. She saw lads begging on London streets and girls taken to shadowy rooms by shadowy men and coming out with snuffed candles for eyes. All these towns and so many lost. She took it all and swallowed it and let it mix with the black bile in her blood. She sang lullabies and children's songs and chirrups and owl-hoots and she said, over and over, 'He will return, she is safe and loved.' And when she could no longer take her own lies, then the black water inside her rose and she stood and sang and cried, and she remembered nothing of it afterwards.

In dusk's underwater light Valentyne lay peeled back like a rabbit ready for the pot. Shay had become so expert that he was spent in twenty strokes, him looking into the fire all the while, Shay watching the heavens. He wiped himself down and pulled a package from a bag.

'A treat for you today, from the hog roast.' The packet was translucent with fat and the smell was so rich that Shay worried it might wake the rest of the crew.

She gave it ten minutes for Valentyne's breathing to slow to a thin shuffle. Ten more as a precaution and then she pulled herself up and placed the meat around the pommel of the cage. She dozed and almost missed Devana's arrival. It was only the scrabble of claws on the top bar that alerted her. She hung her head through the slats and looked up. Devana cocked her head. She glowed a blue-green like a cold flame and even in the moonlight her beak shone slick with fat. One talon squeezed the remaining meat tight, and she gulped a lump down. She gave off a light like fireflies. What had been done to her?

'Good girl,' said Shay. For now she was content to watch the bird eat. Methodically Devana tore strips from the meat and raised them to her mouth. She ate, swallowed, started again. Black eyes tested the night for weakness. Shay talked to her with her gaze averted. 'Are they out there, girl? Is Nonesuch following? Did *they* do this to you?' She raised a hand and Devana ignored it. Only once the bird was finished with the meat did she hop down to land on Shay's forearm. Now Shay could see her whole. She had been outlined in stripes of foxfire across her beak, head and wings. Her talons shone with it. The job had been carefully done, avoiding the flight feathers but accentuating the bird's liquid lines. Devana shone with a blank light as she groomed an errant tail-feather back into place. Twice she shuffled, a little awkwardly, along Shay's arm, bringing up perfect pinpricks of blood. It took Shay a moment to see what was bothering her. A scrap of rough paper was tied to her ankle. Shay flattened it out.

I WILL SAVE YOU

Nothing else. It was blank on the other side.

Devana flexed her talons experimentally and Shay knew from experience that meant she was about to leave. She stared at the note and tried to think. No ink and only half a plan. In her mind's eye she imagined again the paper dragons that had once flown from the Blackfriars roof. Finally, she pricked her fingertip against the point of Devana's beak.

'Sorry girl,' she said as the bubble of blood formed and Devana side-eyed it with professional interest.

Her nail dipped in the blood. K ... I ... T ... The letters thinned so she dipped again. E ... S.

Would it be clear enough? She stroked Devana's crest and the thought that the bird might have been on Nonesuch's arm mere hours before warmed her like brandy.

Devana stretched out her wings, suddenly huge, and Shay had only seconds to set the scene. She kicked Valentyne awake and stood with her arm out at a right angle, Devana stretching out three feet of glowing wings like a shadowy angel. The boy froze, Shay raised her arm a fraction, and Devana was up and away in three giant strokes. Shay waited until the boy's eyes were back on hers and then said, in a voice new even to her, 'They. Are. Coming.'

Uproar. In minutes there were meetings in the galley. There were arguments among the crew. It helped that Valentyne's tale grew more outrageous with every retelling. A ghost bird with eyes like coals and knives for talons had materialised in the cage and it spoke with Shay. It was four feet wide, it was five. It was quiet as snow and beautiful as thunder. And above the barge, as a rejoinder to any doubter, Devana circled like the hand of a clock, far beyond the reach of any arrow.

Shay was dragged from the barge minutes later and the party rode north, swapping teams of drivers along the way and not stopping for twenty hours. The horses steamed like tea kettles. Back on the water the crew avoided her, but it wasn't that wide a boat. If they squeezed past the cage, then she aimed her mouth up at the sky and let fly. Prey-bird cries and the old tunes. Pagan songs intercut with caws and croaks that tore at her throat.

The next night, wiping her hand clean, she whispered to Valentyne, 'I like you, so I'm warning you first. When they come, they'll go for your eyes.'

It was a thrill like the first sip of wine to feel your words scare another human being.

'When who come?'

She was caged, he was free, yet ... 'The birds. When I summon them. Eyes first. Cover your head and then get below deck.'

Below deck was for cargo. There was barely enough room for a mouse down there.

Two days of ceaseless travel, but as soon as they slowed, Devana was back, circling above them. The Commoners pitched up in a bowl of gentle hills like rumpled bedsheets that were bathed in a light centuries older than London's glow. Shay made herself compliant. She asked one of the sword-swallowers to shave her head and then rubbed linseed oil into her scalp to help the tattoo show strong and black. She showed the Commoner boys how to light her so that she shone. More Turkish rugs over the boards so she could go barefoot.

'I don't need your introduction tonight,' she told The Jagger. 'Let me show you how it's done.'

She changed into the bird-dress in front of him and scoffed at his gaze. When she stepped out into the light, the mere sight of her snuffed out the crowd's noise. No words at first. Nonesuch's trick; don't let them get comfortable. The quiet quietened. The dark darkened. She had no script, but whatever she said would work. It didn't matter that she couldn't see around the corner of her words.

She heard herself say, 'I am faster than death.'

Country folk: immediately people crossed themselves and muttered.

'So fast that I see into the future.' A head-tilt, learnt from Devana. 'You, third row. Blue hat.' She drilled her gaze onto his until he looked away. 'She knows what you did. But there will never be forgiveness. Do you understand?'

He nodded; a shy movement from a big lump of a man.

'You won't be forgiven but you can still be saved.'

He nodded so hard that his hat fell off and he said, 'Thank you thank you thank you,' like a catechism.

She kept moving. 'Front row. Blondie with the pigtails. You have lost someone recently.' That wasn't much of a stretch out here in the mud where they died like rats and were buried in heaps. But the girl gasped, and her hand went to her belly. Her smock was too big for her, and Shay struck. She laid her head in the girl's lap and said, 'You lost a little one.'

The girl shook and her voice was masked with sobs. 'A ... boy ... *Michael.*' She said it so quietly that, when Shay repeated the name out into the crowd, they gasped.

'Little Michael.' She knelt and took the girl's hands. She needed to know if he'd been stillborn or weeks old. She took a guess. 'Did he even see the daylight?'

The girl collapsed deeper into herself. 'No. Born dead. What did I do wrong?'

Here and the Murmuration. On stage and in bed. You couldn't just let the feeling take you. Even chaos has its rulebook. Shay lifted the girl's head and, in a quick voice meant just for her, she whispered, 'You did nothing wrong. Nothing.'

She threw back her head and did the barn owl cry. It had been years, but it came out nicely. A short question and then a long one. 'Who, who, *whoo?*'

She spoke to the audience, but her eyes were on the girl. 'When you hear that call next, it will be Michael. "Who, who, *whooo.*" You hear it?'

The girl nodded.

'Those children who die before they see day's light become night-birds. Dunnocks and nightingales and barn owls and nightjars. He will always be near and he will always be talking to you.'

The girl gulped a thank you and clutched her companion's hand.

An hour was all it took. They listened in wonder. Her father's words guided her. 'You break a horse, but you make a hawk.' This audience was no hawk. She would break them and turn them into her weapons. She would arm them with a message that they would spread when Cockaigne was gone. All the way to the Blackfriars Boys, hopefully. She aimed her eyes to the ceiling of the tent.

'Before I go ...' A low moan of sorrow swept the crowd.

'Before I go, I rise up beyond the clouds where I can see the whole of England, and its future and its past laid out like so many fields. I see the hard times behind us.' She was hearing these words for the first time. 'Our famines and floods, our stillborns and taxes.' A murmur of assent ran around the tent. 'Hard frosts and long winters.' Her arms stretched wide like wings. 'And I see our future.'

She gave a falcon cry, harsh in the warm circle of the crowd, and said, 'An army of birds is coming. They glow like the moon.'

There was a commotion behind her and a sharp exchange between the Commoners. Before she could speak again, the curtain was dropped unceremoniously in front of her.

She shouted now. 'Birds that glow like the stars. They will descend with a fury ...' She cawed again and made her hands into talons.

Hands pushing through the curtains. Other hands grabbing her from behind. The whole audience on its feet now, pulling at the fabric until the curtains were torn away and Shay was unveiled like a statue.

'They will blind the tyrants and the slavedrivers and the landowners and the unrighteous.' She tore at her clothes and the cloth feathers fell like snow. Faces pressed close to hers now. The hush of chapel.

When she said, 'They will blind Cockaigne too,' the Commoners had heard enough. They dragged her back across the stage, her heels banging against the boards, but she sang in a voice that tore at her throat:

'Birds that glow, as bright as moons,
With claws to hold and beaks to blind.
Birds that shine above the gloom
And save us from the ties that bind.
We're birds at death and birds by birth,
Our feet will ne'er touch the sullen earth.'

She let a final falcon cry rub sand in her throat, and she ripped at her clothes. The Commoners had to pull her away through a storm of applause.

They packed away in a hurry. The Jagger was everywhere, chivvying his workers with both word and boot. The previous weeks' civility to Shay was forgotten; she was slung across a galloping horse, riders shouting to her left and right, and then loaded back into the cage on the barge. They cast off with half of the retinue still not arrived; Valentyne had to jump aboard while the barge was moving. She asked him what was going on and she could barely hear his answer over the ruckus of bags and boxes being thrown hurriedly aboard.

'We're being followed. Whether by the Black Swifts or somebody else no one seems to know. And there were people in the audience paying to know where we were going next.'

They were here. They were coming for her. The string to Nonesuch tightened; thin as a hair but strong like a spiderweb.

Devana returned at dusk. She kept to a low spiral above the barge with her wings barely moving. Shay held her tongue; not every man was asleep yet and all were armed. The bird was out of range of even the keenest arrow now, but if she descended for food, who knew what might happen. Shay kept quiet and watched. Then something else appeared in the sky. Another bird, perhaps. It glowed an amphibian green, and she couldn't tell if it was vast and distant or small and near. Its wings were swept back like a permanent death-dive and its beak and talons shone. She watched it track across the sky. No real prey-bird flew in such straight lines, but she doubted that the Commoners would know that. Her eyes widened as she spotted another. Then another.

'Valentyne, Valentyne, wake up.'

He was awake in an instant. She laughed. 'Hey, birdfood, check the sky. *They have come.*'

There was something relentless in the way that they patrolled the heavens. Soon every man on the barge was watching and Shay noted that many had kerchiefs pulled up around their eyes; Valentyne must have been talking. She shaped the falcon call in her mouth and aimed it, harsh and bright, into the heavens. Gloriously, Devana called back. Shay didn't see The Jagger until the cage rocked; if it hadn't been for the bars, then his hands might have taken her head off. She cowered at the back, her mouth shaking too hard to make the call again.

He grabbed her shoulder. 'What are you telling them? What are they saying?'

She shrunk from him. But a calm came over her. What could he do to her? She stilled her face and made her voice loud enough for the whole crew to hear. 'They say they're an army. And they will strike soon.'

He shouted, 'Stop the fucking barge,' and pulled a boy from the oars. 'Gag her and cover her ears.'

The boy stepped forward and Shay flew at the bars. She cried from the back of her throat and he threw himself backwards. She leapt and aimed her nails at him. The one who wins a fight isn't the strongest but he with the least to lose. The boy scrambled back on his elbows and she hissed, 'Touch me and you'll be first to die. I'll make sure of it.'

Fear. He was more scared of The Jagger but still, the boy feared her. The Jagger brushed the boy aside and opened the cage door. He was surprisingly deft. Rope around the wrists, cloth in the mouth. Her kicks and scratches bounced off him. A filthy rag, nauseous with lard, was stuffed into her mouth.

After that night they replaced Valentyne with a grizzled old sailor, but as soon as he ungagged her for food and drink she started telling him about the coming attack. He stopped up his ears with cloth and sang hymns to drown out her babble. No matter, no matter. Every time he stopped singing she started up again and he had to increase his volume. Over and over until the occupants of nearby bunks screamed at them to stop. When he was finally forced into silence she whispered tales of the army of birds she commanded and how they would tear the whole circus to confetti.

'Crows go for the eyes and gulp them down in one go. Crows at your eyes, hawks at your throat and phoenix-birds to breathe fire all over you.' Shay breathed out loud and hard and laughed as the man scooted back along the wet deck. 'When you sleep, stay close to the water, it's the only safe place.'

The sailor said, 'We have more arrows than you have birds, little girl.' But that night Shay watched him move his things to a bunk closer to the river.

The next day was quieter but still the rumours swirled. Now, when the crew went off watch, most tied cloth tight over their eyes. In transit, Shay kept her eyes fixed on the skies and whenever she heard bird calls she answered them. Cockaigne couldn't hide from birds. Three days of rain, four. Shay cawed at the crows. Now fully half the crew were blind-folded and boys fought for bunks on the barge's perimeter. Outriders brought news that Elizabeth's Black Swifts were close, dropping coins on anyone who'd seen ghost birds light up the sky. The Commoners' crazed routes couldn't hide them any more. They stopped on some grim northern hillside with sheep as thin as cats, and built Cockaigne in a storm that set the wind groaning around the wooden walls. Hands clasped to hats and the cry-creak-cry of scenery coming down. The men wore handkerchiefs over their eyes when she passed, sending The Jagger into a rage.

'I'll horsewhip the next man who covers his eyes. What's the matter with you? She's a fucking child.'

That night the glowing kites came in flocks. They were a clockwork murmuration up there, ticking in their orbits. Fear swathed the convoy; The Jagger raged across the ship, urging the oarsmen on and promising fortunes to the first archer who brought a bird down. They were too far away for that, but now Shay worried that Devana might stray into range. The kites were driving her lower in the sky and, for the first time in days, Shay kept quiet and hid herself away in the cage, out of sight.

That was a mistake.

'Archers, hold your fire.' The Jagger was watching her. Watching her and watching the sky. He squatted by the cage. 'Not talking with your army tonight? Worried they might come too close?'

Shay summoned some bile. 'I'm worried that they'll kill you before I can.'

That made him smile. He spent an age looking at her and then he barked orders. 'Gag her again. Then, lights out. Archers, be ready but don't fire until I say. The first man who makes a sound goes overboard. The first archer to bring down a bird gets a half-angel.'

Silence and tension. The only sound was the slap of ripples against the bow, the only light was the moon. Twenty archers stood in two rows, bows drawn and arrows trembling in their berths. A row of normal arrows, and a row of the Greek fire-tipped. Shay looked up through the bars. The kites made their solemn circuits but beneath them Devana tipped a wing towards the boat. She was taking her sweet time about it but she was on her way down. Every turn she came a little nearer. Shay moaned through the gag and The Jagger clasped a hand over her mouth. He whispered to the crew, 'Not yet, men. Not yet.'

Devana made no sound. A low circuit, near enough to see her wing-tips ruffle against the breeze. She'd be expecting meat though, thought Shay, and the cage-top was bare. One more turn and then – thank God – she beat her wings. She'd seen enough. One beat, two. Twenty bowstrings drawn tight. Would the archers realise?

The Jagger cursed under his breath and whispered, 'On my count. One, two—' The 'three' was lost under a hiss of arrows. *Pfft, pfft, pfft* into the black, and then the fire-arrows lighting up the sky. White like sunlight on water, and the brightness caught Devana twisting hard against the air, pushing upwards, with her wings back. A trio of arrows hurtled past her and then there was another round of fire, and now she drummed at the air with a panic Shay had never seen in her before. Then, a black arrow caught her between the wing and neck and spun her around, but she shrugged it off – such a human gesture – and tore upwards until even the light couldn't reach her.

Arrows fizzled into the river and torches were relit. The kites were unmoved in their circlings but, wait, just there, there was a smaller bird on a path higher and wider than before. Shay spat out her gag and banged on her bars. 'See. They cannot die. And they never forget.'

The next night the birds were gone. And the night after. But the men still wore their blindfolds. They knew it wasn't over.

36

V ALENTYNE SAW IT FIRST.

'Sir.' He pointed upstream, where dots of light rose from the riverbank. A wave from The Jagger halted the oarsmen.

'Archers, ready.' The snick and snap of preparation as the boat inched onward. The lights rose, at different paces, on different paths, as if the remnants of a dead fire were being stirred. Up and revolving and nearing the boat. An ember fell and fizzled on the deck. Closer now – the nearest ones were almost overhead – and Shay struggled to make them out. Were they paper birds? Scraps of paper folded into the shape of a crane and then set alight? As they burned, they rose, and as they rose, they extinguished, and as they extinguished, they fell. The papers dying smouldering on the water or swept away on hidden thermals. A few dropped, exhausted, on the deck.

Charred, white, paper birds. With black writing on them. The Jagger was up on his feet. 'They're messages. For the girl. Get them. And blindfold her.' Men leapt to grab the burning paper from the sky, and they crumpled whatever scraps had made it onto the boat into pockets and swept more off the side. Shay jammed her elbows against the back of the cage and her heels hard against the door. Valentyne struggled with the lock as burning paper fell all around them. White birds, black writing, bright lines of flame.

'Get her fucking blindfold on.' The Jagger pushed the boy aside and pulled the cage door from its hinges. Shay kicked out with all her might, but he grabbed her ankles and pulled. The bars drove splinters into her hands as she hung on tight. The cage shuddered and cut deep white gauges into the wood of the deck. As The Jagger lifted her and turned her around, she hung, face down, above a torn paper bird fluttering in a puddle. It bore a square of letters:

ART
APO
ELC

What the hell did that mean? Shay's hands slipped, and in moments she was tied and blindfolded.

ART
APO
ELC

She had no idea of the message's meaning. But the Commoners wouldn't know that. She rolled on the ground and howled into her gag. But while she thrashed and foamed, under the surface her mind was working methodically.

ART
APO
ELC

37

THE NEXT DAY FOUR guards ringed Shay's cage but that only served to make the crew more fearful. When they removed her gag for a meal, she fell to her knees and cried up to the heavens, 'Elc, Apo, Art! I'm waiting.' She told everyone within earshot that three bird gods were on their way: pitiless, all-seeing gods with silver beaks and talons of flame.

The Jagger barely slept. He stopped the convoy ten times a day, convinced that he saw movement on the banks. Bowmen patrolled every barge. 'Fire at will,' he yelled, and when the lieutenant asked him what they were firing at, he said, 'Everything.'

Volley after volley, in great hissing arcs. Left and right, fore and aft. Up into the sky. A quarter-hour of wordless work, until the bowmen dripped with sweat, and then The Jagger slumped and said, 'Enough, we move on.'

Without performances, Cockaigne would be bankrupt in days, so they risked a stop on the Scarborough clifftops. There was much quiet discussion over whether it was safe to let Shay perform, but the size of the crowd forced their hand. People from all over the north-east were coming to see her, and the Commoners couldn't afford refunds. Shay felt the world revolve her way. If the countryfolk knew she was coming, then the Blackfriars Boys would too. Maybe the Black Swifts as well.

That evening guards carried her, hands tied, to the main tent. It held hundreds; the canvas walls billowed in the North Sea gales and candle flames were blown near horizontal. It felt apocalyptic. It felt right. When they finally untied her, Shay was all business. 'Roll the carpets up behind me, it's a bare boards kind of night.' By now the Commoners knew to listen to her about stagecraft. They rolled the carpets into columns behind her and ringed the cage with candles.

236

She sat, careless in her cage, sharpening her nails. The crowd surged in in their hundreds, bringing a salt-water chill along with them. They ran for the front seats and watched her like hawks on a rabbit. As the chatter subsided an unseen voice called out from the throng. 'Sharp eyes and blunt knives, Sparrow.'

She searched the crowd. 'Who said that?' It had been a male voice. Nearby.

She kept her voice light. 'Who said that, please?' and again the voice called out. A little further back in the tent this time.

'Sharp eyes, blunt knives.'

The Jagger whispered in an underling's ear and the lad squeezed his way into the crowd. Shay feigned indifference but she knew that phrase meant *show time*; it would happen tonight.

No preamble: 'A person here has lost someone.'

Almost every hand rose. Shay would use the first half of the show to make the crowd trust her, so they would know to fear her later on. Pure instinct drove the performance. She wept with people and upbraided them, she sang and recited and whispered and cawed. And once she had given them wonders enough that they gazed up at her like children in a classroom, it was time for that same old song. She started up and her heart fluttered to hear a hundred voices singing along.

'Birds that glow, as bright as moons,
With claws to hold and beaks to blind.
Birds that shine above the gloom
And save us from the ties that bind.
We're birds at death and birds by birth,
Our feet will ne'er touch the sullen earth.'

Surely it was Nonesuch. Who else had such a sense of theatre? The very last word of her song was buried under three rounded thumps that came from the rear of the tent. Smoke came on their heels and soon it billowed until the entrance was obscured. Shay tasted gunpowder on her tongue. *Whomp, whomp* came another round, and a voice yelled, 'The tent is ablaze. They've come.'

Panic, immediate and total. A hundred chairs knocked over, a hundred terrified voices. A man shouting, 'The birds are at the entrance. Escape across the stage.' Was it the same voice as before? Shay thought so. In an instant, she was caught up in a rush of bodies. Hands and knees and elbows, sharp in the smoke. She threw herself onto a man's back to look for the way out and caught sight of The Jagger being driven back by the weight of numbers. She scrambled left, through a tumult of legs, and prayed she could keep upright – if she fell, she doubted she'd ever get up again. She cut across the crowd and clambered up onto the far corner of the stage, where smoke hung in drifting curtains. Three steps into the murk and she couldn't see another soul. The rolled-up carpets lay across one another and she found the loosest one and squeezed herself into the gap at its centre. She was cocooned within the folds and held her nose against the tickle of fibre as running feet echoed away.

'She got out with the crowd. Close the main gates and check everyone who leaves.' The Jagger sounded firm but Shay fancied she heard a hint of fear too. She tamped down a cough and kept as quiet as she could. If this wasn't what the paper birds had meant, then she was hiding away at the very time she might have escaped.

Art, Apo, Elc: Cleopatra in reverse.

Panic drained from the room and the canvas slapped like flags. Shay kept very still and very quiet as outside people milled this way and that. The rain stopped but the crowds didn't. Then, without warning, the carpet was hoisted up and something dug into her back. A voice said, 'Shay?'

'Mm-hmm.' Mouthful of dry fabric.

'Listen. They're guarding the exits so I'm going to load you into the props cart, and I'll be back for you tonight.'

She couldn't move and could barely talk. The voice was muffled. 'Nonesuch?'

'Quiet now, we're nearly outside.' Every step drove his bony shoulder into her. She tried to follow where they were going but in moments she was disorientated. Suddenly the carpet was flung down. The voice was more confident now. 'Get this on the cart with the rest.'

A voice, querulous, asked something.

'The Sparrow's flown. They say she has an army of birds blinding anyone who follows her.'

Once he'd left, there was a blast of cold air and the jolt of cartwheels on rutted ground. Drivers called out to one another. They were boisterous until the gate and quiet after. Shay stretched out and tried to make herself comfortable inside the rug.

They drove downhill for a long while and then onto a country path that gummed the wheels and slowed them to a crawl. The cartmen whispered conspiratorially to each other but Shay couldn't pick out a word. She pricked herself in the legs with her nails; if she slept, she might snore. The hole at the end of the rolled-up carpet was a grey disc that turned black as night fell. Hours of riding, the horses slowing, voices dying away. They stopped some time before dawn and her cart was manoeuvred back and forth; she guessed they were forming into a circle. She'd spent many a night in Commoner camps. There would be guards and patrols, but the good news was that she couldn't hear any dogs. Her carpet was lifted from both ends and thrown somewhere hard, and it took all of her effort not to cry out in pain.

When it had quietened down, she wormed herself along the carpet and stuck her head out of the end. She was in a store tent, piled high with props. A suit of armour stood sentry and for a second she froze. She wished she could light a torch but Commoners would be sleeping only feet away. Instead, she looked for a costume trunk; her feathered robe and shaved head would be instantly recognisable. She found a chest and rifled through frock coats and loincloths, Pierrot costumes and flippers, before settling on one of the barmaid outfits. It was low-fronted and far too big for her, but at least she might not be the only one here dressed that way and the bonnet would cover her hair.

As she buckled unfamiliar shoes, there was a noise like a sigh. She ducked behind the trunk and watched the rear of the tent. A black V was drawn across the grey of the canvas like a boat's wake. Someone had slit it from side to side, and a head poked through. Trussell.

She scrambled from her hiding place and was in his arms in moments. She pressed her face into his chest and cried for what she now realised was the first time since she'd been taken. He held her, with his hands in her hair, whispering, 'Shush, we're nearly there but we have to move. Take my hand.'

They stepped out and walked between two unlit tents, the ground springy under their feet. Trussell led them on a zagging path avoiding even the merest glimmer of light. Only one tent looked to be still fully awake. It glowed from within, and Shay heard low voices. Trussell whispered, 'We're on an island and the bridge is the other side of that tent. There's no other way out.' They sidestepped left around the back of the tent. He stopped her. More voices and the sound of the door-ties being undone.

'The party must be breaking up. Wait.' He was right. A couple left to a chorus of farewells, and someone threw up noisily only feet in front of them.

'This is no good,' he said. 'They'll close the bridge in a quarter-hour.' Two men chatted by the tent's entrance and their shadows loomed across the grass. Trussell looked ill. Tired and scrawny, though his eyes shone.

'All right. All right. Time to test your acting skills. We're lovers and I'm chasing you.' He nodded at her. 'Imagine that you want me to catch you on the other side of the bridge, out of sight of jealous eyes. You see it?'

She nodded.

'There are men posted at either end, but all the serious boys are off looking for you. We might get away with it.' He pulled the hat down tighter on her head. 'Um ... you could look a little more ... dishevelled? As if we'd already, y'know, started.'

Shay could see his embarrassment. She tucked her skirt into her hose and tore a line of the cheap stitching down the front. Everything, the fresh air, the clothes; she was free already. 'Suitably ravished?' she asked.

'Let's do it.'

She took her shoes in her hand and skipped out past the tent. The men turned and reached for swords, so she tried a giggle and kept herself slow.

'Come back, you little tease.' Trussell was doing his Evans voice: rough around the edges but amused at the world. He moved no more quickly than her and she shrieked with laughter as he tripped, following her. The men relaxed as he said, 'Little hell-cat. Don't you know that it's dangerous to stop a dog mid-hunt?'

He chased her down a slope and her fake laughter built into a kind of real hysteria. Wet feet and already out of breath. That black line in the grey would be the river so she headed that way. At the head of a small bridge, two old men played cards under a meagre torch. She came close, thrust out her breasts and put her finger to her lips. 'Don't tell him which way I went.'

She stepped out onto a bridge that was little more than three planks and let Trussell catch up. The men laughed as the planks bowed under new weight. She ran on, shoe buckles jangling in her hand, until she came to the mainland. The guard there was younger, though still an old man, and she collapsed, giggling, into his arms. 'Oh, help. He's chasing me. He won't take no for an answer.'

She pressed against him and made sure her voice had that breathy chuckle that the London whores used.

Footsteps. Trussell ran and then slowed to a walk. 'My hell-cat's keen to get off the island, is she? Well, that can be arranged.'

He came close to the old man. 'I'll take it from here. Thank you for keeping her warm.'

There was a moment's hesitation as some pecking order was worked out between them. For a moment, the man kept up his grip. Then he pushed Shay away. 'Give her one from me,' he said.

They were nearly gone when the old man stretched out an arm. 'Why aren't you out chasing the Sparrow? I thought only us old boys were left here.'

Nonesuch had been right. The other Blackfriars Boys might be able to act but they couldn't lie. There was a tell-tale moment before Trussell said something about being ill and faked a quick cough, but even Shay had heard his hesitation.

The man said, 'Wait here a second,' and wheezed back across the bridge. Shay and Trussell looked at each other and then, without a word, scrambled down the slope towards the water.

'I have a boat.' The incline down to the riverbank was knotty with tree roots. Shay stepped high, like a show horse, but still caught her toes in loops of root. Mud on her feet, mud on her knees. Trussell thrashed in the undergrowth and then pushed a small rowing boat out into the river. They leapt in together, landing flat on their bellies as behind them lights moved along the bridge. They were close enough to hear shouts of alarm. Trussell slapped his own face. 'Stupid, stupid, stupid. I could have said I was a messenger.'

Shay watched the lights move on the bridge. 'Don't worry, just row.'

He swiped at the surface with the oars, sending grey wings of water up behind them and the boat zigzagged across the stream. Shay said, 'Wait. Trussell, stop. Let me do it – my father is a ferryman.'

She took over, sliding the oars into the water like knives, the work happening beneath the surface, and the boat straightened and sped. 'Do we have a place to hide?'

'No. I didn't think we'd be chased. We'll need to get off the river though. They're twice as fast as us.'

241

Shay had already made that calculation. The Commoners had boats and horsemen so only guile would thwart them. As she rowed, she heard her father's voice: 'Whatever runs is prey.' She slowed her heartbeat and tried to think like a hunter.

An idea. She scanned the riverbank for the right place. No, too open here. Onwards with patience. Twice they passed places that were almost right, but it was a quarter-hour before she saw what she'd been looking for.

'We get out here.' She steered the boat up onto a long C of silt that was overhung with trees. Trussell started to haul the boat up into the shadows, but she said, 'No leave it where it can be seen. Now, follow me.'

She stomped leftwards into the forest making sure that her footsteps showed in the silt, and indicated to Trussell to do the same. Once they were deep enough into the woods that the ground was carpeted with leaves, they cut back to the right. She told him, 'Keep your footsteps light and find a branch that's come down in the storm. One big enough that it'll float even with both of us hanging on to it.'

No moonlight penetrated this deep. Blacks and greys and everything waterlogged. It took minutes before she could see clearly enough to pick out a suitable branch, but at least plenty were down. She stopped by one the size of a small tree. 'This'll do. Help me drag it to the water.'

It was heavy going. The branch snagged and shed leaves like a blood trail. By the time they met the river again, they were both wet with sweat. Still, they were fifty yards downstream of the boat, with no sign that they'd looped back to the river.

'One, two, three, *go*.' They dragged the branch out into the water until they were up to their necks in it, and then clung on as the current caught them. For minutes they stayed that way, arms draped over the branch, occasionally kicking up spray to speed up or slow down until Shay could breathe again. She slid along the branch until their faces were only inches apart. They looked at each other for a long time before, simultaneously, they began to laugh. Laughter that grew until the branch rocked so hard that nightbirds broke for shore and Shay's face was wet with tears.

They didn't talk until they were ashore again, miles downstream, where they lay side by side, soaked and shivering but finally free, and she let the silence claim them. Once the panic had subsided, she said, 'Trussell, where are the others?'

A pause like a feather falling. Trussell turned away and said, 'They're all gone, Shay. It's just me.'

Suddenly she was a long way from home. For weeks she'd imagined the four of them watching over her like birdsong.

'They had to go,' he said. 'There were riots in London, and they targeted the foreigners, as always. Alouette's parents are old. You understand, don't you?'

She didn't answer.

'And Blank heard of a ship. To his island. He's going home. He may already have left, if the weather ever clears.'

How could an absence feel like a living, breathing thing? Shay said, 'They left with me still in a cage?'

'Not at first. At first it was all of us.' There was something in his voice that worried her. Pity, maybe? 'But, as time went on …'

His next question was as careful as a first step onto ice. 'Shay, how long do you think you've been in Cockaigne?'

Edinburgh, Stafford, Leeds. Manchester, Lancaster, Carlisle. So many faces, so many questions.

'A month? Or five weeks.' Something sounded wrong as soon as she said it. She'd been taken in May, she knew that.

Trussell rubbed his thumb on the spot on her palm. 'Shay, it's been six months.'

Suddenly, as if a curtain had been drawn back, she saw the bare trees and the frozen leaves on the ground. Now her final question hung there in the silence, like mistletoe on a tree. She was frightened of the answer.

'You didn't mention Nonesuch. Where is he?'

He took his hand away. 'Not here either. He's in London, I think. We can talk about that later.'

Six months. As long as the time she spent with the Blackfriars Boys. Six months bottled and concentrated and soured like vinegar. She shook her head. The fucking countryside.

38

FOR THE FIRST THREE days, as the black acid of the Cockaigne broth worked its way out of her system, Shay was a wreck. She shivered and sweated and threw up a thin grey bile even before her eyes had opened in the morning. By day, Trussell half carried her through the undergrowth, deep in the forest and far from the roads. The ground swung around her as if she were afloat on an ocean. Sometimes the world tipped and she crawled along a ceiling of clouds with an abyss beneath her. She clung, weeping, to tree roots until Trussell talked her down; she'd never been scared of the sky before. By nightfall, her trousers were ragged and Trussell pulled handfuls of thorns from her calves and thighs.

It was the fourth morning before the storm in her calmed. The night before, she kept her dinner down for the first time and she woke to a sky that was returned to its rightful place. Bars of sunlight broke through the roof of their shelter but they brought to mind her cage, so she dressed in silence and walked barefoot out into the woods. It had been months since no one was watching her and she strolled at random. Bare trees like the bones of lightning, decorated with clots of rooks' nests. Sparrows did their dropped-stitch flight. *The birds are gods.* No Devana overhead – their escape had been too well hidden. She squatted to piss under an oak and there was no sound but her own in these woods that would have looked exactly the same a hundred years earlier. She took huge, icy breaths until her chest ached. Trussell was awake when she returned.

'Where are we?' she asked.

He sat on a tree stump, mending his shoes. 'Somewhere between Ely and Cambridge, I think. Four days' ride from London, if we had horses. Or if we trusted the roads.'

Shay shifted around so that she could see his face. 'We don't trust the roads?' She hadn't had the strength to ask why their route was so convoluted.

He laid down his needle. 'I don't think so. The Jagger will expect you to head for London. And the Queen's men are looking for you too. Apparently, London is awash with stories that you've joined the Commoners, and that makes Elizabeth look weak. We spent as much time dodging the Swifts as we did searching for you. We have to assume that everyone on the roads wants you for their own particular cage.'

They set off perpendicular to the main track and ducked into brambles whenever they heard a noise from the path. It was slow going, but Trussell's hunches were right: after an hour, four men in ponytails and waistcoats galloped by at a fair lick, and soon after, three carts of soldiers rode the other way. Trussell talked as they went and that was how Shay learnt the story of her kidnap and escape, in broken snatches between stands of trees. He told her how they'd followed rumours of Cockaigne. Days watching for smoke on the horizon. And finally sighting Devana. Alouette making the kites and prepping fire-arrows until news of her parents called her home. Trussell had been at Cockaigne for her last three shows; so close at one point that he could have touched her hem. It was midday, though, when the forest was quiet and the road just a rumour off to their right, that Trussell told her the part she'd been waiting to hear.

'So, Nonesuch sold you.'

He didn't work his way up to the story. He just threw the words over his shoulder as he forded a brook. 'The night at Cockaigne, when he disappeared for a while. He found that Jagger man and made him a deal.'

'No.' It was out before she'd thought about it, but already some queasy machinery was turning within her.

'Alouette was suspicious from the start. Those men knew where to wait for us. They had a cage ready for you.'

Shay remembered the way her kidnappers had lolled, unhurried, on their horses. The smell of tobacco. The fiery arrow like a beacon for them.

'No. He wouldn't have.' Cogs turned inside her. 'Trussell, they knifed him. *You* were halfway down the road. I saw his wound.'

245

He wouldn't turn to look at her. He swished at the undergrowth with a stick. 'What did you see, Shay? Just blood. Lamb's blood, I assume. Cow's blood is too thick.'

The smell of iron and shit, and the sound of it dripping.

'Honestly, if he hadn't faked the stabbing then I'm not sure we would have suspected him. But you know that Nonesuch has to be centre stage. Something niggled at Alouette. She got him naked a couple of days later and there wasn't a scratch on him.'

The words slid home. 'Got him naked,' not 'saw him naked.'

'The next day, while he was out foraging, I searched his tent. I found those same French coins buried in the ground under his pillow. The half-angels. Enough to buy him a real title in London.'

Iron and shit, and the smell of tobacco. The way that men lie and laze. His story was true and impossible at the same time.

She spoke. 'You can't buy and sell people in England – that would mean slavery.' But as she said the words she understood. The Queen's Warrant meant that Evans could press-gang whomever he wanted, all within the law. The Queen owned Evans and Evans owned Shay. She wasn't even a slave, she was a chattel, just one more entry on the ledger, next to sets and buildings and furniture and weapons – all the things needed to keep the theatre running. The ten pounds that Evans demanded from Nonesuch wasn't for the ratty costumes and tired scripts, after all. It was for her.

She tugged on Trussell's belt to stop him walking on. 'Where is he?'

'London, I hear. We had the coins piled up outside his tent and we didn't hear him return. He just turned tail. I went after him, but you know he's a better horseman than me.'

Something was suddenly important. 'How much?'

'I ... don't remember.' A wingbeat's hesitation.

'Yes, you do. How much did I cost?'

'A hundred half-angels. And the formula for Greek fire.'

He knelt in the undergrowth and emptied out his purse. Coin after coin after coin tumbled into the mud. They shone brassy against the brown. Her price.

39

T EN NIGHTS IN CLEARINGS and ditches, falling asleep under silent stars and waking to hair damp with dew. Shay felt like the undergrowth that they struggled through. Emotions caught on her like burrs and ideas gnarled and doubled back on themselves. Once they stopped in a hollow, far from the road, where they ate so many blackberries that their lips turned blue, and Shay found an odd plant. It was a climber whose seeds had grown out in the open and the shoots had nothing to cling to. Three tendrils twisted and coiled around one another until the whole teetering mass stretched towards the sun. Trussell couldn't understand why it made her cry. Ten days in knots and then in sleep an untangling. She dreamt of her mother combing her hair and the pain and the pleasure that was mixed in it.

Nonesuch had betrayed her. He had sold her, taken the money, and let others bear the blame. It was too much to think about. Her keenest emotion was embarrassment. How must she have looked, mooning and chasing and excusing and loving? So many memories took on new aspects seen through the lens of his betrayal, like something familiar seen through water: his other girls, her name nowhere on the playbills, Blank and Trussell always playing her lovers for the Ghost Theatre. She burned at what others must have seen.

And if Nonesuch was one problem, then Trussell was another. Oh, Trussell. He loved her, that was plain enough. Had since they met, probably. She tried not to see it, and he was painstakingly, endlessly proper, but still his eyes hung off her. Every night they fell asleep back to back, and every morning they woke curled up like animals in a burrow, wet with sweat and dew, out-breaths hot in each other's mouths. It shouldn't be a burden to be loved, should it? Especially to be loved fiercely by a person who she now realised might be the first real friend she'd ever had. He'd traipsed England after her, and fought and lied and schemed for a chance to see her again. He had slept in ditches and dodged soldiers and never a word of complaint.

And then, from the tenth day, a final, desperate burden: Devana. Shay had no idea how the bird had tracked them under the roof of trees, but now every time they broke cover Devana wheeled above them. The arrow had done some damage. Her silhouette was skew-whiff and she flew a jagged orbit. Shay ached to tend to that wing, but the first time that she called for the bird, Trussell shoved her deep into the undergrowth. He'd never put his hands on her that way before.

'Shay, you *can't*.' His eyes were frantic. 'Everyone knows she's yours. You might as well shout your name from the treetops.'

From then on, Shay pushed them harder towards London, straying ever closer to the road, but with ears tuned to the sound of hoofbeats. Usually that was enough, though once they stumbled across a trio of sleeping soldiers whose horses ate silently by the roadside. With his finger to his lips, Trussell pointed to something peeking from a saddle-bag: a poster. Only the top was visible, but it was enough – two wings of hair and a sparrow tattoo.

There were more fields closer to London, which meant more dangerous open spaces. At dusk Devana circled low above them and struggled against the evening breeze. She'd lost much of her glow and only a few patches of foxfire still showed against her silhouette. She glided lower and Trussell moaned. 'Make her stay back. She'll lead them straight to us.' But Shay had spent her entire life trying to bring Devana closer; she had no vocabulary for sending her away.

By Cambridge, they were making good time. Beaten paths wound through the forest and they walked a quick ten miles without seeing a soul. Ten miles closer to the city and Shay could feel it in her veins somehow. They came across a spot where someone had camped out the night before, and the pair of them sat around a blackened patch of grass as if a fire still burned there. It was quiet. Great tits went after the last of the insects, hanging swathes of invisible bunting from the air, while Shay dealt hand after hand of the bird tarot. Ten of Magpies, the Tower, the Hanged Man. Ace of Sparrows, King of Magpies. Questions, not answers.

'Would you draw me?' she asked.

Trussell propped himself up on an elbow. 'Are you sure?'

'Yes. It's been a while. This might be the longest I've seen you without a pencil in your hand.'

He opened up his sketchbook and flicked past drawings of leaves and moths and branches and rocks. No people, no birds.

'But Trussell,' she said. 'Don't flatter me, for once.'

'What do you mean?'

'You always draw the best of me. You show me as beautiful or clever or brave, but I want to see what I truly look like.'

He looked surprised. 'I don't add anything. You *are* beautiful.' He tried to hold her gaze for a moment but he had to look away.

Shay blushed, as if she'd been the one calling herself a beauty. 'Try drawing me as if I was an object. A leaf or something.'

'All right. But you need to be doing something so that you look natural. Read the cards for me.'

She laughed. 'Now *I* get to ask whether you're sure. We're hungry and lost and pursued, it might not be the cheeriest of readings.'

The look he gave her was folded into itself somehow and a realisation hit her. 'Oh,' she thought. 'He's *happy* here.'

She dealt the Travellers' Hand. A card for departure, a card for arrival, a card for the weather and a card for companions. Despite herself, she couldn't help trying to find the truth in the patterns. The Fool as the arrival card: good sign or ill? What did that Ace of Magpies mean when it was reversed?

'Done,' said Trussell.

She'd only dealt the one hand. 'That was quick.'

He handed her the sketch and she tried to see herself as a stranger might. Plain, certainly. Small features, almost like a child's. Too dark to be English, but too pale to be exotic. It was a face one might grow into. It bore small marks of exasperation – there was a furrowed wake between her eyebrows and a jut of lower lip. Boy or girl? Nothing definite with the hair short and the mouth unremarkable, though Trussell had drawn her leaning over the cards in a way that looked motherly. It was as if her body simply hadn't made up its mind yet. A small, unremarkable youth with a frown and short black hair.

'I'm sorry,' said Trussell.

She couldn't see why. All she needed was to be this girl. Plain like snow, clear like water.

He smoothed out the paper. 'I didn't mean to make you look so beautiful.'

The trees thinned around Hertford, where swatches of land had been enclosed and fenced. Bare fields appeared to their left and right, and Trussell was all for turning back and finding a more concealed route. But Shay could only think of the straightest line back to London – she wanted to lose herself in its crowds. They walked two miles across open ground and Devana flew doggedly above them, low enough that Shay could see the crook of broken wing. She looked weaker than yesterday, and would be weaker still tomorrow. Shay worried that Devana couldn't hunt in this state. She rummaged in her bag for something to feed her with and when she looked up Trussell was notching an arrow into his bow.

'No.'

It was lit and pulled back in a moment. He had tears in his eyes.

'Trussell, please no.'

The arrow spiralled to the right of the bird, spitting sparks, and Devana banked left. Her laboured wingbeats couldn't clear the line of hedges though, and she wheeled around, looking for another way out.

His hands were shaking. 'There's nowhere to hide. Send her away, Shay. I don't want to do this.'

She ran out into the field, yelling and waving her hands, but Devana circled back towards her. She batted at the air as the falcon came in to land, and Devana veered away again. She made a cumbersome, low circle and then headed back towards them.

Trussell drew his bow back again and Shay threw herself across the grass. She slammed into his shoulder as he released the arrow. It flew to the bird's right again, but closer, and Devana tumbled, wing over wing, towards a stand of trees. Sparks bloomed around her head, and she flew low to the ground until a wingtip caught on a branch, sending her tumbling again. Shay beat her hands on Trussell's chest as the bird righted herself and aimed for a gap between the fences. He held her against his body until Devana was out of sight, while he said, over and over, 'Forgive me, forgive me, forgive me.'

A silent day after that. They strayed further from the road as the traffic into London increased. Trussell spoke to the back of Shay's head. 'We should stop here. Walk the last miles when it's dark – that way we can arrive as the gate opens. Less chance of being spotted.'

She made no sign of having heard but when a thick coppice appeared off to their right, she led them that way. They camped by a stream in a bowl of trees and lay separately, looking up through the canopy. Shay saw hawks and a buzzard but no Devana. They lay, back to back, and dozed.

And then there was a noise, gentle like a door opening, and a stag stood before them. His nostrils read the air and froth steamed at the corners of his mouth. He'd been running hard at some point but now his quiet was absolute; the wood pigeons made more noise than him. Something moved in the trees behind him, and his ears rotated, and then without warning he leapt the stream, leapt over Shay and Trussell, and was swallowed by trees before they even had time to turn.

'Idiots.'

The voice came from behind the line of trees. One by one, six archers on horseback stepped out into the clearing. They eyed Shay and Trussell. Trussell and Shay looked back.

'Useless idiots. One stag versus six archers and you didn't even wing it.' Evans' horse was a massive, placid thing with a black coat and a white blaze. He pulled on the reins and looked down at Shay and Trussell.

'Damn, I'm good,' he said.

His hair was plastered flat across his skull to hide an eye that sagged like a saddlebag. Shay recognised the change in him, she'd seen it in her father. The tide was coming in after forty years of going out. He patted his horse on the head and spoke lovingly into its ear.

'I *told* them, but no one listened. I said Trussell will come in from the west because Ludgate is the closest gate to Blackfriars. I said they'll be near the road but not actually on it. And I said that if we take a hunting party, then no one will guess who we're really looking for.' He shook his head. 'I'm right again and nobody who counts is here to see it.'

He shook his head in wonder. 'Cat got your tongues? Sorry, Sparrow, that's probably a sore point.'

Nausea hit her. They were only miles from London. Already a haze rose to their east. 'You've been looking for us?'

'Me and half the country. God might see when any single sparrow falls to earth but that Jagger fellow wouldn't be far behind. And I bet you regret suggesting those Black Swift troops to the Queen. Don't they give you the willies? They do me. Too quiet. Too quick.'

His lip drooped on one side, but his voice was certain. 'You, my little one, are transformed from a sparrow into a golden goose and I am here to sell the eggs. The only question is to whom. The Jagger will offer more in the way of hard cash, but the Queen would be more grateful.'

'We have money.' Trussell spoke for the first time.

Evans kept his eyes on Shay. 'No you don't, boy.'

Trussell opened his purse. 'Thirty half-angels.'

Evans said, 'That's not money, Trussell, not where this prize is concerned. That's loose change. Shush now, the adults are talking.'

'Take me to the Queen,' said Shay.

Evans looked at her with his counting-house eyes. 'Are you certain, little one? She's not sure about you, I'm afraid. I'll vouch for you, but I'd still give three to one on your ending up on the gibbet.'

Why did everyone take Shay more seriously than she did herself? 'She can't be worried about me, surely?'

'She worries about everyone, that's power's burden. Everyone is a threat. Especially a beautiful young girl who's been living with rebels and reputedly now has an army of birds at her beck and call. I guarantee you that there are several meetings going on right now about exactly what to do about you.'

'I'm beautiful now, am I?'

The thin smile wiped years from him. 'As I've always said, you're not to my taste, but you've made the most of what you've got.' He shuffled round. 'Hair a bit longer, good. The girls' clothes help. Let's see those nails.'

Shay held out her hands while she made familiar calculations. The number of men. The speed of their horses. What was wanted from her. But something new was alight within her, too. The voice made of feathers and wind that whispered: *one either hunts or is hunted – there are no bystanders.*

'I'll be at Birdland tomorrow at dusk. Tell her that I'll read the Murmuration for her.'

Evans clapped his hands together in delight. 'Is that an ultimatum? An ultimatum for our sovereign. How fierce. Allow me to counter-offer: I throw you in a sack and dump you at the Queen's feet.'

Shay would never let herself be caged again. 'Do that and I'll foretell that you will overthrow her.'

He beamed. 'So, it's a negotiation. It's been ages.' He walked his horse around them. 'Then I simply sell you back to The Jagger.'

Shay didn't pause. 'I'll tell him that my price for singing again will be the burning of all your lands. In the country, in London, wherever. He'd do it with pleasure.'

Evans' eyes sat deep in his skull: embers with a cold night ahead. 'How complicated. It might be safer to kill you both. Thirty half-angels is less than I expected but it's not nothing.' He tipped his hat at Trussell.

She saw him. Saw right through him. 'It's certainly the safest option, but where's the drama in that?'

She turned and walked towards the main road. 'Birdland at dusk.'

She waited for the arrows in her back. The road was further than she thought. Evans barked something at his men and then trotted his horse to catch up with her. 'All right. I'll tell the Queen. But I'd better make it sound like my suggestion. Contrition, Shay, that's all she wants. Good news and contrition.'

Shay kept her eyes focused on the road. As she stepped onto the track, Evans called out again. 'And Trussell stays here with me. Just until I'm sure that you've been as complimentary as I deserve.'

London was a haze of smoke on the horizon. Birds rode the thermals. Shay didn't look back.

40

ALL THROUGH LONDON SHAY said her lines without thinking and people did what they were supposed to do. The city was a stage set: every house blank behind its eyes and every hawker's apple made of wax. Limbless beggars cried in front of shuttered houses and the sun looked like a gold foil theatre prop. The streets sang with post-plague bustle but Shay walked straight down the middle of the streets with no concern for soldiers or The Jagger or Gilmour's men. A squadron of Elizabeth's Swifts marched past her on Old Change but she didn't bother to hide under her cap. Shay had read ahead in this script. Nothing ended yet.

Extras swarmed around her, but the principal characters were all off stage. Children cried out *Sparrow Queen, Sparrow Queen, sing us a song* and the ferry passengers begged to touch her hem. A long line of figures stood silhouetted on the Birdland horizon. A man with a stick, propped between two others, might have been Lonan, but then again, this was a place full of old men. No matter. The play was in its final scene and the Aviscultans had no more lines.

Alone again then, with just ghosts to walk beside her. Across snow that had melted to dirty ice, leaving the ground the colour of bird shit. The frozen terrain was rough going. Keeping to the tussocks of crystal-lised grass meant an endlessly complicated path, full of doublings-back and dead ends, but it was safer than risking the ice. Shay's hose were soon dark with water, her boots heavy. It was cold enough to tear at her lungs and she brushed ice from her eyebrows and hair.

Drums and smoke. Before she could see the Queen's convoy, that's all they were. Drumbeats that rushed over the marshes and a pall of lethargic smoke as the falling snow extinguished their torches over and over again. The Queen's people were spread out like a wedge of geese with a dark knot of bodies clustered in the centre: footmen, soldiers, ladies-in-waiting, cooks, cabmen, entertainers, advisors and attendants. The entire palace was on the move.

It was a well-oiled process. Servants placed planks across the ice. Mast-long pieces of wood that took six men to move, taken from the back of the convoy and rushed, stumbling, to the front, and then laid down to build a floor as solid as in any house. It was a shifting platform for the Queen on her throne and the various musicians and ladies-in-waiting that she kept close. Servants had dragged these planks, making and remaking the wooden road, for tens of miles; Shay ached just looking at them. Attendants held up painted panels to the sides and the rear of the Queen so that she didn't have to see a single inch of her realm.

Shay shivered in the shadow of the tree. All this fakery – the illustrated walls and floor, the roaring braziers – meant nothing when pitted against the weight of winter. The convoy stopped ten yards from the tree. A knuckle of root protruded out into the marsh, and it set the planks at a slight angle. The Queen's throne leaned gently towards the river. The drums halted and a soldier with a musket stepped forward to check her over. 'Approach,' he said.

The walk felt endless. This close to the tree it was less marshy, but exposed roots had buckled the ground into frozen waves and she tripped twice. Her breath was louder than the sounds around her: banners flapping and the flock of starlings that were beginning to settle in the branches of the tree. Elizabeth was swaddled in dark fur, so voluminous that her pale face looked like a saintly relic on display. 'She's dying,' thought Shay.

Nonesuch would have had much to say about her make-up. It was thick and sloppily applied. The white had crumbled around her eyes and the red blusher made her look clownish. Still, her eyes were watchful.

'I can't imagine one telling a positive fortune in such a desolate place.' She waved a hand in the general direction of Birdland. Thankfully, the starlings were massing behind her.

'It's majestic as well as desolate though, no?' said Shay. She gave a little bow as she spoke.

Elizabeth's glance about the place – the miles of hard grey land, hung over by smoke and cloud – was cursory. She looked up at the tree. 'They are here? You have what you need?'

A restlessness was building in the branches above. Birds arrived from all directions and set the flock moving through the tree. Already the boughs heaved under dark bodies and still more circled overhead.

'God willing, the conditions are perfect. Does Her Majesty have a particular aspect of her fortune for us to focus on?'

A stray gust of wind scuttled across the marsh, lifting the flock from the branches and then setting them down again. A stray curl escaped from Elizabeth's hood: her red hair was pure white at the roots. 'Not my fortune today, sparrow girl, but yours.'

She snapped her fingers and a servant stepped forward to unfold a sheet of paper in front of them. Shay recognised the palette. Yellow paper and black capitals: Ghost Theatre work.

It read:

SATURNALIA NOW!

THE GHOST THEATRE

THE DEATH OF LORD NONESUCH &

THE SPARROW'S RETURN

SOUTHWARK, TOMORROW

Elizabeth's eyes were fixed on Shay. 'There are hundreds of these all over the city. The faster we take them down, the quicker they go back up. It is ... disappointing.'

'I swear I know nothing about this.' The cold was in her bones now and seeing her name there chilled her further. 'I know nothing about it, and if I'd been asked to perform, I would have said no.'

'You've seen him?'

'No. But he knows that I wouldn't be part of this.'

Elizabeth said nothing. She simply sat there with the wind flapping at the panels around her. Rattle of branches and squabble of birds. Her breath smelled of something dying, and of the cloves that were meant to hide the rot. The combination of the two – death and its shroud – was worse than either thing on its own. Her silence begged to be filled. Shay said, 'The Commoners forced me to perform but now I've retired. I'm done.'

She couldn't tell if Elizabeth was listening. The Queen smoothed out the paper in front of her but didn't look at it again. 'Do you know where he is?'

'No.'

'Do you know where he's going to be performing?'

'No.'

'Do you know what he's going to say?'

'No. And I'll warrant that he doesn't know yet either.'

Elizabeth's look then was something deeper. For the first time Shay considered that the Queen might be *scared* of Nonesuch. The whole world knew that the excesses of the prentices were an annoyance to her, what with their riots and drunkenness, but theirs was an unfocused violence that flared and spat and died down as quickly as it had sparked. With a sudden clarity, she saw the source of Elizabeth's fear. Nonesuch might be the one to *fashion* them, to turn them from flock into murmuration, from mob into army, from wildness into weapon. Elizabeth shivered again, even swaddled in her furs, and Shay had the sudden impression that she was just a head – the head of state – lying there on a bed of embroidery. It made her ridiculous and terrifying. Elizabeth clapped her hands and the noise raced across the ice. Behind her, servants started clapping too. Some had rattles. As the racket spread, the starlings took to the air in great ripples.

She took Shay's hand and said, 'Well, we should find out.'

One moment the birds were scattered like pebbles, the next they were a single living thing. A hundred necks craned towards the spectacle and a shape formed in the grey air like cross-hatching. The convoy cried out, as if at fireworks, and Elizabeth squeezed her hand. It was such a human gesture that it took Shay out of herself for a second. The fires blazed around them and made the birds a black smear against the clouds. She couldn't see a thing. Why did everyone want answers? Where did they get you? Nowhere. The world rolled its waves over you anyway. It was like arguing with the sea.

And then, as she readied a lie to cover her lack of inspiration, it happened. A shift like her mind missing its footing. A crack deep within her, ice against ice. And then, inrushing and lifting her, the air came alive and she was inside the flock of birds. They swirled like blown leaves, but everything was calm. Their movement was stillness; their chaos was order. Shay was utterly lost, tossed and buffeted by the wind, not a bird in a flock but a feather on a wing, shaping the flight while being shaped by it. She laughed with naked pleasure. To be thrown down and raised up, to spin like a sycamore seed, to be inches and seconds from disaster but safe in a nest.

'Oh,' said her mind. 'Oh, *this* is what it's like.' It was exactly as she'd imagined, and wholly, shrinkingly strange.

How long did she spend curvetting and fountaining in the breath of the flock? It felt like minutes, but time was soft and fat here, a thing to be moulded. There was something she was supposed to do. What was it? The flock tightened like a sinew, and she was part of it.

HE WILL DIE BEFORE HER, WILL DIE BEFORE YOU

The words were in the noise somewhere, made up of tail-feather and headwind, claw and snow.

THE FOREST MUST BURN BEFORE IT GROWS ANEW

'The forest is London?' she asked without words, knowing the answer and not expecting one.

SHE WILL STOP THE RIVER, HE WILL CROSS THE RIVER, YOU WILL BE THE RIVER

Shay was tossed in a twisting loop that ought to have been terrifying. Inrush, out-breath, and the world tipped over like a glass of water.

AN EMPTY NEST WILL KILL YOU ALL

'How?' she asked, over and over, like breezes in the bare branches.

THE CITY IS A SHADOW OF THE KINGDOM OF THE AIR

'Yes.'

YOU WILL FALL

'No.' The world spun around outside the flock, visible again. Sky, snow, water, earth. The invisible centre around which the Murmuration writhed lost its hold. Birds peeled away into the infinity of sky and the whole flock plummeted, a violin sliding from high to low C.

YOU WILL FALL

How could the earth rise up to hit her when she stood, tight, on her two feet? But it did. A slap from a careless hand and ice ground into the wound. Flat on her face with a hand still in hers. But not the one she wanted. Never the one she wanted. Servants hauled her to her feet with their hands under her armpits. Elizabeth's courtiers stayed close and Shay, as she passed out, saw hands go to knives.

From somewhere else now. Like the voices you hear, far away, as sleep takes you.

YOU THREE WILL FALL

She slept on the floor of her father's house. It had the ingrained cold of a place unheated even by breath for the whole of winter. So, he was gone. Gone from here at least, another ghost in Shay's personal theatre. Her fingers curled and numbed and she didn't have the strength to rub them back into life. Someone came and covered her with blankets but their weight only trapped the cold deeper inside her. Her bones sang with ice and she thought that she might shatter. The moon was at the window. She watched for a bird to fly across its light – a good omen, everyone said – but none came. An empty nest will kill you all. Which of them had said that? The curtains were open and they would never close again.

Hands under her armpits. Conversations in the air above her. A glimpse of milky-blind eyes that saw her and then looked away. Ladders, sleds, boats. So much *work*. Empty hands and the silly old moon above her.

Bear cries. Dog howls. All London's caged things.

41

I T WAS WARM WHEN she woke. The floor beneath her tilted gently and she smelled something too rich for London air. There was only one place where she'd tasted the heat of spices indoors before. 'Blank?' she said.

'Good morning.' He sat on a three-legged stool as he sewed something on to a piece of pale cloth. 'The kraken awakes.'

He put down his sewing and kneeled to brush her hair back. 'You even slept as I carried you up the mast. I wouldn't have thought it could be done.' He looked older; grey tipped his curls and his eyelids drooped. He stood back up awkwardly; the room was at an odd angle. 'Some coffee, I think.'

He fussed with a pan and beans and Shay warmed from inside and out. The room was unchanging in its slope, so she peered out through the flaps. The Thames was frozen solid and had trapped *The Albatross* at an angle. Blank's voice was warm with amusement. 'Your people were extremely keen to be rid of you. A boatman arrived here last night and wouldn't leave without me. Have you been causing trouble?'

Had she? 'I'm not sure. I was with the Queen.'

If he was surprised, he didn't show it. He moved around the crow's nest in bare feet, brewing coffee and spreading butter on thick ends of bread. Shay was instantly, ravenously hungry. He sat down and fed her like a bird.

'Now, what did our sovereign want with you?'

The coffee was too hot, but she needed fire inside her immediately. She sipped at it and said, 'She wanted to know what to do with Nonesuch.'

He nodded. 'He has been rather busy since his return.'

'Has he been putting on shows on his own?'

'I'm not sure I could call them shows, really. Provocations, maybe. Insurrections? And certainly not on his own. There's hardly a boy in the city who hasn't taken part in some way.' Blank looked out, over the city. 'You know he stole a galleon?'

'Nonesuch did? He can barely pilot a tilt-boat.'

'Well, not necessarily him. Someone in his thrall. Or maybe someone out to impress him. Wintour and Fawkes and that lot worship him. Anyway, *somebody* stole an empty galleon and set it afire. Afire and adrift.' He couldn't keep the admiration from his voice. 'It was beautiful, Shay. They daubed it white, like a swan, torched the sails, and set it loose, with every cannon loaded with flour.

'Flour?'

He smiled. 'You should have seen it. Ghost white and aflame down the Thames, and as the cannon burned, they fired great white clouds, like outbreaths across the city.'

Nonesuch did have that gift – putting images in your head. She saw it, clearer than a memory. A spectral dragon gliding across the waves, breathing smoke across the cowering city.

'Where is he, Blank?'

'God only knows. If even he does. Elizabeth certainly doesn't. What did you tell her?'

Shay thought back to the evening before. 'I have no idea.'

She slept without dreaming and the day disappeared between the cracks in the floorboards. London's clockwork whispered to her: hawker cries and church bells, street songs and the constant sound of building. Blank went in and out. He left in sailor's whites and came back smelling of rum and smoke. As the light began to fade, he returned again. Shay struggled to sit up and he examined her carefully. 'Awake? Alive?'

She nodded and he handed her a handbill.

SATURNALIA NOW!
THE DEATH OF LORD NONESUCH & SACKERSON UNBOUND
THE GHOST THEATRE ISSUE PARDONS
THE SPARROW SHOWS HER CLAWS
SOUTHWARK, TOMORROW

Blank looked pensive. 'There are thousands of them between here and the bridge. It's provocative. Deliberately provocative. The prentices are

261

like animals on Saturnalia anyway and it wouldn't take much to push them over the edge.'

Shay pulled the cover more tightly around her. 'They won't let it go ahead, surely? The Master of the Revels will shut this down in an instant.' Elizabeth's Black Swifts too, she thought.

Blank said, 'It's not quite that simple. No one knows exactly where in Southwark it's happening and Nonesuch has built quite the following while you were away. By the time the Master knows the location, there will be thousands there, and there's no way that his men will take on a crowd like that.'

Shay pulled back the cloth to look out over the water. The frozen river was thick with figures making for the southern shore. Their shouts and the clink of ale-jugs carried across the ice. She watched a drunk boy slip and be hauled laughingly to his feet by his friends. 'It's busy out there already.'

Blank bent over his coffee. 'Everyone wants to be in Southwark tonight. I heard that rooms were renting for a shilling apiece already. Everyone wants to be prepared.'

Shay watched the stream of people. How could there be so many? She had the sense, as she often did, that London was endless and its population immeasurable. The city was England's drain, and everyone spiralled around it, pulled from the wide open spaces to huddle in one of London's unlit, unheated rooms. It chewed them up and threw them out and the next generation came happily to take their places. And now the flotsam drained towards Southwark. Most were laughing and most were drunk. Children really, but still they came. Dusk fell and the numbers grew. Those who'd thought to bring lanterns cut straight across the frozen river, while the less prepared wandered and fell and could only be tracked by their curses as they went over for the third time. Southwark was a glittering gem on the southern shore. You could even hear it: a low crackle like embers, made up of thousands of voices. Shay dozed and dreamt of a cold, empty nest.

A noise woke her. A subterranean crack that echoed in her bones. It was like trees coming down; the crow's nest vibrated with a deep shudder.

'Blank?'

'Hmm?' He was silhouetted against a square of moonlight, dressed for going out.

'What's going on?' she asked.

He turned back into the room, a black shape. 'They're smashing up the Thames.'

She wrapped herself in a blanket and looked out. At first it appeared as if the river itself was aflame, but as her vision cleared, she made out a string of men holding torches. In front of them, other figures swung axes. Men cried, 'Three, two, one, go,' and then a wave of axes broke onto the ice. A moment of rest and then again. Two times, three, and then came that crack. The line of men shuffled back a couple of yards and the torchmen followed. Shay looked west along the river. The line of men stretched all the way beyond the bend of Westminster. Blank pulled on his boots.

'What are you doing?' Shay asked.

He tied a bow. 'They're going to cut off Southwark. They'll break the ice for miles and then close the bridge. If the Queen orders the rivermen to stay home tomorrow, then there will be no way in and out of south London. They won't care if whatever Nonesuch has planned stays in Southwark.'

He tossed her some clothes from the costume pile: trousers lined with fur and a monk's habit. Gloves and socks. 'Come on. You don't want to miss this, do you?'

The gloves hardly helped against the ice on the mast and the rope ladders. By the time they stepped out onto the Thames, she couldn't feel her fingers or toes. They cut along the river, close to the bank, where the ice was still intact. Shay half walked and half slid across the surface, and the motion made her feel like a child again. One Christmas when she was small, the whole family had strolled the frozen Thames to watch the city folk all dressed up for midnight service. She could feel it now: the thrill of being awake so late and her mother's hand in hers as they slid across the ice together. And then the memory, buried deep in her muscles, of being carried home, draped over her father's shoulder, as secure a feeling as she'd ever had.

It took them ten minutes to reach the ice-breakers. Shouted orders and the cymbal-crash of axes on ice; it sounded like war. Blank cut diagonally away from the bridge and they overtook the first of the men. Moongleam flattened the ice until it was like walking on air. In the centre the surface was thinner and twice she had to guide Blank around darker patches. They could hear the river still rolling somewhere deep beneath them and every minute or so the ground reverberated with deep clangs.

Southwark was a lantern. Torches blazed on every wall and braziers glowed in sheltered corners. The taverns shook with song and every brothel had a queue down the street. Prentices, wreathed in their own breath, whistled at passing girls and Shay pulled her hood tight around her. Ghost Theatre posters plastered the walls, and they heard the same names from every drunken street corner: Nonesuch. Sparrow. The Queen. *Tomorrow*. Nothing to do but walk. They strolled along the bank, with the Thames whispering somewhere beneath the ice off to their left. Blank still hadn't asked about Nonesuch and Shay was grateful for that. Somewhere in the distance, broken ice clashed with a grinding sound and along the shore lights showed, yards out into the river. Blank pointed. 'See that? They're merchant ships trapped in the ice. They'll have a berth for an old sailor. If you could bear pretending to be a boy again then it will be warm, at least.'

Shay was done with men and talk and tiny rooms. She wanted silence and space. A familiar building loomed behind them, and she said, 'You go. I need to see an old friend. I'll find you in the morning.'

42

T HE BEAR PIT'S HUGE fireplace was topped with a wide chimney and Shay had to wedge against the sides to lower herself down. The brickwork was lined with inches of built-up soot, and as she pressed herself against the walls, they started to crumble and slide. The dirt fell in a black sheet and her left arm shot after it, spinning her horizontal. She straightened and forced herself rigid. Bricks scraped her skin and she had to dig in deeper. She let out a cry of pain and came to a juddering halt with her shoulders and feet pressed hard into the walls. Soot fell and she kept her mouth closed as she shimmied down. One foot, opposite shoulder, other foot, other shoulder: an inch at a time, the walls as rough as sandpaper. Inch, inch, inch. A trickle of blood ran between her shoulder blades. Inch, inch, inch, until her arse touched something, and with relief she let go and tumbled the last foot into the hearth. Spent logs crumbled under her, the grate dug into her back and her mouth filled with ash. She coughed and spat and rolled out into the room.

Pitch black. She stifled a cough and listened. Soft noises. Soft but not small. Breaths with some heft behind them. *Thud, thud, thud* and Shay saw those paws in her mind. Leather pads with knives attached. She sat still and made the dove call.

The steps stopped. She cleared her throat and tried again, and a whine came from directly in front of her. She cooed and felt sudden wet leather at her neck. Wet leather and hot breath. Sackerson's nose read her, carefully. The vein in her neck, her wounds. Her hair, between her legs. She kept her hands by her side and whispered, 'Good boy, old friend, you can smell the cage on me, right?'

Her knuckles had been skinned on the flue and Sackerson began to clean them. His tongue was like a gloved hand: rough but gently wielded. As slowly as possible, she reached out. Could he see in this light? The way he snuffled with his nose made her think not. She touched fur and he growled, a sound that came up through her feet, but it didn't worry her. Growls are all he has, she thought, and stroked his belly. They went on like this for a couple of minutes, his tongue on her wounds, her hands in his fur and his growl unceasing.

And then he was done. He lay back down with a sigh and arranged himself into a crescent. Shay curled into his belly, trying to leech some of his warmth. She chattered the whole time. 'Do they come after you in your sleep, boy? They do? Me too. They won't let us have even a minute to ourselves. Tonight, though, their attentions should be elsewhere. We'll see each other when we sleep. Where shall we go?'

In her dreams she flew, low and fast, through a snow-shrouded forest. Trees so thick that at a distance they looked like a wall, but as she sped closer, the perfect gap opened up between the trunks. She didn't even have to alter her course, just on and on with snow beneath, the boughs above and icy air whistling around her. Twice she saw bear tracks curling off into the distance, but she couldn't stop. She couldn't even look around.

And then it was morning. Grimy light shone in from a ring of windows high above the pit. Still, she wouldn't have known that Nonesuch was there until he cleared his throat. He sat in the front row of the circle, looking down. Shay had never seen him in the audience before.

He clapped, slowly. 'What a first scene. I couldn't have written it better myself. "We open on the Sparrow, blackened and torn, in the embrace of a mighty bear." I am agog.'

He wore the same holed jacket that he'd had on the first day they met, but it was now greyed with age. His face was the same faded hue: candlelight skin. A stage crown sat angled down over one ear. He shifted forward in his seat, keeping his distance. He still knows where the light suits him best, Shay thought.

'So what's scene two?' he asked.

Shay sat up, trying not to disturb Sackerson. 'I have no idea. There's no script. You're the one advertising a performance. Advertising *my* performance.'

He held his hands up. 'I'm sorry about that. But today very much needs arses on seats and, though it pains me to say it, you're quite the draw. No accounting for the public. Of course, you're even more popular since your little northern jaunt.'

Shay kept her voice low. 'Northern jaunt? Use the proper words. My enslavement. My betrayal. Your cowardice.'

He shook his head. 'Well, whatever it was, it's done you a world of good. You're looking well.'

Shay had planned, many times over, what she would say to him when they next met, but here, now, words weren't adequate. 'How did you know I was here?' If Nonesuch could find her, then so could her enemies.

'I didn't. I came for the bear. The only real star out of the three of us.' Sackerson had been on the poster, Shay remembered.

'You're going to have him fight?'

He waved a hand. 'Lord no, I'm going to free him. I'm going to free him and all of the city's prisoners. He can go drink at the Old Swan or order suckling pig at Emerson's. I'll grant him the freedom of Southwark.'

Sackerson shifted beneath her. A huge paw scratched at his ear from somewhere deep inside sleep. 'So, freedom for everyone except me?'

There was irritation in his sigh. 'Oh saints, it was necessary, Shay. Our drama called for it. The tragedy.' He stood. 'Surely you saw it, right from the beginning. Nonesuch and the Sparrow, the Sparrow and Nonesuch. What a tale! It had everything. A bird girl and a changeling boy. Queens and magicians. Treasure and treason. But it could only be a tragedy, you must have understood that. When the low-born reach for the sun, then the world will burn them up.'

His words were black ice, but she stood firm. 'Remember that first night in the bunk? We were going to make something new. We were going to raze their old stories to the ground.'

He nodded. 'We were. We did. Ah, but those old stories never really die.'

A still fell across the bear pit. Sackerson's breaths calmed her.

Nonesuch passed his hand across his eyes. 'I was a fucking *magician*, Shay, once. I transformed the stage into a ship. I made London into Rome. Blackfriars became Babylon.' His voice rang. 'I was Cleopatra, Caligula and Constantine.' As he spoke, those characters flashed across his face and then disappeared. 'But I had nothing.'

He collapsed in on himself. 'Evans took the money, and I got the flowers. Do you remember all the flowers, Shay? Armfuls of them. Half as pretty as me and dead before sundown.' He wiggled a finger through his blouson. 'A tragedy of a boy. But then, but then …'

He threw his arms wide. 'I built the Ghost Theatre and I was reborn. I snuck into a thousand prentices' minds and a thousand rich girls' dreams. My words were a plague that infected the whole city, and those old stories couldn't claim me.'

He sat back down. 'And then you opened your mouth. Without so much as a thought. You started to sing, and the coins spewed out. Birdsong. I was second on the bill to birdsong.'

He stared at her with blank eyes. 'Shay, have you any idea how hard I worked to escape? You can't imagine the things I did, the lies I told, the sins that I ate.' He spat. 'Everything that I spent my life working for, you found in your back pocket. You didn't even know it was there.'

He rubbed both hands down his face, pulling his skin so he looked like a bloodhound. 'The Sparrow, the Sparrow, the fucking Sparrow. Oh, the mystery. With her tits like pancakes and her arse like a serving board. She's boy and girl, she's man and bird. Make up your fucking mind. Sixteen years old and never had to make a decision in her silly life. So I made up your mind for you. Isn't it every child's dream to run away and join the circus?'

Words. The moment that you tried to fight words with words, you were lost. But she had nothing else here.

'You sold me. *Sold* me.' She took a handful of coins from her pocket and tossed them up into the stall. They fell with a dull clatter. 'You were sold as a boy, and you sold me. You're everything you hate.'

He shook his head and stepped out into the bear ring. 'People like you and me, Shay, we were born sold. I just chose your buyer.'

He came close and reached out his hands, and automatically she reached back. He stepped her into a dance position and whispered, 'One-and-two, one-and-two.'

Even in the straw and shit of the bear pit, he danced well. One hand in the small of her back and one in her palm. 'That first day I saw you, on the rooftops, oh my word. With each leap, I thought to myself, that's it, she's going to *fly*.' With his hands under her armpits, he lifted her, but barely a couple of inches. 'I truly thought it would happen. I could *see* it. The men and the dogs all looking up into the heavens and you gone into the light.' He stopped. 'But down you came, every time. We can't escape our roles, Shay. We can only play them with some style.'

Shay stopped the dance. 'Did you love me?' The question was automatic, an out-breath.

'Yes.' He didn't stop to think. 'Yes. A hundred times over. I loved your stubble-rash and your stutter and the way you cried when I was inside you and your scars and your sailor's smocks and your fierce, fierce nails. I loved your feet on the roof overhead and your hand in mine and your animal-kick dreams and the way you ate and the way you slept.'

He looked weary now, like he was listing violences done to him. 'I loved your kindness to the stage-door girls and your scuffed knees and elbows and your big stupid joy at a magpie or a blue jay. And your leaps and bounds and your bird calls and trances and your singing and your laughing and your stage fright and your tattoos.'

A swollen river of words. How much he'd seen and how much she'd never managed to hide. She felt stripped. Words tumbling out like they were on stage. But an image crossed her mind: Trussell's drawing of her.

'That isn't me. Those are just things I did. It wasn't me that you loved, it was just my role.'

His eyes were black discs but he smiled for the first time that day. 'Maybe so. But oh Shay, *what a role.*'

Someone pounded on the main doors. Sackerson's nose twitched and Shay went back to comfort him.

'That'll be my blades come for the bear.' The door swung open into a blazing rectangle of light and Nonesuch's boys barrelled in. Street kids mainly, in torn military uniforms all decorated with thick red Xs across the chest. Sloppy painting like plague-house doors. They filled the space with chatter and ale-belch and the clanking of chains. Shay's eyes hurt from the light as the boys surrounded her and the bear. They looked more wary of her.

'What's it like out there?' Nonesuch leant on a stick and picked at his teeth.

'It's wild. Everyone has cleared out. No Watch, no owners, no rules. Gilmour's men are out there looking for someone' – at this, the boy gave Shay a sideways look – 'but they're keeping their heads down. There's ten of them and thousands of us.' He flung his arms wide. 'Southwark is ours.'

'Did you bring food for the bear?'

'Of course.' He opened a sack and the air filled with the smell of cooked meat. 'Swan. Venison. The good stuff.'

Sackerson rolled his thick shoulders and snuffled his snout even as he slept.

'Collar him first, then feed him.'

It was like Shay was the one being chained. The clunk of the lock and the groan of metal, she felt them in her teeth. Nonesuch tugged a drumstick from a swan's carcass and it rippled nausea through her. He saw her shoulders heave. 'Sorry, we didn't know you were going to be here. Anyway, one man's god is another man's lunch.'

Sackerson hauled himself upright and his muscles rolled like hills. He turned his head sideways, touched the meat with the dimpled end of his nose and then took it gently in his mouth. He fell back onto his behind and chewed contemplatively. When he spat out a long bone and brushed it from his fur, Nonesuch made the sign to leave. He pulled another hunk of meat from his bag and Sackerson eyed it. The bear could be nimble when food was involved. Up onto all fours with Nonesuch's boys waggling the haunch of venison.

'Get me up there.' In moments, he was on the bear's back. Sackerson craned his neck to see what was going on but finally settled down to chew.

'Join me,' said Nonesuch to Shay, as if they were idly discussing a scene. 'Our public awaits.'

'Your public. I'm done with audiences.'

Nonesuch puffed his cheeks out. 'Come on. There are only a couple of pages left to the script. Don't you want to see how it ends?'

He dug his heels into the bear's flank like he was riding a horse. Out, blinking into the street, where the air was glassy and cold. Sackerson sneezed twice – short barks – and Nonesuch lolled on his back.

'Good boy, here we go.' Arms around his neck like a lover. The boys surrounded the bear and Shay thought of the Queen and her household. She stood in the doorway, blinking into the light. Gulls bayed at her for her lack of food. She walked in the opposite direction, down towards the river to see if the merchant boats were still there; Blank would know what to do.

The river was quieter than Shay had ever seen it. No boat in any direction and even the waterwheels had stopped. Sheets of ice the size of carpets collided idly in the tide. Shay walked down to the water. A group of men had been hidden by the overhang of a jetty. Men in black leather with a map out in front of them. She thought nothing of it until one started at the sound of her footsteps. He watched her and then turned to talk urgently to his companions. Of course, they were Gilmour's men.

She turned tail as unobtrusively as she could, back past the bear pit and then right, following the noise of Nonesuch's procession. At Cross Bones Graveyard she risked a look back. They were a street behind and only had eyes for her, even as the spectacle of Nonesuch riding a bear through the waking streets unfolded. They bunched together to talk and then broke into two groups. One set made for the river and the other followed her. With reluctance, Shay sped up to join the parade.

Southwark was a mess. Boys slept in doorways and the streets were spattered with blooms of vomit. Crows picked over the debris, hopping into arguments, and high in the blank bowl of the sky, hawks waited. She watched, but no Devana. As she walked, the procession thickened. Outriders banged on drums, waking the drunks and throwing open windows. Nonesuch tossed occasional coins behind him and the parade grew a long tail of children. Kids who skipped in and out between the boys, and prentices who'd slept where they fell, slipped into the queue without asking where they were going. Drums and pipes and the rain of coins. Sackerson's sporadic bellows and the cawed fury of the crows.

Gilmour's men pressed closer. She recognised them now, she could see their expressions. She moved up through the ranks, now so close to Nonesuch that when Sackerson raised a leg to unfurl a steaming arc of piss, the smell scraped at her nostrils. Would the men dare snatch her here? She thought not. Prentices called out, 'Give us a song, Sparrer,' and slapped her on the back. However ramshackle a fighting force they might be, they were numerous and raw. Gilmour's men would wait.

West through streets where boarded-up taverns had been jimmied open and the wreckage of ale-jugs turned the streets to obstacle courses. People joined from side streets and, as they did, the blades daubed their shirtfronts with red crosses.

'A red cross means you're dead. And you. And you.' Despite the words, there was a festive air to it. Children giggled as they were daubed, running in circles and throwing themselves backwards into the mud. 'I'm dead. I'm dead.' Dripping paint turned the mud black. White faces, red crosses. Shay didn't recognise a soul. Was this what it was like going off to war?

West, west, west. East was the people, west was royalty. Drum and pipe music pulling the gaggle up the hill. Shay realised where they must be going.

43

P ARIS GARDEN. OF COURSE. The only place for gentlemen south
of the river. The grand building offered a chance to explore the
delights of Southwark without getting one's feet dirty. Paris Garden
whores, it was boasted, bathed twice a day and their fighting cocks
ate grain from silver salvers. Shay had never been inside before. She'd
passed the columned entrance, where liveried footmen kept the likes of
her away, and she'd seen the boats that disgorged parties of gentlemen
onto its private wharf. But today the doors stood wide open, and a thir-
ty-foot red X had been daubed across the facade.

In she came with the others like a rip tide. The great hall had been
cleared and given a sloppy coat of whitewash. Paint dripped from the
famous chandeliers and made ghosts of the portraits on the walls.
Nonesuch and Sackerson sat on a rough stage that had been erected at
the rear of the room. A painted map of the city was their backdrop. It
showed the outline of every house to the north of the river. The south
side was blank.

Nonesuch sat on a cardboard throne and rested his chin on a long
wooden sword. The procession had grown hundreds-strong and stragglers were still coming in at the back. More boys pushed their way inside
and Shay was crushed between a mass of bodies. She was among the
shortest there, trapped at armpit height in a sea of people. A tightening
claustrophobia caught her, like stage fright but with no exit, and she
cried out.

'Sparrow, Sparrow, Sparrow.' The cry went up and instantly hands
hoisted her aloft. Prentices passed her forward, ever so gently, like a
package with tuppence extra promised if delivered undamaged. A boy
placed her on the edge of the stage and Sackerson regarded her with
interest. Behind the bear, the back of the hall was piled with the crudest

of weapons. Pikes and clubs. Rusting swords and staffs. The map of London shimmied, and Shay couldn't work out where the breeze was coming from.

Nonesuch raised a hand. 'Blades, we have spent our lives in a play.'

Each word drove the volume of the crowd down, and by 'play' there was silence.

'A bad play. A poor play with poor actors as the leads. Yet you and I are forever in the background. We're serfs and water-carriers, prisoners and slaves. We've spent twenty years playing the same old parts while our lords and ladies take the bows.'

He sat on the edge of the stage and necks craned to catch his words. 'Why?'

No answer.

'Why? In the theatre the best roles go to the most gifted.' He gave a bow. 'Granted, that's usually me, but not always. Any one of you could be a king. Any one of you could get the girl.'

Shay scanned the room. At least three-quarters were boys.

'But this is real life, and in real life people like us aren't allowed to choose our roles.'

He paused and Shay heard raw breaths from the front row and a rowdy bunch of crows outside.

'Until today. Saturnalia. The one day when servants are masters and masters are servants. They deign to give us this one day. But we shall turn it into forever.' This last in a hissed whisper.

'Who's first?'

A boy jumped on stage. Jug-eared and wet-lipped, he executed a series of bows: to Nonesuch, to Sackerson and finally to Shay. His painted cross ran from shoulder to hip.

'Kneel,' said Nonesuch, and the boy slid to his knees. Nonesuch took a slip of paper from a pile and touched the boy on each shoulder with his sword. 'I dub you Lord Gresham of the Dead. Your lands await.' He handed the boy the slip and behind him a lad drew a red cross on the map, marking a house up near Bishopsgate.

'Next!'

A queue formed and boys scrabbled up onto stage to be knighted and given a parcel of land. Hundreds of them. Even with Nonesuch at his fastest, it took an hour. Sackerson snuffled around the stage and ripples of laughter and applause erupted through the hall, seemingly at random. Children dripped with paint, clutching swords longer than their arms, chattering like it was the last day of school. 'Where did you get? Who will you have to kill?'

Shay didn't understand the show. It was metaphorical, like something the old Nonesuch would have done. What would happen when every boy had his piece of land, and they were stuck here in Southwark?

Lord Lothbury of the Dead, Lord Billiter. She recognised the names: great houses and city estates. Places that she and these boys would never see inside. With every boy who stepped on stage, the map was further covered with red crosses. Boys picked up clubs and pikes and tried them out against each other. She couldn't see the point of it, but that was probably for the best. By nightfall everyone would be dead drunk, so until then they could play at being lords and no one would get hurt. The map dripped in red now and the queue had become a trickle. Nonesuch dubbed a one-legged boy, who couldn't have been more than twelve, 'Lord Lombard,' and then laid down his sword. He stood and hushed the crowd.

'Who wants to see their new lands?'

A joyous cheer.

He walked to the map and tugged on a rope. The map fluttered to the ground. Behind the canvas, the whole back wall of the building had been removed, and you could see out across the river. A river now paved with boats. Hundreds of them. Jammed together like a wooden walk-way all the way to the far shore. Barges and wherries and tilt-boats and rowing boats and ship's launches and floating platforms, all alongside each other and roped together tightly. The north bank was in walking distance.

'Take the city. Take the city. Take the city.' Nonesuch started the chant, but in moments it was taken up by the crowd and he sat, silently smiling.

'Take the city. Take the city. *Take the city.*'

44

'N o.'
Her voice was swallowed up. She could see what was about to happen. The boys would flow across the water in a mad rush to their new lands, driven on by Nonesuch's promises and the mob at their back. And then. Knives and swords, guns even. Quiet men with a bird emblem on their shoulders. And a hundred dead prentices staining the snow scarlet.

'No.' She said it again. '*No.*' She stamped her foot, like a child having a tantrum.

A boy turned.

'Stop.' She stamped again. The boy shushed his companion and then silence swept across them as easily as the chant had. She stood on the throne so they all could see her. It wobbled under her feet.

'Stop. You will die.' It wasn't her voice that caught the crowd, it was her frailty. She lowered herself to her knees and kept the emotion from her voice. She was just delivering a message: 'I saw the Queen last night and she expects this. The noblemen expect this. They will be waiting and you will die.'

The crowd exhaled and Nonesuch stepped forward. 'We can't be killed. We are already dead.' He dipped a finger in the paint of his red cross and smeared it across his face. 'The Ghost Theatre can't die.'

Under his breath he started the chant again. 'Take the city, take the city, take the city.' It began to spread. 'We cannot die, and I'll prove it.' He handed her his knife and tugged down his ruff to display a crescent of white throat. 'Try it.'

She took a step back. 'Nonesuch. No.'

'I beg you. Try it.' He turned to the crowd. 'We cannot die on Saturnalia, and Saturnalia is forever.'

He turned back to her. 'Do it. They'll see.'

Back at the theatre there had been all manner of fake knives. Blades that retracted into the pommel when a button was pressed, or daggers made of rubber. But she knew Nonesuch's own blade; she'd used it often enough. There was even a tree, somewhere deep in the forest of the Midlands, where she'd used it to carve their names into an ancient oak. The boys milled and watched and pushed against the stage. The scene froze and she found herself in the bird-time of the Murmuration. She could get up and walk around the boards. She could examine Nonesuch with his shirt pulled down, showing rib and potbelly, and one pale nipple. His expression was some indecipherable mix of laughter and something grittier – desire, maybe?

Do knives want? The tip is an arrow, pointing where it needs to go. Look, *here and here*. Heart. Neck. Wrist. Ending places. *Here and here.* Shay touched the point against his neck, right where the muscles sank beneath the jaw, and felt him, almost imperceptibly, flinch. She applied enough pressure to make his skin dimple, but he didn't move. Instead, he leant into it. The skin at its limit. A bead of sweat worked its way down his temple. The mind may be still, but the body has its own fears.

Quiet now. She couldn't shake the impression that the room was frozen. Open mouths and not a breath of wind. That single sweat-drop.

'Stage fright?' she asked.

A beat. His blood blue at the neck. 'Always.'

And then he was taking her hand away and she was letting him. And the look in his eye wasn't the triumph that she'd expected. He placed the knife to his neck and pushed carelessly until he bled a little, no more than a splash of colour, and then said, 'We. Cannot. Die.'

Silence and then a cheer; a twist and a dribble of blood. 'We. Cannot. Lose.'

His head pushed back as if it weren't him holding the knife. His voice echoing from the ceiling.

'Take the city.'

And they were up and gone like a single animal, scattering chairs and tables with a belly-roar from somewhere deep in the crowd. Barefoot, up and over broken brick, and then sliding along frozen ground, with boys tumbling over and picked up, brandishing knives in the air like the sky was their enemy. Sackerson was driven before them, the bear for the first time facing a creature larger and less fearful of death than himself.

Shay was carried with them, in the crush, with her feet off the ground. A fish in a living river that crested and dropped, and then she was over, upside down and in the dirt, and she was crushed and stepped on, so she rolled hard, left and left and left, feet striking her shoulder and back, and she rolled faster because these weren't boys any more; they were a flood and floods don't wait to inspect the damage. She pulled her arms around her head and when the silence had ebbed back, she sat up and looked out at the river.

The boats rocked under hundreds of pairs of boots, but the platform held fast. When the vanguard of the mob had made it two-thirds of the way across, a shower of impotent arrows sprayed from the soldiers on the bridge, but they were much too far east. A cry went up. Their enemies were useless. Their arrows were nothing. Nonesuch was at the front and Shay saw his mouth moving but the words were lost on the wind. The rocking of the boats and the press of bodies gave the mob a fearsome forward momentum. Shay imagined a Devana-eye view of the front row of boys – white horses breaking on the northern shore. How would it be met? Swords, arrows, muskets? Men and dogs?

But the noise stayed joyous. She climbed onto a low roof to watch the first wave hit. Empty shore and empty boats. Boys swarmed the wharves like rats and met no resistance. Shay scanned the skyline for raised bows or cauldrons, but it was just chimneys and birds. In fact, doors stood open in the riverside properties. It took a few minutes, but London swallowed up the crowd, as it swallowed everything. Shay waited for noise of disaster, but none came, so she brushed herself down and followed the path the boys had taken. Once she'd finally picked her way across the platform of boats, she found herself in a city as quiet as a Sunday.

London had been abandoned and every building stood open. This wasn't the dereliction of a plague city – it was an invitation. Shay walked up St Andrew's Hill, where she could see through open doors into the dining rooms of merchants' houses. In each one a table was set for dinner. She chose a house at random: a three-storey with a cloth shop at street level. The floor-rushes were askew where someone had dragged something heavy out into the street, but the furniture was where you'd expect it, and a meal was laid out in the dining room. Coney and oysters and a bread pudding with dates. She touched the coney. It was stone cold and there was a film on the soup. She worked it through in her mind. They'd cooked a meal, laid it out and then fled with their valuables. An empty nest. It was a trap, obviously, but how had they known that the boys were coming, especially once the river was impassable? She sniffed at the wine, but it smelled fine. Last night echoed off empty walls: *she will stop the river, he will cross the river*. Who had said that? Her? The wind? Whoever it was, Elizabeth had been listening.

The same scene was replayed all the way up to St Paul's. Boys had claimed their new estates and in every second house a feast was taking place. Lads tucked wall-hangings into their smocks as impromptu serviettes and carved roast beef with broadswords. She saw wine drunk like water. On Paternoster Row two boys, no more than twelve, had pulled a dining table out into the street and were arguing about the cutlery. A yard-long roast trout was laid out in front of them.

'Join us, Sparrow,' they said in unison. 'Eat.'

It was unnerving to sit on such a richly embroidered chair in the middle of the street. She crumbled a bread roll for the sparrows as one of the boys served the fish.

'Where are the owners?' she asked.

'Run away,' said one boy through a mouthful of chestnuts. 'We haven't seen a soul since we claimed our street.' He made a face as he polished a fork on his shirt and then hooked a thumb back to point at a stone building. 'That's our house. Nice, right?' His paper was pinned to the door with a knife: Lords Paternoster and Paul of the Dead.

'And the food was waiting for you?'

'All laid out. Brandy too.' The boy mimicked a gentlemanly drawl. 'Though someone's in for a thrashing when I find out who let the fish get cold.'

Could it all be poisoned, thought Shay. *Was there even enough poison in the whole city?*

'You trust whoever left it for you?'

'It's Saturnalia. They have to give us this one day. I think it's the law.'

'It's tradition,' said the other, and they both nodded.

Shay looked at the paper pinned to the door. 'Saturnalia's only one day though. Nonesuch was claiming that this was forever.'

The boys were unconcerned. 'Well, that's what he *said*.'

She watched them. The cutlery was too big in their hands and their feet barely reached the floor.

'So, you don't think he's telling the truth? That this is all really yours?'

'That would be amazing. Imagine having this house to yourself. Imagine the servants. I'd have an army of maids. Fat little things.' He trailed off and looked at her. 'Sorry, Sparrow. I know Nonesuch says it'll be forever. But you know how actors are.'

She picked at her trout and then said, 'Listen, you know who I am, right?'

The boys nodded seriously.

'Promise me you'll be out of here by midnight. If you can't get to your parents' house, then sleep on a rooftop. There's a good one on the corner of Ivy Lane.' She didn't think they recognised the danger they were in; this was a game to them. 'They will make someone pay for this, understand? Make sure it's not you.'

She walked north past open doorway after open doorway. Prentices went visiting from house to house and children sat outside their new estates like homeowners at the Lord Mayor's Procession. 'Go home,' she called out to them as she passed, but they waved and called back happily.

A boy trundled a burning cartwheel down the centre of the street and then bowed, ceremoniously, to Shay. Two younger boys slashed wildly at wall hangings with the punctiliousness of housework. Cheapside was a ghost street; Shay had never seen it empty before. She walked down the dead centre of the road and a lone barn owl appeared on wings quieter than breath. It glided above her, and its grace reminded her to call for Devana again; no answer. Would the falcon have returned to her mews? Perhaps she'd tired of her freedom. With nowhere else to be, Shay headed east to Eltham House. She found its grand double doors wide open, but inside it was untouched. As she climbed the stairs, she wondered about the servants: the butler and the cook who'd brought her cherry cake. The Elthams had a country home too, but the London staff would be fending for themselves; the fields beyond the city walls would be full of serving folk tonight. Shay climbed those dwindling staircases and stepped out into the kind of evening that she loved best – glass-bright and ice-cold. The mews sat like a miniature palace in the corner of the roof, and she moved noisily enough that Devana would hear her approach if she were home. At first glance the mews was empty, but Shay caught a glimmer of light. She put head and shoulders inside.

Devana was hunched at the far end up against the wall. She perched in the deepest shadow – the glimmer was her one open eye, a black gem on black cloth. The hawk-gloves still hung there, and Shay put them on.

She extended a hand; no movement. She tried a call and Devana shrunk deeper into the gloom. Shay moved back and switched to a sparrow chirrup, something old and unthreatening. There were long moments of silence and then Devana sidestepped, with difficulty, along the perch. She looked wretched. A patch of feathers was burnt away around her right eye, and the socket itself was just a dark absence. A slick of oil smeared her breast and one foot dragged uselessly behind the other. She hopped nearer. The wing and foot both looked broken. The Jagger's arrows or Trussell's?

'Hey, my beauty.' Shay put her hand as close as she could get, but Devana didn't move.

'All right. I'm going to pick you up, just this once. It doesn't mean anything.'

She placed her bare hand around the bird's body and Devana gave a trill, a thin noise that Shay had never heard from her before. She peeled her from the perch and that ruined right leg hung down.

'Here.' She placed her on the glove. Devana's left talon tightened and then relaxed. Shay could barely feel the claws through the leather.

'Rough couple of days? You were so brave with those arrows.' Shay kept the panic from her voice. The bird was scarily light; how long was it since she'd fed?

She took off the glove and tried again, placing the bird on her bare arm. Again, the talon tightened and Shay watched her skin pucker. 'That's it. A bit deeper.' Beads of blood blossomed, and Devana turned her head towards her.

Their eyes met before Shay thought to look away. One mirror eye. Another warning squeeze of talon but it barely registered. Still, Shay kept her eyes on the floor; the falcon had earned that. She brought her closer and the bird's head lowered, gratefully, to Shay's breast. The last remnants of luminous paint clung to the bridge of her beak and her crown was a wasteland of burnt feather shafts.

'Good girl, would you want your hood on? I have it here.'

With her free hand she pulled the hood from her pocket. Devana cocked her head while it rested on Shay's chest. One black non-eye was set amid blunt stubble.

She eased the hood on, and the lilac leather was an affront to the scuffed oil and black patches of the plumage. Devana gave the same strange trill and lifted her wings behind her. The feathers on her right wing were torn back to the bone. A flash of pink like uncooked meat. She flourished her wings one more time and then pulled them tightly around herself. That wing needed setting and Shay couldn't do it here, she would need tools and candlewax. She fastened her blouson up half-way, cradling Devana into the warmth of her body. A chirrup won a reply, something lower than sound, fluttering against her skin.

In the street below, boys sang drunkenly and there was something sad about it, an end-of-night sound. She talked to the bird. 'What do you think, girl? Is there any way that this doesn't end badly?'

She would find food and wax for Devana and then she'd try to make the boys leave. This empty-nest city could only be a trap. She tried to think the way that Elizabeth might. The boys were scattered and sated because they'd met no resistance; that would have been her idea. Her advisers would have wanted to meet force with force. Fighting felt inevitable only because it was what men always chose. So the Queen had prevailed for now, but Shay didn't need the cards to know that the Swifts would be here sooner than later. Where though?

Devana was fragile against her chest, so Shay kept away from the roofs. She walked south towards the river and found only a scattering of boats remained on the Thames. She walked east to the city wall. As she'd predicted, makeshift camps had sprung up in the farmland. Lamps were on everywhere and servants stood guard over carts full of possessions. She had nowhere to go, so she just walked and chattered the whole time: news and gossip and trills and chat, to cover the fact that she hadn't felt Devana move since the river. West London was lit up and the palace was ablaze with torches. She got as close as she could, but troops patrolled the walls. The danger would come from the north, then. She would find a butcher's shop and a candlemaker on the way.

Later, she couldn't work out exactly when it was that Devana died. Somewhere between Eltham House and Lombard Street, where she broke the hasp on a butcher's shop door to get at the suckling pig hung inside. She knew as soon as she undid her buttons. Something had gone from the bird, her lightness. She was still warm but somehow dulled.

Shay wrapped the body a little tighter and then headed back the way they'd come. Rain began to fall.

She escaped to the emptiness of the rooftops; enough of boys and their clamour. She walked across huddled houses, relishing the still, icy air, and let the moon guide her northwards until a noise brought her to a halt. A soft stamping like far-off thunder. It happened twice more, so she crouched behind a turret to scan the area. Dead chimneys stood cold against the stars and the weathervanes were all in agreement. Cripplegate lay to the north and the sound could have come from there, so she shuffled on her belly to the edge of the roof. The scene was hard to make out. A squadron of shadows going through some kind of drill – step left, step right, knives out, knives away – all in near silence. The only substantial thing about them was the sound of their feet moving in unison. They wore black clothes and black slippers, and she couldn't make out faces. When the moon peeked from behind a cloud she saw why: every man was blindfolded.

Someone whistled off to her right and the shadows started to move. She heard the clack of ladders being lowered onto the roof of St Alphage. If they moved that way, then they'd come right past her, so she pushed herself flat against the thatch and held her breath. The figures crossed the ladders on all fours, still blindfolded, and then walked in formation, each with his hand on the shoulder of the man in front. They were so close that she could hear them breathing. Close enough to see the bird insignia stitched onto their tunics and the knives at their waists. They passed her and stepped across onto the rooftops of Addle Street. Some of Nonesuch's boys were on Addle Street – she'd seen them play-fighting on the way over – but the road was quiet now. The Black Swifts lined up in neat rows on the roof's edge.

It happened fearsomely fast. Ropes were thrown around the chimney, a captain touched shoulders, and eight men removed their blindfolds. They scaled the walls in one swinging movement. Black rope and soft shoes. Down, soundlessly, and then noises from below. Shouts of alarm, heavy objects hitting hard surfaces, and then an ominous quiet. The men were back on the roof in moments, getting their breath back and retying one another's blindfolds. They were Elizabeth's men, all right; the Swifts were a tool, a knife. Shay once saw a man stabbed on Cheapside. The blade slipped in and out with the man still talking, and then he touched his back, and his hand came away red. A second later he was dying on his knees, coughing up blood.

How well could the men see in this half-light? The blindfolds would give them an edge and that might be all they needed. While she calculated, a whispered command rang across the rooftop and the Swifts began to head south. What to do? She could cut around and warn the boys she'd seen earlier, but that would risk getting caught herself. Instead, she cut towards Silver Street. Below, two boys sat in huge armchairs, which they'd pulled out into the road, singing softly to themselves. She cleared her throat and it made them jump. One lad waved his torch in her direction. 'Sparrow! We heard you were here with us.'

'You have to get out. Head east. There are troops coming and they can see in the dark. Don't take anything, just go.'

The boy scratched at himself. 'There's nowhere *to* go. They've barricaded all the gates.'

It would be a massacre. 'Go south then. Get to the river and then cross to Southwark.' She couldn't convey the urgency to them. 'Hundreds will die – don't be among them.' It infuriated her; at this rate, it would take hours to convince all of Nonesuch's boys to leave. She needed to find an escape route.

'Do either of you know Alouette?'

'Flanders girl? Face like a mule?'

Shay nodded. 'That's her. Have you any idea where I might find her?'

'You should try St Paul's. All the foreigners have shut themselves away in there.'

The boys started to pack up their booty, but still seemed reluctant to leave. Shay calculated: St Paul's was only three streets away, so it might be quicker at ground level. The roads were quiet; boys had retreated inside, and fires blazed in grates. Broken glass piled up in the streets and her feet were soon sticky with wine.

From outside, the church sounded like a party. The towering front doors had been thrown open and the air steamed in the lantern light of the entrance. Shay slipped inside. The path through the church, St Paul's Walk, was the city's crossroads, and it was here that rumours bloomed and deals were done, fashions started and affairs ended. But she had never seen it like this. At one end boys jousted, riding on shoulders as they ran at one another with curtain poles and staffs. The lads in the front pews – some watching, some sleeping – were spattered with blood and Shay saw teeth on the floor. At the other end, young blades aped the perambulations of fashionable London couples. In costumes too big and dresses too small they paraded from one end to the other, to the hoots and jeers of their friends. Bonfires of broken pews and bibles burned; the font was filled with wine.

Two steps inside and there was a sight that made her heart sing. Trussell and Alouette and Blank with their heads almost touching over some document. In better times it would have been a script, with Alouette describing the way the lights would play, Blank working the fingerings on his trumpet and Trussell sketching. Instead, all three faces were drawn tight with worry. Even with time so short, Shay stopped to watch them for a moment: her friends.

'Oh, thank God.' Trussell squeezed her so tightly that she couldn't see his face. He breathed out hard into her skin and then held her by the shoulders. 'They dumped me by the gate last night, but I couldn't get across the river. I've been scouring the city for you.' He looked into her eyes. 'I was hoping I could follow Devana to you but there's been no sign of her. Is she …'

All Shay could do was shake her head, and Trussell's joy fell away. 'Oh, Shay …'

But then there were more embraces. Alouette and Blank and Trussell talking over each other: the show and the ships, the boys and the river. The three of them were guarding a huddle of families who took up five rows of pews near the back. Quiet, serious people all dressed in black; three generations who held hands and prayed together.

'From Flanders, they're Alouette's people,' said Trussell. 'Alouette walked the whole community out to Bishopsgate but soldiers sent them back. We thought that here would be safest until daybreak.'

Shay had almost forgotten what she'd come there for. 'Nowhere in the city is safe. They're coming over the roofs. Hundreds of them. They can see in the dark and they're as quiet as mice.'

Alouette glared at her.

'Really Alouette, it's not magic. They have blindfolds and slippers and black-suits like stage hands. They're prepared. We have to get all of your people out. The boys too.'

Shay pictured the route through to the river. It was all skinny, unlit streets that would present bowmen with a shooting gallery. Moving this many people would need space and light. The three crowded around her and she felt the familiar fear of having no answers. Their faces were expectant, so she just let herself talk.

'Listen. The Swifts blindfold themselves so they can see in the dark. So we need to light up the city. Then we'll take everyone here down

Thames Street.' She'd run that route a thousand times. Streets wide enough for two lanes of carts. She pulled Alouette close. 'Do we have fire-arrows? We need to light up a path for everyone to follow.'

The lines of concern were wiped from Alouette's face. 'Oh, we have better than that. Come and see.'

She pulled Shay into a corner of the nave where wooden boxes were stacked. The lids were already unfastened and Alouette opened the nearest. Tubular rockets were wrapped in straw and paper-wrapped cones peaked in a twist of wick. The tray underneath was filled to the brim with rough green spirals that smelled of sulphur and lilacs.

'Are those fireworks? All of them?' There were maybe thirty boxes.

Alouette couldn't keep from grinning. 'It was supposed to be Evans' gift to the Queen. A Christmas show from his glass house. It took me six months to make them all so there was no way I was leaving them in the workshop.'

Shay pictured a path of white fire leading from St Paul's to the river. 'Do we have enough to light all the way to the Thames?'

'Easily. But what do we do when we get there? They broke up the platform and boatloads of soldiers are patrolling.'

'We can't get across?' She'd given no thought to what they'd do once they got to the Thames; to her, the river was safety.

'I think that we can.' Blank had joined them. 'The bridge.'

Alouette frowned. 'There are more archers on the bridge than here. It would be a bloodbath.'

'Not if we go underneath.' Blank pulled them in closer. 'You know the metal rings on every bridge support?' He looked around the blank expressions. 'You Londoners should learn your own history. In case of invasion, chains can be pulled across every arch to stop ships sailing upriver. If we were to tie boat-ropes across, it'd be like a bridge across the surface of the Thames.'

Shay pictured the froth and violence of the rapids and shivered. 'And how do we get from arch to arch to tie them off?'

'For that you would need an expert swimmer.' Blank executed a bow. 'At your service.'

They waited; somehow, Shay was in charge. 'All right, you get the ropes and I'll lead the boys. Alouette can set off the fireworks.'

She saw a quick glance between Trussell and Alouette. 'What?'

Trussell took her hand. 'The Flanders crowd won't follow you. They're frightened of *me*; God knows what they'd think of you. Alouette has to go with them. I can set off the fireworks.'

He'd be lit up and exposed in the midst of a battle; she dared not ask it of him, but he was already stuffing handfuls of rockets into his jacket.

'Give me five minutes to get up onto the roof and then I'll start to light a route south.'

They embraced again and the soft bundle of Devana pressed against her breast. Trussell was gone before she could say thank you.

In the nave a fencing match had broken out. One huge boy took on two girls in a duel that flowed back and forth along the aisle. Money lay in piles on the floor. Boys were betting with the loot from their new homes: candlesticks, spices, tapestries. Getting their attention wouldn't be easy. Shay looked for a good spot. An unlit gallery ran around two-thirds of the nave and the walls looked easy enough to climb. The crowd ignored her as she started up the sides. She shimmied up mouldings and statues and scuffed her hands on walls icy to the touch. Up and out and pulling herself onto the second floor. The gallery was dark and the warmth of five hundred boys had barely touched it. She crouched like a gargoyle and tried a hawk-call. The sound made her instantly, blazingly, lonely but it stilled the church. Faces turned her way. A sky full of pale moons.

Her stage voice. 'The Black Swifts are on their way. Hundreds of them. They've already slaughtered everyone between here and the gate. You'll be next. So, we leave now.'

There was silence but no one moved. 'Join me. Fireworks will light our way.' Still they watched, uncertain. What was the voice that would convince them? What were the words?

But then Blank was shouting from across the hall. He stood on the far side of the gallery under a triptych of thirty-foot-high stained-glass windows that painted him in underwater tones. He took a staff and drove it through a pane of the glass.

'Come and see what she is talking about,' he shouted.

The sound of glass raining to the ground roused the crowd. Boys streamed up the staircase that led to the spire and with pikes and swords they smashed out every last clinging shard of window, until hundreds of boys stared out over long slivers of London.

'Now, Trussell,' Blank called. For a moment, the city remained an inky pool and then the first firework whistled overhead. A crack like a whip and white fountains sprayed. Every roof from St Paul's to the marshes of Moorfields was lit up and on every one black figures waited. The glare faded too quickly to see whether there was any end to them. Whistle, crack and crack. Red fire and then white. The fireworks framed the Swifts from two directions and in two lights. The men were moving, making for the edges of the roofs, a frozen ant-swarm.

In a moment the boys were a mob once more, but this time in retreat rather than advance. They swept back downstairs, gathering others around them, and charged out through the doors into the cold. Shay ran to get ahead of them and Blank elbowed drunk boys aside. He shouted, 'Follow the Sparrow.'

A crowd ten wide and fifty deep pushed at her heels. The rear of the crush was swallowed in shadows. Alouette had guided her flock of families there; they would have been trampled otherwise. The street was narrow and piled with rubbish but the crowd at her back drove Shay on. Fireworks blazed above them as they crossed Knightrider Street, and now knots of boys began to appear from side alleys, joining the rush unthinkingly. A roar went up with each addition. It was darker now, and frosty underfoot. Shay slipped and was caught by dozens of hands before she even touched the ground. She couldn't tell whether she was leading them, or they were driving her. She planned to take them along Thames Street, but as the crowd swept that way, a fresh crop of fireworks carpeted the sky. A vision like lightning: Black Swifts were waiting in a line across the street with swords drawn.

'Up here.' A shed made an easy step up onto a low roof and then it was just a yard's jump to St Peter's Church. Boys climbed up behind her and she set off as slowly as she dared. She knew every roof from here to the bridge and she could pick a path as easily as her father did through the marsh; there would be no dead ends or sudden gaps for her boys. Shapes moved to her left and right. Boys were finding their own way up onto the rooftops and she called out, 'Follow my footsteps and you'll be safe.'

Whistles off to the north and the sky was painted with light. For a moment she could see almost all of the city. A V of boys fanned out behind her, helping one another over the gaps and laying planks between buildings. She ran, feeling hollowed out. The city unfurled beneath her, and she tossed herself carelessly over chasms of streets. Wherever the fireworks landed, fires ignited and now smoke began to rise in columns from every direction; the rooftops glowed like embers. Rockets came in rapid bursts and, in minutes, the city was a black sea dotted with fiery islands. The true shape of London emerged. Roads were looming black trenches, churches threw long shadows, and she could see to the river. All around her boys scrambled, dazed, onto the rooftops.

Movement to her right. Fighting was scattered across the turreted roof of L'Erber. The Swifts had the technique, but the boys had the numbers. More and more poured onto the roof and the red crosses began to overwhelm black bodies. Shay stopped, breathless, on the roof of the Old Swan. She'd fed Devana a grass snake here once; fucked Nonesuch under summer rain too.

Ahead, a battle was being played out on the roof of Fishmongers' Hall. Ten black shapes surrounded boys with red crosses. Swords met knives. Cracks of wood or bone. Arms raised and bows drawn back. Three huge fireworks erupted overhead, and when the third burst, only the boys in red remained. Flash. A boy fitted the stage crown back over his curls and Shay could hear his laughter even from there. They saw each other at the same time. Maybe thirty feet apart, both a hundred yards from the bridge. Nonesuch tipped his crown and took off towards the river. Shay's feet moved even before she'd told them to. West towards the lights of the bridge, jumping Wolsies Lane like it was nothing. She was faster than him. She was stronger than him. He leapt the lane with one hand on his crown and he came down with a bump before struggling on. His blades followed.

'They have the bridge.' His voice was joyful. 'It looks unguarded but they're stationed in the houses a few yards back.'

Shay used a weathervane to spin her across a half-built roof. She came down cat-quiet. Nonesuch clapped and shouted, 'Show-off.'

The boys were far behind her, but the fireworks would show them the way. Nonesuch's blades struggled to keep up with him. Who were his loyalties to? Just to the drama of it all, she thought. She'd find out soon enough.

'We're going under the bridge. Blank is setting the ropes now.'

She could hear how hard the running was working him now. He tried to say something, but it was lost in the air. Then …

'Stop.' His voice still had some steel in it. She pulled up, the river like black oil down to her right, and he held up a hand. Noise behind them. Boys catching up, slipping and cursing. 'Wait. Ahead.'

A firework went off mere feet above them and it framed a row of Swifts kneeling on the roofs of the last street before the bridge. They were low and silent, and she would have run straight into them. She held up her hand and behind her boys slowed. She had more men than they did. They could probably punch through the line but so many would die. There was a theatrical stillness to the scene. Lines of men listening hard on the rooftops, facing each other. Shay let her breathing slow.

And then, to her left, all was light. Nonesuch stood with two fire-arrows spitting sparks in his hands. The harsh light turned his features demonic, and he howled upwards at the moon: 'Saturnalia now.' And then he threw himself towards the line of men.

Fireworks went off again and again, and Shay watched it like a series of tableaux: Nonesuch sporting fiery wings. Nonesuch careering over the tiles with his mouth open to the sky. The line of black shapes breaking. Men coming out to meet him on a flat stretch, the sky glistening with light. Like a stage curtain drawn and opened. Three black shapes, five. Then arms raised, so many, each holding a sword or a knife. Nonesuch's arrows snuffed out. One-and-two. A white starburst captured black shapes hunched like crows over carrion, and a crown rolling back and forth across the tiles, and then Shay was leading her boys down a ladder onto the shoreline, and the fireworks piled up against one another until the very sky was alight.

The boat-ropes were enormous things: plaited monsters thicker than a man's leg. Blank and Shay took the end of the first one as the boys snaked off through the streets, the rope making them look like a giant caterpillar in the distance. They bunched in a darkened alley and Shay risked a look around the corner. The entrance to the bridge blazed with lanterns and it looked almost inviting. The gates were open, and no soldiers guarded the entrance, but Shay was sure they were there somewhere. She turned back. Hundreds of boys stood with the ropes slung over their shoulders, talking in whispers and smoking, as if waiting for curtain-up.

'Nonesuch said they're hiding in the bridge houses. How do we get down to that first stanchion without being shot at?' she asked Blank.

He looked back at the crowd of boys and the lights of the entrance. He bit his lip. 'We don't.'

Shay looked around her. 'Then how do we get to the first stanchion without too many dying?'

Blank said nothing.

Faces piled up behind her, hungry in the torchlight. It was the Murmuration again and she still didn't have any answers. A spire rose to their left, clad with scaffolding that made it look like a skeleton. That new roof would mean tile rather than thatch and it gave her an idea. She asked Blank, 'Could we get in there?'

Sheer numbers had the door down in moments; a tide of prentices threw their bodies at the locks. Once it was down, they spilled into the space behind it. The bones of the building rose around them, framing the stars in geometric constellations, but the ground was invisible in the gloom. 'Be careful,' she said. 'We want roof tiles, if you can find them; if not, then anything that you can use as a shield.'

It was mayhem. Boys slipped and shouted out. A few found planks that they held out in front of them. Blank discovered a pallet of tiles in an unlocked shed and distributed them to any boy still empty-handed.

Back out in the street, rain was falling hard now, furring the bridge's glow. Shay said, 'Ten lines of ten. One hand holds the tile over your head. The other holds the rope.' She showed them what she meant. To her surprise, they formed into a tight oblong immediately; they were no strangers to being told what to do, she guessed. The rope holders held tiles over their heads until there was a flattish roof above them. Boys were still arriving. They took tiles and joined the convoy at the back.

'All right. We move fast and straight down to the right side of the bridge.' She shouted it to the latecomers. 'Do *not* enter the bridge. There are soldiers there. Go down to the shore at the right and then we'll loop the ropes across. Keep a hand on your neighbour's shoulder, keep the rope tight and keep your heads guarded. Are we ready?'

A joyous roar filled the street and the boys lurched forward. In the moonlight they looked like some scaled, mythical beast. The tiles rose and fell in time with their steps and the beast clanked and swore. At first, they jostled and bumped, but then, like a theatre crowd, they fell into some kind of unison. The tiles undulated in rhythm and their feet beat out a drumroll. They broke into a run and there was no response from the bridge. Shay was just thinking that maybe the bridge was unguarded after all when the sky filled with arrows. In the main they skittered harmlessly off the tiles; Shay heard cries but not enough to slow their advance. She pulled a tile over her head and ran alongside them. Still, they picked up speed. Shoes clattered on the cobbles. Only yards from the bridge now. She risked a look. Soldiers sprouted from every high place, and she saw the machinery of archers: hand back for the arrow, notch, pull, aim and fire, in one smooth movement. But it didn't stop them.

Then an older soldier stepped into the light and yelled something to the troops. The boys ran on, the lights of the bridge reflecting in their rain-soaked tiles, but now the archers fired almost horizontally, aiming solely at the front row. Arrows skidded along the floor or snapped on tiles, but many more reached their target. Holes appeared in the group as boys fell to the ground, but they were moving too fast to stop now. They careered forward to where the road dipped down to meet the bridge and Shay was pulled along with them. They swept over the wreckage of that broken first wave and things cracked or cried out underfoot. Down with her feet wet and shoulders jammed into hers and something pinging through the forest of legs, and the boy next to her falling and dragged back behind her before she could even turn to see what had happened, but too late anyway because she was sliding down the bank on her arse, boys whooping around her like they were sledding, down into cold water up to her ankles, her shins, her knees. The bridge glowed overhead and boys waded out as far as they could go. Up to their necks in the river, with arrows whistling around them, but in moments they'd reached the shadow of the buildings that lined the bridge, some three storeys high, and the archers lost their line of fire.

Boys crowded onto the first support and shoved Shay forward. Blank was already standing in the shallows, tying the rope around his waist. In the shadows she could only see the glint of his buttons and the white V of foam forming around him as the river rushed through the arch.

'We need to be quick. They're piling up behind me,' she said.

He nodded. 'It will be easy enough across these first arches. The water is pretty quiet. It's nearer the centre that I worry about.' Blank took off his coat, rolled it into a ball and placed it on the stanchion. Then, without a word, he dived into the water. He cut a diagonal path, swimming upstream, away from the bridge with the current battering him back towards it. His arms came out of the water in huge thrashes and the spray rose all around. One stroke across and then the current pulled him back, one stroke away, then pulled back. In half a minute he was on the next platform. He called out, 'Secure,' and Shay led the first boys across. The water pulled at them, but the rope was taut. Halfway across, the rope slipped, and Shay was swept deeper, out beneath the arch where all was night and the water raged.

'No more men on the rope,' Blank shouted. 'Ten at the most. Otherwise it'll never hold.' The message was passed back and then the rope tightened again. She inched across until she climbed, panting, on the platform where Blank stood shirtless and soaked. Water dripped noisily from his hair. He took her by the shoulders. 'Don't let too many onto the rope, we'll never hold it.' And then, again, he was in the water.

Shay could sense the effort of it. Swimming hard against the current, his strokes almost perpendicular to the bridge, but still he was dragged back. Twice he disappeared into the shadows under the arch and twice he managed to haul himself back into the light. It took longer for him to tie up this time. Longer for him to tug on the rope. As she dragged herself along the line, the water raged at her now, turning her clothes to sails and pulling at her hair. She concentrated hard on the inky shape that was Blank; if he could swim across then surely she could walk. Her hands were raw against the rope and when she reached the next arch she looked back. A line of heads all the way to the shore. She strained to hear if there was still fighting but the crashing of the water covered everything. She grabbed Blank's hand. 'How are you feeling?'

He grinned. 'I've been worse. The next couple should be similar. It's that centre arch that worries me.'

Shay wasn't sure how Blank managed it. By the ninth arch, the current tore at her like a banshee. Even with the rope hooked tight under her armpits the water drove her legs out almost horizontally and she had to inch forward, rope burns from her hands to her chest. Twice she heard noises behind: a cry, a splash and then a worrying silence. And still the queue behind her grew. The bridge's central stanchions were huge things and Shay and Blank lay, getting their breath, on a stone platform as big as a stage. Lads clambered, shivering like rats, out of the water behind them. All their earlier boisterousness was gone.

'Bollocks,' said Blank. It was the first time Shay had heard him swear.

'What's wrong?' The span was wider here, but the water was calmer, less brutally funnelled.

He looked back upstream. 'There is a boat out there.'

Shay stared out over the river. It was a black field, and she couldn't see anything. She concentrated on the sound. Was that oars? Oars hard against the current?

Another knot of boys climbed onto the platform.

'Nothing to be done but try, I suppose,' he said.

In he went. A neat dive. He cut upstream and made good progress but as the water deepened, so did the rush of current. Shay could barely see him, but he slipped back, further back, until he was level with her, then behind her, his arms flailing against the great invisible hand of the Thames and then the rope jerked so tight that she was almost pulled over and down. She went slipping across the stone, hands reaching for anything to hold on to, knees scraping. She was tugged to the edge of the platform, with just blackness behind her, until a prentice grabbed her by the wrist and pulled her back. It took four lads, held firm against the rope ring, to haul first her, and then Blank, back to safety. He was sodden and bruised. Blood ran from somewhere in his curls. He coughed up water and lay there. His voice though, when it came, was matter of fact. 'Well, it appears that won't work.'

Tink. An arrow struck the arch and fell harmlessly to the ground. A boy picked it up. 'That came from the river.'

Shay stared back upstream. She could see them now. Not the men, but their struggle. Grey spray from twenty oars pulled hard against the tide and the rise and fall of the bow. So, bowmen in the water, bowmen on the bridge and bowmen on the northern shore. Shay was sick to her stomach. The only option left was the water itself and she doubted if one in ten of the boys could swim. Maybe they should wade back to the very first arch where the water was slower and the shore closer. She'd been wrong, they would have been safer back at St Paul's. An arrow flopped into the water at her feet, and she prepared to order the boys back.

'Thomas à Becket.' Blank was telling her something over the cymbal crash of water. 'The chapel.'

She leaned out to look up at the bridge. Buildings bulged further out over the side here, blanking out the stars. The Chapel on the Bridge had been sold and turned into warehousing years ago, but it still had an ecclesiastical grandeur, and people still called it the Thomas à Becket. Shay had never been inside.

'There was an entrance here once, for the ferrymen.' Blank held her by the shoulders. 'So they could pray before they shot the arches.' He shouted to the boys huddled, soaking, on the stanchion. 'We're looking for a door up into the chapel. It'll be somewhere above the waterline.'

Those with torches relit them, prompting a spatter of arrows. They were closer now and Shay fancied she could see the outline of the boat. Torchlight played across the walls and underside of the arch.

A boy's cry. 'There.' At some point, metal rungs had run up the inside of the arch here but only a couple had survived. Those that remained pointed a path to a bolted wooden door set about eight feet up in the arch. It was the same seaweedy green as the walls.

'On my back.' Blank steadied himself against the wall and boys lifted Shay to stand on his shoulders. The bolt was rusted solid, the metal fused together with rust, but the wood itself looked rotten with sea spray. She threw her shoulder against it, and it gave a little.

'Take a step back,' she told Blank. He did as she said and then launched her against it again. The wood was soft as putty around the hinges, and she left a deep dent in it.

'Again.' Three more times, her shoulder stinging as she caught it on the hinges, and the wood began to crumble. A hole opened up and she worked her hand in behind it. A chunk came away and she dug her fingers in deeper and pulled. Half the door came crashing down, hinges and all, and she threw herself in though the gap. For a moment she hung, half in and half out, and then she tumbled through onto a solid floor. From the ground she kicked the rest of the door out.

She could see dry stone stairs and a handrail of rotted twine. Up she climbed and it was nearly ten feet before she found somewhere she could attach her rope: a one-winged stone angel too heavy for her to shift. She tossed the rope back through the hole and shouted, 'One at a time. I'll see if there's a way out.'

The underchapel was a long rectangular hall lined with vaulted ribs that made it feel like being inside Jonah's whale. Prayers would have been said here, hymns sung, but now it was just warehousing for the shop above. It smelled musty and rich with odd undertones: incense perhaps, and wet dog. Shay had no torch so she let her eyes adjust to the dim light. As shapes came into view, Shay crouched and held her breath.

At first, she thought it was another bear pit; shaggy creatures stood, unmoving, as far as she could see. She edged closer. No movement and no sound bar the river below. She was inches away when she realised what she was looking at. Furs. Neat rows of Russian furs on wooden mannequins.

Blank and the boys were close behind her. They walked in a hush between the mannequins, some stroking the soft pelts as they passed. One whispered, 'Good boy,' and there was a peal of nervous laughter. Blank put his finger to his lips. They were only feet underneath the bridge itself now; the stairs in the corner must lead to the chapel proper. Above them the ceiling boards were ill-fitting, and lines of moonlight sliced the gloom. Blank whispered, 'Extinguish your torches,' and Shay corralled the boys into a long line.

'We're looking for a way out of the chapel as close to the southern bank as possible,' she said. She tried to sound confident. 'Then it's just a short walk to the Southwark end of the bridge.' It was a peculiar kind of silence. Hundreds of boys, either drunk or hungover or shivering from cold, trying to walk noiselessly across an echoing chamber. Halfway across, Blank halted them as the sound of running feet came from overhead. One by one, the shafts of moonlight extinguished and then illuminated again, and the boys stood stock still until whoever was above had passed. Once all was quiet again Blank led the boys up into the chapel.

Portraits of saints stared balefully down at them, and the roof was so far above them as to be hidden in darkness. Shay risked a look out of the window. To the left, the northern end of the bridge was lit up like fireworks, but to the right the exit to Southwark was lost in shadow. A hundred feet away; if she could keep the boys quiet, they might make it. She halted the crowd with her hand and waited for the moon to go behind a cloud. As soon as it was dark, Blank opened the door and led the first boys out onto the edge of the road. With her finger to her lips, she guided them quickly through the shadows. Shops were boarded up and houses wore the cold stone of abandonment. They came to Nonesuch House and Shay reached out and touched the nameplate, imagining Nonesuch in the back of the cart that had brought him to London; it hadn't been just some story.

Shivers and stumbles. Footsteps and tears. The boys were doing their best. Shay looked past the ragged train of figures at the lights of the northern shore. There was no sign that they'd been spotted. She imagined running feet and torches ablaze, but no, the boys filed roughly past and already the stragglers were here. They might just make it.

'Oh, damn it.' Blank was only steps ahead of her, but he saw better in this light than she did. She stopped and saw it too. The drawbridge was up. A flat rectangle rose from the road like a black wall. That was why there were no men guarding this end.

She caught him up. 'Where does it raise?'

'There's a winch on both sides. Ours is across the road.'

It was a wooden wheel the height of Blank. It would take at least a couple of boys to move it.

He pulled at it experimentally. 'It makes a hell of a commotion though,' he said. 'I could hear it at night from the crow's nest.'

Shay remembered the noise. Her father had brought her here as a child to see the big ships come upriver, vast bristling cities that swarmed with sunburned men and fluttered with a thousand flags. Their favourite spot was at the side of the drawbridge, where you could lean out to touch the masts as they passed. She remembered the infuriating, slow arc as it was raised and the grind and clank of its chains. The soldiers might not be able to see the drawbridge from the northern end, but they'd surely be able to hear it. Without some kind of distraction, the drawbridge would be the death of them.

Shay tucked two unlit torches and turned north. She took Blank's arm. 'Wait until you see me light these before you start the winch.'

Blank followed her eyes. 'No, they'll shoot you.'

She shook her head. 'I don't think so, not tonight. I'm going to have to try anyway, so just wait for your cue.' She took his hand from her shoulder.

'Please. No. We can lower it before they have any idea what is going on.'

She saw it from a falcon's view. The wings of the drawbridge spread like angel wings, their slow passage across the sky. The soldiers running, slowly and then fast. Lights, fire, noise. And then young bodies piled against the side of the drawbridge.

'You know that's not true. We owe it to them to try. If you do get them across, then raise the drawbridge again. But leave a twenty-foot gap. No more, no less.'

He shook his head, but she was already walking away. A dead torch in each hand and Devana at her chest. 'Yes. Twenty feet. I'm the only person on this bridge who can jump that.'

It was oddly peaceful. Shay realised she'd never seen a London street properly dark before. Even after curfew, insomniacs' candles peeked from upstairs windows and bakery ovens lent whole streets a fiery glow. But here, with her dead footsteps and the whisper of distant water, the houses were corpses, flat and cold and damp.

She talked to Devana. 'Should I light a torch? D'you think they are more likely to kill me if they can see my face? Or less?' It was as quiet and dark as the marshes. She let the dead torches swing as she ran through her repertoire. What could she perform for a gang of murderous soldiers? She'd think of something. She quietened her footsteps. Not nervous, she realised, for the first time – late, so late. Not even a hint of stage fright.

She waited until she was about ten yards from the northern entrance. It was well within arrow's range, but she needed them to feel that they could take her, if they wanted. Glow of fire and a soft burble of voices. She hauled herself onto the guardrail at the bridge's edge. Her legs stung with the effort; it was nearly five feet high and rounded smooth from decades of London hands.

What to sing? 'Every Lost Lamb'? One of Nonesuch's drinking songs? Never mind. It was only seconds away, but she'd think of something. With unsteady hands she lit one torch and then the other. She held them high so that Blank would see them, back near the southern end.

She felt, rather than saw, the soldiers' attention move her way, like some huge, slow animal turning. London had taught her that, at least; she now knew when she was being watched.

She started with a small voice, the one you'd use to sing to yourself. 'To live is to fall, to live is to die ...'

She could see the soldiers now, as they turned and lit their lamps. At first, they were just a straight line of bows, all drawn and aimed her way, but she made herself look past the mouth of arrows to the faces behind them. Boys, all of them. Boys playing at fighting while the men sat at home and waited for news of how it had gone. The kind of boys she'd seen at the theatre many times: boisterous and beautiful and sad. Her vision felt hawk-like. She could see the twitch of biceps held tight against the pull of the bowstring. The beads of sweat and the damp crotches.

'To live is to fall, to live is to die ...'

No friendly eyes on her. No Devana above, no Nonesuch below. Trussell and Alouette were God-knows-where, and Blank was trapped behind her. Instead, faces glared from behind arrows. 'They're more scared than me,' she said to herself, and then, as if in answer, a deep thud came from behind her, a noise which she felt through the soles of her feet. The drawbridge. She stepped forward and walked the guardrail like a tumbler. Was that the grind of the winch she heard behind her? She raised her voice stage-loud.

'To live is to fall like a stone from the sky.'

Some soldiers lowered their bows now. She turned her toes inwards to better grip the guardrail. Sea winds buffeted her.

'We fall through love, we fall through war.'

She could hear the creak of wood behind her, but the soldiers were focused purely on her. It might be the best audience she'd ever had. She waited for the familiar feeling, for the sky to take her up so she could gaze down on herself from Devana's viewpoint. She wanted to shrink to that delectable point where she didn't matter any more. But it didn't happen. She just stood there, shivering on the guardrail of London Bridge with flames in her hands and winter in her blood.

'We fall with grace and we live once more.'

She tossed the torches to her right in a long, end-over-end arc that set them sparkling like Catherine wheels. At the same time, she threw herself sideways down onto the bridge. Hopefully a hundred sets of eyes were now following the torches' descent down to the black Thames. She landed awkwardly and took off back along the bridge, keeping low and near to the house-fronts, where it was darkest. She kept an even pace; she'd need her strength for the jump. She walked as quietly as she could, but it was no good; her footsteps echoed out across the bridge, and she saw the front row of soldiers break and begin to follow. She ran hard but not so hard that she'd be too winded to leap the drawbridge. The footsteps behind gained and she dared not look back. The centre of the road was in darkness but after twenty yards she could see the lights of Southwark ahead. Then her heart sank. The drawbridge was angled steeply upwards; not the kind of gentle slope she might leap from. She heard voices: Blank yelling, 'You've made the gap too wide, for God's sake, get it lower.' Figures worked the draw-wheel, and she watched the lip drop another foot, but the pursuers were almost upon her. A final burst of speed, low and hard, up onto the slope of the drawbridge as fast as she'd ever run. Scrambling up, momentum carrying her, bare feet on old wood, up she went, and somewhere on the other side boys were cheering, urging her on, until she was facing the sky at the drawbridge's end, and launching herself off at a hopeless angle, twisting in the air and looking down and then, and then … and then realising that she wouldn't make it, that it wasn't even close, and the lights of London tumbled all around her, and the cold, dead arms of the Thames rose up gratefully to snatch her from the air.

45

IF YOU WERE A falcon that next morning, high on the thermals as the line of dawn crested the horizon, what would you see below? The grey river and grey marsh are dead to you; a mere backdrop to the business of killing. Every part of you is tuned to the scurries and nibbles and dashes that mean prey.

Then a black bundle floats downstream. Its stillness means that it's probably already dead and therefore of more interest to the carrion birds than to you. It might still be edible but if it doesn't run and it doesn't fear then where's the sport in that? Your attention snaps elsewhere: a thrilling rabbit's dart across blank grass or a fledgling's tumble from the nest. You make an adjustment – a slope of wing – and become a living missile. Down below something is dead but doesn't know it yet.

The black bundle – wind-battered and broken and about the size of a girl – floats on.

46

THE FERRYMAN WORRIED AT first that the man might be a pickpocket. He was maybe a little old for a crook, but he had that mix of watchfulness and anonymity that characterised a good dabber. It wasn't good for business if the yokels got robbed before they even disembarked so he kept an eye out, but most of the passengers left at Horsleydown and the man remained quietly alone at the rear.

A couple of miles downstream and the man came and sat beside him. He was apologising almost before he'd asked whether they could stop at the pier up ahead. The ferryman hadn't known a working wharf there since his father's time. He said, 'I can do it but there's nothing left. And at this time of day, you'd be stuck out there for the night. I wouldn't trust that path in the dark.'

If the man heard, he didn't show it; he just handed over an extra penny.

The wharf was rotted right through. He had to jump from support to support, with the coffee-muddy Thames waiting beneath crumbling boards. You couldn't really call it beautiful. There was grandeur in the blank scale of the place – the way the blue of the sky weighed on the pencil-line horizon, the broken mirror of the marsh pools – but it was oppressive too. His shoes were soon soaked through, and his teeth chattered. He pulled up his collar and made for the wreckage. A path between moulding wooden stakes was overgrown and twice he had to double back to get around trenches of water. It was a maze, he thought, that was doubly frustrating because your goal was right in front of you. It looked like a shipwreck: bleached beams at crazy angles and rotting nets trodden hard into the mud. Dusk leeched colour from everything: the sky, the grass, even his hands looked grey.

The tree was dead back in his day and it was dead now, unchanged by decades of wind and rain. He sat beneath its branches. It was cold as stone against his back as he unpacked the bag. His voice was small in this echoless plain.

'So, Shay, I'm not sure if this is what you wanted.'

He crumpled his oldest pictures first and placed them in a hollow near the base of the tree. The drawings showed Shay fresh from London, wild-eyed and wild-haired. The next was her asleep on a channel boat with her arms tight around herself as if she were clutching something. Then later, the pictures from Flanders. Feeding a sparrow from her hand. Or this one: arms outstretched against the wind and face to the heavens. On and on, drawing after drawing, until he was screwing up the last of them. He didn't look at it, but he didn't have to – he knew that final face better than his own. Worry lines, age lines, and finally, so late, laughter lines. A softness to her that he thought had died in that Cockaigne cage.

Once the pile was built, he took out a jar and tipped the ashes on top, a grey snow covering the pyre's peaks. He placed the skull in the centre. Its beak was like a hooked knife and its deep sockets, even in death, seemed to pull you in. It was the same spoiled white as Birdland's beams and the lowering clouds.

One more day, that's what he asked her for, every day of that last year. One more day to hold his hand and watch the birds. And, bless her, she'd tried. The morning that he'd found that black bundle snagged in the Thames rushes, he'd not expected her to survive that day, let alone decades. One more day, he'd asked, and she'd answered, her hand lighter and stiller every time, until one day she was gone.

The paper took a moment to catch alight. Black splutter and then a line of orange racing across the drawing. Was it his imagination or did the first starling arrive just as the fire started? The balled papers twisted and blackened. As above, so below. The birds came the way she'd described it to him. In ones and twos and then all together, like a rain-storm's beginning.

the birds are fire the birds are water the birds are muscle

No warmth came off the fire; just threads of smoke that rose now, fanned and funnelled and driven into the heavens by a thousand thoughtless wings.

they are a wing they are a fin they are a mouth

At one time he would have got his sketchbook out for a spectacle like this, but now, who would he show? One more day was a gift greater than all the treasure in all the holds of all the ships in all the ports of all the cities in all the countries of the world. A hand in yours and eyes to see it.

the birds are flame the birds are rain the birds are death

A chorus of wings hoisted the ashes up, back where they belonged. Now they were part of a living, pulsing thing that bloomed instantly into great dark fireworks and just as quickly were gone.

Back into the air.

ACKNOWLEDGEMENTS

First and last and always, thank you, Anissa.

My thanks to two writers whose work I love – Ever Dundas and Mariana Enríquez – who were kind enough to read *The Ghost Theatre* in early drafts. Their thoughts helped mould everything you've just read, and Shay wouldn't be Shay without their insights.

To Leo Robson and Johnny Daukes for hours of lockdown walks and coffees where I ironed out those annoying last wrinkles, and my brother for his constant support, (and occasional commiseration, too).

Huge thanks to Victoria Hobbs. On our first meeting I said I needed someone who did for a book what a producer does for a record, and Victoria has turned out to be a veritable George Martin. Thanks too to her assistant, Jessica Lee, for so much valuable input.

To Emma Herdman at Bloomsbury. There's barely a page of *The Ghost Theatre* which hasn't been polished or sharpened by Emma and she's managed the neat trick of making me appear a better writer than I am. Thanks too to Madeleine Feeny and Sara Helen Binney for all their help.

And finally, thank you to the real Blackfriars Boys – John Chappell, John Motteram, Nathan Field, Alvery Trussell, Philip Pykman, Thomas Grymes, and Saloman Pavey – and to the red kites of Windsor Great Park.

A NOTE ON THE AUTHOR

Mat Osman is an author, journalist and founder member of British rock band Suede.

A NOTE ON THE TYPE

The text of this book is set in Adobe Caslon, named after the English punch-cutter and type-founder William Caslon I (1692–1766). Caslon's rather old-fashioned types were modelled on seventeenth-century Dutch designs, but found wide acceptance throughout the English-speaking world for much of the eighteenth century until replaced by newer types towards the end of the century. Used in 1776 to print the Declaration of Independence, they were revived in the nineteenth century and have been popular ever since, particularly among fine printers. There are several digital versions, of which Carol Twombly's Adobe Caslon is one.